CLOSE-UP

a novel

Michelle Herman

Columbus State University
PRESS

Excerpts of this novel appeared, in somewhat different forms, in *Townsend Literary Journal* and *Valparaiso Fiction Review*.

Library of Congress Control Number: 2021941884

ISBN 9780578905280 (paperback)
ISBN 9780578940533 (e-book)

Printed in the United States of America

26 25 24 23 22 P 5 4 3 2 1

Columbus State University
PRESS

Published by Columbus State University Press
Distributed by the University of Georgia Press

For my father

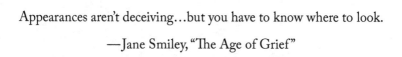

Appearances aren't deceiving…but you have to know where to look.

—Jane Smiley, "The Age of Grief"

Just before walking on:

    —*Load champagne bottle in pants*
    —*Put fruit in jacket pockets for final load of Cups and Balls*
    —*Make sure deck in left jacket pocket is stacked in Si Stebbins order*
    —*Rose for volunteer (girl/woman) pinned in jacket*

Open with Miser's Dream to music

Climax with Champagne Production from bucket to end Miser's Dream

Invisible Deck

Paper rose to rose

Close with Cups and Balls

PART 1

PART 1

BARTLEBY

The plan was to use the bird in his act, but Jacob didn't have the stomach for it. The way to make a bird disappear was to dump it into a little pouch, and the only way to get the bird into the pouch was to flip it over very fast, so fast that it—*she*—would lose consciousness for a few seconds.

Jacob's mother had tears in her eyes. "Oh, sweetheart, that's awful. No wonder you couldn't do it—poor thing." But of course she meant sixteen-year-old Jacob, not the bird. She set her wine glass down and raised her arms to him.

Jacob stayed put in the doorway, his own arms folded tight across his chest.

His mother's tears infuriated him, just as they always did (when he was younger, he remembered, he had been touched—sometimes alarmed—by his mother's crying, but he could not remember why). Mostly he was angry with himself. Why on earth had he paused in the doorway as he passed between the kitchen and his own room and acknowledged that he even saw his parents there? Why had he told them anything at all?

"Oh, yes, poor Jakey," said his father. "Poor kid, he's so sensitive."

His father's sarcasm, his mother's crocodile tears.

When he was older, telling the story of the bird—a cockatiel he'd named Dolores because she had seemed so sad—to his new girlfriend, junior year of college (he felt ancient, thinking of the boy he had been four long years ago), he would say that what he pictured when he looked back on his childhood were such moments as these. His parents both expectant in their separate corners, ready for a battle—like boxers. Or like the black and white rooks on a chessboard. (Jacob's father had insisted he learn to play chess, which he disliked and never played again once he left home for college. What was the point of all that strategy and slyness, of having to think so far ahead, when there was no beautiful effect, nothing to dazzle anyone—no audience *to* dazzle—at the end of it?)

Yes, he could see them still, in their customary poses with their customary props: his father in the big red leather armchair that his mother hated, a thick book in his left hand and a heavy square glass full of amber-colored Scotch and one big ice cube in his right; his mother with her slender paperback and a fragile-looking glass of wine that matched the couch she'd just had re-covered for the second time, in a color she called *ecru* but that Jacob's father said was only *yellow, Jesus, Gloria, just call it pale yellow for the love of God—why do you insist on such bullshit names for things?*

Jacob in the doorway itched to get away from them. But he knew that if he bolted, his mother would follow; she would want to talk. And he would want to say, "Leave me alone, would you?" but he would not (if he did, she would begin to cry outright, and the brimming eyes were bad enough). Or he would want to tell her, "Go talk to your husband. It's his job to listen to you, it's not mine." But of course he wouldn't say that either. It would be cruel, and he wasn't cruel. (*That* was his father's job—or so his father seemed to think.)

His mother sitting on the couch, perched at its very edge as if poised for flight. His father reclining, his feet in socks and slippers on the ottoman that matched the leather chair, his birthday present to himself in 1994 when he'd turned forty, the same week his seventh book came out to excellent reviews (Jacob's mother had said, "No—is this a joke?" when the men delivered the enormous chair and ottoman, and she had wept as the couch, the color of baked salmon then—*bittersweet coral*, she had called it—and garnished with a row of small, square pillows, *seal gray* and *bone*, four of each, as hard and inflexible as teeth, was pushed back against the wall in order to accommodate it). "Other men buy sports cars," she had told his father, who had laughed and said, "Indeed they do, or else they have affairs with women half their age. So you might be grateful for my midlife good sense." And he had turned to Jacob, who was fourteen then, and said, "What do you say, kid? Am I right or am I right?"

Jacob had kept silent. Anything he said would give one of his parents ammunition for the quarrel he could see was just ahead.

Just as he should have stayed silent about the bird.

Jacob at sixteen knew perfectly well that if he had been serious about using a bird in his act, he would have bought a dove, the way other magicians did. The way Jackie, who owned his favorite magic shop, had told him to when he'd asked for advice about a bird effect. Jacob knew the difference between a pet and a prop. A dove was not a pet.

But that was why he had not bought a dove, he knew. He had kept this a secret from his parents.

In his studio apartment a block south of the campus of the college he had chosen for no reason other than that it was hundreds of miles away and big enough so that among the many thousands of his fellow students, there were likely to be plenty who had never read his father's books, who'd never even heard of Martin Lieberman, Jacob told his girlfriend about how, for his entire childhood, when he'd begged for a pet his father had laughed and said, "Are you kidding? It's more than enough trouble just to keep *you* fed and watered." And how, even at the age of five or six he'd understood that this was meant to be a joke but not why it was funny. By the time he was thirteen, his father liked to say, instead, "I'll tell you what, kid. When you're grown and have your own apartment, you can fill it up with seven pairs of clean beasts, seven pairs of fowl, and two of every other living creature."

Was it any wonder he'd concluded that it might be better not to talk at all?

His father in particular disliked it when Jacob kept silent. Often he'd refer to him as "Bartleby"—an allusion Jacob would not understand until after he had gone away to college, when he read the depressing nineteenth century short story in a course he took to fill a Gen Ed requirement for three credit-hours of "literary analysis" (he had chosen the least boring-looking class in which there was no chance that any of his father's books would be assigned or even mentioned). He would ask himself then if his father had supposed he'd understood the reference all along—but almost certainly he hadn't, almost certainly his father hadn't (then, or ever) stopped to think about what his son did or didn't understand; almost certainly it had been for his own amusement that he would make such observations as, "Bartleby, I see, is keeping his own counsel," or, "Bartleby would rather not cast pearls before the swine among whom he so grievously remains obliged to live."

What he remembered best about his childhood was his father's sense of humor, which was mean, and his mother's brimming eyes. The way his father mocked them both—the way he couldn't seem to help it, or maybe it was only that he didn't really even notice them, so how could he care about their feelings? The way his mother sat so upright at the edge of any surface that she perched on, as if she were about to flee.

The day he brought the bird home, he'd been so excited he'd called out to both his parents without thinking—and, remarkably, both of them had come, his father from his study, where he had as usual been working, and his mother from the kitchen. They stood beside him while he coaxed the cockatiel out of the cardboard box punched full of holes and into the cage he'd bought and set up on his dresser; the three of them together watched it settle itself in among the bells and balls and multiple assorted perches and the spray of millet Jacob had clipped to one of the cage's bars, and he told them all about the bird breeder, Veronika, whose ad he had discovered in the *Voice*'s back page classifieds, and her small apartment downtown full of parrots that spoke with German accents just like hers and what seemed like a hundred other birds, cockatiels and lovebirds and canaries, chirping and trilling, singing, calling out to one another. His bird—the one he had picked out himself—was quieter than all the rest. Contained, composed. More dignified. It was why he'd picked it. Her.

But on the ride home on the 1 train, the bird had been so silent and so still inside the cardboard box that he had begun to think that she was sad.

"I think you might have been projecting just a little bit," said Jacob's girlfriend four years later.

He should, no doubt, have returned the bird to Veronika, as she'd asked him to if things did not work out. "Promise me," she'd said. He'd had one foot out the door by then, the box poked full of breathing holes secure in his hands. "Why wouldn't things work out?"

"Ach," she said. "Who knows why? Some people are not meant to live with birds, that's all."

Meant to live! one of her parrots screamed. Another cried, *That's all! That's all!* The rest of them called out, in their German accents, *Goodbye, Farewell, See you later, I'll see you around.*

He hadn't made the promise, really—he had only not *not* made a promise.

And now it was just his father and the bird—the poor bird, Dolores, that he'd sworn he needed for his act, but which had ended up as something halfway between a discarded prop and an abandoned pet—alone in the apartment in New York.

Dolores in her cage and his father and his many books and his square glass of Scotch and his red leather chair and ottoman that Jacob's mother never had to see again, and the couch she had re-covered one more time (stripes: *eggshell* and *slate*) before Jacob left for college.

He had been right about his college. Almost no one here cared about novels, at least not as much as they cared about football. His girlfriend, an English major who wrote poetry, complained that even among those who did—her classmates, her professors—she could count on her fingers those who cared about *living* novelists, much less poets. Jacob wondered when—or if—he'd tell her who his father was, or even that his father was a writer. He preferred not to. He hoped he wouldn't have to.

"What makes you so sure your father kept the bird?" she asked him. They were sitting on his bed, crosslegged, a pizza box between them.

The question shocked him. "He wouldn't have given her away without asking me first."

"But how can he ask you if you're not talking to him?"

"Exactly," Jacob said.

"Oh, Jacob," she said. "Why don't you just call him? What kind of person stops talking to his own father?"

"You don't know," he told her. "If he were your father, you wouldn't want to talk to him either."

"I guarantee I would."

"We'll have to agree to disagree," Jacob said. "I've found that not talking to him has improved my life considerably. I imagine my mother must feel the same way."

"It's a pity you can't ask her, then."

If anyone else had said this to him, he would have supposed there was some cruelty behind it. But *she* didn't have a cruel bone in her body. When she said "it's a pity," that was what she meant: she actually pitied him.

For a little while they were both silent. Then she said, "Jacob? Tell me this. If your dad didn't want you to have a pet and only let you get the bird because you said you needed it for a trick, why did he let you keep it when you didn't end up using it that way?"

"I have no idea."

"Do you think maybe he thought there was a lesson in it?"

"A lesson? What kind of lesson could I possibly have learned from that?"

"For him, I meant," she told him. "Not for you."

"You think he was teaching *himself* a lesson? How would that even have worked?"

He thought about telling her then who his father was. But what if it changed everything between them? What if it changed *anything* between them?

One of the reasons he loved magic was that he was in control of everything about it. Even as a child, when he'd first started doing tricks, he'd understood that if he ever got good enough at it he could guarantee the outcome, every time. And for a long time now he *had* been good enough at it. More than good enough.

So instead of telling her that the famous writer Martin Lieberman was his father, he told her about how, on the night when he had told his parents that he wasn't going to be able to use the bird in his act after all, his father had smirked and said, "Poor Jakey. He wanted to kill two birds with one stone," and his mother had wept and said, "Martin, please. Can't you see that he's upset?"

Both of them putting on a show, one that had nothing to do with him.

His father, laughing, with his feet up on the giant ottoman he could have rested ten pairs of his slippered feet on. His mother who pretended to care so much about how he felt, but who had left him too when she had left his father. He had been right about her all along, then. All those tears, just for herself.

His girlfriend had tears in her eyes too now.

"What?" Jacob said. "I'm fine. We're all fine. My mother got out. I'm here, with you. It's all good."

"You should call your father."

He took her hand in his. "Trust me on this. I should not."

"But he's all alone."

"And whose fault is that?"

"Is that what matters? Whose fault things are?"

"Isn't it?" he said. "Isn't that at least one of the things that matters?"

"I hope not," she said.

Two birds with one stone—what kind of joke was that? A terrible joke. No joke at all.

So what was it then?

It was nothing, that was what it was.

It was nothing, and nobody had learned anything.

ARCANA

Grassman loved his wife—he loved his children. What kind of monster doesn't love two intelligent and pretty children? Those heads of thick black curls! Those saucer-eyes, those somber and beseeching expressions! What sort of man does not admire, does not marvel over, the young mother—fair, unsomber, unbeeching— who looks after them? Who looks after Grassman, too, gently sliding shut not one but two sets of etched glass doors each day when the twins burst into the house shrieking, chattering, trailing friends and neighbors, flinging their schoolday detritus, lunchboxes and rainboots, jackets, bookbags, hats, gloves, flyers and instructions and permission slips on colored paper everywhere throughout the lovely home she's made for them and which she, the irreproachable Margaret Grassman herself, chases down—bowing, scraping, collecting, sorting, shutting into closets, hanging up on hooks, lining up on shelves. All so that he, the utterly reproachable Daniel Grassman at the piano in his studio, is able to continue without disturbance. Grassman thought of Tolstoy, who complained in his diary: "Family happiness completely absorbs me, and it's impossible to do anything." One hundred and twenty-seven years later, as Grassman's children stood beside his piano on a Sunday afternoon and performed for him a charming song of their own composition—Julian played the flute; Hannah, the cello—Grassman willed himself with all his might not to wish the delightful song to end; not to interrupt them; not to ask Margaret, her arms folded like a sentry in the space vacated by the doors that had disappeared into their pockets at her touch, to take the children outdoors or to another room. How much better he would love them all, he knew, if only—like the moon—they did not appear in his sky every day.

—Martin Lieberman, *The Grassman Sonatas*

When Caroline met the famous writer Martin Lieberman—when he flirted with her (if that was what he was doing; she wasn't sure herself, but her friend Natalie insisted it was so) as they stood talking after his reading at the Arts Center; when he invited her and Natalie, the English majors with whom he'd struck up a conversation, to come along with him and Professor Rosen to the Faculty Club for a drink; when, at the Faculty Club, he told Caroline (and he was definitely talking to her and only her, then: he took hold of her left wrist and leaned in as close as the table between them would allow) that she ought to meet his son, "a handsome devil, not like his old man"—and here he paused to allow a protest, and it was Natalie, more confident, more experienced than Caroline, who obliged him—she was both repelled and charmed. *Equally* repelled and charmed. Something she had never experienced before.

And so, just as Professor Rosen had taught her to do with "any new experience that should happen to come your way," Caroline turned it over in her mind, trying to make sense of it as she sipped her Diet Coke with lemon.

Martin Lieberman drank Scotch (*straight up, a single malt please if you have it*—but they didn't), quite a lot of it, actually—four drinks to Professor Rosen's two, and *she* was drinking white wine (*whichever of these Chardonnays is the biggest—would you know, by any chance?*—but the waitress didn't). Caroline would have liked to order a glass of wine, too. She would have ordered just what Professor Rosen had—and then perhaps they could have exchanged a sympathetic glance after the first sip from the first disappointing glass. But the drinking age was strictly enforced on campus as it wasn't always in the bars across the street, or in the grocery around the corner from her house—her mother's house—where she had lived all her life (where in her darker moods she feared she'd live forever). Thus she nursed a single Diet Coke, just as Natalie did, while turning over in her mind the mystery of Martin Lieberman's effect on her—the mystery of Martin Lieberman himself—and making an effort to contribute to the conversation even as she simultaneously tried to memorize every single thing that was happening, both within and without.

That was a phrase she had learned from Professor Rosen: *within and without.*

It was also from Professor Rosen that she had learned, albeit not directly, to drink wine. It was thanks to a poem about wine—*ostensibly* about wine, as Caroline had told Natalie: on the surface (*without*) about wine—which Professor Rosen had written and which Caroline had come across this past fall in *Poetry*, one of the journals she had taken to leafing through at Borders. The poem, a villanelle, was so beautiful it had inspired her to put a bottle of wine—the very type of wine named in Professor Rosen's poem—in their shopping cart when she and her mother were at the store that evening, and later, to her mother's evident amusement, to pour a glass of it to drink with her spaghetti dinner.

Her mother, who drank beer, hadn't said a word when Caroline put the bottle in their cart, but then, at dinner, in an exaggerated, purposely terrible French accent, she read the label aloud. The she said something astonishing. "Your father drank tequila, you know."

You know. As if this were not the first new piece of information about him that she had offered up in years.

"Right down to the worm," she said. She *laughed*. "Fool. Fool like only a man can be."

Caroline held her breath. She knew better than to say a word, to ask any questions. If she did, her mother might even pretend that she'd misheard her. *Who said anything about tequila? Who said anything about fathers?*

But it didn't matter. She was done. She was already talking about something else, just as if she hadn't contradicted what she had been telling Caroline her whole life long: that she did not recall a single thing about her father except that he had been tall and had long hair—"long and blond and wavy, just like yours." And that he'd never known that she was pregnant, that he'd left town without knowing.

Later, she had tried to write a poem about this moment, this conversation with her mother over dinner, but it wasn't very good. Professor Rosen had said that she needed to find the right details to make it come alive, to make it *new*. Like what? she wondered. The spaghetti with sauce from a jar that they were eating? Her glass of Côtes du Rhône, her mother's sweating can of Bud Light? The fact that it had been at least five years since the last time her mother had uttered the words "your father"? How about the way her mother had so casually changed the subject, asking her if she'd remembered to stop at the SuperX near campus to pick up shampoo on sale, and if Nat's sister Felicia was still looking for babysitting jobs, because someone at work had asked if she knew anyone?

When she was little, Caroline remembered, she'd thought the cover of a record album was a picture of her father and his friends. One was taller than the others and had longer hair, the same color as hers. Would that detail make her poem any better?

It wasn't as if she didn't believe Professor Rosen. It was just that sometimes she didn't know what to do with the advice she offered. The problem, as she saw it, was that she didn't know enough yet to be able to make use of her teacher's wisdom. Natalie teased her when she said things like this. "Does she walk on water, too?" Nat said. And, "Does she travel in a shiny pink bubble and tell you, 'You had the power all along, my dear'?" But it wasn't awe or worship she felt. It was trust. And gratitude. Ever since she'd started at Kokosing State last year and had the good luck to have Professor Rosen as her freshman seminar teacher, she felt her whole life had become new, even if it hadn't changed at all in its ordinary details. Same best friend. Same mother, obviously. Same small, ugly house just south of campus—same small bedroom off the kitchen that she had tried for years to make pretty until finally, just this past year, she'd given up because it didn't matter anymore: it was just a place to store her stuff and sleep. She went to the library to do her homework, to write poems, to read—or, if the weather was good, she sat outside on campus and worked there. It was the same campus she'd been walking past and walking *through* forever, but it felt so different now. *She* felt different—new. No, not just felt. Was.

Even her mother had begun to notice this. Just this morning, when Caroline was getting ready for school as her mother was getting ready for work, she'd stopped what she was doing—digging through her purse to make sure she had everything she needed for the day—and scrutinized her. "What?" Caroline said. She had dressed carefully for the visiting writer's reading later in the day, in a belted pale blue linen dress and dark blue platform sandals; she had wound her long hair into a loose bun atop her head, an approximation of Professor Rosen's hairstyle. "Do I not look okay?"

"You look fine," her mother said, letting out a little sigh and resuming her muttered recitation of *keys, lipstick, tissues, gum, change, lighter, cigarettes.* ...But then, without looking up again, she said, "It's just that sometimes I think I don't even know who you are anymore."

"You say that as if it were a bad thing," Caroline said lightly— or so she had intended. But her mother looked up and she could see that it had landed harder than she'd meant it to. Her mother didn't say anything. She just zipped her purse shut and patted it, the same way she did every morning, as if it were a living creature that she counted on, and hung it on her shoulder by its long strap. But Caroline had seen something in her face, just for a second.

It occurred to her now, as she sat listening to Martin Lieberman talk, that her mother had a kind of dignity. It was a surprising thought. That her mother had never made much of an effort to please her—to *win* her—Caroline had always considered one of the many indications of her lack of normal motherly feelings. And maybe it was. But maybe— oh, this was a novel idea!—she consciously held back. Maybe it took effort not to try to make her daughter like her more than she did. To keep from seeming desperate—to keep herself in check.

Martin Lieberman didn't keep himself in check at all—and that, Caroline realized, was exactly what bothered her about him. But it was also (strangely, illogically) what made him so appealing.

The way he'd read at the Arts Center from the manuscript of his new novel—the way he kept interrupting himself to sigh and say, "Well, *this* will surely change in the next draft. Forgive me, boys and girls"— had confused her. She had assumed that once you'd published nine good novels (or, more accurately, four good, three excellent, and two truly brilliant ones) and were so famous that even people like Caroline's mother had at least heard of you, *and* you'd had movies made of two of your books (not the two best, but the two that had been bestsellers, one of which Caroline's mother actually had a copy of, in the movie tie-in paperback edition), you wouldn't ever be apologetic about what you had written. Which suggested that he wasn't really apologizing but was just making a show of it, hoping for reassurance, for praise—even if only in the audience's minds, even if he only wanted them to *think*, "Oh, this is so good, how funny that he doesn't know it!" But why would he need that if he weren't insecure about his work? Or was he pretending to be insecure, displaying false humility? And wasn't that a type of conceitedness?

It was hard not to wonder why a famous writer would bother with false humility, why a famous writer would *be* conceited, instead of simply, quietly, self-assured. If he still needed to be flattered—if he were still, despite everything, insecure—it was hard for Caroline, in her front-row seat at the Arts Center, not to feel sorry for him.

And what about the way he was so obviously showing off right now, telling a long story about a couple, "dear, dear old friends" of his—a famous painter and a famous playwright, long married, and both of them, he said (raising one thick black eyebrow like a cartoon villain, but knowingly, as if everyone at the table were in the know, too), *famously* drunks—and the opera singer with whom the playwright had been having an affair for decades? It was a story in which the Italian Alps, Prague, Budapest (he pronounced it *Budapesht*) and Paris figured importantly—as did the Tony Awards, backstage at the Metropolitan Opera, and "half a dozen bottles of Bollinger Les Vieilles Vignes Francaises." As the story went on, she began to feel embarrassed for him. It didn't even matter that she *was* impressed. You'd think someone like Martin Lieberman would be beyond wanting to make an impression, you'd think he wouldn't care one way or the other. You'd think he wouldn't *have* to care. That he did seemed to Caroline almost unbearably poignant.

And then there was this: she had expected to be fascinated by Martin Lieberman, had expected him to be brilliant, witty, philosophical, effortlessly knowledgeable, *wise*—just like his novels. But he wasn't. He was terrifically smart, of course. There had already been several times she'd wanted to take out her notebook just to write down words to look up later, or complicated ideas he didn't slow down long enough for her to fully grasp, but she didn't dare. (Even if the visiting writer *and* her teacher were to let that pass without comment, Natalie never would have.) He knew a lot of things, too, and he moved at lightning speed from one subject to another, sometimes faster than she could follow. But it didn't add up to what she had imagined. She had expected meeting him to be like reading him, and it was hardly like that at all.

Right this minute, for example: he was finished with the painter and the playwright and the mezzo soprano and was somehow on the subject of bridal dresses (perhaps the playwright was going to leave the painter and marry the singer, and she had missed that part of the story?). "Did you know that the tradition of the white wedding dress, to which you girls have undoubtedly given some many hours of thought, dates back only to Queen Victoria?"—and then all at once he was talking about marriage itself, and then about divorce. Divorce, and then child custody. Did they know, he demanded, that it was not until 1886 that granting custody of children to their mother became a matter of course? "It's ironic, really. Just as divorce laws became more 'liberal'—not in the contemporary sense, to be sure—domesticity was on the rise. Indeed, it's been said that domesticity was an invention of the nineteenth century."

"Like Christmas," Natalie interrupted him to say. "We just talked about this in my Victorian Lit class. Professor Sammler's," she said, turning to Professor Rosen. "He's very cranky," she added in a stage-whisper, then turned back to Martin Lieberman. "Trees and Santa and all that? An invention of the Victorian era."

The novelist smiled. "Indeed."

And now, already, he was talking about something else: the flowers on the table! He had reached for one pale yellow tulip, plucked it out of the round vase that was in the center of the table. "Do you know the story of how tulips were first introduced in Holland?" Caroline was still thinking about that "indeed." Did it mean that he was irritated that Natalie had changed the subject—or that he was glad she had made the connection, the way a teacher might be? (Though perhaps not Professor Sammler. Natalie said he'd made it clear that he disliked it when his students spoke in class for any reason and forbade the raising of hands—*You are here to listen, not to offer your opinions*—which Caroline found hard to believe, though when she was younger she had believed everything Natalie told her.)

He had just read a fine nonfiction book about tulips, Martin Lieberman declared, and Professor Rosen interjected to speak of a poem about tulips that she liked very much, and this led the two of them to talking about still life paintings—now they were talking about seventeenth century Dutch still life paintings, and Professor Rosen said something about the Rijksmuseum. Which, it seemed, housed a painting Martin Lieberman was particularly fond of, Rembrandt's "The Jewish Bride." Which led him back to wedding dresses. "Ah, yes, I was talking about Queen Victoria and her bridal dress! Do you know, she wore white when she married, in 1840, which was quite original and daring of her. Before that, from early Saxon times on, at least up through the eighteenth century, only the poor wore white. It was a symbol of 'nothing to bring to the marriage.' In the sixteenth and seventeenth centuries, teenaged girls wore pale green—presumably for fertility. A girl in her twenties wore brown, and older women might wear black. And then Victoria set the new standard, and there was no going back."

So in a *way* he was like his books. One had to hold on and fly along with him, as Professor Rosen did, as he bumped and careened along from place to place. The difference was that in his books everything fit together in a way that made all the pieces more meaningful than they would have been if taken one by one, and even the transitions that required great leaps, or leaps of faith, made sense—if not immediately, then eventually.

Maybe the trouble was that in a single afternoon's conversation there *was* no eventually.

The difference between Lieberman on the page and Lieberman in life, thought Caroline, was that by the end of a chapter—or at least by the end of the book!—the answers to the questions one couldn't help asking oneself (*Why are you telling us about bridal gowns? Why tulips?*) were always clear, even if they could not easily be put into words. But perhaps this could only be true in books.

Was it true only in books? In life, wouldn't everything—eventually—fit together to make sense? To make a whole?

And now the novelist was on to something else: an anecdote that he described as having taken place in his own "long-ago youth—that is, in near ancient history," he said, and Natalie took up her cue. "Oh, it couldn't be so long ago, Mr. Lieberman. My parents grew up in the sixties and they talk like it was just yesterday, and you're much younger than they are."

"Martin, please," the novelist said, "and thank you—what a nice girl you are. But I'm afraid I very much doubt I'm any younger than your parents. I have fond memories myself of the infamous Summer of Love, three long decades ago. I was *at* Woodstock, as readers of my first novel will have guessed." Here he winked at Caroline, which made her anxious (she had no idea what to do in return—smile? Wink back? She had never winked in her whole life!) and at the same time pleased her. So Martin Lieberman knew—assumed—that she had read his books. And (so it would seem, for he had winked only at her) he assumed that Natalie had not. Which was a perfectly accurate set of assumptions. (The truth was that, as much as Natalie seemed to be enjoying herself now, she'd had to be dragged to the reading. She was an English major only because she couldn't think of what else to major in, and because Caroline was.)

"Fifteen years old, having hitched a ride with the older sister of my best friend. Now, *that* was a time. As was the summer of '72, when I hitchhiked across Europe with that same older sister—but minus the friend. Ex-friend." Martin Lieberman laughed. "Ah. Memories. And when Harold Hartfeld, the titular 'hero'"—he made quote marks in the air—"of *Hartfeld*, makes his cross-country jaunt in 1973? That trip bears an uncanny similarity to one of my own. Like Hartfeld, I traveled with the lovely young woman who would later become my wife. Of course, Hartfeld, wherever he is now, may well still be married to the woman with whom he did his best to trace Lewis and Clark's travels. Indeed, I would like to believe this. It was an ambitious undertaking for us both." He paused. "The marriage, I mean. Not the road trip. The road trip was a lark, just a few months after we met."

"Hartfeld's wasn't a lark," Caroline said bravely. "When Hartfeld asks Joanne Grofsky to spend the summer traveling with him, it's out of desperation." But now she was blushing. She should not have used the word *desperation*, she thought. She should not have told Hartfeld's creator how Hartfeld had felt. "I just mean it seemed urgent. To me, I mean. When he asks her, and also when they go."

Martin Lieberman gave her an appraising look. "One of those road trips is fiction. One is not."

"Martin," Professor Rosen said, at the same time Natalie said, "You're divorced?"

"Something like that," he told Natalie.

Professor Rosen had turned pale. "I didn't know. I'm so sorry, Martin."

"What about your son?" Natalie asked. "Did your wife get custody of him?"

"*Natalie*," Caroline said.

"It's all right," the novelist said. "My son, as it happens, is about the same age you girls are—rather too old for concerns of custody. He'll be twenty this June."

"Will he?" Professor Rosen said. "Oh, my. It's been so long since I've seen him, I supposed I'd lost track of time."

"When you don't have a child yourself, it's easy to do that."

There was a freighted silence. The look that passed between the two of them was uninterpretable to Caroline. She watched her teacher.

"So he's halfway through college then," Professor Rosen said. She said it in a friendly, cheerful way. The bad moment, whatever it had been, had passed. "Where is he at school, then?"

"Well," Martin Lieberman said. "He's here, actually."

"*Here?*" Natalie said, and all of them—Natalie, Caroline, Professor Rosen—looked around as if he'd meant the Faculty Club.

"Not in this room, ladies. Here at this university."

Caroline took note of how astonished Professor Rosen looked. Astonished and confused—and angry? Could that be?

"I should have told you, I know," the visitor said gently.

"You could have, certainly."

Should, could. Caroline tried her best to understand what they were saying—what they meant. She had never seen the professor so flustered (or was it agitated?). She had never seen Professor Rosen flustered or agitated at all.

"But I'm having a marvelous time. I'd forgotten how much fun this could be, really. You know, I gave up this sort of thing years ago."

"I do. You've said so countless times."

"Not countless. Two or three."

"Or seven."

Unruffled, the novelist said, "I was telling you the truth twice or thrice or seven times. At some point, a long time ago, I began to find these college visits wearying."

"I was pretty surprised when you said yes this time."

"I should have told you why. I'm sorry." But he did not sound sorry. "I'd been hoping you would ask again. I'm afraid that things have been quite difficult. Forgive me. I was so certain he'd turn up today. I thought, all right, he can't bring himself to pick up the phone, or to respond to a letter or even an email, but when push comes—"

"Hold on," Natalie said. "You and your son don't *talk*?"

"I talk. He doesn't."

"Wow. What did you do to him?"

Caroline flinched. She had often wondered if there were anything Natalie wouldn't say. Apparently there was not.

But the novelist did not appear to be offended. "Oh, I'm not altogether sure what my son is angry about. I'm not even sure he *is* angry. He may be perfectly happy, living hundreds of miles away from me. I have no way of knowing."

"I can't believe you didn't tell me he was here," Professor Rosen murmured. "I might have been able to do something."

"Don't be foolish, Jill," he said, and Caroline couldn't decide what was more shocking: the *foolish* or the *Jill*. "Remind me, how old was he when you last saw him?"

"Three or four? Very young. And I've only seen him twice, all told." She said it coolly. She looked composed now, too—she looked the way she always looked. Her thick dark hair streaked with gray piled glamorously atop her head, her large dark heavy-lidded eyes leveled steadily on the visitor. She never wore makeup. She was beautiful anyway.

"Ah, yes. You were at the bris, weren't you."

"I was. Gloria cried, I remember that. I wanted to comfort her, but I didn't know her well enough. I didn't know her at all. So I kept waiting for someone to go to her. But no one did. She just stood there weeping."

"That was a long time ago," Martin Lieberman said.

Caroline was amazed to see that his eyes were wet.

For a little while all of them were silent.

"It makes no sense," the novelist said finally. "He loves the city. He loves our neighborhood. He loves the apartment. He could have gone to Columbia. I was sure he was going to *go* to Columbia. He got in, I know that—I saw the letter myself—and it's a short walk from our apartment. Whoever heard of a kid getting in to Columbia and declining the offer in favor of"—but he managed to stop himself. "I'm not being a snob. He accused me of being a snob, but that's not it at all. I just don't get it. If he wanted to be on his own, I would have gotten him his own apartment. If that wasn't enough, he could've gone to NYU, moved down to the Village. That would have made at least a little sense. And if he was so set on mingling with the masses, he could've gone to City College. I got a hell of an education myself at City College. So did you, Jill. But this? How would this even have occurred to him?"

"Surely you don't think I had anything to do with it, Martin."

"Of course not. He has no idea who you are."

"Of course not," Professor Rosen echoed. "Why would he?"

Caroline looked back and forth between the two of them anxiously. Was this how the children of bickering parents felt?

An absurd thought. Where had that even come from?

"For all I know, he applied to colleges all over the country. He never talked about it. He never talked about any of it. I knew about Columbia because I asked. 'Are you going to apply to Columbia?' 'Yes, Dad.' 'Did you get your application in to Columbia?' 'Yes, Dad.' 'Did you get *in* to Columbia, son?' 'Why, yes, Dad. Here's the letter.'"

"I wish you'd let me know that he was here."

"I was going to. I had every intention of letting you know. But then, just after he left, so did Gloria. I believe at that point my mind went blank."

"Wait," Natalie said. "Why did she leave?"

"I have no idea."

"That can't be true." Natalie turned to Professor Rosen. "Can it?" It was one of the few times Caroline could think of that Natalie, so sure of herself always, had seemed uncertain.

Instead of answering her, Professor Rosen spoke to him. "Where did she go?"

"At first, to stay with a childhood friend in California. I believe she's still somewhere in California—who knows where, exactly." He rattled the ice cubes in his empty glass. "It would seem that everyone is happier when hundreds of miles away from me."

"I'm so sorry," Professor Rosen said.

"She made no bones about the fact that I'd begun to bore her. Perhaps I'd always bored her—perhaps once her beloved son left home for college she saw no reason to endure it any longer."

"Oh, Martin. You are a great many things, and not all of them are charming. But boring? Never."

"Ah. Dear Jill. You were always such a fine cheerleader for my sorry self. But you've never been married. In marriage, everyone is boring. *Marriage* is boring. Whether boredom is justification for flight is another matter. And it may be that boredom in fact played no part in her decision to flee. I shall never know. She refused to explain herself at the time, and now she refuses to speak to me at all. Just as her son does."

None of them said anything then, not even Natalie. And in the silence that followed, Caroline found that she could suddenly picture Gloria Lieberman. It was as if a series of vague, half-formed images had snapped sharply into place, like shuffled cards reformed into a deck. She *saw* Martin Lieberman's wife: saw her as Joanne Hartfeld and also as Loraine Silverman and Marianne Gold, as the young Dianne Terzetti in Lieberman's fourth novel, *The Old Trouble*, and as Margaret Grassman. It was funny that she had never once considered that they must be variations, versions, of one real-life woman.

She had also never considered how, in approximately half the novels, the protagonist and wife (always so restless and impatient and dissatisfied!) had a precocious son: in one, a precocious violinist, in another a child actor, in a third a mathematician—and then there were the Grassman twins, one of whom was male, a boy who was good at everything. She tried now to summon up the fictional son—or sons—but he was harder to envision than the mother/wife. The son was always a much less important and more sketchily drawn character than his mother—even in the two books in which the mother was dead in the narrative present (and in two other, earlier books, he was a daughter, not a son—which on the whole did not seem to make any difference, now that she thought back on them). It would be interesting, wouldn't it, to examine the question of what it might be in these various depictions of the protagonist's child that was like the real-life child, and what was not?

But in order to do that, one would have to find the real-life child. It was what she would do if she were in a novel.

But a novel wasn't life. And none of this was any of her business.

That evening, after Professor Rosen had taken the visitor to the airport and put him on a plane back to New York, after Caroline had dinner—take-out Middle Eastern—with her mother and half-listened to her stories about rude customers and someone she'd run into at the food court on her lunch break, Caroline wrote down everything she could remember about the afternoon. She wrote sitting on her bed, in her ugly room. She didn't want to take the time to walk back to campus, to seek out some private corner of the library. She felt as if she'd grown up even more today—grown up so much she knew it was time to stop being precious about *where* she wrote, knew it didn't matter. She filled page after page of her spiral-bound notebook, trying to get it all down before she forgot any of it. The handsome, angry son who stayed away. Natalie's whispering in her ear, as they'd left the Arts Center for the Faculty Club after the reading, that the visitor was flirting with her, when Caroline was sure now that he wasn't. The way Natalie enjoyed stirring things up; the way she read everything as being about sex, or romance. And Nat's own flirtatious and obsequious, then tactless—outright rude—remarks as they'd sat talking over drinks. The pastel-colored tulips on the table. The waitress who had brought the drinks and set them down on the white tablecloth—whose nametag said

Chelsea/Textiles Major, and who didn't know anything about the Chardonnays on the wine list.

Page after page, writing so quickly she wasn't sure she'd be able to read her own handwriting later—but she had no choice, she had to get it all down, quickly, before it was gone. The bris (she'd had to look up the word). The opening lines of a poem she only now understood were *about* a bris, a ritual circumcision. That must have been about *that* bris. The poem was from Professor Rosen's second book, *In the There-and-Now.* It was called *"Blessed be he who comes."* Caroline knew the first few lines by heart. She didn't have to consult the book before she wrote in her notebook

> *The shotgun shacks and railroad flats*
> *And upstairs-from-the-store*
> *Have been abandoned—and good*
> *Riddance—for the classic six prewar*
> *W/doorman where we've gathered for*
> *The mix of ritual and pastry, seltzer, wine,*
> *A little blood. The mother's Niagara tears.*

If she'd known what a bris was—and if she were Natalie and not herself—she would have asked about the poem today.

If she were Natalie, she might have recited what she remembered of it, then and there.

The last stanza began

> *Elijah's here but doesn't say a word*
> *As usual, while all the other Jews won't shut up*

She wrote those lines down too.

She wrote down the other words she'd remembered to look up (*xenial, caducity, coadunate, synechiology*—oh, that was her favorite: *the union of all things*), every question that had crossed her mind about Martin Lieberman and his work and his wife and his son, and an exhortation to herself to gather up the nerve to ask Professor Rosen the next morning in Twentieth Century Poetry if the novelist had managed before leaving town to contact his son, or if his son at the eleventh hour had contacted *him*.

The curious exchanges between her teacher and the visitor. The looks that passed between them. That he called her Jill. *And what did I think?* she wrote in her notebook. *That her friends call her J.T.? That her friends don't call her anything?* How discomposed she—*Jill*, J.T. Rosen, the professor who had changed Caroline's life by recognizing that she was a poet (anointing her, granting her the right to *be* a poet)—had fleetingly been. What it had felt like to see her this way for the first—perhaps the only—time. What it had meant to her. What the whole afternoon had meant to her.

According to Professor Rosen, she was not only to write down everything that happened—everything she saw and heard, and also everything she felt and thought—but to think about what all of it meant. "It's the privilege of being a writer, the chance to pause and think. And if you think your way through by writing your way through—why, that's what will *make* you a writer."

Caroline had never known anyone before who used "why" in this way. Or who called people "my dear." But she would *like* to say "my dear" herself—she would like to say "why" in just the way Professor Rosen did ("Why, memory itself is no more than simple storage," she'd told Caroline last week, in office hours. "It's notoriously untrustworthy. Rely on it, and you may find that precisely the lost moment that you most require is the one you cannot retrieve"). She would like someday to say, "A glass of Chardonnay, whichever of the Chardonnays is the biggest. Something lush and buttery, creamy. Nothing crisp, please, nothing bright."

What would it take to become the kind of person who could say such things?

And at that moment, writing in her notebook on the bed she'd slept in since she'd graduated from a crib, in her room that was hardly bigger than the bed, she understood something. The understanding came to her forcefully, as if it were breaking through a solid layer—a thick panel of glass, or a stout wooden door…or the hard-packed dirt of the small yard behind this house, where she'd played as a child (she wrote down all three images, just in case one of them turned out to be useful for a poem)—exactly as Professor Rosen had promised it would if she thought things through, if she *wrote* them through.

But perhaps it was less an understanding than it was a glimpse of something—the beginning of understanding. A crack in the glass. The center panel of the door about to splinter. A quarter-inch of green shoot pushing out of the hard ground. It was a glimpse that "eventually" would come. A glimpse that it didn't have to be only the protagonists of novels who would have the chance to turn into the kind of people they hoped to become. That it wasn't only in books that everything might come together—*fit*. That someday everything about this day, about (*literally!* she thought, and wrote—or wrote, and thought; she could no longer tell which came before and which came after) *her place at the table* (as if she had belonged there!) with the likes of Martin Lieberman and J.T. Rosen, would make sense.

That someday everything about *this* day, about her place at the table (literally! she thought, and wrote—or wrote, and thought; she could no longer tell which came before and which came after)—as if she had belonged there!—with the likes of Martin Lieberman and J.T. Rosen, would make sense. That she would understand that he had a son he loved and grieved for, of whom he was proud and of whom, in his books as in his conversation, he made use when it suited him—and that he was irritating, childish, needful, a windbag full of facts and trivia, arcana…*and* that he was brilliant, and that he had charmed her. That he was likable, too, despite the desperation and the endless recitation of the many things he knew. And that he deserved, like anyone, to be loved, didn't he?

She had filled the entire notebook.

She put it in the top drawer of her dresser, tucked under the tangle of unpaired socks and underwear and tights. She would buy another one tomorrow, on her way to her first class. She closed the drawer and thought of this: that perhaps one of the pleasures of a novel—a good one, and that included all of Martin Lieberman's—was that it portrayed life as much more various and shaded than you ever could experience it when you were only *yourself*, living your own life. In a novel you could see more sides to things than it was possible to see in life—you could see behind the corners and you could see underneath; you could see what wasn't even there but was only alluded to. You could even see before and after, if the author chose to let you. You could get the whole picture, all at once, of everything.

But it was also true, wasn't it, that even as a novel let you see all the complexities as they unfolded, in a novel things were simpler than they were in real life, too. A good one stripped away all the irrelevancies and distractions that kept you from understanding what the real story was as your own life unfolded.

If you could manage in your life to make sense of things as they occurred *without* simplifying them—if you could hold in your mind all the complications and contradictions and mysteries as they played out—then it would be as if you were the author of your own life. The author and the reader, both.

This was what she was thinking as she fell asleep. And when she looked back—when enough time had passed and enough had happened for *eventually* to have come, as she had glimpsed on this night that it might—she would think of this as the start of the story of her life. Her life as she wanted it to be, the life she was the author of. The beginning of everything, really.

PHOENIX

Even in the presence of the holy—art, God, language,
Love—there's trouble. On this day, too, the eighth,
The blessed, it's here, boiling up and threatening
To burn us all alive. Even the baby's furious
Kicks only remind us of promises unmet.

—J.T. Rosen, *"Blessed be he who comes"*

For years—decades—Martin Lieberman had moved through the hours of his days, day after day, week after week, in an invariable routine: awake before seven, at his desk by seven thirty. By noon, the serious work of the day was done; he took his lunch. And after lunch, there was a walk. The walk, a familiar circuit around the neighborhood, was less for exercise (although, as he aged, his wife noted that he was "lucky" he already had the habit—and he could not resist, as he no doubt should have resisted, telling her that luck had nothing to do with it) than for the change of scene and the demarcation it made between one part of the day and the next.

On Saturdays and Sundays, also by long-established habit, he took the rest of the day off. Monday through Friday, he spent his afternoons and evenings on pragmatic minutia—bill-paying and obligatory correspondence—as well as on whatever he had promised but put off and which on any given day could be put off no longer: a book review that was already ten days late, a blurb that he should never have agreed to write. And then there was what he thought of as his real correspondence. Even after nearly everybody else had given up on proper letters, he still wrote them, single-spaced on watermarked bright white bond paper, folded into thirds and then inserted into envelopes to which stamps had to be affixed. He carried them downstairs and dropped them, one at a time, into the mail slot in his building's lobby.

Letters came to him, too. At one time many of them were from friends; now they were almost all from strangers. His old friends, among which he counted both his agent and his longtime editor, had switched exclusively to email. But the people who read his work, who cared about what he wrote, were often the kind of people who might still be moved to write a proper letter, in care of his publisher. And his sister still wrote to him regularly by old-fashioned mail—handwritten letters in blue ink on thick, cream-colored stationery. Anna was more of a Luddite than he, who had traded his typewriter for a Macintosh computer and a printer long ago. He had persuaded her to purchase a computer—"for your children's sake, at least, unless you *mean* for them to remain unequipped for the new century"—but even when she used it to email him, as she did infrequently, she followed up just minutes later with a phone call asking if he had received her email (thus defeating its purpose, but by now he'd given up explaining this) and because invariably she was forced to leave a message on the answering machine, the question would be paired with a complaint about how hard it was to reach him (when the plain truth was that it was easier on both of them not to talk, even briefly).

Another click in the day's routine: at just after seven every weekday evening, emerging from his study, he would check the answering machine and greet his wife, who would be making dinner. He would read until dinner was ready; he would have a drink. And after dinner, Gloria would join him with her own book in the living room. When Jacob was a child, he too would join them (when he was very young, he would only pretend to read, holding his book carefully and frowning at it, the way Martin must often have frowned over whatever he was reading). Later, when the boy lost interest in spending time with his parents, he would flee immediately after dinner (if he had deigned to grace them with his presence even for the meal). Martin didn't mind his absence, for Jacob as he'd fumbled into adolescence was restless and noisy: his sighs and groans and throat-clearing, the impatient flipping of pages, his constant rearrangement of his body, made it impossible to concentrate. Even the noise of the television, which Gloria turned on at ten o'clock each night, did not disturb him as his teenage son did. He was acclimated by then to her television shows as he could not—would not—grow acclimated to the adolescent manners and behavior of his once-gentle, easy-to-please son.

It was Gloria, of course, who minded Jacob's absence. Or so she said. "You'd think he'd want to spend a little time with us. Before we know it, he'll be off to college. You would think he hated us." (And perhaps she had been right. Perhaps he'd hated them—or him—for years.)

(And was that why she'd left, once Jacob left for college? Was it that the *constant* absence of her son then was unbearable to her?)

The final clicks each day: the half hour, ten to ten thirty, during which he went on reading while Gloria shifted from her book to television (journalists, cops, lawyers, doctors arguing, declaiming, falling into bed); at ten thirty he left her to her television shows and headed for the bedroom, where he would continue reading for an hour. At some point, without waking him, she would take her place beside him. Night after night, year after year.

He had imagined—foolishly, he now understood—that his life would continue in this way for the remainder of his days. Day after day. Year after year. He would awaken every morning a few minutes before seven—he needed no alarm clock—and after he'd shaved and showered, would dress quickly and quietly in the dark bedroom as his wife slept on. Then he would fetch the *Times* from the doormat outside the apartment. There would be the single, large cup of black coffee, which he had always made himself, using the same type of single-cup plastic Melitta device he'd been relying on since before he had met his wife, even as she unremittingly upgraded her own coffee-making equipment, from Mr. Coffee to Gevalia to a French press to et cetera, right up to the brand new Technivorm that still sat on the kitchen counter next to the old pop-up Toastmaster, where she had set it when she had removed it from its box and then abandoned it, and him, soon after.

His daily cup of coffee. His toasted bialy with cream cheese.

Gloria bought bialys in batches of a dozen every twelve days and sliced them in half and froze them within an hour of their removal from the baker's oven. He had only to take one from the freezer, pry its halves apart, and drop them in the toaster. Toast them crisp, coat them with cream cheese. Gloria made sure there was always cream cheese.

It had now been just over a year since he'd last heard from her. *You've taken my life away from me*, he had intended to tell her the next time she called. He would be serious—he would speak from the heart. She would not be able to accuse him of doing otherwise. It was just as well that he'd not had the chance. He knew what she would have said— if she bothered to respond at all, if she did not hang up on him as she so often did, sometimes only minutes into the call. *I didn't take your life away. I took my life away.*

He had had this conversation with her in his mind so many times in the last year, there were days when he believed it had transpired.

Happy anniversary. He raised his coffee mug in salute to his vanished wife. The last time she had called—the last time, it seemed, that she would ever call—he had made the mistake of pointing out that the first anniversary of her abandonment of him lay just ahead. "Should we celebrate?" he'd asked. "We could sit talking on the phone, coast to coast, and drink a glass of Champagne 'together,' as it were." But Gloria was not amused. "Not everything is a joke, Martin," she said.

He laughed—what else was there to do? "Tell me something I don't know," he said.

But she did not. She did not tell him anything he didn't know.

Presumably if she were dead someone would inform him.

He would not have been aware that today marked two years since she had announced that she was leaving him if the date had not been circled on the kitchen calendar. If Gloria herself had not written *G. home from Calif. trip today - flight due in @8pm LGA* in the little box she'd circled in red (just as she had circled the box right above it, seven days before that, where she'd written *G. leaves for Calif. trip - flight @10:55AM LGA today!*). If the calendar were not still hanging there, below the kitchen clock, two years out of date.

Gloria had been the one to buy the calendar and hang and annotate it, just as she had been the one to buy the bialys—just as she had been the one to keep him in stamps and envelopes, paper and printer ink. He bought English muffins now (the bakery was not in the immediate vicinity, and a second, separate shopping trip beyond the supermarket seemed a great deal of effort simply for the gathering of food) and walked to the post office himself to buy his stamps; he ordered reams of paper and boxes of envelopes and ink cartridges over the internet.

He would tell Gloria this if he ever heard from her again.

He turned his back on the calendar and reheated his cooling coffee in the microwave oven for the second time, took his English muffin and his now too hot mug into the dining room, and sat down at the table.

Before Gloria had left, the single change in his morning routine of so many years had been the switch, which she'd insisted on some years ago, to reduced fat cream cheese (which was not "cream cheese" at all, of course, but Neufchâtel), and what a ruckus he'd raised over it. But now this was habit too. Shopping for himself, he bought Neufchâtel, dropping it into his shopping basket at the Food Emporium along with his package of Thomas's English muffins and a bag of apples or a small bunch of bananas and a juggler's worth of navel oranges—he did this once a week, on Monday afternoons—and not without a certain satisfaction in his competence, this demonstration that he could look after himself after all, which Gloria, it seemed, assumed that he could not. Or—as was more likely now—she didn't care if he could or could not manage to look after himself.

But when had she ceased to care?

He had actually asked her this, the last time they'd talked. Asked, *When did I stop mattering to you, if you don't mind my asking?*—though he knew she'd mind his asking (she had made it clear that he was not to ask her anything, had hung up on him more than once after this sort of "provocation"). And so he'd asked and then at once regretted it. "I'm sorry," he said quickly. "Don't hang up, please. I'm just curious, that's all. How can I help it?" And then regretted that as well. Regretted *curious*— that poorly chosen adjective. Regretted its diminishment by way of the adverb: *just* indeed. Regretted the supplication. Regretted everything he'd said except "I am." Regretted only its contraction.

And still he pressed on. (In for a penny, in for a pound—and she hadn't hung up on him *yet*.) "I mean it, Glor. I need to know. When did you stop loving me? When did you start hating me?"

"I don't hate you."

"You don't love me."

"This is what you want to talk about? *This*, of all things? My God, Martin. When did how I feel become of any interest to you?" And before he could answer—before he could begin to think about how he might answer—she said, "Never mind. Forget it. Look, I've got to go."

And then she was gone. And this time—but how could he have known that?—she was gone for good.

It was a failure of his imagination—he saw this clearly now—that he had never once imagined that he would be alone in middle age. He'd met his wife when they were both nineteen years old, at a party thrown by Stuart Fleischer, a boy who'd been at Stuyvesant with Martin and was with him then at CCNY, as was Gloria Hirsch, who was Stuart's second cousin—and by the end of the next day Martin was certain they would spend their lives together.

Stuart lived with his parents (they all lived with their parents then) in a small walk-up apartment on Convent Avenue. The parents were out of town—thus the party. Martin encountered Stuart's pretty cousin in the Fleischers' kitchen, where he was holding court. She was a lively, lovely, surprisingly blond, blue-eyed girl, slender and small (Martin, who was not tall, had to bend to hear her at the noisy party) but for a considerable bosom. They drank gin and tonics and ended up necking and making a date for the next day, which, it turned out—drunk, and in the midst of their kissing, they had both forgotten—was Mother's Day. Gloria called him at ten in the morning to say she couldn't meet him at noon as she'd promised: her mother expected her to have lunch with her family. "If you really want to see me, you could come," she told him. "It would be the worst first date in history." But he took her up on it, and after lunch he brought her to his parents' store and introduced her to his mother—it seemed only fair—and hustled her away before his father finished with a customer. They spent the rest of the day in Riverside Park, talking earnestly about the future. Then Martin bought her dinner.

Jacob was already a year older than he had been then.

But he steered away from that thought, as he had trained himself to do now from all thoughts of Jacob. What had happened to that lively girl who hung on his every word? The twenty-seven years between that Mother's Day in 1973 and this November day that marked two years since she had called from California to tell him she wasn't coming home was an entire lifetime. His lifetime—his *life*.

Middle aged was a temporal notion to which he'd paid little attention before Gloria had left him. Like all the other things she did so that he didn't have to, she had taken on the task of worrying about his aging. She nagged him about annual checkups; she tried to impose more changes in his diet—most recently to downgrade his lunch (the pastrami or corned beef sandwich or the ham and cheddar omelet that for years she had set out for him) to a salad with a slice of whole grain bread, no butter, next to it. He had objected strenuously; they had argued. In the end he won, after several days when he left the downgraded lunch untouched.

(Surely this was not why she'd abandoned him?)

She must have known that he was grateful (yes, even grateful for the salads that he wouldn't eat, because they were evidence that she'd wanted to keep him alive). She knew very well—he had told her often enough—how much he disliked thinking about food in the way one had to in order to prepare it for oneself. "The Great Man does not think about food," she would tell their friends. "I shudder to think what he would feed himself if left to his own devices."

And did she shudder, now?

Certainly she would be amused (or gratified—or disdainful) if she knew how much difficulty he had had at first. Whole days would sometimes pass during which he didn't eat at all; then, ravenous, he'd rush from the apartment to the diner on the corner or the Chinese restaurant across the street and order far too many things, wolfing them all down, hoping he would not be hungry again for a long time.

Finally he'd come up with a system, which comprised the keeping of the delivery menus from seven nearby restaurants in a little stack next to the kitchen phone. He went through them in order, one for each night of the week. For lunch he chose among the last few nights' leftovers.

And every morning now, his English muffin and his low-fat "cream cheese."

You see? he would have liked to tell her. I've figured it out. It turns out that it's not so difficult to manage after all.

In the dining room on this November morning in the year 2000, Martin ate his daily English muffin, which was cold now.

He knew that he was not supposed to miss his well-done (which was to say, nearly burnt) bialy, knew that this would seem to be a trivial concern. And yet the crisp morning bialy—oh, the knowledge that there would *be* bialys in the freezer for him to toast every morning—how could one not miss, not mourn, a ritual of so very many years?

Still, it shamed him. It shamed him not only to mourn it, but also that he had believed so thoroughly in the necessity—the *stability*—of all of his rituals. And that he'd believed his family to be so gracefully, so happily, complicit in them. (But had not both his wife and son, when they had call to use the toaster, turned the setting back to "darkest" after they had finished with it? Had not they known to leave his daily *Times* unspoiled until he'd read all sections of it?—known and *understood* that otherwise he could not read it?) It was only in their absence that he saw that every gesture they had made of thoughtfulness, of tending to his needs and expectations—which had pleased him, which had moved him (he had not, as Gloria insisted, taken them for granted)—were only routine for *them*: that both his wife and son had merely had the habit of ensuring that he was not irritated, thwarted, disappointed.

And now something new—and dark—rose to the surface as he sipped cold coffee. Was it possible that they had feared him?

He had a temper, it was true, and when he was displeased, yes, it erupted—but to what end? His temper was alert and quick, but not long-lasting, never violent—certainly never physical, as his own father's had been. How could they have been afraid of him? They could not have been afraid of him. At most, they'd been alert to him. Perhaps it had been that that was habitual.

He wandered with his coffee mug into the living room, where he set it down on the low table at one end of the couch he never sat on, the couch (gray and white striped in its final incarnation) he thought of as Gloria's—placing it intentionally one inch to the left of the silver coaster she had left there. By now there was a set of interlocking rings tattooed into the wood, a Venn diagram of his life over the last two years. In the old days, by now he would have been at work for hours.

For the first few months after Gloria had left, he had not been able to work at all. The days had passed, one after another—lopsided, mixed-up days in which he slept at odd hours, mostly in daylight and never more than two or three hours at a time, and spent his nights prowling the rooms of the apartment as if they were a series of interconnected cages. He would turn the television on, then off, then on again. He remembered middle-of-the-night phone calls to Claire Alter, his literary agent, who was also his oldest friend. And those infuriating, too-brief conversations over the phone with his son. A few infuriating, and not nearly brief enough, phone conversations with his sister.

In the old days, even when his work had not been going well, when all he could do was undo what he'd done the day before, he had never missed a day. Even before he and Gloria had moved uptown, when they were living in the Village in a tiny studio apartment, he had written every day, working at the "kitchen" table (that was what they called it, but it was their only table; it sat in the corner near their only sink; the toilet was behind a curtain in a tiny alcove of their one oddly shaped little room). When Gloria came home and began the dinner preparations, he'd pick up his typewriter and manuscript and set them on the floor beside the bed. She used the table as her kitchen counter— the "kitchen" itself a two-burner stove beside the small square of a sink, the refrigerator in a corner of its own.

And then after dinner, she sat at the table to make lists of things that needed to be done. Their whole life, he used to say, reading over her shoulder, was summed up by these lists: *buy bananas, rice, milk, kidney beans; cigarettes; wine/whiskey? bank & post office; story to* Paris Review; *call M.'s father!* She checked each item off as she accomplished it, or as she made sure he accomplished it. She was the one who noted deadlines for grant applications, who reminded him that one was approaching ("Five days, Martin," then, "Three days, Martin," until she snapped, "*Now*, Martin, *today*" and asked him irritably why on earth he had to put things off the way he did, and he would kiss her forehead and say,

"They call it a deadline for a reason"). She was the one who made the trip to the post office with the envelopes that needed to be mailed in some particular way (certified or registered, return receipt requested, or *do not send certified or registered*—which she also kept track of).

She had known that he'd been grateful for her help, had she not? He had teased her about her list-making—as if everything that mattered could be planned for, then attended to and crossed off—but she had kept *him* on track too with her lists. When she no longer had to think about submitting manuscripts for prizes or for publication—when his publisher did the submitting and the prizes to be won were bigger, when Claire Alter was the conduit between his writing and its publication—he'd imagined that she was relieved. Still, he should have thanked her then for all her years of service.

Or perhaps she hadn't been relieved at all. Perhaps she had felt obsolete. Perhaps she missed the years when he'd relied on her for everything.

How could he know? How could he know anything if Gloria had kept it to herself? Was he to blame if she had never let him know she was unhappy?

He was not to blame. How often must he tell himself this? How could he be blamed? He had asked Jacob this the last time they had spoken. *Was I supposed to read her mind? Is that it? No one has to tell me anything—I am just supposed to* know?

"No one can tell you anything," his son said, so affably that for an instant Martin thought he was agreeing with him. But Jacob went on, "You know everything, so what would be the point?" Only then did Martin understand that Jacob (too?) was furious at him. That both his wife and son now so disliked him there could be no reasoning with either of them. But how had this happened? *When* had it happened?

Gloria had loved him once, he was certain of that. How happy she had been after his first great successes! How happy they both had been when they left that squalid Village room and moved uptown to this apartment. The good-sized advance for *Hartfeld*, its glowing reviews and brisk sales, the Guggenheim Fellowship he was awarded in its wake—all of this felt like a bet the universe had placed on him. When they signed their first lease on the apartment, at a rent that would have sounded like a joke to them just two years before, he told Gloria—who was happy, yes, but also nervous (though not nearly as nervous as she was when, before long, their building, like virtually every building in New York in the eighties, went co-op, and they had to buy or else move out)—"If a bet's been placed, you've got no choice. You have got to call and raise it. Otherwise you're out." It went without saying that he wasn't going out, that he was in the game no matter what by then.

Looking back, he thought that *he* would not have placed a bet on the earnest and arrogant young writer of his first book—those dutifully Chekhovian short stories—or, for that matter, on the early draft of *Hartfeld* for which Claire had somehow secured that generous advance. His learning curve, as he saw it now, had been comically long: he'd had no idea how to write a book that anyone would want to read, no sense of how to handle himself when he talked to other writers, no clue how things really worked. The Guggenheim was the direct result of *Hartfeld*'s rapturous reviews, when at the time he had felt sure it was a fluke—a wild coincidence that things had just started happening for him. Unlike the young writers he met at PEN and other literary functions, or that kid who had reviewed his last book for the *Times*—the Jewish kid whose own first book had been described by its publisher as "the literary love child of a drunken pairing between Martin Lieberman and Cynthia Ozick: wisecracking yet wise, seesawing between crackling, street-smart wit, crazy-clever highjinks, wordplay, and the cold steel of an intellect with which one dares not argue or even think of contradicting" (Martin knew which was which and he resented it)—he had been a rube, a greenhorn.

Thankfully, his first book, *The Ladies and Their Pet Dogs*, was long out of print, all but forgotten. It had been praised upon its publication, but once the first reviews of *Hartfeld* started coming in, he understood what he had not been wise enough to see two years before: that the polite, respectful praise that had meant so much to him, the solemn acknowledgment of the influence of Chekhov—as well as Henry James, Saul Bellow, and Flaubert—was the sort of praise that meant absolutely nothing. By then even he had lost all patience with his writerly good manners, for after three too-careful drafts of *Hartfeld*, he had started it from scratch again and made a breakthrough: "kicking all his influences to the curb—kicking contemporary literature's *ass*," in the words of the *Village Voice* review that Gloria affixed to the refrigerator with a 1010 WINS magnet (*You give us twenty-two minutes, we'll give you the world*) next to her current to-do list.

The publication of *Hartfeld* changed their lives. Gloria herself told everyone it felt as if they'd won the lottery. On the day the lease was signed on this apartment—with as grand a flourish as if it were the Magna Carta—laughing, flushed, he hurried home with Gloria and made love to her in the corner of their studio they'd actually called their "bedroom." The new apartment had *three* bedrooms— they marveled over this as they lay naked in each other's arms on Christopher Street. Real rooms, each with its own closet, its own windows. "So many rooms!" He remembered how they had said this to each other, remembered how enormous the apartment had seemed to them—although perhaps not so enormous as it seemed to him now, a man alone in too many rooms. Still, enormous enough—enormous and *elegant*. That was the word Gloria had used, a word she used too often (about clothes, parties, restaurants—people—and it maddened him but he could not break her of the habit). For once, however, he'd agreed, it was the *mot juste*.

When they first moved uptown—*back* uptown for him, and not so far from where he'd lived most of his life—it was as if he'd passed from one dimension to another. Just four street blocks and two avenue blocks (a distance that in other places would have been called half a mile) from his father's store and the apartment upstairs from it where his father by then lived alone, they might have wandered over to a different planet. His father said as much the first time he came to see them there, the first of only three or four times that he ever did. "Ach, it's a different world," the old man said—and the son, constitutionally unable to agree with anything that came out of his father's mouth, said, "Nah, it's not all that different. An apartment's an apartment."

"It seems to me very big," his father said. "We made out just fine with four of us, didn't we, in our place on top of the store." This was not delivered as a question. Martin managed to restrain himself, to keep from saying, "Oh, yeah? Mama would have liked more room, I guarantee it." Or reminding him that *he* had moved out just as soon as he was able, or that Anna had been in so great a rush to get away soon after that, she'd married the first boy she'd dated—that she had made a hash of her life just because she wanted out so desperately.

"It's not all that big."

His father laughed. "No? For two people?"

Gloria spoke up then. "Martin needs a room to write in, Dad. And we're hoping there'll be three of us eventually."

But this was a tactical mistake. "Eventually? You're hoping?" He fixed his gaze on Martin. "So she talks like this is for somebody else to make decisions. When it's up to the two of you, nobody else. Make up your mind."

Martin knew what was coming next—it was an old story already. His father disapproved of their relationship. "Either you're married or you're not married," he said at every opportunity. "A life together and also not together. One foot in and one foot out. What kind of sense does that make?"

And if Martin told him that it made sense to them and that was all that mattered, the old man would say, "Oh, so *that's* all that matters? What a world it would be if the only thing that mattered was what made sense to one person in particular."

"Two people," Gloria would put in then and the old man would turn on her again. "*You* should be smarter, at least. From you, I always expected more."

And Martin would say, "That's enough, Dad. Time to give it a rest."

He realized with a start that he had wandered back into the kitchen while arguing with his dead father.

He glanced up at the clock—it was past ten already (how, he didn't know)—and then, below it, at the calendar once more. He ought to take it down. He ought to throw it out.

He could hang a picture there if the blank spot beneath the clock disturbed him.

But what picture? He could not imagine.

Gloria had left, he sometimes thought, for reasons having little, perhaps nothing at all, to do with him. She might have told herself that her despair, frustration, boredom—whatever it was she was feeling that she kept to herself—was his fault, but really if she wasn't happy, wasn't that her own responsibility? With Jacob off at college, she had no excuse not to do something with her life, not to fill her days as she chose with something that would *make* her happy. Instead she chose to flee.

He had fled the kitchen for his study, where he was now hiding from the woman, Dorrie, who came in to clean for him. Not hiding, no. At ten-thirty, he belonged in his study. In the old days, he'd have been three hours into his workday by now.

Still, while Dorrie did her own work, instead of doing his, he sat remembering that first apartment he and Gloria had lived in, in the Village. As insufficient to their needs as it had been, for five years they had lived in it. One would think if they were able to do that, the rest would be smooth sailing. But in fact those first years had been their best. He thought now about the argument they'd had, not long after they had moved uptown, when he decided to quit teaching, to devote himself to writing full time. The advance Claire had secured for him for the as-yet unwritten *Gold's Will*, after the success of *Hartfeld*, made this possible, yet Gloria insisted that it was a "rash decision, arrogant, short-sighted." She told him he was "burning bridges" and he told her that this was just what he wanted to be doing. "I've landed safely on the other side. I'm not going back."

And then came the movie deal that brought in so much money even she could see that he had made the right decision (not that she admitted this—but she stopped talking about it).

Even so, she had kept *her* job, working part time in a law office—she kept it until only days before Jacob was born. She liked working, she said. "But then at least there must be something you would enjoy doing. There's no need to keep doing *this*." But she swore that she did enjoy her little job—that she was happy to be answering the phone and greeting clients, typing letters. She liked getting dressed up and having somewhere to go each day for four hours. She liked that the lawyers depended on her. And she liked that it was work that didn't interfere with her "real life." Unlike his work, he understood her to mean, which *was* his "real life." And her "real life," he also understood, was him. And then it was also their son.

Her real life, which she had left behind.

Twelve-thirty.

He read over the paragraph he'd written yesterday—it was all he'd written yesterday, although he had wrangled with it for a long time then—and decided that he liked it, or liked it well enough to move on from it. He wrote another sentence, the start of a new paragraph. His real life indeed.

It was possible he'd gotten back to work after those first few months simply because he didn't know what else to do with himself. He had never done any other sort of work, except in those early years when he'd taught others how to write (his father, if he were alive to say it, would have scoffed: "You call that work? I'll show you work. You never worked a day in your life") and, before that, proofreading and filing for a few years during college—also work his father had scoffed at. When he was a boy, the old man had expected him to help out in the store. His mother had encouraged him in his resistance. "He's a student, let him study." But maybe she hadn't done him any favors.

He heard the door close, the key turn.

Dorrie was gone.

He stood and crossed the room, opened the door. Silence and that mildly toxic scent she left behind. It made him think of a bath with lye soap, or the taste of having one's mouth washed out with soap (both of which had been inflicted on him in his childhood: the former by his father's mother, who didn't mean it as a punishment, and the latter by his father, who did). It was the scent his apartment deserved to have.

In the kitchen, he opened the refrigerator and considered the delivery containers lined up on the top shelf. He was hungry but there wasn't anything he wanted—not last night's baked ziti, not the night before's eggplant with garlic sauce. From three nights ago, there was lamb vindaloo. Nothing appealed to him. But he couldn't think of anything that did.

He considered calling someone. When was the last time he'd sat across a table from another human being? With a menu in front of him, with the social contract implied by meeting a friend in a restaurant, wouldn't he be able to pick something? But who was there to call? There was nobody he wished to see, nobody he wanted to talk to.

Long ago, he'd had plenty of friends—in high school, in college. Unlike Gloria, he had not accumulated new friends every year. Thanks mostly to her, however, the whereabouts of all their college friends were known to him. Gloria had sent holiday cards—a great many of them—and she kept her address book up to date. She kept up with all the milestones in their old friends' lives too somehow; she would bring them up in conversation with the new friends she relentlessly collected, mentioning that their "dear old friend Alice Rubinstein, who teaches history at Berkeley, has just married a Nobel Prize laureate in physics," or "our wonderful friend Manny Grodman—you may have heard of him? He's an expert on civil rights law and his last book has won a Pultizer—is running for Congress, heaven help him." But Martin could not recall the last time he had talked to Alice or Manny or any of their other City College friends. And neither he nor Gloria had kept track of the people they had known before then. Except for Penny Markowitz, Gloria's best friend from her old neighborhood, her best friend since kindergarten.

Martin barely knew Penny. He had met her only twice over the years (and he had not been impressed—and he gathered that the feeling was mutual) but she and Gloria had remained close, talking on the phone several times a week even in the years when long distance was a luxury. They had lived on opposite sides of the country since they were freshmen in college, which meant that they'd been friends long distance longer than they had been neighborhood and school friends, but despite the distance, the passage of the years, and all of Gloria's new friends—it seemed to him that every month she found somebody to befriend—they had continued to think of themselves as "best friends."

(Would Gloria have gone if she hadn't had somewhere to go? Would she have gone if she had not already *been* gone?)

Somehow he had ended up in Jacob's room. It seemed he had been wandering from room to room without being aware of it, and now here he was. Here was his son's bed—neatly made, as it had almost never been when Jacob lived at home—the blue-and-black striped blanket pulled tight, with four inches of blue topsheet folded over it; two pillows stacked at one end and an extra blanket at the other. The folded blanket was pale gray, fringed, softer looking than anything else in the apartment. Gloria had foresworn *soft* ages ago (Martin had gone along with it because the furnishing and upkeep of their home was in her jurisdiction—he had never had a say in it). He hadn't known that Jacob (or *how* Jacob) had managed to hold on to a soft extra blanket. (But wasn't it curious that he hadn't taken it with him?)

(But he had taken hardly anything with him.)

On the bookshelves, he saw, there were a few gaps where Jacob must have grabbed handfuls of books he thought he couldn't live without. They looked like a mouthful of teeth after a bar fight. It was unlike Gloria not to have closed the gaps herself, pushing together the books their son had left behind, adding bookends to keep the shortened rows from falling over like dominoes. It was less surprising that Dorrie, who was in here every day to dust and look after the bird, had not touched them. She was a thoughtful, careful housekeeper, and Martin himself had taught her to be particularly cautious when it came to books and manuscripts. (In the old days, when she came to clean once a week for Gloria, she would often move a stack of books or papers, re-shelve books wherever she perceived an opening without attending to where they belonged, and close books he'd left open, face-down. He would lose his temper then, and Gloria would scold him. But he and Dorrie had now come to terms. How difficult would it have been for Gloria to make what he required clear?)

He had sent Dorrie away when she showed up the first Monday after Gloria had left, but four months later he had called her and rehired her when he recognized that he required her services. "Recognized" was a misnomer: it was Claire who told him this after she bullied her way into the apartment. "Good lord, it's even worse than I imagined," she said, and demanded he find someone to keep things in order. "None of that once a week crap either," she said. "You need someone five days a week just to pick up behind you. Not to mention scrubbing away your filth."

Jacob's room was very clean, and like the rest of the apartment in the first hours after Dorrie left each day, chemical-scented. He could not remember the last time he had set foot in it, last set eyes on the bird abandoned by his son. It eyed him now, suspiciously, from behind bars. Dorrie tended to it daily, bringing from her own home little plastic bags filled with chopped-up fresh vegetables—"Only seeds is no good, Mr. L," she said. She even stopped in on the weekends for a moment (her idea, not his; he would not have asked her) to take care of it. He heard her susurrating to it as she cleaned its cage—he supposed she had become attached to it. She'd scolded him for the poor care he'd taken of the bird during those first months he'd been left alone with it. (Thanks to her, he no longer had to care for it at all.)

He spoke to the bird now. "Dolores, right?" The bird held his gaze briefly, coolly, then hopped onto another perch and turned its back to him.

"Fine," he said. "I completely understand."

The bird was none of his business and he was none of its.

He sat down on Jacob's bed, halfway between the pillows and the dissident soft extra blanket. He had not sat on this bed since Jacob was a little boy and he would read to him at bedtime. No—that wasn't true. He remembered now: he had last sat on Jacob's bed right after Gloria had called to say she wasn't coming home—when he'd hung up the phone and without thinking went directly to his son's room to tell him what she had said. It was only as he crossed its threshold that he was reminded that Jacob was elsewhere, that he'd left for college months before. He didn't know what else to do and so he went in. He sat down on the bed. He might have sat there for a long time, stunned. So both of them were gone. Had they planned this together—to leave him alone? Or had she left both husband and son? It was inconceivable to him, it struck him then, that she would have left both of them. He would have sworn that for years it was Jacob who had mattered to her—that it was only Jacob.

When he had reached his son by phone that night, he did not ask if he had known and Jacob didn't volunteer this information. By now there was no one he could ask. By now he wasn't sure it would make any difference.

But during the ten weeks between the day his son had left for college and the day his wife had left for what was to have been a week's vacation, he had often walked by the open door to Jacob's room and seen her sitting on his bed. It startled him each time (startled him even after it should not have startled him, after he should have grown used to it, expected it). She never acknowledged him as he went by.

He never spoke to her about it. They had lost the habit long ago of having conversations of that sort. If they had ever had the habit—honestly, he wasn't sure. It was hard now to remember what they used to talk about, before their conversations were about logistics—or weren't conversations at all, but were terse, ill-humored exchanges. Or were outright arguments. She never spoke to him of how much she missed Jacob, and while he supposed that she was suffering—supposed that it must have made her feel better to be sitting among Jacob's things—he'd never asked. And once she was gone he wondered if maybe she hadn't sat there missing Jacob after all. Maybe what she had been thinking was, *All right, he's really gone. Now I can go too, can't I?*

Well, he would never know.

From the bird's cage came a soft grinding sound, like someone zipping and unzipping a suitcase. Martin looked at the bird, whose head was tucked under its wing as if it were asleep. The zipping sound continued for a moment and then ceased. Martin had the feeling that the bird was waiting patiently for him to go away, that given the choice between his company or none at all, it by far preferred solitude.

"I'm not that bad," he told it. "You know, if given half a chance."

The bird did not acknowledge that he'd spoken. Well, that was perfect. No one who'd ever lived in this apartment, not even the failed magic prop he had been stuck with, was on speaking terms with him.

Indeed, the only creature with whom he had ever lived who spoke to him was Anna, and they hardly ever *spoke*. But she wrote to him faithfully, and he to her—they were on writing terms. This almost made him smile.

He glanced once more at the bird, pretending to sleep on a perch made to look like the branch of a tree. Or maybe—who knew?—it was really asleep. Maybe it wasn't angry with him; maybe it was so uninterested in him, so unmoved by his presence, it had dropped off to sleep out of sheer boredom.

And maybe he was losing his mind, trying to understand the way a cockatiel's brain—a brain the size of what? A poppy seed?—worked.

He ought to have rid himself of the bird long ago. He should have found a family to give it to—a proper family that lived in an apartment with more than one person in it. A family in which everybody talked to one another even when they weren't living under the same roof anymore. In which, when a kid went off to college, he called home, visited on holidays, came back for a whole summer.

The truth was that he never should have said yes to the bird in the first place.

What he should have done was let the kid have a dog. That was what he'd really wanted, just like any kid. It was what *he* had wanted too—what he had begged for—as a kid, until his old man slapped him and said, "Stop this begging. You are acting like a starving dog yourself."

He had never said this to his own son. Nor had he said, as his father had—as his father said *his* father had (and as Martin knew his old man would feel free to say again if he told him he had brought a dog into his own home for his own child)—*The Cossacks had dogs, Jews don't have dogs.* Still, he had thought it, and it was not the first time—and also not the last time—that his old man had spoken up inside him. It was not the first or the last time that he'd successfully suppressed his father's voice, his father's words. Instead he spoke to Jacob calmly of commitment and responsibility and how much work it was to have a dog. He mentioned how much of a mess a dog made—this with the hope that Gloria would chime in, back him up, and she did. *So* much mess, she said, and who do you think will be cleaning up that mess?

And Jacob—he was a small boy when he first asked, but so much more tenacious than Martin had been at that age—said earnestly, *All right, then, how about a cat?*

And later on: *Why not a guinea pig? Why not a turtle? Why not a snake, a rabbit, an iguana? Why not fish?* His son was not a boy who gave up easily. (Martin had secretly admired him for it—and admired himself a little for it too, for had he not been the one raising the boy to ask questions, to push back? Not to be cowed the way he had been as a child?) And then the tenacious little boy became a sullen teenager and it was finished. Or so Martin had thought—until, out of thin air (like something out of one of the boy's tricks), came the demand for a live bird he deemed essential "for the act."

For the act. The effect on Gloria was instantaneous. *Oh, if he needs it for the act! Well, then, that's a whole different story!*

And that was how he'd ended up with Jacob's bird.

Or at any rate it was how the bird had ended up in Jacob's possession.

Gloria was wild for anything that had to do with his "career," perpetually offering the kid encouragement and arguing with *him* when he suggested that perhaps their son was spending too much time on magic, taking it a bit too seriously for what it was. "But he's good at it," she'd say. "He's ambitious, and his ambition is paying off." She would point out that he was earning money at his magic, that he was winning prizes for it. And it was a serious pursuit, she said, like playing the piano or the violin—it was not like collecting baseball cards or banging out three chords on a guitar. It was not *trivial*, even if performing magic tricks was not, she granted (but she said it sarcastically, as if he were the one who was wrong, as if *this* were the risible idea), "making great works of art."

Slyly, she'd add, "He's younger than you were when you began to publish your first stories."

But here was what was risible: *he* had been the one to get the kid started on magic—he had been the one to teach him his first trick. And more than that, that *he* knew just *one trick*. He had taught his son the only trick he knew, and that was all it took: the kid fixed on the idea of becoming a "magician."

And because Jacob was a kid who didn't give up, who held on to any idea he happened to stumble on long past its universally understood expiration date, he never wavered from this goal. It was the damnedest thing.

What if he'd taught him how to tap dance—one painstakingly memorized dance number, let's say, at an impressionable age? Would he be on Broadway now? Or—hell, how to make the perfect lokshen kugel? Martin's mother had made delicious lokshen kugel. What if she had taught her son and then he'd taught his own son? Would Jacob have devoted the whole rest of his childhood to learning to make brisket and knaydelach, then grow up to open a deli?

But Martin did not know a tap dance routine, and nobody had taught him how to make a noodle pudding or even how to scramble eggs. He was destined for higher things—that was how his mother had seen it. And so all he had was writing and reading, which did not impress the child. And that stupid magic trick, which did.

He had learned his one trick—it was called "the phoenix trick"—in high school. He had practiced it and practiced it until the trick was something he could casually pull off to charm girls at parties. He had never bothered to learn another one—and why would he have, when it had taken so much practice to get this one right? Besides, one trick was all it took to serve his purpose. (Indeed, one was sufficient. More than one and he would have been "the guy who does magic tricks," which he had zero interest in becoming. He had other fish to fry.)

He was in his sophomore year of college on the night he did his trick in Stuart Fleischer's kitchen, the night he met Gloria. He was pretty sure, in fact, that this had been the last time he had done it until he did it for Jacob on a day the child was stuck at home—he was in second or third grade and it was some kind of holiday, or maybe he was sick?—and Gloria had gone out for the afternoon. He remembered very well, all these years later, how she'd fretted, how she'd tried and failed at the last minute to reschedule whatever it was she was doing, and how something (desperation? boredom? seizing the rare chance to dazzle him without Gloria on hand to make it her business to *undazzle* him?) had inspired him to perform the trick. He managed it beautifully too, as smoothly as if it had been days instead of years since his last performance.

He was absolutely sure that *that* had been the last time he had done it, because after that it became Jacob's trick.

It involved a book of matches, and there was a story you told while you did the trick—or, as Martin had liked to think of it, there was a magic trick you did to illustrate the story you were telling. His son was enthralled and asked for it again and then again, and Martin was reminded of how it had been between them when Jacob was very small, before he'd started school, before the whole world came between them. Oh, he could do no wrong then! Gloria had complained of it: *He thinks the sun rises and sets on you.* All *that* little boy had wanted was for his father to read him another book, make up another story, sing him another song…and then read it again, tell it again, sing it again. But the three-year-old would fall asleep after a while; *this* Jacob was inexhaustible. His father, of course, was not. Eventually he told him to find something else to do.

And that would have been the end of it except that what Jacob had found to do until Gloria came home was sit in his bedroom with the book of matches he had surreptitiously picked up after Martin did the trick for the last time—and then, once that book of matches was used up, another, and another, and possibly *another* book of matches to which he helped himself from the kitchen drawer—until he figured out, all by himself, how the trick was done.

From that point on, the kid was hooked. And unless something had changed since the last time he'd talked to him, it did not seem that anything the boy was studying in college was derailing, or even nibbling at the edges of, his determination to make a career of magic. From what Martin was able to gather when his son still deigned to take his calls, he was juggling that career with his life as a college student (who had not yet, Martin had noted—though not nearly as frequently as he was tempted to—declared a major). On the occasions when Martin had ventured to inquire into the academic side of his life ("Aren't you having to miss a lot of classes, traveling so often to perform? Don't your professors mind? Don't your grades suffer?"), Jacob said that everything was fine, his grades were fine, his teachers were all very understanding (there was the occasional professor, yes, who was not on board at first, but he always won them over just by doing solid work all term despite his absences—and, if they asked, he'd even do a trick or two in class). He seemed as certain as ever that this was what he wanted, that this was what his life would *be*. A life of magic tricks. Illusions, games. Applause from those he fooled.

Who would have supposed that such a thing could happen? Well, who would have supposed that the boy would choose a college on the single criterion, it seemed, that it was far from where *he* was?

He thought about the evening when Jacob first performed the trick for him and Gloria, how after she applauded wildly (and before it became clear to her that eight- or nine-year-old Jacob, practicing this trick, had been lighting matches in his room all afternoon), he asked if she remembered it and she looked at him blankly. "The night we met? At Stuart's? You watched me do this trick in Stuart's kitchen. It was what made you like me." He winked at his son. Jacob looked at him as uncomprehendingly as his mother had.

"It wasn't the trick," she said, and because she gave each word exactly equal weight, he didn't know if what she meant was that it hadn't been the *trick* that had caught her attention, or that she believed that it had been a different trick that he'd performed that night. He was going to set her straight—she was wrong either way—but Jacob was already talking about how hard he had worked, how his father hadn't told him how to do the trick, he'd only *shown* it to him, and that was when she understood about the matches and she scolded him (she scolded Martin too, for negligence) and Jacob cried. And then she started crying too, because she always cried when he cried—even when he was a baby and cried all the time.

Martin closed his eyes. He felt a little dizzy. He should probably eat something. But he could not bring himself to stand up, to leave Jacob's room. He was stuck there, it seemed. Stuck in Jacob's room, on the bed that had been Jacob's bed. (Whose bed was it now? It was no one's bed.)

He lifted his feet from the floor that was now no one's floor and swung his legs around, swung himself around, until he was lying down.

Thanksgiving was a week away. It was the only holiday that Gloria had ever made much of, the only holiday they celebrated as a family. The holidays that had meant something to their parents (Passover had been the only one in Martin's childhood household; in Gloria's, a Seder was the least of it, her mother making an event of *every* major Jewish holiday, Sukkot and Shavuot as well as Yom Kippur and Rosh Hashanah) by mutual agreement were not marked in any way, and early on he had also persuaded her that the fatuous, purely American elevation of Hanukkah, a minor holiday, into something that stood up to Christmas was beneath them. (Christmas, it went without saying, was ignored.) Jacob got plenty of presents on his birthday every year in June. They were not a family who needed so many holidays, Martin had liked to say.

But for Thanksgiving Gloria would cook for days, and decorate with gourds and ears of flint corns and bouquets of autumn leaves. She invited guests, sometimes upwards of a dozen. It all mystified him. But he had grown used to it.

When she left him—or, rather, when she *told* him she had left him, a week after she had set out on vacation with a single suitcase, one she'd bought just for this trip—it was only a week before Thanksgiving.

Stupidly, when she said she wasn't coming home, he'd said, "But what about Thanksgiving?"

"What about it?" she'd replied, and this had been almost as shocking as what she had called to tell him.

Jacob had never enjoyed their Thanksgivings (so many grownups, so much drinking and talking about matters that were of no interest to him, and when there happened to be children present, they were strangers—they belonged to whatever friends his mother had acquired that year and were always the wrong ages and wrong temperaments). Still, he had put a brave face on it. And by the time his first Thanksgiving after leaving home for college was approaching, he was making jokes about it: when Martin told him that his mother would be taking a vacation just before it, "resting up before the onslaught, I guess," his son said, "Great, maybe she'll bring some new friends home with her from California. Surfer dudes. Or maybe movie stars." And when he had to call him with the news that his mother wasn't coming home—not for Thanksgiving, not at all—Jacob had not said, "Then I won't come home either."

But just three days later, he called to tell Martin he had changed his mind about Thanksgiving. He was sorry, but if it was all the same to him, he'd skip it this year. He had too much schoolwork to do anyway.

It was not all the same to him. He should have told him that. All he had said was, "All right, son. I understand." But it wasn't true. He didn't understand any of it.

A month later, Jacob did come home for winter break, but only nominally. He had booked a lot of shows, some in town but more of them in other cities. And then he went back to school right after New Year's—which he celebrated with his childhood friend Roberto, with new friends of his at Juilliard—without their having had a single conversation face to face about his mother. But even on the phone, they didn't really talk about her. Martin would report that she had called—in those days when she was calling—but he didn't dare ask Jacob if he too had heard from her. And when he asked Gloria herself, her temper flared: *this is not your business.*

He could remember just one conversation about Gloria with Jacob, besides the one they'd had the very last time they had talked. It was only month or so after she'd left, a few days before he came home for that winter break. It was the only time Jacob had volunteered the information that he'd heard from his mother: a postcard had come, he said.

"And?"

"And nothing. It was a postcard. It said the kind of thing people say on postcards."

"Wish you were here?"

He should not have made a joke. Jacob went silent. If he apologized, would it make it worse?

"Well, it's good that you heard from her," he said instead. "I'm glad. Even if she didn't have much to say this time. Maybe next time."

That was when Jacob said, "You were a jerk to her." He said it without anger. He said it flatly, as if it were a truth universally acknowledged.

"I wasn't," Martin said. And then, "Was I?"

"For sure."

"In what way?" he asked. He genuinely wanted to know. Even if it wasn't true (it *wasn't* true—he was confident it wasn't), he wanted to know why Jacob thought it was.

"If you have to ask," Jacob began, and Martin said, "Oh, give me a break. Your mother used to say, 'If I have to ask, then it doesn't count.' It was maddening. How can that be so? I'd want to know. How can you get what you don't ask for?"

"But that's not what I said, is it," Jacob said. "What you were asking me was not *for* something." He sounded patient. He was still patient then, in those first weeks. "You were asking me what you'd done wrong. And just the fact that you don't know suggests—"

"I'm trying, Jake. Okay? I'm doing my best."

"Then your best isn't good enough," he said. Yet another thing that Gloria would say, infuriatingly, when they had argued. "It would be great, too, if you didn't interrupt me when I'm talking," Jacob said. And then, abruptly: "Look, I've got to go. I've got to study." And he hung up—no goodbye. It was inauspicious.

Still, he was unprepared for Jacob to stop calling him, not long after his one visit home. And even then, at first, if Martin called *him*, he would pick up the phone; if Martin emailed him, he'd email back, if tersely, obviously grudgingly. But by the start of his sophomore year, after a summer of Martin calling and emailing (perhaps too often, but who could fault him for that?), asking if he wasn't going to come home for at least a short visit, and how was it that he didn't feel the need for a vacation…and what kind of kid does not come home from college for the summer after freshman year? (and Jacob responded, during one of their tense phone calls, to just one of Martin's questions: "Going home would not be a vacation, Dad"), he stopped taking his father's calls; he stopped responding to his emails.

At first it seemed an oversight, an accident. The boy was busy starting a new year of school. He was busy with his magic. What were a few emails left unanswered, a few phone calls unreturned? He himself was guilty of such lapses. But the months piled up, and the number of phone messages that disappeared into the void, the volume of unanswered emails and then postal mail, which Martin added to the mix—thinking that a proper letter might be harder to ignore (he was mistaken)—made it clear to him: his son was gone, just like his wife.

Thanksgiving weekend that first year, he hid away in the apartment. He did not answer the phone, the three times it rang, and he turned off the answering machine so that he didn't have to hear Jacob's apology— if, indeed, it had occurred to him that an apology was owed—and if Gloria had anything to say, he didn't want to hear it. Not just then, not when he wasn't up to a debate, or to hear a catalog of all his faults. And there was no one else who knew he was alone, no one who would call to speak to him. Thanksgiving meant nothing to his sister, just as it had meant nothing to him until Gloria decreed that it had meaning.

On Thanksgiving Day he waited tensely for the doorman to buzz up (he would have ignored that too) but Gloria must have rescinded all her invitations. Perhaps she'd made a list: *Things to do when I leave Martin*. Perhaps she had affixed it with a magnet to her friend Penny's refrigerator, checking off each item just as she'd done in the old days.

He left home for an hour, that first Thanksgiving that he spent alone—late in the evening, and only then because he hadn't eaten all day long (or eaten much of anything the day before) and all at once he found that he was famished. He had dinner at the Greek diner (roast turkey, mashed potatoes, stuffing, a perfectly reasonable facsimile of a real Thanksgiving dinner), accompanied by that day's *Times*. He didn't read the paper—in those days he couldn't read the paper; he didn't want to know about the world—but he propped it up so that if anyone tried to make conversation, it would be clear that they were interrupting him. No one tried to make conversation.

That first Thanksgiving, he kept what had befallen him a secret. Eventually, of course, he told Claire; he told his sister. The doormen in his building all knew. Dorrie knew. He didn't speak of it in interviews, although presumably the next time he was newsworthy (if he ever finished the book he was working on—if he ever finished anything again) it would all come out in the wash. By now it made no difference to him. He was used to the idea of having been forsaken.

So he repeated to himself, as often as if it were now his mantra—or a prayer.

Last Thanksgiving, Claire had prevailed upon him to join her and her then-boyfriend and her two grown daughters from her second marriage (one came with a husband; one, newly divorced, without) and the boyfriend's own grown daughter and her husband and child. This year he would be joining Claire and her new boyfriend, who had no children, and the boyfriend's stepmother, and Claire's two daughters (the one who'd still been married last year was now separated; the divorced one had a girlfriend now and would be in attendance with her own two daughters). Martin had tried begging off (last year had not been much fun for anyone, he reminded Claire: "I brought everyone down, I ruined your party"), but she said, "I'm so sorry, darling, but you're just not that important—no one's fun was in the least affected. Besides, Thanksgiving isn't about fun, it's about family."

Should he have said something like that to Gloria, long ago? (Could he have said it with a straight face?) More to the point: was there a relationship between her leaving him and her filling their home with strangers every year for dinner on her favorite holiday?

And how had *she* spent the last two Thanksgivings? (He had asked about her plans last year—another question she'd declined to answer during that last-ever phone call. *It's not really your concern now, is it.* She had expressed no interest in what he'd be doing. He did not tell her that he hadn't talked to Jacob since mid-summer, and she didn't ask.)

Now, for the second year in a row—and possibly for the rest of his life—he would spend Thanksgiving with his agent and the current incarnation of what she called family. It was not the worst way to spend the day. Claire cared about him, she worried and fussed over him (in her mordant, Alteresque way), she understood him. She had been his agent and his friend since he was twenty-two years old. That made her his oldest and closest friend, without a doubt. Perhaps, by now, his only friend.

He closed his eyes for a moment. It was possible he fell asleep.

When he opened them, he was startled to find himself still in his son's room. He turned his head on the pillow and looked at the room from this angle. A desk, a desk chair, a tall dresser, a nightstand. The surface of the desk—Jacob's desk (it was no one else's desk)—was clear. He considered this, his cheek still resting on the pillow. He blinked once, twice. Ah, he was wrong about how much the boy had taken when he left. How had it escaped his notice that there was nothing at all on the desk? Or that—as he now saw—the tops of the dresser and night table were bare, too.

So his son had taken everything: clock, reading lamp, the raised-relief globe Martin had bought for him on an impulse during one of his post-lunch walks years ago (it was in the window of a shop that had just opened in the neighborhood; when he saw it he remembered how much he had wanted one himself when he was Jacob's age, and how it had been every bit as out of reach as Europe, Asia, Africa). What else had been here? A semicircle of trophies. A signed baseball on a stand.

He propped himself up on his elbow. The posters on the walls remained—Houdini with his bound wrists and quizzical expression, Carter the Great playing a game of cards with the devil. But above the desk there was just bare, pitted cork, dotted with blue thumbtacks. Whatever had been hanging there—ticket stubs from Yankees games? postcards? photos?—Jacob had decided was worth taking with him.

Gloria's decision was that nothing was worth taking with her.

But then Gloria had not known she was leaving. She had packed up only a week's worth of clothing for her trip to visit Penny Markowitz.

Jacob hadn't known that he was *leaving* either, though. He was just going off to college. He would be back for Thanksgiving and again for winter break, then spring break, then the summer. He hadn't planned to leave for good.

Martin sat up. Then he stood. He crossed Jacob's room and opened his closet.

A scattering of hangers. A stack of board games on the shelf.

Had he planned it?

But he had bought his airline tickets for Thanksgiving. He had told his father his flight number and the time of his arrival.

And then he hadn't arrived after all.

Monopoly, Careers, The Game of Life, Clue, Trouble.

Martin closed the closet door.

So the boy had taken all his clothes—that was not so strange, was it? For all he knew, it was what all children did when they went off to college.

What was strange was that Gloria had left behind all of *her* clothes. There were so many blouses, dresses, skirts, scarves, pairs of slacks, blazers and cardigans and who knew what else jammed in on the two rods that faced each other in her closet—so many towers of shoe boxes stacked up along its back wall, so many belts hanging from hooks, a winter bathrobe, a summer bathrobe—it was hard to imagine that she had removed anything when she'd packed for her week away.

And when she'd called to say she wasn't coming back, he had asked (sardonically, yes, but still he had *asked*) if she wanted him to send her any of her clothes, she'd said, quickly, "No, I don't want anything. Just leave it."

His wife had left everything behind, so eager was she to start a life without him. While his son had taken everything he had.

It felt as if together, miles apart, his wife and son meant to teach him a lesson. But what was the lesson? That whether one moved on unburdened or weighed down, escape was possible? From where he stood, they were only two ways of being gone. It was the *gone* that mattered. A full closet or an empty closet—what difference did it make?

He left Jacob's room, closing the door behind him. He would not make the mistake of entering it again—this room that was like a looted museum.

And the rest of the apartment? An intact one.

In the two years since Gloria had left he had not altered anything, had not discarded anything, had not so much as set his hands on anything except what he had no choice but to touch. Why had he not put Gloria's ludicrous coffee-making machinery into a cabinet? Or better yet, given it away? (Better still, thrown it away?)

He returned to the kitchen, where he scowled at the coffee maker and wrenched open the refrigerator, taking out the container of eggplant with garlic sauce. As he set it on the counter, he noticed the blinking light on the answering machine. In the old days Gloria had turned the telephone's ringer back on as soon as he was done with his day's work, then switched it off again before she went to bed. Now he kept the ringer turned off at all times; the answering machine too was set to silent, and he listened to his messages when he felt up to it—sometimes going days without checking the machine (and when he did, there would be a stream of messages from Claire, interrupted only by hang-ups from solicitors or pollsters or wrong numbers, so that he often wondered why he kept a phone at all).

He poured himself a glass of water and stood by the sink, eating his cold Chinese food out of the container with a pair of disposable chopsticks. He had a whole jarful of them, gathered and stored by Dorrie. Indispensible Dorrie, who was all that stood between him and chaos. He thought again about the bird, alone in Jacob's nearly emptied room. The bird that despised him. As the sun went down, the room would darken and the bird would sleep. It would wake when the room lightened and wait for Dorrie to come to take care of it.

Not that he cared whether it woke up or not.

Dorrie could be counted on to care, to speak cheerfully to it, to feed and water it and clean up after it. Just as she cleaned up after him each day. What must she think of all of this? He recalled how she and Gloria would chatter at each other all day long when she came once a week—how Gloria seemed to follow her from room to room, talking louder when the vacuum cleaner was switched on. How the sound of their voices taking turns, rising and falling, sometimes dropping to a whisper, sometimes giving way to laughter, irritated him as he sat in his study. How sometimes, if his work was going badly, he would throw open the door and beg them to be quieter.

He and Dorrie exchanged few words, but she followed his lead without his asking her. She left everything as it had been: the tall, high-heeled black patent leather boots that Gloria had left under the bedroom window, which stood alertly waiting for their owner to return and step back into them; the bottles of perfume lined up like little soldiers on the dresser top; the book that Gloria had left face down, its spine cracked, on the nightstand on her side of the bed—the book she had been reading in bed on the night before she'd left for California; the clip-on book light she used when she read beside him while he slept.

He remembered her picking up the book—it was the first volume of the complete collected Chekhov ("The Darling" through "Three Years")—thinking out loud about taking it, deciding not to, saying, "Maybe I'll take something new instead. Something fun for the plane trip." And she had glanced at him, as if to challenge him to challenge her, to say something about the word "fun," to mock her or provoke her. He remembered his decision not to—because he didn't want to argue with her (he didn't want her to argue with him) before she left for a week. And so instead he said, "You know, there's a pile of bound galleys in my study, and every single one's a novel coming out this winter. Would you like me to see what I can find for you?" He remembered that he'd said this in a friendly way, that she had said, "No, that's all right. I'll buy something to read at the airport. It'll be an adventure."

The abandoned Chekhov. The battery-operated book light. The box of tissues, the jar of expensive hand cream, the pair of drugstore reading glasses. The white plastic case with her custom-made bite plate inside. She had meant to pack that—she'd mentioned it on the phone the first time she'd called home, when she still believed—or when he believed she still believed—she would be coming home. "Oh, well," she said. "Maybe I won't need it. Maybe while I'm on vacation I won't grind my teeth."

Perhaps she hadn't needed it. Perhaps that was why she'd stayed away. Once she had discovered that there was no need to protect her teeth from themselves as long as they—she—were thousands of miles from him, perhaps she had asked herself, *Why go back? Life is good here, where my teeth are unclenched and the lemons grow on trees.*

He leaned against the counter and thought about the volume of Chekhov he had not been able to bring himself to close, much less put back in the bookcase where it belonged. He thought about what she might be reading now instead of Chekhov. She might have been relieved to settle back into her former self, to give up Chekhov and Flaubert, Ozick and Coetzee, to read all the potboilers and slick magazines she wanted. Or not to read at all. To watch as much television as she liked instead.

Or perhaps it was not relief she felt. Perhaps it was fury. *The hell with him and his godforsaken books.* If so, she was hurting only herself. What was it to him? And in time she would come to see that one could not survive on an intellectual diet of television shows and *Elle Decor*—or that one *could*, just barely: survive, but not—assuredly not—thrive.

The way I thrived all those years with you?

It was what she would say, if she were speaking to him. If he could tell her what was on his mind and expect an answer.

And yet she had been grateful, those long years ago, when he had taken up the cause of her intellectual life, when he had taken her seriously enough to do so. She hadn't been resentful or hurt—she had been pleased. "I don't know anything about literature," she'd confessed when they'd first started dating. "I'm sure I haven't read what you would consider a 'good book' since I was in high school."

He had started her out, slyly, on Jane Austen. Then he moved on to Edith Wharton, then to Henry James (stories at first, then *Portrait of A Lady*). From *Portrait of A Lady* it was on to *Madame Bovary*. Then came the Russians, which was where he struck gold.

You never knew what would take, what the books were that would win a given reader's heart. They were in college then, where Gloria had majored first in sociology, then in psychology, then anthropology—a march through the *ologies*, he'd teased her. It was with Gloria that he discovered, before he ever taught a college class, that you could coax someone to read—that you could, in fact, lead someone to a book *and* get her to read it. If you knew her well enough, if you paid enough attention to the things she said, if you chose cleverly enough, you could make someone a reader. And if you continued patiently, book by book, writer by writer, you would find the one that would not only be appreciated or enjoyed but truly and dearly beloved.

For Gloria, it was Chekhov. She read two stories, the Constance Garnett translations of "The Darling" and "Misery," in a paperback *Selected* Martin bought her at the Strand, and she loved them. He suggested that she read "The Lady with the Dog" and "The Kiss" next; he handed her another (then another) volume of the stories—and when Ecco Press brought out the complete set, he bought it for her, for her birthday, and unlike every other gift he'd ever given her, she wasn't disappointed by it. He had never been good at discerning her taste in scarves or sweaters or perfume or jewelry. He'd even gotten gloves wrong once. (You'd have thought it was impossible to get wrong a pair of soft, fur-lined, very expensive leather gloves, but she'd said "Brown?" when she peeled back the tissue paper. "Martin, you know I never wear brown." But he hadn't known.)

As to the Chekhov: he did not believe it was a matter of his having at last guessed correctly what she'd like, or even that he'd accidentally put in her hands the right book at the right time. What he believed was that he had changed her taste. That he had changed *her*. Because what you read was what you were (and he knew firsthand that what you read could *make* you what you were—what you would eventually be).

And yet now, when he thought of the book she'd left behind, the paperback she had reread so many times that multiple pages had come unstuck from their binding, so that there was a little fan of yellowed page-ends beyond the edges of the book's splayed cover, he wondered if he had made a mistake—if he had planted a seed in her mind, all those years ago. If the seed he had planted there himself had finally germinated. All those characters who were revealed to have deluded themselves. All the regrets, the doubts, the almost comical mistakes, the second-guessing. So tenderly portrayed. Such *inviting* sorrow.

All those years that he had had the satisfaction of watching her across the room from him with a book in her hands, it had never crossed his mind that she was studying up on her own *dis*satisfaction.

Had he taught her to see herself in Chekhov's stories? Had she come to imagine herself as one of those thwarted characters? And what did that make him? Did she truly think he'd thwarted her? But thwarted her in what?

When she told him she was leaving him, the only explanation she'd proffered was that she had "deluded" herself for too long. "I never saw things clearly until now," she said.

What things? he asked her. Him? Their home? Their family? Their *life*?

"You're bullying me," she said.

Was it bullying to ask her questions?

It was, yes.

But he could not stop asking. Did she really think she was going to live in California? Did she think she *belonged* there? Did she not recognize that this was a cliché—and not just a cliché, but an outdated one? Did this not embarrass her? And did she not recall that she had not thought much of the West Coast when they were there together?

That was in 1973, she said. I've got to go. I'll call you.

Really, Martin thought, the cut-off conversations and the absence of an explanation that made any sense—the sheer repetition of their truncated, senseless exchanges—and finally the silence that fell and then lingered, and then lasted (apparently for good—the very ending of his marriage), were—it must be said—less Chekhov than Kafka.

Kafka, he thought, if Kafka had ever troubled himself with the small domestic matters with which Chekhov was so much preoccupied.

His chopsticks scraped the empty takeout container. Ah, done, then.

But there had been in fact no *ending* of his marriage. His marriage had stopped—that was different, was it not, than an ending? It was an "ending" only in the Chekhovian sense, an ending that did no more than suggest that things would go on somehow (who could say how?) from this stopping point.

If he had let her be—if he had never put a story of Chekhov's in her hands—would she at least have felt obliged (would she have simply been inclined) to provide an ending for him that was not merely a *stop*? It would have been a kindness to him. (She did not believe she owed him any kindness. But there had been a time when she'd believed that every story required a clear-cut beginning and a middle and an ending—it was his own fault that she'd learned otherwise.)

It was ironic, he supposed, that it was he who found the lack of a clear ending so unsatisfactory. (If he did not know better, he'd suspect that she'd intended irony—but this was not her strong suit.) Not knowing why she'd left or why she had stopped calling him, not knowing where she was (*was* she still in California—or was she by this time in Paris or in Prague—or, for that matter, back here in the city?), not knowing if he'd ever know—not knowing if Jacob knew and not knowing if he'd ever know what Jacob knew, if Jacob knew anything. Not knowing if he'd ever hear from either one of them again.

One could not live this way, however. One's life was not meant to be a story written by Chekhov.

That Gloria had taken no steps toward divorce—what was he to make of that? Was it her intention to leave him—keep him—in limbo? Was that meant to be his punishment? Or did it seem to her not worth the trouble (she could not be bothered with him anymore, not even to dissolve their marriage)? The depth of her unhappiness with him had evidently been so great that she was willing, eager, to leave everything behind—every last book and pair of boots and bottle of perfume and blouse and bracelet. What was he to make of that? Was he to spend his life surrounded by her things? Still married and yet not married at all?

He should sell the apartment—the thought came to him suddenly. Yes, he should sell it and move to a smaller place. What was keeping him here? Hope? Nostalgia? Fear? Inertia? Laziness?

He had never in his life been lazy.

He imagined it now: packing up his papers and his books and his computer, his desk and desk chair, his good reading chair, his clothes— doing what Jacob had done, taking only what he needed and what mattered to him. Donating or discarding all the furniture that Gloria had chosen and arranged and rearranged, re-covered, fussed and fretted over. All the clothes and shoes and scarves and purses—everything that she had left behind. And her jewelry—Claire would know what was worth selling and where it could be sold.

He heard something then. At first he could not place it—a loud click, giving way to a low whirring sound—but then he recognized it as the answering machine collecting a call. He moved toward it unthinkingly, but its volume was turned off: without turning it on, he could tell nothing about what was happening within. He stood for a moment with his eyes on it. Then, cautiously, he slid the dial up. His outgoing message was still playing—he caught the last few words of the message he'd recorded years ago ("…at the infernal beep, please")—and then there was the beep itself. Then: "Dad, this—"

He lifted the receiver. "Son?"

He flushed—he had never once addressed Jacob as *Son*. But Jacob laughed. Laughed! "That's me," Jacob said.

"Jake. My God. How are you?"

"I'm fine," his son said. "You?"

"Also fine." He said it carefully, walking the receiver on its long cord to the dining room. He had to sit down. He felt struck through the heart, lightheaded.

"Well, listen," Jacob said. But then he was silent.

Martin waited, his face hot, his heart thudding in his ears. His son could not be calling because it was the anniversary of his mother's leaving. Martin was sure *he* would not have known but for the circle on the calendar. But why, then? To tell him he'd heard from her? Because something had happened?

To her, or to Jacob?

Or could it be that he just missed his father?

Martin almost laughed then. But instead he said, "I'm listening."
And then, into the silence, "Jake? Are you still there?"

"I'm here," Jacob said. Martin could hear him take a long breath.
"So, Dad, I was thinking I might come for a visit."

"Were you?" *Careful now*, he told himself. "Well, I would welcome
that. That would be good." He thought of the way one approached a
stray dog. Trying to coax it near enough to read its tags, to offer help.
Not wanting to frighten or provoke it. Hoping that it wouldn't bite.
"When is it you're thinking you might come?" He made sure not to
emphasize the word *might*. "Were you thinking of Thanksgiving?
Because Auntie Claire—"

"No, not for Thanksgiving. Sometime after. We have plans for
Thanksgiving."

"You have—who has?" His heart had sped up. It was beating so fast,
so hard, it was as if something alive were trapped in his chest. Beating
on the bars of its cage.

"Christ, Dad. You sound as if you're about to have a stroke."

He *felt* as if he were about to have a stroke. Or maybe a heart attack.
"You're spending Thanksgiving with your mother?"

"With my *mother*? Are you out of your fucking mind? My girlfriend
and I have plans. With *her* mother."

"You have a girlfriend?"

"I do, yes. Don't sound so surprised."

"I'm not surprised. I mean, yes, I'm surprised. I'm surprised to hear
from you. And I don't know anything about your life so all of it is bound
to come as a surprise. But of course you have a girlfriend. I look forward
to meeting her."

"I suppose I should tell you that this wasn't my idea, it was hers."

"To spend Thanksgiving with her mother? I should think so."

"No, Dad. To come see you."

Martin laughed.

He laughed because it was funny—and because he was not having a stroke or a heart attack. And because it was classic Jacob. Of course he had to make sure Martin knew that he did not want to see him, that someone else was pushing him to do it.

"So you haven't heard from your mother."

"It's been a while," his son said. Then: "She thinks I'm being pigheaded about you."

"Your mother does?"

"My *girlfriend* does."

So Jacob and Gloria had not been in cahoots. Or if they had been once, that alliance had come to an end. Martin felt a flicker of relief, then shame.

"So your girlfriend thinks you're pigheaded," he said.

"Not generally. Only about you."

Martin laughed again. "Tell her I like her already, will you?"

"You can tell her yourself when we come."

So they'd gone from *might* to *when*. And *I* to *we*.

"So when are you thinking of making this visit?"

"Sometime in March, most likely. We have a break between winter and spring quarters. That's the first chance we'll have."

"March is a long way off."

"Not that long."

"Well," Martin said. "All right, then."

"All right," Jacob said.

And then he was gone. Not even goodbye first. Just gone.

Like mother, like son.

But Martin banished that thought quickly. No. Not like his mother. *He* was coming home.

PART 2

YOUNG ENOUGH

The poet Jill Rosen had always intended—had always *planned*—to publish her first book by the time she was twenty-one, although she could not have said how she had determined that such a thing were possible (and yet it *was* possible: in her late twenties she would hear of someone who had done just that—a friend of a friend of a friend from her pre-Iowa, post-City College days—and she commiserated gladly and perhaps a little meanly on the phone with the old friend who passed this news along, but commiserated only to a certain point, as the friend herself, who had just turned twenty-nine, already had two books behind her to Jill's one, and a Whiting *and* a National Endowment for the Arts grant, and had recently secured a tenure-track teaching position, even if she'd had to leave the city for it).

It was likewise a mystery to Jill where she had ever gotten hold of the idea that "poet" was an occupation to which one might aspire—but she had written proof that she had so aspired by the age of eleven, for she had filled in the blank beside "future career" in her sixth grade (zippered, silver) autograph book with the single uppercase word followed by a multitude of exclamation points. (For "best personality trait," on the same preliminary page of questions—favorite book, song, "saying," best subject in school—she'd filled in *intelligence*.) By then she had been writing poems for years, since at least the second grade. (She had evidence of this, too: a poem about Elvis Presley, entitled "Why I Like Elvis Presley" and written in a form surprisingly close to the Spenserian sonnet—missing only the final couplet—on a piece of wide-ruled faded yellow paper, with her name and date and class, 2-1, in the top left corner.)

Yet it was not until she reached the age of twenty-seven that she published her first volume of poems, and although she was pleased with the book itself—slim, elegantly made, with thick, cream-colored pages, the poems set in type (Caslon Old Face) she would have picked herself if anyone had asked her, and a book jacket designed around a close-up black-and-white photograph of the stone face of an apartment building—still she spent autumn 1978, when *Fire Escape* came out, in a gloom of conviction that her time had passed. Even at her own book party, at her editor's dazzlingly large apartment on the Upper West Side, she could not shake the sense that she'd already lost the race. Besides her editor himself, who was over fifty (even his blond wife, a modern dancer, was younger than Jill—she asked), the only people at the party for her book who were older than she was were her parents.

She had returned to Manhattan only a few months before. During her sojourn away it seemed that half her friends had fled—and, unlike her, had failed to return—and she had somehow managed to lose touch with the half who hadn't. Everyone she met now was a new arrival, fresh from college or the Peace Corps, late of Scarsdale or Long Island or the deep South. They were actors and composers and playwrights and novelists and other poets, and every one of them was younger than she was.

How could this have happened? For years—for practically her whole life—she was famously the youngest one, the girl who'd skipped the third and seventh grades, who'd graduated a semester early from high school (which was laughably easy—all she had to do was double up on gym—so why didn't everyone? she had naïvely asked her then-best friend, Gail Skolnick, who pointed out that, a) not everybody raced through the requirements of the NYC public school curriculum so that, except for gym, they had completed everything ahead of schedule, and b) even if they had—as indeed, Gail noted, *she* had—normal people, herself among them, *liked* being high school seniors and didn't want to miss out on half of the best year of their lives so far). Two weeks after she'd been sprung from that mind-numbing, supposedly best year of her life, she was enrolled for eighteen credit hours at CCNY and was thus through with college at nineteen.

She hadn't properly appreciated this (youth, as ever, wasted on the young). In her early twenties she'd waved off remarks about her work (admiring, hostile, envious, defensive, or only surprised) that paired praise or even evidently neutral observation (*I see you have a poem in the new* Paris/New England/Virginia Quarterly Review) with the never-neutral observation of her age. Now, as she neared fifty, no one spoke about her age. There was nothing to say—there would *be* nothing to say until she was very old: *Eighty-seven and still writing such magnificent poems!* Or: *Eighty-seven and, poor thing, she ought to have quit years ago. Have you noticed how she is simply repeating herself?*

No-longer-a-prodigy had crept up on her. At Iowa, she had not been among the youngest because she'd held out after college for five years, insisting that there was no reason for her to pursue a graduate degree. Had Emily Dickinson? Had Yeats? (Wallace Stevens had earned his degree in law—perhaps she ought to do that, she had said archly to a boyfriend who was himself enrolled at Brooklyn College in a graduate creative writing program, and was, like everybody else she knew in those days, older than she, which he seemed to think conferred upon him the authority to offer her advice.) When she did at last decide on graduate school, it wasn't because anyone had changed her mind about it—it wasn't even that she'd changed her own mind, but only that she was exhausted, tired of scrambling to make ends meet, tired of freelance copyediting and proofreading and temp jobs as a typist, tired of everything about her life in New York City, including the string of boyfriends, of failed relationships, of "friendships" that could be counted on to irritate, upset, or bore her—and then there was her family, which could be counted on for all of the above plus disappointment and the occasional bout of rage.

The two years away, however, had only made it harder to eke out a living, as her three best freelance contacts were among the people who'd thrown up their hands and left, presumably returning to wherever it was they had come from (really, she thought, it was as if people had just been waiting for her to look the other way before they made a run for it). And her illegal subletter, a twenty-three-year-old aspiring actress from Milwaukee, had slept with her next-door neighbor, Roger, half a dozen times before he (he too!) left New York for California, having landed a small role on a TV show—Jill had come home to find a subletter in *his* apartment—and now she kept calling Jill to ask if she had heard from him, and if so what he'd had to say about her. (Back then Jill was ready to bet somebody ten dollars that the actress would go back to Milwaukee before *she* was twenty-seven. For all she knew, she had.)

All of this would not have so depressed her if the aspiring actress wasn't one of the only people she knew in the city by then. She wondered sometimes why she had been in such a hurry to return to New York. (Well, but where would she have gone? Where could she go *now*, for that matter, if she wanted to go somewhere? Unlike the lovelorn actress Maryellen from Milwaukee; unlike Roger, who'd broken Maryellen's heart and who, if things had not worked out in LA and then still did not work out back in New York, could always have returned to wherever it was that *he* was from—somewhere with a V, thought Jill, who had lost touch with Roger years ago: Vermont? Virginia?—she had nowhere to return to. Unless she were to move back to Queens. To Flushing. But nobody returned to Flushing.)

In July, almost exactly a year after her return, she packed up to leave—temporarily again, and this time only for six weeks, but oh, what high hopes she had for those weeks! She was off to Yaddo, the artists' colony, to be cossetted, protected, perhaps even inspired—so she had been promised by one of her teachers at Iowa ("*If* you get in," he said. "Don't take it personally if you don't. It's very competitive," which she recognized as understatement, and which of course made her determined to compete successfully, as indeed she did). She took an early bus up from the city, then a taxi that wound through a path lined with tall trees—and when she saw the mansion looming, she was filled with anxiety: did she actually *want* to spend six weeks in the company of other "artists"? Would they all be famous poets, as her teacher was? (Or famous symphony composers, famous painters, famous avant-garde performance artists whose work she wouldn't understand?) Would she feel small and unimportant in the midst of them? And then there were all those trees—how could one tell where was one was in the midst of *them*?

She was shown around by a young man in shorts and a Sex Pistols tee shirt who identified himself as a conceptual artist. He pointed out landmarks and gave her a map she could not make heads or tails of, directed her to the lunchbox that had been packed for her, and deposited her in the room to which she'd been assigned—where, with the curtains drawn against the forest, she got right to work. By dinnertime, having accomplished more in a few hours than she had over the last few months at home, she was quite cheerful. She thought about how Yaddo had once housed Sylvia Plath, James Baldwin, Leonard Bernstein. Carson McCullers, she hummed to herself, descending the stairs. Flannery O'Connor. Langston Hughes.

And of course her former teacher. Who was a good poet even if he was kind of a self-important jerk.

Katherine Anne Porter. Elizabeth Bishop. Robert Lowell.

This was the state of mind she was in when she entered the mansion's dining room. Thus she was caught off guard—shocked, really—by the buzzing hive of industry that greeted her. Or rather that did *not* greet her (even now, two decades on, the memory of that first Yaddo dinner made her wince), for no one spoke to her; even the conceptual artist who had been her tour guide didn't seem to recognize her. The conversations she caught snatches of seemed vulgar—too worldly, too businesslike. As she filled her plate and took a seat, as she ate her dinner silently, she heard talk of book tours and advances and reviews and prizes and commissions, gossip about editors and art dealers and agents; there was chatter about who was leaving and who was or might be coming (many of the residents—the "colonists," they called themselves—apparently knew one another from previous visits, or other artists' residencies): "Oh, Fiona's due on Thursday, late. I can't wait to see her" and "Have you heard that Henry's coming?" and "I can't believe I missed Stephen *again*—we missed each other at MacDowell last year by just one day."

At breakfast, she took a seat at the morning "quiet table," which had been pointed out to her as part of her tour, "for anyone who doesn't like to talk so early in the day." While all around her greetings and inquiries were exchanged ("How did you sleep?" "How late did the ping pong game go on after I left?"), she sat reading the new Auden *Selected* over cereal and toast and coffee. No one joined her at the quiet table, but no one seemed to be offended or surprised—or even seemed to notice—that she'd opted for silence.

If only there were such a table at dinner, she remembered thinking as she hovered at the entrance to the dining hall that evening while others moved past her, heading decisively to a place at the long table or to one of the smaller tables from which people called out greetings to them. There was a great deal of laughter and exclamation, a clattering of dishes and lively conversation, and her hesitation reminded her unpleasantly of junior high and her first months in high school, before she figured out that if she took an extra class, she'd miss lunch altogether—a bonus, she discovered, of successfully petitioning to take a second foreign language. Just as she had then, she felt the heat on her face. The fabric of the gauzy kurta she'd changed into for dinner (a little bit but not too much dressed up, the way many of the other women had been the night before—she had taken note) was dampening under her arms. She'd made no progress when someone behind her—male—said, "Want to sit over there with me?"

She turned. He was good-looking, around her own age, maybe a little younger. Longish very black and curly hair. A Yankees cap. Black tee shirt, jeans. Not tall—built like a wrestler. Dark eyes, no glasses. Not a writer, she thought. His arms were too good. A sculptor, she guessed. Jewish, and overcompensating.

"All right," she said. And added, "Thanks."

From the long table in the room's center came the roar of many people laughing at the same time. He took her elbow. "You were looking a little lost," he said quietly, directly into her ear, to make sure she could hear him as he guided her toward one of the smaller tables.

"You could tell that from behind me?" She glanced at him. He looked familiar. A *little* familiar, as if she'd seen him on TV or in the movies. She was sure they hadn't met before. Perhaps there was an actor he resembled? He was handsome enough. But more likely she'd half-noticed him last night, or this morning at breakfast before she had settled in with Mendelson's beautifully restored selected Auden.

"You were standing there for a long time," he said.

"So were you, then."

He laughed and kept her moving forward. "Mel, Lucy, Paul, Naomi," he said as they neared the table, "this is"—he paused—"who is this?"

"Jill." He drew out a chair for her like a waiter (or, okay, she thought, a gentleman) and she sat down. She thanked him.

"Just arrived?" one of the women asked.

"Yesterday afternoon."

"I arrived four hours ago," said the wrestler-sculptor who looked like a movie actor. To Jill he said, "But I've been here twice before. And once to MacDowell—Lucy and I overlapped there by a day. I met Paul earlier today, when I picked up some mail that got here before I did. Naomi and Mel I've been at Yaddo with before, but we've also run into each other in real life."

"Something like real life. A book party for Bernard Malamud that I wrangled an invitation to," one of them—Naomi or Mel—said. And the other said, "A post-reading thing after Martin's debut at the 92nd Street Y. His life is more surreal than real these days—wouldn't you agree, Martin?"

Jill turned to him, puzzled.

"Oh! I'm sorry," he said. "I haven't introduced myself." He raised his hand—a gesture that was half wave, half nothing-but-the-truth-so-help-me-God. He was Martin Lieberman, and he was not a sculptor—or a wrestler—but a novelist. Jill recognized his name as soon as he said it. His second book had been published to great acclaim last year. And she had read it. That was why he looked familiar—from his book jacket photograph, the same one that had accompanied the numerous reviews and interviews (he looked more bookish and more serious in the photo, though: he wore a button-down white shirt and a tweed jacket and his hair was short and tidy).

She'd liked his novel very much. More than his first book, which she'd read too—a collection of short stories that had come out during her first year at Iowa, and which had created a big stir among the fiction writers there, because its author was just twenty-two, fresh out of college, and *The New York Times Book Review* had granted him a full page. Everybody in the Workshop was reading the collection—three or four copies of the new hardcover were being passed around. She'd thought it admirable and intermittently absorbing but overall a little careful and as a result a little dull—like Roth's *Letting Go*, or Ozick's *Trust*. It was the kind of book that let you know the writer was eventually going to write a very good novel. She would not have guessed (who could have guessed?) that the very good novel would come only two years later.

"I've read *Hartfeld*," she told him. "I liked it a lot."

"Oh, I'm so glad," he said. "It's kind of you to tell me that."

"It seems to have made him a bona fide literary celebrity," said the one whose name turned out to be Mel. She had a blond pixie haircut, a high forehead, a pointed chin—she looked like an elf.

Martin Lieberman laughed. "That's less kind, Mel. But yes, I'm afraid it's true. I'm doing my level best to enjoy it. But it's also confounding. It's what one hopes for, I suppose, but when it happens—"

"*When* it happens? Do you promise?" said Mel.

"We all want to be Martin Lieberman when we grow up," the one who Jill now guessed was Naomi said. "Well, except for Lucy."

"I write poetry," Lucy said. "So there's no hope of it."

"Not much," Jill agreed. "I'm a poet too."

"Lucy Porter," said the other poet. She half stood to extend her hand to Jill from across the table.

Jill clasped it. "Jill Rosen. It's nice to meet you." She could see Lucy—who looked the way Jill imagined people thought a woman who wrote poems should look: pale, with tragic-looking bluish half circles below her eyes and a lot of light brown hair piled atop her head, secured with jewel-tipped bobby pins—thinking hard, trying to decide if she had heard of her. Lucy Porter didn't ring a bell with *her*, so it would be just as well if Lucy didn't know her work. She hated that lopsided moment when two poets met and one had read the other's book but not vice versa. Since her book had come out, this had happened several times. It was almost as bad as meeting someone whose work you knew and disliked.

"Jill Rosen," Lucy Porter murmured. "Have you a book yet? My first is coming out this fall. So's Naomi's novel—we've been talking about having a joint publication party."

"My first came out last year. Around the same time as *Hartfeld*, actually." She thought about making a joke about how her book might have made a bigger splash if not for Martin Lieberman's cannonball jump into the literary pool, but it would not be funny. Everything that had come out last fall had been buried—drowned—by *Hartfeld*, but a slim volume of poetry would have slipped into the water soundlessly under any circumstances.

"Oh, wait," Martin Lieberman said. "I know who you are. You're J.T. Rosen! I knew you looked familiar. It's amazing to meet you. I haven't read *Fire Escape* yet, but I've got a copy in my suitcase. I picked it up at Shakespeare & Co. just a few days ago, right after I read that poem of yours in the new issue of *The Nation*. It was fantastic. I can't wait to read your book—it's the first one on my read-at-Yaddo list. I can't believe you're here."

And just like that, the two of them were friends.

But other people didn't like him. She could hear it, as the days passed, in the way they greeted him—the irony that suffused the customary dining room questions about how one had slept and how the workday had gone—and the scarcely veiled sarcasm with which they responded to anything *he* said. She couldn't figure out if they were all just jealous (there was plenty to be jealous of, but it seemed to her shockingly petty to dislike someone only because you were jealous of his outsize success) or if there really was something about him that displeased and irritated everyone but her.

And "everyone," she learned, included the small group—a clique, she realized—with whom they'd had dinner the night she and Martin met. A few days later, on a hot, humid afternoon when she had knocked off work a couple of hours early, she sat dangling her legs into the swimming pool from its cement edge and heard Paul and Naomi, on the grass behind her, laughing and agreeing with what Mel had just said, quietly (although not quietly enough)—that while she did not "personally" wish Martin any ill, she would be much happier if he would live and be well somewhere else. "Yes, please," Paul said, "anywhere but here," and Naomi said, "For sure, let him be celebrated and revered. But as the rabbi says about the tsar in *Fiddler on the Roof*"—she shifted to a singsong Yiddish accent—"*far avay from us.*"

Perhaps they didn't realize it was she, in a swimsuit with her back to them, or perhaps they didn't care—or did they somehow assume she would agree with them, despite the evidence of her friendship with Martin? She and he sat together every day at both breakfast and dinner, and after dinner they sat talking in whatever quiet corner of the mansion they could find, or else they took a walk. She saw people exchanging glances when they peeled off alone together from the after-dinner drinks and parlor games crowd. She was a curiosity to them. Martin didn't seem to notice any of it. Or, if he noticed, he could shrug it off.

His confidence, she thought, was genuine—unlike the puffed-up, put-on confidence that seemed to be built upon deflating anybody else's, which she'd encountered everywhere in grad school and now again at Yaddo. Martin's confidence made *her* feel confident—it was contagious. He made her feel optimistic, too, which was unlike her. He was so enthusiastic about everything that interested him (and what was there that didn't?) and so *eager*, so excited. He was like a puppy, she thought sometimes, wanting to get into everything, attentive to minutiae that nobody else could see (she thought of this often during dinner, when he went on about something he found fascinating and she watched the others at the table losing patience after trying futilely to redirect the conversation, like irritable dogwalkers whose leash-tugging had no effect).

Halfway through her second week, somebody she didn't know said, "So you and Lieberman are pals?"

"Sure," she said. "I guess." *Pals* was a strange word. It put her on alert. The man who'd spoken was a novelist, at least a decade older than she; he'd arrived two days before. Jill had recognized him—there'd been a profile, accompanied by a large photograph, in the magazine section of the *Times* (his third or fourth novel had been something of a sensation a few years ago), and it had been intriguing enough so that she'd sought out the book (and she'd liked it, too, although not nearly as much as she had liked Martin's)—but they hadn't spoken until he made this remark as they stood side by side in the Linoleum Room, where Jill had come to see if she had any mail and he was collecting packages he'd sent ahead. "That book of his is pretty good," he said, and Jill looked up from the envelope in her hand. It was from her mother, and she was trying to decide whether to open it and read it quickly and be done with it, or if it would be better to put it away and read it at another time, maybe even days from now—or if she should hand it to Martin later and let *him* open it and read it out loud to her. Then it might seem funny instead of depressing.

"I thought the book was great, actually," she told the other novelist.

"Did you? That's interesting." He said this without looking at her. And then she watched him turn and go, cradling the stack of packages in his arms. She might have helped him with the door to the back porch if his tone had not been so unpleasant.

And the next morning, as she took her bowl of oatmeal to a table—Martin was across the room guarding the toaster as he waited for his toast to pop up, for he had to re-press the lever once it did since he liked his toast nearly burnt—the writer she had met the day before (or sort of met—they had not even exchanged their names) sat down beside her and resumed their conversation as if fourteen hours had not elapsed. It was his opinion that "too-early success is never healthy for a writer," and that Martin's, in particular, had come too easily. Martin was heading toward her with his toast and hers, so she had only seconds to think of something to say. What she landed on was, "I don't know a thing about success myself. Do you?"

She said it sweetly, and then greeted Martin, thanked him for her toast and asked him if he knew the novel she'd begun to read in bed last night—she'd found it in the Yaddo library—and which had kept her up late. Naturally, he knew it (she had yet to ask him about anything he didn't know), though it had been out of print since soon after it was published. "Ten, fifteen years ago," he told her. "It's a tragedy. A travesty. *Stoner* is a hell of a good book. John Williams is a hell of a writer." And then he was off and running: about *Stoner*, about Williams, about other underappreciated writers ("Ever read George P. Eliot's story collection *Among the Dangs*? That collection alone—plus his essays, which are really something—should have established him as a major writer"). After a while she heard the man on her other side gathering his dishes, and she saw that Martin was poised to speak to him, but she asked a question about a line in the Williams novel that had especially moved her—"the epiphany of knowing something through words that could not be put in words"—which distracted him.

As new people arrived over the days that followed and were seamlessly absorbed into the ranks of those who found Martin (or at least his success) insufferable, the two of them drew closer. It occurred to her that the other colonists might have concluded they were lovers. She never spoke of this to him, but it must have crossed his mind too, and most likely it amused him. (It did not amuse her, but then she was not as easily amused as he.) What they did speak of sometimes by then was the others' envy of the attention *Hartfeld* had gotten, the attention *he* had gotten.

"Who can blame them?" Martin said. "I wouldn't like it either, if I weren't me."

"You think it's just human nature to be covetous?"

He laughed. "Would there be a commandment that outlawed it if it weren't?"

"*That's* how you determine human nature?"

"Absolutely," he said cheerfully. "Anything that's forbidden by one of the Ten Commandments. Or else is on the list of the seven deadly sins. Oh, and also the stuff that had to be addressed by the Bill of Rights—but that's more complicated. Like, it's only natural to want to be free from unreasonable search and seizure, but I'm thinking that it might also be natural to want to unreasonably search and seize."

"You're very silly," she said. But when she woke up the morning after this exchange over the lunch they'd made a picnic of, on the grass between East House and the Wood Shop, before returning to their work, she was still thinking about what he'd said—and four days later, after dinner, while everyone else was out on the flagstone terrace, she handed him a draft of a new poem (she had titled it "Human Nature") from her perch on the giant carved oak chair in the great hall, as he sat on the carpet below her. She could not recall the last time she'd shown anyone a poem she had just written. Even at Iowa, she had revised for days—weeks—before she'd bring a poem to workshop.

When he looked up from the pages, he said, "Yes, that's good. I like it."

"It's still rough."

"I just said I liked it."

"Right. Thank you. I'm glad."

"I don't care for the title, though," he said thoughtfully. "And the epigraph? It's from such a gloomy poem. That's the one about looking out at the ocean and stealing the view from people who have more of a right to it than you do, isn't it?"

"Something like that," Jill said, though the line, from Marianne Moore, was *taking the view from those who have* as much *right to it as you have to it yourself*, and in the line before that, the first line of the poem, Moore had used "sea" and not "ocean," which made a sort of pun with "looking." Martin would have corrected her if she'd made this mistake. She was pleased with herself for choosing not to correct him.

The epigraph she'd used, from Moore's poem, was

> *it is human nature to stand in the middle of a thing,*
> *but you cannot stand in the middle of this*

and Martin was right, she realized, about the title, which relied both too much on the Moore and on what amounted to a private joke between her and Martin. But she wasn't losing the epigraph. She told him that.

"But Moore's poem is about death and yours is about figuring out how to live. Don't you think that's something of a bait and switch?"

"Don't you think it's just the opposite of bait and switch? Who baits with death?"

Martin ignored the question. "Also, you should drop the first ten lines, right down to

> *Don't be greedy. Don't look*
> *now. Don't spare the rod*

and then drop down to

> *Spare change? Drop it*
> *in the bucket. Keep a clean square*

> *of embroidered hanky safety-*
> *pinned above your heart. Brush*
> *your hair, your teeth, yourself off."*

"Stop," she said. "I can't bear it."

"Really? I thought you *wanted* notes."

"No. I do. The poem, I mean. I can't listen to you read from it."

"All right," he said. He handed it back to her. "But it's a good poem. Make the cuts. Call it 'How to Live.' Trust me."

"All right," she said. "Maybe I will."

She did trust him, which was a little shocking. She was usually slow to trust. But she felt at ease with him. She liked his erudition and intelligence, his enthusiasms and his cleverness, his wealth of assorted knowledge. At dinner he held forth on books and art and theater, music, modern dance, and film (silent, French, circa-1940s Hollywood, Robert Altman, Terrence Malick). He had much to say about the history of the United States, which had been his college minor, and the history of science, which seemed to be a hobby. He knew all about—and was happy to speak of to any newcomer who innocently wondered aloud about any aspect of—the history of Yaddo itself, and could speak knowledgeably of architecture, the six manned U.S. moon landings, and the weather (she had started working on a poem that was the direct result of Martin's disquisition, over Sunday morning pancakes, on cloud formations).

She was reminded of a character in *Stoner*, which she had by then finished reading—David Masters, the friend of William Stoner's youth, who declares himself "too bright for the world" and unable to keep his mouth shut about it ("a disease for which there is no cure")—and thought of Martin tenderly, as if what others must perceive as boorishness *were* a disease. It made her feel protective toward him at the same time that it made her want to tease him. She did tease him ("Oh, please *do* tell me fifteen more facts about patterns in nature! Quick, before I have my first cup of coffee!")— somehow he brought this out in her, as if he were her younger brother (just as she had been both her brother Norman's protector and his tormentor when they were children). Martin, for his part, would say, "You're the mean older sister I never had," and Jill would tell him that somebody had to keep his head from swelling; he would point out that this was exactly why he had a girlfriend: "Just ask her— that's *her* job." Gloria, the girlfriend (his "long-suffering girlfriend") doled out praise and criticism in "perfectly equal measure," he told Jill. "If I surprise her with a Western omelet on a Sunday morning, she'll be sure to tell me it's delicious, but she'll also mention that the onions and green pepper are a little underdone. Or if I'm all spiffed up for some high-class *lit'rary* event of the sort she has no use for, she'll say, 'Very handsome. I like the new suit—but you did a lousy job tying your tie, and you need a haircut."

He spoke often of Gloria. He had mentioned her during that first conversation over dinner (*duly noted*, Jill had thought) and, indeed, by the time they had parted that evening, after talking for a long time after dinner, too—first on the terrace, Martin smoking one cigarette after another; then, when the mosquitoes drove them indoors, in the mansion's drinks room; and when others drifted in as well, trailing a composer who held a bottle of gin in one hand and one of vermouth in the other, out to the great hall, to sit cross-legged and facing each other on the floor by the hearth, under the mosaic of a phoenix rising from flames—Jill had learned that Martin had met his not yet long-suffering girlfriend in the spring of their sophomore year at CCNY (they'd begun there just three months after *she* had graduated) and was living with her by the following winter.

"What was the big hurry?" Jill asked, that first night. "You were what, nineteen?"

"Why were *you* in such a hurry to finish college?"

"That's not the same thing at all."

"I think it is. You were in a rush to get to the next part of your life. So were we."

Days passed before he told her that his mother had died of a massive heart attack not long after he and Gloria had started dating. There was a chance that this had had something to do with how quickly things had escalated between him and Gloria. Living with his father and his younger sister, Anna, with his mother gone, was unendurable. "I missed my mother horribly. So did they, I'm sure. But my old man never talked about it—he never talked about her at all—and Anna couldn't stop crying. And if she tried to talk about it, he would fly into a rage." Anna had wept when he moved out, "but she'd been crying for months anyway," he said. "I didn't think things would get that much worse for her. But I'm not sure I was right about that."

"And Gloria?"

"Things didn't get worse for her, either."

Jill sighed. (Was it this tendency to be a wiseguy, she would later ask herself, that made people dislike him?) "I mean, how was it that *she* was ready to start living with her boyfriend so soon? You were both so young, and you'd known each other for, what, six months?"

They were walking through the pergola, to the rock garden—far from any of the others, who rarely ventured beyond the lawn. "Gloria didn't love living with her family, either. And we both had part-time jobs, and school was free. We knew if we pooled our resources, we could handle a squalid little studio somewhere. It wasn't a hard decision. It didn't even feel like a decision. We were in love. We took an optimistic leap into the future together."

Was she disappointed, that first night, to learn that he lived with someone? She was not. Was she attracted to him? Sure, but not unmanageably so, and she had an iron-clad, utterly unchallengeable rule about married (or might-as-well-be-married) men, which had served her very well for years. (If only she had managed to devise and stick to other equally fixed rules—about depressives, alcoholics, narcissists, or liars… or actors, musicians, other poets, or the pathologically dependent—she would have been spared so many ill-fated relationships)

In truth, it was a relief to her that they were destined to be friends. A friend was what she needed, not another failed romance. And Martin was an excellent friend, a friend of a sort she'd never had before. Not only was he the first friend she'd ever had whom she was not a good bit smarter than, Martin was *landsleit*—as her mother would have put it—someone she knew in her bones, someone who was from the same place she was.

Metaphorically, she meant. The people who were literally from the same place she was—Flushing, Queens—had never seemed to her her *landsleit*. She had been an alien among them. As Martin had among the people with whom he had spent his childhood. Nobody understood what he was up to. His parents, like hers, were mystified by his determination to grow up to be a writer. (They also had in common one combative, disapproving parent each as well as one baffled, gentle, mostly ineffectual one.) All eight of their combined grandparents were from the old country (but not *landsleit* either: his family Litvaks, hers Galitzianers); all four of their parents had spoken Yiddish before they spoke English. Both of them were the first in their families to go to college.

But the differences in their upbringings were a source of endless conversation too. She never tired of hearing him speak of Lieberman's Homegoods and the dark, crowded apartment upstairs from it on Amsterdam Avenue, nor he of the sunny semi-detached brick house with an upstairs and a downstairs "just for living in" (so his mother would have lovingly and longingly described it, Martin said) with separate bedrooms for her and her brother and a den in which her parents watched TV and her father, who went into "the city" each day to work in an office, sat at a small desk and paid the bills.

After she showed Martin that first poem, they traded everything they'd written. Jill read aloud to him as soon as she had a complete draft of a new poem (but never again *handed* one to him, the way he handed pages to her; *he* was not afraid that she might read his work out loud). He gave her the first three chapters of the novel he was working on—everything he'd written of it before Yaddo—and once she'd read them and they'd talked, he brought new pages to her, whatever he had written that day, almost every evening.

She thought the new book was wonderful, every bit as good as *Hartfeld*. She was glad for him. And not just glad but relieved, too. She knew how much pleasure certain people would take if the follow-up to *Hartfeld* was a disappointment. That was what Gloria worried about, Martin told her. "She says, 'The reviewers will *kill* you.' She's said this a thousand times, that they'll bury me if it doesn't live up to their expectations."

"But has she read what you've done so far? There's no chance of it not living up to anybody's expectations."

"I haven't shown her any of it yet."

"*Martin*. You have to show her. Then she'll stop worrying."

"Or she won't, and my life will be a living hell."

What he said about Gloria was hard for Jill to put together. She was a pessimist, a worrier, *and* she had taken that "optimistic leap into the future." She managed his career as if she were his secretary—

making calls, *taking* calls so that he could work uninterrupted, handling his correspondence—and she was also sure he'd fail. But asking Martin to account for this, to explain it (explain *her*) in a way that she could understand, seemed to Jill a line she couldn't, shouldn't cross.

Although he had no trouble asking her about the men with whom she'd been involved. (Of course, all of those men were in her past, so this perhaps was not equivalent.) He was especially persistent in his questions about the most recent one—the man she'd dated while she was in grad school. Not another writer in the program, but a med student named Tomas. He had wanted to marry her.

"Really?" Martin said. "You're serious?"

"You don't have to sound so flummoxed."

They were sitting on the second floor landing, halfway between the palatial bedroom suite that had belonged to the house's owner, which was Martin's for the time being, and her much smaller room. "I'm not *flummoxed*," he said. "Just slightly thrown. I hadn't figured you for someone who wanted to be married."

"I'm *not* someone who wants to be married. Tomas is. That was the trouble." For just an instant she closed her eyes and conjured Tomas's face. He'd had—he *had* (as far as she knew, he was still among the living)—a beautiful face, a mournful and sensitive face, with his sad brown eyes, his long, thin nose. It was a face out of a fifteenth century Netherlandish portrait. She did not tell Martin that.

She almost never thought of Tomas's face anymore. She almost never thought of Tomas. At first she hadn't let herself, but now he was simply gone. They had agreed not to speak to each other once they'd parted—Tomas's idea, not hers: he had told her it would be too hard, it would keep him from meeting someone else. And once he did meet someone else, he would not be inclined to stay in contact with a former girlfriend. It made him uneasy that she was in touch, however slightly and irregularly, with so many of the men she had once dated. He did not want to be one of them, he told her—he said it gently, but it still stung.

Tomas had been the only one she could allow herself to relax with, to speak freely to, when she was in grad school. With everyone else she knew in Iowa City, and even when she was alone, she felt she was working. Drinking coffee, doing laundry, walking along Dubuque Street—somehow this all felt like work.

She had met Tomas, in fact, during one of her aimless, anxious walks through town. The rest of the poets were elsewhere (for all she knew, they were all together). She was walking after workshop had let out—up Gilbert, down Linn, not ready to go home, uncertain what to do next. She had paused to look in a shop window. Tomas had paused beside her and made a joke—she could not remember the joke. But it led to their walking together, and finally to a cup of coffee. Both of them were surprised by this. Both of them, she thought later, were surprised by everything about their relationship—it was that unlikely.

"He loved me," she told Martin, "and he's the kind of person who wants to be married to, and to have children with, the woman he loves. As soon as I understood what his intentions were, I told him I wasn't interested in marriage, I wasn't interested in staying in Iowa and looking after children while he went about his business of being a country doctor, I wasn't interested in *having* children."

"And so you broke up."

"And so we broke up."

"But you loved him." He said it the way a child repeats a line from a story he's heard again and again until he knows every line of it by heart.

"I did."

"But not enough to have children—tell me again, how many children was it he wanted to have?—and be a farmer's wife."

She sighed. "He's not a farmer, Martin. He's a doctor. And the number of children he hoped for hasn't changed since the last time you asked me. He wanted at least six. Maybe eight."

"Eight children? Was the man insane?"

"Catholic and Czech and a Midwesterner, but not insane, no."

"Did he want you to convert, too?"

"To being Czech and a Midwesterner?"

"Seriously, Jill. Did he?"

"We never got that far."

She wasn't sure why she had said this. It was the first time she had lied to him.

"But you loved the guy," Martin said again. His voice was full of wonder.

The next night, they sat on the terrace drinking sherry, which an abstract painter—a tall, pale, beautiful woman in her forties—had produced and offered to share with anyone who wanted to partake, in honor of her last night. "Or in mourning, really," she said, "and to soften the blow before my return to real life." Real life was Connecticut and a husband, an oral surgeon, and a teenaged son. She drifted across the flagstone in a long dress, white lace and mesh, on bare feet, refilling glasses. "To Alicia!" someone cried, raising his plastic cup. Alicia, the painter, paused to bow. "I do hate to go," she said. "Is that awful? I wish I never had to leave."

"I do too," Jill heard herself say quietly.

Martin took her hand. He didn't speak.

Jill looked down at their hands. She did not remove hers—it was enormously pleasurable, the feeling of her hand in his—but she thought, *I should.* They did not touch, ever, except to smack each other lightly on occasion when one was teasing the other to distraction—and once, when she'd stumbled as they went down the ravine steps, he had caught her and taken her arm, but he let it go when she said, "I'm all right." Now they sat holding hands for what seemed a long time, Jill drinking her sherry with her left hand and Martin drinking his with his right. She thought, absurdly, *It's a good thing I'm left-handed,* and then she thought, *Good? Really? Are you sure of that?*

Still, she did not take her hand from his.

It was by then the end of their fifth week, with a week left of her residency and three weeks left of his. She had thirteen new poems that she believed were finished and had made a good start on four more; Martin had a hundred and fifty-two new pages of the novel and had begun to revise the portion of the manuscript he'd brought up to Yaddo with him. It was possible, he told her, that if he kept working at this pace—new pages in the morning, revising in the afternoon—he'd have an entire draft done before returning to the city.

The painter, Alicia, circled the terrace again and stopped to refill their cups. Jill thanked her, and then Martin did, and Alicia tipped her head toward Jill and said, "You're welcome," and then turned to Martin and offered him a look so chillingly evaluative Jill wondered if she had been underestimating how *much* Martin was disliked, or if the hostility toward him might be more complicated than she'd guessed. She glanced at him as the painter moved on and stopped to talk to an elderly novelist, who was also leaving the next day, and a group of much younger writers who had recently attached themselves to her. Martin seemed unfazed by (or unaware of?—but that wasn't possible, was it?) the painter's chilliness.

For the first time Jill wondered what he might be up to after they had said goodnight each night. After he wished her sweet dreams and she said, "See you at breakfast," and he said, "Not if I see you first." Did he go straight to his suite above the porte cochere? He often looked tired at breakfast, and she would ask him if he'd slept well. "Never," he said. He said it with a smile.

She shook her head—a small, quick movement, one she hoped he wouldn't notice—trying to shake out the thought that had lodged there.

For all she knew, he had slept with any number of the women here. For all she knew, he had affairs all the time.

She extracted her hand slowly and brought it to her cup of sherry, as if it were only natural to drink two-handedly. *He has not,* she thought. *He most certainly has not. And he* does *not.*

There—it was gone.

All through her final week, Martin often took her hand. Or took her arm, or propelled her gently forward with a flat hand to her back. It was very pleasant—why should she forbid it? Martin now kissed her on the cheek when they said goodnight; he touched her elbow or squeezed her hand when he said his ritual "Not if I see you first." Once, when they had both knocked off at four and met, without planning to, at the swimming pool, he hugged her and said, "What a nice surprise to find you here," and then after he had swum short laps for half an hour and she sat enjoying the sun and reading Lore Segal's *Lucinella,* they sat together in their swimsuits at the pool's edge, legs dangling in the water, holding hands and talking until it was time to change for dinner. *Holding hands—what's holding hands?* she asked herself. Still she was ashamed. But even so she looked around defiantly, silently daring anyone to say anything. Daring them to think anything.

On her last night he kissed her. They were walking arm in arm through the allée, under the giant spruces, at dusk. "What will you do with yourself after dinner without me here?" she had just asked him. She had said it lightly, teasing. "You'll have to make a new friend. That will be painful, won't it?" And instead of answering—instead of saying what she'd supposed he would, something like, "Yes, it will be painful, but I'll steel myself to the task," or perhaps, "Are you kidding? Not a chance. I'll put myself in solitary confinement"—he stopped walking, so that she had to stop too, and turned to face her, unhooking his arm from hers. He set his hands on her shoulders and then he kissed her, hard. She gasped. And pulled away.

"Oh, Jill," he said sadly.

"Martin. We can't."

"And why not?"

She gaped at him.

"I'm sorry," he said. "Jill, look—it's all right. I'm *sorry*. Please. Just stop."

Stop? she thought. *Me?*

And then she realized she was crying.

"*Jill.*" He moved toward her and took hold of her elbows, then let them go. Then he clasped both of her wrists, then dropped them too and stepped back again. "I am so sorry. I didn't mean to upset you."

"I'm sorry, too," she said, still weeping.

"You have no reason to be sorry." He reached for her hand. "We should just pretend that never happened. Can we do that?" She hesitated before closing her fingers around his. "Okay. Come on. Let's go back. It's all right."

It wasn't all right, though. She went over it again and again in her mind—the instant before the kiss, the kiss itself, what he had said, what she had said, her tears. She went over it later that night, and the next morning as she showered and packed up to leave, and as she sat with him at breakfast talking about nothing, or not talking at all as the others chattered all around them and the china clattered and people shook cornflakes into bowls and someone said, "I can't eat cereal with a *tea*spoon," and after breakfast, after they had said goodbye in the foyer (he took both of her hands in his; he kissed her lightly on both cheeks and told her he'd call her when he too was back in the city), on the way to the train station, where she would get the Trailways bus, and for all of the four-hour trip down to the Port Authority. She went back over it in an endlessly repeating loop, and it got her nowhere. She didn't even know where she wanted to get. And because she couldn't seem to rewind past the kiss under the spruces, she couldn't even try to figure out what she could have done differently, or even if she wished she had done something differently. At twenty-seven she'd already lost hope of a romance that would end well—which was to say: one that would not end at all. Even the most promising romances ended. Here was one that would have had no promise.

Back in the city, in her hot, dusty apartment with one rattling, ineffectual exhaust fan in the window overlooking the weed-filled courtyard below, she was bereft, unreasonably broken-hearted. Martin sent two postcards—pictures of Lake Katrina and of the rustic bridge at the outlet of Lake Christina—with jokey messages about late-night chats with the ghost of Spencer Trask, whose bedroom he slept in (*he offered financial tips, alas—no help with the novel*) and the mysterious sandwich fillings that turned up in his lunchbox, and one short, informative, and blandly friendly letter: his work was going fairly well; most nights he went back to it right after dinner, skipping the communal wine and all of the performances and open studios; a horde of new people had arrived—*summer's last gasp.*

And finally he was back on West End Avenue—just four miles instead of two hundred miles away. It took him ten days to call, but then at last he did, and they met for coffee at the Caffe Reggio.

He seemed distracted and he talked much less, and far less animatedly, than was his custom. She talked too much and too excitedly (and afterwards she could not remember what she had talked about). After an hour and a half, he said he had to go, he was meeting his agent at a bar in Gramercy Park. Next time they'd have more time, he said—next time they'd have a meal. He was so sorry to rush off. She ought to come up to his place, meet Gloria. He'd call her soon.

Which he did, a few days later. He and Gloria were going out of town, he told her. They had been invited to "the beach" by new friends who had a year-round house. "A brownstone in the city and a 'cottage' in the Hamptons—I'm betting it's a cottage like the Trasks' cottages," Martin said, and Jill mustered a laugh. "They want us to come out before the weather changes." He'd call when he was back and they'd get together then.

It was irrational, she told herself, the way she missed him. How *much* she missed him. She missed him far more, for example, than she missed Tomas, whom she had loved, whom she might have married—who would have married *her*. And yet she thought of Martin every day. She scolded herself whenever she caught herself at it, and she took on extra freelance work, more than she could handle—took on work she hated and would never have sought out if she had not been trying to distract herself (proofreading a legal dictionary and a scientific reference book, copyediting a lurid mass market celebrity biography). She tried to write but she could not. She did not trust herself to try to finish any of the poems she had begun at Yaddo and she could not write anything new—and she so mistrusted her instincts and her ability to think clearly that she did not allow herself to reread the poems she had written there and had considered finished.

She could still read other people's books, but not for very long. She wanted to talk to Martin about what she was reading. When she went out, when she spent time with anyone, she was disappointed in the conversation. Everyone she spoke to bored her.

And she and Martin had been only friends—that was all!

Oh, not *had been*, she corrected herself. Not had been—were.

Well, and that was why she missed him so much, wasn't it? This silence, this absence, was worse than a breakup with a boyfriend because there had been, there could *be*, no breakup. There was nothing to break.

But she wasn't certain of this. She wondered about it, worried about it. A single kiss could not undo a friendship, could it? She wanted to ask him about this, but that was impossible. What had he been thinking? Was it just a moment, an impulse, a mistake—something easily undone, forgotten?

Not forgotten.

She no longer replayed the kiss itself, that fragment of film strip in her mind—just before the kiss until just after it. Repeated viewings had exhausted it, had drained all meaning from it, so that it was even harder to make sense of now than it had been at first. Now it was like staring at a word for so long that it ceased to be a word, so that all that could be seen was a handful of letters that meant nothing.

She stopped staring. She let go of the kiss—the kiss and just before it and just after.

But then it was worse, because she found herself scrutinizing everything else that had ever passed between them, trying to coax meaning out of *every* moment, every interaction, and she could not remember *every* moment—and even what she could remember yielded nothing that was helpful to her. Had she misunderstood their friendship? Had he? Was what happened on her last night an anomaly or the logical conclusion of something she had never understood?

It was no wonder that she couldn't write. She was *stuck*.

Stuck was different than blocked—she had never made such a distinction before, but it seemed clear to her now. She was stuck trying to make meaning out of something that had probably been meaningless— but she could not stop poking at it, turning it around, taking it apart. How was she to make meaning out of anything else while she was thus preoccupied?

A week passed, then two, and then a month. Perhaps they never had been friends at all. She remembered what some of the others had said about the artists' colony. "Summer camp," they'd called it. Nothing like real life. But did summer camp friends really give up on each other once they'd all gone home? Especially if they'd gone home to the same city?

She'd never been to summer camp. How was she to know?

Finally, she called him. She understood that the hours of conversation every day, the evening walks, the daily exchange of pages and reports on how their work was going—none of this was realistic now that they'd returned to their real lives. But this utter silence was strange, wasn't it? Too strange, after so much talk. She called him on her birthday—it was as good an excuse as any. "Would you like to wish me a happy birthday?" she asked as soon as he answered the phone. He laughed. "I would. I do."

"So you're alive," she said.

"I am," said Martin.

"But are you okay?"

"In a manner of speaking," he said.

"But what does that mean? Has something happened?"

"Something has," he said.

Gloria was pregnant. They weren't telling anyone for another few weeks, until she had passed the first trimester mark.

"But you're telling me."

"I am."

She waited for too many beats before she thought to say, "Congratulations. That's great news—a baby."

"And it's not the only news. We're getting married, too. Another thing we're not telling anyone yet. Next month—right after Thanksgiving, probably. We're just going to go down to City Hall."

This time she didn't say, "But you're telling me." She said, "Mazel tov. A double mazel, as Shirley Rosen would say."

"Your mother?"

"My mother."

"Well, don't tell her. You never know who she might know."

It was a strange enough thought to silence her.

"Are you aware," he said, "that *mazel* is the word Jewish mystics use for the most important part of the soul? The mystics say our bodies contain only a single ray of our souls. The main part, the 'mazel,' shines down on us from the heavens. I've been thinking about how that would work for a newborn baby. Does the mazel start shining down at birth? Or does it take a while? Or is it already—"

"Martin," Jill said, "when's the baby due?"

"June 12, they say. But our own calculations have it as June 5."

After she was silent for too long, Martin said, "Want to hear an old wives' tale? If you combine the mother's age at the time of conception— that would be twenty-five—with the number of the month you conceived, which would be nine, and the resulting number is even, as it is in this case, then the baby is a boy. So I suppose that we'll be having one of those."

"A baby boy in early to mid June," Jill said. "Noted. Invite me to the bris."

"I will."

And that was the next time she saw him—at Jacob's bris, when the baby was eight days old. He was born on June 5, just as Martin had predicted.

Three months later, she paid for a membership in the Modern Language Association and received its job list in the mail. She applied for twenty teaching jobs—none of them in New York City. Well, there *were* no jobs in New York City, or even in New Jersey or Connecticut, though there was one upstate, at a second-rate SUNY college, and she put in an application for it—she put in applications for every job teaching poetry that did not require a PhD and/or more than one published book, with the exception of the jobs in Kansas, Wyoming, and Alaska, which seemed to her beyond the pale. She was glad there were no jobs listed for Iowa—she would have felt foolish eliminating them because of Tomas. (*Would* she have eliminated them because of Tomas?)

She was invited by fifteen colleges to send further materials and in the end she had nine interviews at the MLA conference in Houston, which led to five campus visits in January and February 1981, and finally to offers from three schools, all of them in mid-sized Middle Western cities. She chose Kokosing State—the easternmost of the three—in part because it was the closest to home, in part because she'd liked one of the people who had interviewed her better than she'd liked anyone she'd met at either of the other schools, and in part because the Thai restaurant that she was taken to for dinner on her campus visit there was better than the restaurants at which she'd eaten on her visits to the other schools. This last reason was the only one she mentioned to Martin when she called in March to give him her news. He laughed and approved. "Decent Thai food is the least that they can offer you if you're in exile."

Before they hung up, he told her that he and Gloria would have her up to their place for a farewell/celebration dinner in the summertime— an invitation that never materialized, but then she had not supposed it would. She left town in August without saying goodbye.

When her birthday came around again, she didn't call, and he did not call her—well, he couldn't, could he? He didn't even have her new phone number! (though he could have looked it up: she was not unlisted)—she wrote him a letter. She wrote it before bed that night. She'd just completed half of her first quarter as Assistant Professor of English and she had just turned thirty. This seemed sufficient reason for a letter. And she was writing poems again—she wanted to tell him that too. *I suppose it's possible that having* less *time to write has sharpened my focus—or maybe it's just forcing me to develop better "time management skills," as my brother Norman would probably say.* But after she wrote this sentence she remembered that she had never told him that she wasn't writing. And she could not remember if she'd ever told him anything about her brother beyond his existence.

She added a sentence about Norman, who taught linguistics but talked like a businessman, and then she wrote about her students and her colleagues and the classes she was teaching and committee meetings; she told him about the literary journal she'd been asked to edit, for which she was proud to have negotiated a course release once every other year. She wrote about life in the Midwest: the enormous supermarkets that stayed open all night long (*and they call New York the city that doesn't sleep!*) and how she would have to learn to drive because what passed for public transportation there was laughable, and the charming Craftsman house that she was renting from a retired professor of anthropology who couldn't bring himself to part with it even though he lived year-round on Sanibel Island. She wrote about her plan to buy a small house of her own as soon as she'd saved up enough for a down payment. She mentioned what she was reading and she asked him about his writing and what *he* was reading, she inquired about Gloria and Jacob, and she offered up her phone numbers—both home and office—and both addresses, too. It ended up being quite a long letter, and without saying so directly, she made it clear that she was ready to renew their friendship from a distance of five hundred miles.

Evidently so was he, for he wrote back right away and equally exhaustively. For several months then there was a great flurry of letters, and sometimes one of them would send a package, a copy of a book he or she insisted that the other had to read. His letters were full of news about the new book, *Gold's Will*, and about the *Hartfeld* movie that was being shot mostly in Manhattan—he had gotten to know its director and stars, so his letters were sprinkled with anecdotes about them, along with long asides on the nature of celebrity—and also about what he was reading on any given week and what he thought about it, and all sorts of facts he'd picked up since the last time he had written, and then, at the very end, there was always a paragraph about his son. She was never able to decide whether the placement of the paragraph meant that it was an afterthought, or if the rest was all preamble—or if it suggested a certain ambivalence about talking (writing) about Jacob (to her? or in general?). Whatever it meant, it was plain that he was proud of the child, whose accomplishments so far were on the order of uttering the words "banana" and "noodles" (the latter mispronounced as *noon-els*).

When her father had a heart attack and died that April—suddenly and unexpectedly, with no history of heart trouble, just as Martin's mother had—and she flew home, she thought about calling Martin. She went as far as lifting the receiver on the wall phone in her mother's kitchen, but she did not dial his number. It had been so long since they'd last talked, any conversation now was likely to be awkward, and she didn't have the fortitude for awkward. She was shaken by her father's death, shocked and sadder than she would have guessed she'd be. He had been so *quiet*, much less present than her mother all her life—but she had loved him, and even though she didn't feel as if she'd really known him, she had liked him in a way she'd never liked her mother. He was kind, and he was proud of her, which was something she'd learned only recently. Perhaps he'd started out proud of *banana* and *noon-els* too, but when she was growing up he had retreated even as her mother advanced: *he* had never made a fuss over report cards or awards or skipping grades or graduating early.

But just over those last two years, he'd let her know that he was proud of her, that it meant something to him that she had written a book (even if, as he claimed, he "didn't understand a word of it") and that she was teaching at a university. On the only two occasions he had written to her, he'd addressed the envelopes to "PROFESSOR! Jill T. Rosen" and he mentioned—in both letters, as if he couldn't think of what else she might like to hear—that "practically every day!!" he wore the tee shirt, windbreaker, and baseball cap emblazoned with the KS logo she had sent him.

What she needed now was to be comforted, and this wasn't something Norman or her mother could provide. They were suffering too, of course, each in their own way, but the truth was that no one in the family had ever been much good at comfort—it was as if consolation was a language none of them had learned. She thought of Martin and his father and his sister, the way Martin had fled them in his grief. It was Gloria he had turned to.

Martin would not be able to console her. Not on the phone, certainly. And there wouldn't have been time to get together, she told herself once she was on her way back to Kokosing, even if he'd wanted to see her. And even if there had been time—even if she'd stayed a little longer instead of rushing back to teach her Tuesday morning class, and Martin had been free to meet her—what point would there have been in it? He was not the person to whom she should be turning for comfort in her sorrow.

There was no one to turn to. She thought about this on the flight back and she thought about it on the taxi ride home from the airport; she thought about it as she opened the door to her rented house—the first time she was returning to it after having been away for longer than a day on campus—and looked around her at its furnishings, all of which belonged to the retired anthropologist whom she had never met, and at the silent phone and the unblinking answering machine beside it. There was a man, a colleague, whom she slept with from time to time, but she had told him next to nothing about herself. She hadn't let him know about her father's death, had mentioned only that she would be going home for a few days. She would not have told him even this much if she hadn't run into him in the department office, and if he hadn't asked if she was busy Friday night.

She watched him arrange his face to demonstrate concern. "Everything okay there?"

She assured him that it was.

He was a first-year Assistant Professor of English, like her. He was not a writer—she was the only writer, or at least the only writer who'd been hired *as* a writer (there was a Joyce scholar who occasionally published his short stories, and someone in nineteenth century British who wrote young adult novels), but his area of study was twentieth century American poetry and his dissertation had been on Frank O'Hara and William Carlos Williams. Impulsively, as she stood holding the stack of student poems she'd come in to pick up, she asked if he'd cover her honors seminar in modern poetry so that she didn't have to cancel it while she was gone. It was a course he'd hoped to be assigned to teach, he'd told her when they'd met for the first time at a department meeting in the fall, and instead he'd been assigned a lower-level survey course. It was as if she'd offered him a gift. "I'd be delighted to," he said. "I'm glad to help."

"Just the one session. I'll be back before the class meets again."

"Whatever you need. Just say the word." But she felt as if he were rubbing his hands together. And when she turned to go and he called her name as she reached the doorway, to ask if she perhaps wanted him to take her other class as well—her poetry workshop—she spoke as gently as if he were the one needing comfort.

"They'll be fine," she told him. "They'll use the time to write. But thanks, that's very generous of you."

By the end of that spring quarter, he was dating an art history graduate student, and Jill had started sleeping with—not *seeing*, as she took pains to make him understand; not *dating* (she wasn't "ready" for dating, she told him, and he did not ask why, or what this meant)—a young tenured professor of Russian. This did not last long either. After the Russian professor came others. She went on one or two dates that led nowhere with a few of them, but for the most part she preferred to skip the dating—which she found unproductive, stressful, and exhausting—and invited them (not *them*, but one; one at a time, for several months or sometimes only weeks) into her bed. Into the anthropology professor's bed.

More than two years passed before her next trip to New York. She missed the city (at times she missed it the way she had once missed Martin—desperately, hopelessly—and her separation from it confused her and filled her with sorrow) but it seemed to her that it would be worse to return for a few days and then have to leave than not to go at all. Still, two years was a long time, and her mother was beginning to threaten to visit *her*.

And really it had been more like three years, for when she'd returned for her father's funeral, she had hardly taken in where she was. And she had not left Queens at all except for the drive out to Long Island for the burial.

This time she got in touch with Martin. Their letter-writing had not been consistent—it had waxed and waned since the early flurry— but lately they'd been corresponding frequently again. She wrote to tell him she would be in town for a whole week and that she was staying with her mother (*Ah, well then*, he wrote back, *clearly you need to make as many plans as possible*).

They met in Central Park, the day after she arrived. He brought his little boy, which took her aback her when she saw them walking toward her (but she should have known, for why else would he have proposed the Alice in Wonderland statue as a meeting place?). And yet after a few minutes she found that she was glad that he'd brought Jacob. He was a beautiful little boy with the serious face of a nineteenth century folk portrait, easy to be around, polite and well-behaved ("All his mother's doing," Martin said after the child greeted Jill by shaking her hand and saying, "How do you do?"). He walked between the two of them, holding tightly to one of each of their hands—she'd been surprised by how willingly the child had taken her hand, and even more surprised that he did not interrupt them or complain of being bored or tired or hungry, but waited until there was a lull in the adults' conversation before speaking. When they passed the statue of Robert Burns, and Martin broke into song—*Should auld acquaintance be forgot, and never brought to mind?*—his son laughed as if this were the most wonderful thing he'd ever heard.

They spent two hours together, walking idly through the park, stopping twice in playgrounds, where Martin pushed Jacob in a swing for ten or fifteen minutes before they moved on, and once for ice cream, which they sat down on the grass to eat. When they parted—when Martin declared that it was time for Jacob's nap—she bent to say goodbye to his son. She told him how happy she was to have met him and how much she'd enjoyed their outing. "Thank you," he said, and then, "Did you like the Balto statue better or the Alice?"

"I like them both," she told him. "Don't you?"

"Dada told the Balto story better," the child said, and Jill looked up at Martin, who laughed.

"Everyone's a critic," he said. And then, to Jacob, "Would you like to give Jill a hug before we go?" Evidently he would, because he immediately wrapped his arms around her. She kissed the top of his head—he had a headful of black curls just like his father—before she straightened up.

Martin said, "Very good to see you" and kissed her on both cheeks—just as he had when they'd said goodbye at Yaddo, in the foyer by the fountain pool, four summers ago—and told her to "feel free" to call if she needed to escape, "if your mother starts to drive you mad before the week is over." She took this to mean: *don't call.* And it seemed to her too that she shouldn't. One visit with him in a week was enough after all this time. Twice would leave her wondering how often they were supposed to be in contact afterwards.

Instead she called everyone else she could think of who might still be in the city. By now, it turned out, some of the people who had left in the late 1970s were already back. The actor, Roger, who had lived next door to her, was back in his old apartment, back to auditioning for stage plays ("California was crap. Television is crap," he told Jill over bowls of soup at the Front Porch). He talked about giving up, going home to Vancouver. "I'm thinking of opening a karate studio. I've taken up karate—it's more satisfying to me now than acting." He was gloomier now, not nearly so much fun as he had once been.

Or perhaps it was she who'd changed.

She managed to find people to have dinner with every night and to fill her afternoons with coffee dates and bookstores and museums. She thought often of the moment just after she and Martin had set off in opposite directions in the park, when she had stopped and turned around. He had picked up his son and put him on his shoulders. His hands were on the child's back, holding him in place, as he weaved through the crowd that was moving too slowly to suit him.

Afterwards, they continued writing letters for a time and then not writing letters, falling silent for months or a whole year. They almost never talked on the telephone, although when her second book finally appeared, nine years after the first one—she had sent him one of her precious ten complimentary author's copies—he surprised her with a phone call in her office, and as soon as she picked up with the brisk "J.T. Rosen, English" she had mastered long ago, he cried, without saying hello, "J.T. Rosen! The mail is here and I am holding your beautiful book in my hands as I speak!"

They talked for only a few minutes before he told her he was hanging up so that he could "start reading right this very second." And then a letter arrived just over a week later, full of effusive praise, and a P.S. that expressed his gratitude for what he called the "entirely unearned honor, which delighted me" of her having thanked him in the book's acknowledgments. In a second postscript, he wrote: *I hope you'll be coming home to do a reading from this gorgeous book soon. I'll be there with bells on.*

But although she went "home"—it no longer felt like home— three times that year (once to give a reading at the Jefferson Market Library, her old branch public library in the Village; once as part of a bill of four poets at NYU; and once, with her brother, to help sort out what they'd left behind in their old rooms in preparation for their mother's selling of the house and decamping to Florida), Martin was out of town each time.

After *In the There-and-Now*, after her mother's move away, she returned to New York with decreasing frequency. She went only if she was invited for a reading or a talk—and once, in 1992, the MLA conference was held there and she went as part of the hiring committee tasked with the replacement of her long ago former paramour, the twentieth century American poetry scholar (who had improbably enough written a modestly successful, scandalous biography of a famous, recently dead poet and had been poached by UCLA). Sometimes, but not always, she would call Martin when she was in town and ask if he wanted to meet her for a drink, but they never managed it—he was up against a deadline, or else he was traveling to promote a book; or she had only a few hours free and those few hours corresponded with a crucial and unbreakable appointment. Still, when he came across a poem of hers in a magazine, he'd send a postcard with a line or two or praise—and since she often published in journals he was unlikely to see, she would sometimes photocopy the poem, if she thought it was one he would especially like, and put it in an envelope along with her latest letter.

And she was always on the list to be sent galleys of his books. Each time a new one appeared, she wrote to him about it.

The friendship felt as if it mattered, still. She felt there was a slender yet strong thread between them.

Thinking of you with affection, he would write. And: *This new poem is a quiet devastating marvel—I'm so glad you sent it.*

She wrote: *Grassman breaks my heart. It's strange, but I feel as if I can hear his music. Like Proust's Vinteuil's.*

By the time Caroline Forester first turned up in a class of hers—a freshman seminar, in autumn 1998—Jill had not seen Martin in fifteen years. They hadn't been in touch even by email for a year by then. The last time she had heard from him was after her third book came out, in 1997—ten years after her second. She'd half-expected him to call when he received the copy she had sent him. Later, she learned that he had been traveling—as usual, there was a book to promote. But he sent a thoughtful, charming email upon his return to New York, where he'd found his copy of *On the Bergère* in the pile of mail waiting for him on his desk. He'd read only the first three poems, he said—*the title poem and the two sestinas, all of which wowed me (your best work to date, I think)—* but he didn't want to put off writing until he had time to read the rest, *so please take this too-brief note as a down payment.* He was leaving town again in three days and would take her new book with him—he was so looking forward to reading it. He closed the email, *More soon, much love.* Two years had now passed since then.

She had been teaching for seventeen years. She lived alone, with the exception of a dog she had acquired several years before, in the pretty little turn-of-the-century house she'd bought some years before that. There had not been a new man in her life for a long time, but she no longer minded that. She had decided she didn't mind. She had been promoted finally to Full Professor. She would be fifty before long and it seemed to her that living alone, in the company of a good dog, and having work she loved, was plenty. She had decided it was plenty.

And her students—she was fonder of them and more interested in them each year. Not all of them, naturally. But there were always a few—always there were enough—who were serious and smart and gifted. Some years there were more than a few. Some years there were some who meant to become poets, come hell or high water, just as she had.

The first time Caroline Forester came to her office—the girl was trembling; she was eighteen years old and had bravely brought poems for her teacher to read, although the class she was enrolled in was not a poetry workshop but a seminar Jill had devised for first-quarter freshmen (Arts and Sciences 159.04: Why Poetry Matters)—she confessed within the first five minutes of her visit that she'd never for a moment wanted to be anything *but* a poet, that she had never dreamed of growing up to be a ballerina or a kindergarten teacher or a movie star. Her eyes were brimming, her voice unsteady. "But I never *told* anyone. I mean, who can you tell that to?"

"I understand," Jill said. She put out her hand, palm up. "Well, let's have them, then." The girl looked frightened. "Yesterday after class you said you'd bring poems. I assume you did."

Caroline nodded, but she had gone pale. She reached into her backpack and produced a manila folder from which she slowly removed two sheets of paper. "I've brought just the two best ones—the ones I think are the best."

Jill took the pages from her. She read the first four lines of the first one and looked up. "Ah," she said. "Yes." The girl looked perilously close to tears, but before she could speak, Jill held up her index finger. "Give me a minute." She read the rest of the first poem, then read it a second time. She looked up and smiled. "You've been reading poems, thank God. Quite a lot of Emily Dickinson, yes?"

The girl nodded. Her face was very white.

Jill read the second poem. "And Elizabeth Bishop"—the girl's eyes widened—"and some contemporary poets too. Louise Glück?"

Caroline looked as if she were going to faint.

"These are all good influences. You're reading well and you've taught yourself a great deal." She sat back in her chair and considered the girl. "You're starting in the right place."

The color was coming back into Caroline's face. "Can I ask you a question?"

"That's what I'm here for."

"Can you tell that I've been reading Heather McHugh's *Hinge & Sign*, too?"

Jill laughed. "No, I can't. But good for you. That's a wonderful book." She handed back the poems. "It's not a superpower or a magic trick, you know. I'm not a mind-reader. I've just been doing this for a long time." She considered the girl. "What else have you been reading lately?"

Caroline blushed. "Just what you're assigning for the seminar. And I'm taking another freshman seminar—Professor Kittredge's Great American Short Story—and so far we've read stories by Hawthorne and Melville and Flannery O'Connor. And in Professor Gallet's survey course we've been reading Chaucer and we're about to start on Spenser. I haven't had much time to read just for, you know, myself. I'm taking Intro to Psych and a science Gen Ed too."

"That seems quite a lot."

"The freshman seminars are only one credit each. So that's only seventeen credits."

"Only seventeen? My goodness."

"I thought I would take twenty next quarter."

"Twenty is too much. Are you in a great hurry to graduate? You've just gotten started here."

"I'm not in a hurry at all! I don't want to graduate early. I just want to take everything I can while I am here, you know?"

"Ah," Jill said. "I do know. I'll tell you what, then. When it's time to register for winter, why don't you save ten of those twenty hours for me? Take my introductory poetry workshop and my upper level seminar in prosody—you won't feel out of your depth in a class with seniors, will you?"—she did not wait for an answer—"and if you're casting about for what to do with the other ten hours, you might think about spending five of them on a foreign language. I'm guessing you have enough credits from high school so that if you choose to, you can use them to fulfill the requirement here. But don't do it. Stick with that language—is it French? Yes?—until you have excellent reading proficiency in it. And then you might think about adding another language as well. Though perhaps not this year."

"I was already thinking about taking Italian. I hadn't thought about continuing with French."

"Do. Do both—add the Italian next year. Then in your senior year you can take the translation seminar the Romance languages department offers. All right then—you're set." She watched the girl slide her poems back into the folder and insert the folder into the backpack, carefully, between two oversized textbooks.

"Thank you so much," she said. "This has been amazing." She hoisted the backpack onto one shoulder that did not look nearly sturdy enough to bear it. "But I still don't think I can tell my mother that I'm going to be a poet."

"I understand." Jill smiled. "And no one says you have to. What you do with your life is nobody's business but your own."

"Wow. Tell that to my mother."

"Well, you might not want to put it quite that way."

"I'm not going to put it *any* way," Caroline said heatedly. "There's no point even trying to talk to her about it. She thinks it's silly enough that I've declared an English major. 'What are you going to *do* with that?' is like her mantra. But if I told her I was going to study poetry, that I planned to *write* poetry—you know, for a career—it would be as if I were saying, 'I'm planning to go live on the moon.'"

"She'd be worried, yes. But you know what? She would be right to worry, because no one earns a living as a poet. You'll have to find something to do that will keep a roof over your head. When you do decide to talk to her about your future, make sure to talk about that, too. I got lucky, honestly. I have this"—Jill spread her hands to indicate what was around her: her desk, piled high with books, the books on her many bookshelves, the tall window that looked out over the Quad, even Caroline herself—"and I don't know how I would have managed otherwise."

It was only after the girl had left that Jill thought, *Nonsense*. She knew just how she would have managed. She would have kept on temp-typing and freelancing. She would have proofread scientific manuals, copyedited unauthorized celebrity biographies and dreadful "novelizations" of popular TV series and movies. She would have *managed*, just as others had. Trollope worked at the post office. Faulkner wrote *As I Lay Dying* while working the night shift at a power plant. Joseph Heller wrote *Catch 22* while working in advertising. Wallace Stevens and William Carlos Williams were anomalies, like Chekhov— like Toni Morrison—in having other work that truly mattered to them. Maxine Kumin and her horses. The librarians, Borges and Larkin. But most only *managed* somehow, just as she would have.

She had been very lucky indeed. Even if there had been times— long periods of time—when she hadn't seen it that way. When leaving New York City for a teaching job in the Midwest had seemed to her a kind of failure. When the too-many years between her first and second books (when she began to wonder if there'd ever *be* a second book) had her believing that she'd squandered all her early promise. When that "promise" hadn't seemed early at all. (And yet how young she had been then! What could she have been thinking?)

There had been a night at Yaddo—she remembered it perfectly, though it had been so long ago—when she had spoken of herself to Martin as "over the hill." She'd said it humorously, laughing at herself, but he had scolded her. Had told her she was beautiful and brilliant "and when you're old, you'll still be beautiful and brilliant, but why rush it? Where's the fire?" She remembered that she'd blushed and, to distract him (to distract herself, too) from noticing how pleased she was, said, "So what's old, then, Martin?" and that he had said, without an instant's hesitation, "Forty."

And she had agreed. Forty was old. Forty was not just over the hill but over the river and through the woods (and thus her house, which she loved and had lived in now for so many years, would be "grandmother's house"—except that she was nearer now to fifty than to forty and had borne no children and would never have grandchildren).

She was very old now, by young Martin's standards. By her own, too.

How had she not been able to see at the time how young she was? She looked at photographs that had been taken fifteen, twenty years ago (she even had one of Martin and herself and two other people—two composers who did not share in the general antipathy toward Martin—from that summer at Yaddo) and she was taken aback by how much prettier *and* younger she had been then than she'd thought. She looked like a girl. She had still *been* a girl.

Caroline Forester, she reflected on that autumn afternoon after their first appointment—the first of many, as it would turn out—had ten years to go before she'd be as old as Jill had been that Yaddo summer. And even then, she—Caroline—would still be very young. And she herself would be approaching sixty.

This was the sort of thing about which she had to remind herself: how old she was now, in comparison to the very young people by whom she was surrounded. For just as she'd imagined herself, when young, as already old, now that she was…if not *old*, despite what she and Martin had once thought, then certainly no longer young, she sometimes imagined a much smaller distance between herself and her students than there actually was.

One was never the age one felt oneself to be.

When she was as young as Caroline Forester, she had been in such a hurry to get on with it! To be through with her schooling, to be on her own, to get her first book written, to establish a career—to start her "real life." She had so longed to be grown up—she'd felt as if she *were* grown up, felt older than she was (why couldn't everyone around her see it? she'd lamented all through college)—and then all at once she *was* grown up and thought herself "over the hill."

Fifteen months had passed since Caroline's first visit to her office and she had emerged since then as one of her best students—gifted, yes, but also more engaged and dedicated than most undergraduates. If she returned a poem to Caroline marked up with edits, questions— challenges, complaints, and even arguments—Caroline would be back in her office two or three days later with a new, much better draft; if she suggested, regardless of how casually, something she might want to read, Caroline would read it and then show up for Jill's office hours eager to talk about it (an annotated copy of the book in hand). She reminded Jill of her young self.

Perhaps the time had come to speak to Caroline about her future. Not that there was any rush—she still had two years to go at State—but it was not too soon for her to set her course. Jill as she sat in her office, finishing her notes for class, thought about what she might tell her. That there were more reasons not to spend one's life writing and reading poetry than there were reasons *to*—and that this lopsided equation didn't matter if a life of making poems was her true calling. That it was her willingness to keep on doing something hard (and not only hard, but that meant spending many hours alone and was repaid with very few rewards) that would define her. And that—pragmatically—there was no reason to delay grad school for longer than a sensible two years.

And what would she be able to tell Caroline about the experience of graduate school itself? She remembered little of it besides the hostility of certain of her classmates, especially after she'd signed the contract for her book (their names and faces and the poems they'd written—all of that was gone). She could not remember the address of the apartment she had rented, or anything she had been taught in workshop, or anyone she'd known to whom she had been sad to say goodbye—except for Tomas, but Tomas was not supposed to have been part of that experience at all. Tomas was a sort of happy accident—a happy accident that had turned sad.

And so it was because she was thinking of Caroline on this December afternoon in 1999 that she found herself thinking about Iowa, and about the girl she had been then, and about Tomas. Which was why what happened next was less astonishing than it would have been otherwise—because when she logged in to check her email before heading upstairs to teach her last workshop of the quarter, she found a message in her inbox from Dr. Tomas Vítámvás. The subject line was *Across the many miles and years.*

A message from the universe. Or from the inside of her own mind. She clicked on it.

> *Dear Jill!*
>
> *I am sure you are surprised to hear from me—I hope not unhappily so.*
>
> *Naturally, I have thought of you often over the last 20+ years. I am not so technologically sophisticated, however, so any efforts to see how you were and where you might be proved unsuccessful (blame AltaVista and something unfortunately called HotBot) and it is thanks only to my eldest, who today introduced me to Google search, that I believe I have found you now. (That is, if you feel thankful, rather than distressed. If the latter, I apologize.)*
>
> *Besides Adam, my eldest, who is 14, I have 7 others. The youngest, Lucie, is 5. The twins, Tereza and Katerina, are 8. Nina, Max, Sofie, and Samuel are everything in between.*

He had been married nearly fifteen years, he went on to say. His wife had been a nurse—*predictable, I know! Sorry to have turned out to be such a cliché*—only a year out of nursing school when they'd met, sixteen years ago, and she had left her job when Adam was born. He had, as planned *(you will remember this, I'm sure)*, remained in Iowa. *We bought the farm (50 acres)—not in the euphemistic sense, but actually—when Adam and Samuel were babies.*

He was glad to see, thanks to the World Wide Web, that things had turned out so well for her. He was proud of her, he said. *Three books! And through the wonders of the internet, I have now ordered them and they appear to be on their way to me. And you are a tenured professor, too! I am very glad for you. I remember how much you enjoyed teaching as a grad student.*

He was also teaching, he said, though not as much as he would like to. He had admitting privileges at three different small hospitals and he ran a clinic out of one of them that catered to a low-income, geriatric population—he explained that after his residency in family medicine, he'd gone on to specialize in geriatrics—and he was in private practice too, in a group with four other "family docs." But he was planning to scale back his private practice. More and more, he wrote, teaching in one form or another was becoming the most rewarding part of his job. Family medicine residents from the university rotated through his clinic, and he had taken groups of medical and premed students interested in practicing family medicine on "medical missions" to the Czech Republic, Latvia, Ukraine, Belize, and Ecuador. His eldest son had come along on the last one, last summer. *He wants to follow in the old man's footsteps. So do Max and Sofie. The others are more interested in sports—except for Terry, who says she wants to write books (!) and Lucie, who likes dinosaurs. (But who doesn't like dinosaurs?)*

Between work and his family, he was very busy—*too busy, maybe? No time to stop and smell the roses*—but still, all told, he was happy. He hoped she was, too. It appeared that she had gotten everything she wanted out of life. He sent his love.

She read the email twice. Then she read it again. And even after that, until she had only ninety seconds to get to her class, she sat staring at the screen.

As she walked up the stairs to the third floor, her arms full of books and papers, with more books and papers in her heavy shoulder bag, she thought about Tomas. How big was fifty acres? How big was an *acre*? It sounded very big. And eight children! Well, that was what he'd wanted. He was happy, doing just what he had wanted to do, living just as he had hoped to live.

And she was too. *It appears that you have gotten everything you wanted out of life.* It was true, she too had what she had wanted all those years ago.

She did not have what she had not wanted.

She paused at the third floor landing before pushing on the double doors.

Was she sometimes lonely? Yes. But so was everyone—wasn't that so? This included everyone she knew who was married and had children. For all she knew (for all his cheerful reporting after all the years since she'd last seen him, talked to him—known him), so was Tomas.

No—not Tomas. She pressed the doors open with her shoulder and pushed through. Tomas had always known how to find happiness— how to *be* happy. That was a gift one had or didn't have. Like the gift for writing poetry, or for music or for drawing—for any art. Happiness was an art, too. But it was not enough to have a gift. One had to make use of it. And Tomas had.

And she? She had made use of her own gifts.

At the doorway to her classroom, she stopped, just out of sight, and stood listening for a moment to her students talking and joking around the seminar table. Then she stepped into the room, into the sea of conversation. "I'm here, I'm here," she said—she was nearly singing. "It's your last chance this quarter to be brilliant for me. Everybody ready?"

Caroline Forester smiled at her from under the curtain of pale yellow hair she wore too short and yet still managed to hide behind.

Jill dropped her books and her students' poems and her heavy leather bag on the table. She nodded at Caroline.

"Get us started today, won't you? Read yours out loud."

Caroline cleared her throat. "All right," she said. "Always Always Land." She looked up from the page in her hand. "As opposed to Never Never Land. From *Peter Pan*. You know?" Jill nodded. "Um. And it's a sestina." She cleared her throat again.

> *Wendy would have gone there*
> *If she'd known she had a choice.*

Jill did not allow herself to smile as she listened. Caroline was gifted, yes—but would she make use of it? She was still so young. She looked like a child with her too-short hair, the too-long bangs she was constantly brushing her fingers through, pushing them away from her eyes. Today she was wearing a too-big, shapeless sweater—a thrift store find, no doubt—with sleeves so long she had to shake her arm to free those fingers; the hand she held her poem in was invisible.

> *Think unlovely thoughts, choose*
> *to prefer not to—why not? You won't*
> *miss it—that much I can promise, darling.*

By now—the start of the sixth stanza—some of her classmates were nodding approval, and when she had finished reading the poem there was a murmur of appreciative laughter, followed by applause, as was the custom. Only then did Jill allow herself to smile. "Thank you. Beautifully read."

Caroline shook the bangs out of her eyes and whispered, "Thanks."

"All right, then, folks," Jill said. "Shall we talk about the form? There's something sly going on here. Would anyone care to tell me what?"

Nick, a senior, one of her two thesis students, had a hand up. "Before we talk about the form, could we address the shift from third person to second by the fourth stanza? Because that confused me. And then that interplay, or whatever—sort of a conversation—between the second and first person from then on?"

"How about form first, point of view second?" Jill said.

"Sorry. Okay. Well, then, I'm not sure how I feel about 'compromise' and 'promise' being treated as variations of the same word," he said. "That's 'form,' right?"

Several of the others started talking at once.

Jill held up a hand. "Ah, so you *are* all going to be brilliant today. Terrific. One at a time, please, though. Andrea—you first."

Andrea defended promise/compromise. She had a question about "there" as an end word, however. Especially in the envoy line *You get the last word—so there.* "Doesn't it seem a little…I don't know, wishy washy or a little boring—sorry, Caroline—"

Maureen interrupted to say that "there" was "the best *ever* end word, and not just because of the whole 'their/they're/there' thing, but because it suggests, like, everything. Everything outside the world of the poem."

"I also kind of love the idea of one of the six end words being one that's a noun, a pronoun, an adverb, and an adjective all in one—not to mention the way she uses it in that final triplet, as an interjection I guess? It's—"

"It's like, though, is there any *there* there, in 'there'?" This from Eric, who considered himself a great wit.

Jill let them go on, interrupting one another, for a while.

They were all so young. They were young enough to know how young they were. Younger, then, than she had ever been.

"Now let's talk about the point of view shift," she said. "Nick? You're up."

Nick began, then Jordan chimed in. Then Samantha. Jill let them talk. She felt as if she could let them talk forever. As if she could close her eyes and listen and there was no chance, no chance at all, that they'd run out of things to say.

HISTORY OF ART

Sense, sincerity, and sensibility, the solemn
sensitivity and sweetness of the same
three chords repeated night and day and you
are the one, the one, the one-two-three-four.

— *Caroline Forester, "Perfect"*

Caroline's first boyfriend, Clifford Delgrange, was smart, polite, earnest, and handsome in the way only a painfully thin, awkward, guitar-playing seventeen-year-old boy can be. He had a sweet smile and pale blue eyes and long blond-brown hair he wore in a ponytail. He was a good student, too—not one of those smart boys who didn't bother doing his schoolwork because it bored him or because it was uncool to do it, like most of the boys Caroline's friend Natalie went out with. The rest of them, as Natalie herself said cheerfully, were "dumb as dirt," so that even if they had done their homework they still wouldn't be getting good grades (but that was all right, Natalie said, because they were *very* good-looking, and to be that good-looking a boy had to be stupid—and who was Caroline to argue, when she had never even held hands with a boy before Clifford Delgrange, senior year of high school?).

Compared to her friends, and especially compared to Natalie, Caroline was a late bloomer. She'd been waiting for the right person, she told anyone who asked, including her mother. What she didn't say was that she'd made a list of everything that she required in a boyfriend, and Clifford Delgrange was the first boy she had encountered who met all of these requirements.

And if he had not approached her in the hall during the second week of senior year and started talking to her, they would probably not ever had a single conversation, much less started dating. They weren't in any classes together—they hadn't been, he told her, since AP Bio sophomore year ("I know you don't remember me from then," he added quickly, "not from Bio and not from Freshman Humanities the year before either, right?")—but he fell into place beside her as they walked down the third floor hall. He said something about Emily Dickinson. He knew the IB English class was reading Dickinson, he said. The AP class was too. "So what do you think of the poems?" he wanted to know.

She was glad that Natalie, who had no patience for Dickinson ("Seems like she needed to get out more," Natalie had said in class last Friday), wasn't there to roll her eyes when Caroline told Clifford how much she loved the poems. Natalie was out sick, or pretending to be sick, which was why she was walking alone for once.

"You were always with her," Clifford told her later. "That's why I never talked to you before. The two of you together just seemed so impenetrable."

"That's not true," Caroline said, but she knew it sort of was. Natalie had rules about her own boyfriends during the school day: she sat with them at lunch, and if they happened to have a study hall at the same time she did, she'd spend study hall with them, but she always walked from one class to the next with Caroline, even before junior year and the International Baccalaureate program Natalie had joined too just so that they'd have the same class schedule. And while they walked, they talked—quietly, their heads close together, ignoring everybody else. It was how they'd walked through halls at schools since kindergarten.

Caroline told Clifford all the things she never had the chance to say in class: that she thought the poems about the passage of time, like "There came a Day at Summer's full" and "I held a Jewel in my fingers," were about how precious things were, how quickly they were gone ("relationships, life, everything"), and that all the poems about loneliness were about the reason it made *sense* to be lonely. And when he agreed with everything she'd said, and added, "Yeah, and like, how can we *not* feel isolated and strange when we're just...*specks*, just here and gone? When the only permanent thing is nature?" it struck her that he wasn't bad-looking. That he was *nice*-looking. That she liked his longish dark blond hair, his smile. The way he looked in his faded black Mott the Hoople (who or what was Mott the Hoople?) tee shirt. He had nice arms.

"So which poems are your favorites?" Clifford asked her.

"Too many," she said. "Maybe 'It sounded as if the streets were running,' or 'As imperceptibly as grief'? Or, I don't know, 'Like mighty footlights burned the red'?"

"The love poems," he said. "Those are all love poems to nature, love poems to what lasts."

She stopped walking and stared at him.

"You know what kills me about Dickinson? When you read the poems out loud, they don't sound like poetry. Like, in ''twas later when the summer went,' which is one of my favorites. You can see how, in the lines 'Yet that pathetic pendulum/Keeps esoteric time,' she uses 'pathetic' and 'esoteric' for their syllable count, because '*poor* pendulum' and '*strange* time' wouldn't fit the meter. I get that. But it sounds normal anyway. It just sounds like someone's talking."

"Ha. Tell that to the kids in my class," Caroline said. And, disloyally, "Tell Natalie."

"I just wish I knew how she did that. I wish *I* could do that."

He wrote poetry? Here was something she hadn't even thought of putting on her list. "So...you're a poet?"

"Oh, no. I wish. I just write song lyrics. You?"

"A little," she lied. She wasn't used to telling anyone. She'd never even told Natalie, and she'd been writing poems since they were in the second grade. She'd written her *first* poem about a trip Natalie's family had taken her on, to a lake—the biggest body of water she had ever seen, and the first time she'd ever been *in* water other than a bathtub or the rec center pool—and she'd felt she had to do something with how that had made her feel, something more than talking to Natalie about it. Since then it had seemed natural to turn things, to turn everything—arguments with her mother, weird facts she learned in school, even some of the stupid conversations she had with her friends at lunch—into poetry. "What kind of songs?" she asked Clifford.

"I'll play them for you sometime if you want."

And then they were making plans to meet outside of school.

By their second date, he'd written a song for her and she'd shown him some of her poems. A week later, he'd written another. (And this too—the songs, the singing, the guitar-playing—had not been on her list. But *someone who reads* had. And so had *bonus item: who reads poetry.*)

She made the mistake of telling her mother about the songs, and after that she was always asking, "So has Clifford written any more *songs* for you?"—pronouncing *songs* as if this were the single most ridiculous, embarrassing thing anyone could do, when Caroline knew she didn't think that. Her mother was crazy for singer-songwriters: James Taylor, Joni Mitchell, Cat Stevens, Jackson Browne. What was ridiculous to her was the idea of *Clifford* writing songs. And even more: of Clifford writing songs for her.

But then her mother seemed to think everything about Clifford was ridiculous. Or else just wrong. She'd say, "Why is that boy so quiet around me? What's he trying to hide?" Caroline hated that she called him "that boy." And she always did. That boy or just "he." She never said his name. "That boy really ought to get some sun."

And: "He's so skinny. Don't you think he's too skinny?" She pointed out how *serious* he was (as if *serious* were a flaw). She even complained about his hair. And her mother liked long hair—Caroline knew this for a fact.

"Maybe she's jealous," Natalie said.

It was late October, already cold. They were walking to Natalie's house after school as usual and, as usual these days, Caroline had been complaining about her mother's irrational dislike of her boyfriend.

"Jealous? No, that's crazy," she told Natalie. "It's not as if she and I were spending that much time together before I met him. If anyone were going to be jealous, it'd be you, not her."

"Me? Nah. I'm too psychologically healthy for that." Natalie sounded happy. She always sounded happy. It was possible that she always *was* happy. She had a new boyfriend, Eli, and for the moment she was enthralled by him. He was one of the smart but too-cool, easily bored ones—the kind she liked best. "Really," Natalie said, "I am deeply and purely happy for you. Just like you're happy for me. You're not jealous of Eli. You've never been jealous of any of the guys I've gone out with."

Caroline couldn't think of how to say that none of those boys had affected their relationship—it would sound as if she hadn't taken any of them seriously. Well, she hadn't taken any of them seriously. She had just waited them out, one after another (and once—when there were two boys at the same time, when she and Natalie were fifteen—she had waited for the predictable crisis, and the double breakup). But this was one of the few things they never talked about.

Eli had been in the picture for nine days. Caroline figured he had less than three weeks left. But what she said was, "You always make an effort to keep me from feeling excluded."

"I'm wonderful that way, aren't I?"

"One of the many ways," Caroline said.

"Anyhow, I'm too busy to feel neglected. Plus, you haven't actually been neglecting me all that much—honestly, you should probably be neglecting me *more*—and *plus*, if you ever do start spending more time with him than with me, it'd give me more time to spend with my own boyfriend, because then I wouldn't have to worry that I was neglecting you."

Caroline was about to object, but they'd arrived at Natalie's house and she was yelling, "We're home, Ma," as they went up the stairs to the room she shared with her younger sister, who wasn't home from school yet. They dumped their book bags on the bed and Natalie said, "*Plus*, that wasn't even what I meant." She unzipped her bag and started pulling books out of it, tossing them to the floor. "I meant that she's mad that you have a boyfriend and she doesn't."

"That's not jealousy. That's envy."

Natalie rolled her eyes. "Same difference, bookworm."

"You're wrong. But the point is, she isn't envious *or* jealous of me. She has no interest in having a boyfriend."

"Are you so sure about that?"

"I am, Nat. I am completely sure." She took out her math book. "Can we get started on the math? I promised Clifford I'd stop in to see him at work at the String Shoppe before I go home."

But hours later, watching her mother across the dinner table, she was still thinking about what Natalie had said. Her mother had worked late at the mall and brought home Chinese food. She was reading a two-week-old *People* magazine as she ate her General Tsao's chicken. Caroline had *The Age of Innocence* propped up on a stack of textbooks and was just starting it over her kung pao shrimp, but she was distracted by Natalie's question—*was* she sure her mother didn't want a boyfriend? Her mother talked about men not just as if they were another species, but an inferior one it was impossible to communicate with. She had a bumper sticker on her car that said *If they can put men on the moon...why don't they?* She didn't even have any male *friends*. And she had not been on a single date in the seventeen years since Caroline was born.

She stole another look at her mother over the top of her book. She was frowning at something in her magazine.

There had been a brief period, when she was nine or ten and blazing through a Young Adult book (or two) every day—books that put lots of ideas in her head that wouldn't otherwise have been there (all those suicides and eating disorders and angry divorces and car accidents that left everybody paralyzed)—when Caroline had been on a campaign to *get* her mother to go out on dates. The girls in those books all had Single Mothers or Single Fathers and they were *always* dating (well, okay, maybe there were some who had two parents—but if they did, there was some truly awful problem: the father beat the mother, or both parents were alcoholics or drug addicts, or one of them or even both of them were dying of some terminal disease). Why she should have considered these novels a model for anything in life, she could no longer say, but for a while, whenever they went anywhere, she pointed out the men who looked presentable and said, "Would you want to go on a date with him?" Her mother thought this was hilarious.

At least that was what she said. Maybe she didn't mean it. Maybe she was lying.

Her mother lied about a lot of things. She lied about stupid things, like whether or not she'd ever seen a certain movie, read a certain book, tasted a certain food—but she also lied about big things. Until she was nine, Caroline had believed her when she said that her own father, Caroline's grandfather, had been a television actor. It turned out that he had only sold insurance. And she was almost sure her mother was lying about not remembering anything of consequence about the man who was supposed to be her father. Not even his name.

So maybe she *was* envious. She hadn't even made an effort to pretend to be pleased that Caroline had found someone she liked and who liked her back. What if she had started dating someone and *that* boy (would her mother have called him *that boy*?) had turned out to be a jerk? Maybe then her mother would have been satisfied. Maybe that was what she had been urging her to stop waiting around for. *Get your heart broken. Be disappointed. Be hurt. Be sorry. Be anything but happy.*

Join the human race.

Join the human race!—she hadn't thought of that in years. It was what her mother used to say when she was little, whenever she wanted to stay indoors to read or just to think and her mother insisted that she go outside to play. It didn't sound like something nice, the way her mother said it. It didn't sound like something inviting, something you'd *want* to join. The first time she had ever said it to her, it had made her cry. *I don't want to race. I don't like racing. I'm too slow.* She had been very young then—not even in school yet. Her mother had to explain what "the human race" was. But even after that, she didn't like the sound of it. Or maybe it was just the way her mother said it.

Her mother never did warm up to Clifford Delgrange. Even after they broke up, amicably enough, when Clifford went off to the University of Chicago and Caroline stayed in Kokosing, her mother made it clear that she had never liked "that pale, quiet boy with the long face and the long hair and that gloomy music" without ever once coming out and *saying* that she hadn't liked him.

Her mother didn't like the boyfriend after Clifford, either. Or the one after that, the last few months of freshman year at State. She didn't like any of her boyfriends, until Jacob Lieb. And *that* she came out and said. She said, "I like this one. I think he could be a keeper."

Which was astounding, really. And if Caroline had been a little less mature (she was perfectly aware of this, because she could feel it twitching inside her—the much less mature response, the *natural* response), she would have rejected Jacob simply on the basis of her mother's approval. Because her mother's judgment was by definition suspect. And because there was no reason to believe, Caroline told herself, that her mother had her best interests at heart.

But this time her mother was right—by accident, maybe, but still right. And maybe it was not an accident that her mother approved of Jacob. Maybe she had seen that there was something missing, something important, something that couldn't or shouldn't be overlooked, in the boys that came before him.

No—that was giving her mother too much credit.

But it didn't matter. She met Jacob, they fell in love, and her mother didn't say a word against him—not even when Caroline moved in with him, the summer after they finished their junior year at State. Her mother smiled, her mother was tearful, her mother *hugged* them—she hugged both of them. She was *happy* for them. Jacob had no idea how unusual this was.

"That's one parent down," he said. By then she knew about his father. By then she'd even met him. Well, met him *again*—met him as Jacob's father. Her mother was easy by comparison. Who would have imagined that?

They had been dating for six weeks before Jacob told her who his father was, and at first, just for a minute, Caroline did not believe him. Not that she thought he was lying—this would never even have occurred to her. She just figured he was kidding. So she laughed, even though it wasn't funny. She laughed to be kind.

"Don't laugh," he said. "Trust me, there's nothing funny about it."

What he'd said, out of the blue, as they sat at his kitchen table studying for an exam (Dadaism, Surrealism, and Early American Modernism), was, "You know that writer Martin Lieberman? The one whose books are all about how hard it is for a man to just be himself, what a lonely place the world is, and how nothing is ever as good as you thought it would be when you were young?" and she'd said, "Sure," although this was not the way she would have described these books, and she was about to add that she not only knew the books but that she'd actually met the man, that he'd been on campus last year and did Jacob know that?—because what a pity it was that he'd missed the reading—when he said, "I should tell you, then, I guess, that he's my father."

If his name had been Jacob Lieberman instead of Jacob Lieb, she might not have thought for so much as a millisecond that this was a joke she just didn't get (it would not have been the first time he had told a joke she didn't get). She would have known that it was not a joke, because she had been looking for the son of Martin Lieberman since late last spring.

Natalie made fun of her for it. In the huge psych class that they were in together this term, she was always leaning over and whispering, "What about that little guy in the third row, the one with the black curly hair and those tiny wire-rim glasses? Could that be him?" or she'd point to some big frat boy in his giant sneakers and long cargo shorts walking up the stairs toward one of the top rows and nudge her: "Check out this guy—so cute, right? That could definitely be him. Why don't you go on up to him at the end of class and ask him, 'Hey, so what does your daddy do for a living?'"

If Jacob's last name had been Lieberman, she would have known he was the writer's son as soon as he had introduced himself, which he had done right after the first lecture in the History of Art class they were both in. He'd been sitting next to her in the front row, and as they stood to gather their belongings, he'd asked her if she'd "ever seen any of these paintings in real life"—a pretty good line he swore later had not been a line—and when she said no, she hadn't, he told her which of them *he* had seen, in museums all over the U.S. and in Europe. So obviously she had to ask him why he'd been to all those places, and that was his chance to tell her he was a magician, that he traveled to perform and to give lectures on magic—and the rest, as her mother liked to say, *was [art] history.*

Even that very day, in the class that they were in together—the two of them and 278 others—even at the start of that class, twice a week, after she'd *met* Jacob (even after they had started dating), she had sometimes wondered, as she'd watched people filing in before the lights went out for slides, *Is Martin Lieberman's son one of them?*

So he would have to excuse her, she told Jacob, if she had to spend a few minutes now *adjusting* to this news.

He hadn't meant to keep the secret from her for so long. He'd thought about telling her—of course he'd thought about it. For the first couple of weeks, as they talked and talked—staying up all night, taking breaks from sex to talk, taking breaks from talk for sex—he waited for her to ask. *So, what kind of work does your father do?* If she'd asked, he would have told her. They were a month in before it dawned on him that he had *met* her mother and still didn't know what kind of work she did. The trouble was that he had spent too many years among people who knew who his father was before they knew who *he* was. Even after he'd begun to be known in his own right in the world of magic and magicians— even when a national society named him "best young magician" before he was seventeen and someone came to interview him for a profile in a magazine—he was "the well-known novelist Martin Lieberman's only son." So he had forgotten—or maybe he'd never known—that most people didn't care what anybody else's parents did.

"Why tell me now?" Caroline asked him.

"It was just time," he said. "*Past* time. I realize that." But this was not the truth. Or—it was, it *obviously* was, but it wasn't the whole truth.

The whole truth was that he had just had a revelation. As they sat at the formica table in the corner of his studio apartment that he called the kitchen, making notes on a shared legal pad (they took turns: for one chapter, she dictated and he wrote; for the next, they swapped) about historical context and artistic influences, and eating handfuls of both plain and peanut M&Ms and popcorn Caroline had dusted with cayenne pepper and extra salt, it had come to him: he could not do without her.

The thought had stunned him. There had never in his life been anyone he'd felt he couldn't do without—and this, he would have said if anyone had asked him, was a good thing. He *was* doing without everyone, was he not?

And *I can't live without you* in "romance," he'd been sure, was only the stuff of fiction—movies, pop songs, *Romeo and Juliet*. He'd had to write a paper in his nineteenth century lit class on *Wuthering Heights* and he had written it about the novel's (as he saw it) central fallacy (he'd gotten an A, too). So it hit him hard when he looked at Caroline across his kitchen table and thought, *This is it—this is forever.*

It frightened him. Not because he was "afraid of commitment," as he had been accused by girls he'd liked just fine until he didn't anymore, or just didn't like *enough* when they were claiming love and wanted him to claim it too (they flung this diagnosis at him when he broke up with them, no matter how regretfully and gently). And not because he feared he was in danger of losing Caroline—because he was not afraid of that; because one of the many things he loved about her was her willingness to let him know she was devoted to him, as if she'd never heard that keeping a certain distance, maintaining at least a hint of ambivalence, was attractive to men. She had liked him from the start and she had let him know that—and when she began to love him, she let him know that too (so cheerfully and non-coercively—*announcing* it, saying, "Hey, guess what? Apparently I love you"—he knew it wasn't meant to be transactional). *She* had probably known long before this night that neither one of them was going anywhere without the other. She had probably been waiting patiently, matter-of-factly, calmly, confidently (that was Caroline—that was how she was, and it was why he loved her) for him to catch up.

And now he had caught up, quite suddenly, while they sat contemplating images of boots with fleshy toes and plaster busts wearing dark glasses and Frida Kahlo holding hands with Frida Kahlo, and what frightened him was that he'd kept a secret from her for so long—too long. That he'd already ruined something that could have, would have, been perfect.

So he put down his pen, and he released the fistful of plain M&Ms he'd just scooped up from the blue Pyrex bowl Caroline had put them in (she had a rule about things being served from bowls or plates or platters, since she had grown up with bags and boxes, bottles, jars, cardboard containers, plastic tubs and cartons "just plunked down" at mealtimes and was now determined, she said, never to put anything still in its package on a table—so she poured cream from a creamer and spooned sugar from a sugar bowl, and even junk food was decanted into bowls—she'd *bought* a set of multicolored Pyrex bowls for him, just for this purpose, when she started spending so much time in his apartment). Now he took her hand—the free one; her other hand was in the bigger, yellow, popcorn bowl—and told her the truth.

She did not react in any of the ways he had imagined when he had considered telling her. He'd thought there was a chance she would be *too* happy (she was an English major, after all), that she might shriek the way girls who liked pop stars did. He had considered that she might become more interested in him than she had been (not that she'd love him more—he didn't go that far, not even in his gloomiest projections—but that she'd find him more intriguing, which he would have hated) and he had considered too that she might be *less* interested, that she might begin thinking of him in terms of his father, or (worse still) his father's books—comparing him unfavorably to them.

And he'd been prepared for anger (wouldn't he be angry if she'd kept something about herself a secret?). He'd been prepared for her to say she wasn't sure that she could trust him anymore (and what if it turned out that she couldn't?).

He had imagined every possible response, he thought, except for laughter followed by confusion. He'd forgotten to consider that because he and his father didn't share a name, he'd have to assure her that he wasn't joking. He had to explain that he'd been Jacob Lieb for a full one-third of his life—at first unofficially, when he was thirteen, because the new name "fit better," he told her. "Fit better?" Caroline said. "Fit better *how?*"

"Just, you know, *fit*. On flyers, posters, tickets, all that." He tried not to sound impatient. He had been glad to shed his father's name professionally but he never thought about it anymore—it was old news. He made the mistake of saying that.

"Not to me it isn't," Caroline said. So maybe she *was* angry.

He apologized. He told her that the summer after he turned seventeen, he changed his name legally. That because he was a minor, his father had to—

"And he didn't mind? That you were giving up your name? His name?"

No, his father seemed to think it was amusing. On the day they went together to the courthouse, his father told him he'd had uncles who had gone by Liebman or by Liebmann. For that matter, there was no agreement about the spelling of Lieberman/Libermann/Liberman. And *his* father, Jacob's grandfather, had once told him (Jacob's father said) that *his* father, in the old country, had been Lipmanowicz, "so my old man felt sure he had some second cousins who would go by Lipman. He made a joke of it. 'Jews and their names,' he told me. 'That's the thing—they're never set in stone. Except when they actually are.'" Caroline didn't laugh. "After they're dead, he meant," Jacob explained. "He meant, etched on their gravestones."

"Yes, I got that."

"Hey, it was his joke, not mine."

But now she wanted to talk about how his *mother* had felt when he'd gone to court with his petition for the name change, and if she'd been sorry later that she'd let him do it—if they ever talked about it anymore or if they all were so accustomed to it that there was no point—he saw that telling her the secret of his parentage was just the start of all the things he had to tell her. That one thing would lead to another.

And so this was the night he told her everything. Or almost everything. Everything except for the whole truth about the reason he was telling her. He had to work up the nerve for that.

This was also the night, then, that Caroline began her campaign to get him to call his father. "It doesn't matter if he's selfish, self-absorbed, detached, a pain in the ass. He's your father. If he drove your mother away, if you want to punish him or punish both of them for not giving you what you believed you needed—"

"What I 'believed' I needed?"

"—it makes no difference, Jacob. You should be in touch with him."

It didn't sway her when he told her he had come to the conclusion that his father was incapable of seeing him as his own person, separate from *him*, and that the only way he'd ever see his son as anything but an extension of himself was if he severed their connection. He'd had a glimpse of this, he told her, when his mother left: after she was gone, it seemed to him that both his parents counted on him to fill in for *her*. "How fair is that?" he said. "*She* escapes, and she expects—what? That I'll look after him *for* her? That's not my job, is it?"

No, Caroline said. It wasn't his job. It wasn't anybody's job. And he was right, it wasn't fair. But that didn't matter. "If you'd never had a father, you'd feel differently," she said.

"If you had had a father like mine, *you* would feel differently."

"You realize, don't you, that these counterfactuals make it impossible to have a reasonable discussion?"

"This *subject* matter makes it impossible to have a reasonable discussion. Besides"—he took her hand; he smiled hopefully at her—"you started it."

She smiled back, which was a relief. "Jacob, believe me, I know he's not perfect. Just from the one conversation I had with him last spring, with—"

"Multiply that by 365 days a year by eighteen years—"

"*Jacob*. You're being childish."

"I'm allowed to. I'm his child."

"You are. That's why you should call him. You should have heard the way he talked about you. He wants to see you. It seemed obvious that the whole reason he made that trip here last spring was that he hoped he'd see you. It was also obvious how much he missed you."

"Why does his wanting to see me count more than my not wanting to see him?"

"It's not that it counts more. It's that it doesn't cost you anything to do it, and it would mean—"

"Oh, it would cost me something, all right."

"Okay, maybe it would. Still, it's worth the cost."

"You're changing arguments."

"I know."

You might have thought, he told himself, that this single-mindedness of hers, this stubborn certainty that she was right, would have made him doubt his revelation. Shouldn't it have made him love her less? But it had the opposite effect. As days passed, then a week, and they continued arguing about his father, he was moved by her certainty, moved by how passionately she cared about something that had nothing, really, to do with her. He marveled over her willingness to brave the possibility that he *would* be driven off by her insistence that he call his father when he'd made it so clear he didn't want to.

Had he ever known anyone who cared so much? How was it possible, he wondered, to care this much about something that would make no difference in her own life? (Or was she able to project into the future in a way he couldn't? *Would* it make a difference in her life? He did not dare ask her: it would have meant their talking about something that made no sense to talk about less than two months into their relationship.)

He thought a lot about what she had said about his father, that it didn't matter if he was "detached" or self-absorbed, that all that mattered was the *fact* of him. *If you'd never had a father, you'd feel differently.* When she talked about the mystery of her own father— the invisible man, the man it was clear she would never know, a man who (it seemed clear to Jacob) hadn't been worth knowing—who had passed almost invisibly (invisibly except for her existence!) through her mother's life—her sadness dumbfounded him. Everything she cared about, whether it was worth caring about or not, she cared so much about.

She was, he thought, the antithesis of detached—the antithesis, then, of his father. And of his mother, too. The antithesis of both his parents.

Attached. That was what she was. It was all he'd ever wanted.

He was lucky, Jacob thought, that she was focused on his father, on repairing *that* relationship. If she had decided to go on a crusade about his mother, if she'd begged him to try to track her down, he wouldn't have known where to start. In the beginning, after his mother had first left, she'd sent a few postcards and a letter—and the letter might as well have been a postcard, for all it had said. And only the second of the postcards, which had come in April of his freshman year, four months after the first one and five months after she'd left, had included a return address. He'd waited several weeks before he sent a postcard in return—a picture postcard featuring the small lake in the center of his campus, to match the scenic view she'd sent him of Bird Rock in Marin County, saying as little as she had, nothing more than *Yes, I'm still alive, everything's fine, no need to worry.* After thinking hard about it, he'd provided the address of the off-campus apartment for which he'd just signed a lease, beginning July 1. Her third postcard had reached him there, soon after he had moved— *Hope all's well, Love, Mom*—and then, not even two weeks later, before he'd finished thinking about whether he would answer, and while he was still wondering if the address that she had sent in April was still good (the card was postmarked Oxnard, California: hundreds of miles north of that address—he'd looked it up), there had been the "letter" (which consisted of three sentences that told him nothing, only that she had been traveling "up and down the coast" and how beautiful it was, that "all's well here," and that she loved him and, oh yes, hoped once again that all was well with him), but it was unclear where "here" was, since the letter's postmark was Eureka. She'd traversed over six hundred miles since the last time she'd written. "If she wanted me to write back, she would have included an address," Jacob told Caroline. "Not putting a return address on an *envelope* is a decision a person has to actively make. I think she was letting me know she didn't need to hear from me again. And I haven't heard from her since. Which is fine, really."

"It's not *fine*, Jacob. None of this is fine."

"Okay, it's not 'fine.' But it's history. It's just how it is."

"Which is all the more reason for you to stay in touch with your father."

It always came back to that.

Finally, of course, he gave in. And she was so happy! She fluttered around, chattering about the trip she'd made him promise they would take to see his father. She talked about it endlessly at Thanksgiving dinner with her mother, though the visit was still months away; she talked about it all through finals week and winter break, insisting that he call "home" (her word) on New Year's Eve just after midnight to say Happy New Year (and the old man cried—*that* was a first). Her happiness infected him—he could not protect himself against it.

Even so, it was not until mid-March, after winter quarter ended (a ten-week period during which his father called him twice—without tears either time, thank God), that he told Caroline why he had come clean that night in November.

It happened this way, on the night before their New York trip:

Caroline was all keyed up. And so was he, but while *she* was happy and excited, what he was feeling, he thought, seemed a lot like stage fright—and he had not had stage fright since his earliest performances, when he was a child. He was agitated, jumpy. He felt sick, actually—his stomach hurt; he was a little nauseated. He had just returned from Minneapolis, where he'd been paid outrageously well for doing strolling magic at an enormous corporate event, and he had suffered badly, missing her, the two days he'd been gone. He hadn't told her that.

Now he was in her dorm room with her, watching her pack and repack her suitcase—she could not decide what she should bring. She was dancing around the tiny room and periodically dipping to kiss him or alight for an instant on his lap where he was sitting on her bed.

"Stop for a second," he said. "I want to show you something."

She dropped down beside him, a sweater in each hand. "I don't know which to take," she said.

"Take both. If you run out of room, you can put it in my bag."

He took out his wallet and extracted the check he had come home with. He handed it to her and her eyes widened. "That's a lot of Chinese takeout, Jake."

And Jacob heard himself say, "Chinese takeout nothing. This is let's-get-married money."

Ah. So that was what was happening. No wonder his stomach hurt.

Caroline laughed uncertainly.

"Not a joke," he said.

"You want to get *married?*"

"Yes," he said. "I do."

"We're twenty years old."

"I know," he said. "Let's get married anyway."

Caroline leaned toward him. She put her head on his shoulder. "Okay," she said. "I'll take both sweaters. And yeah—let's get married."

Jacob could have sworn he felt his heart stop beating. It took a moment before he could respond. "Really?" he said. "You'll marry me? You're serious?"

"Obviously. You're the one who makes jokes, not me. And I've known I couldn't do without you practically since we first met. *You* had to go to Minnesota to figure it out. You're way behind."

And so he had no choice, he felt, but to tell her that he wasn't—that he'd known for months. "I think that's why I told you about Martin," he confessed.

Caroline laughed for real this time. "You're such a strange boy, Jacob."

"And yet you're going to marry me."

"Of course I am."

"You're sure? You won't change your mind?" And then, as if he meant it as a joke—he smiled before he said it, to make sure he could claim it as a joke if necessary—he said, "Should we do it right away, then? Like, as soon as we get back?"

She smiled too. "No. We are not getting married in a *week*." She kissed his neck. "We don't have to rush. I'm not going to change my mind. I'm promised to you now. We're promised to each other. We're *betrothed*."

He had to turn his head away. His eyes had filled.

"We've pledged our troth," she said. "We're affianced."

"You just like all those words," he told her.

"I do like the words." Her arms were around him. "I like all words. But I like you too."

"So what now?" he said. "Do we go get a ring?"

She drew back. "Jacob Lieb! Don't you dare spend any of that money on a ring! We'll put it in the bank. We're going to need it."

We'll. We're. "Is it okay if I tell you how happy I am that you're telling me what to do with my money?"

"Our money." She was grinning at him.

He waited until the next morning at the airport, as they sat at their gate waiting to board the plane, before he asked her, "How long do we put it off, then? How long is an engagement?"

"We'll see," she said.

"But *what* will we see? Is there some specific thing you're waiting for? Do you have a secret plan?"

"You're the secret-keeper," she said. "I'm an open book."

"Read it to me," Jacob said. "Tell me what are we waiting for."

"We're waiting long enough so that it won't seem intemperate. Precipitous."

"To who?"

"To everybody." Caroline stood up. "Give me the boarding passes, Jacob."

"What? What did I do?"

"You didn't do anything. They've called our row."

He handed her the boarding passes and picked up both their carry-ons. "Who's going to think we're being intemperate or precipitous? Your mother? She'll be thrilled. She loves me. Or do you know something I don't know? Has she been faking? Does she *not* like me?"

"She likes you more than she likes me."

"So who? Natalie? She couldn't possibly think this was precipitous. She doesn't even know the word precipitous."

"Natalie isn't stupid, Jacob." She put one hand on his back and pushed him gently toward the boarding line.

"Are you worried about my father?" He stopped and turned to face her. "Why would you worry about my father?"

"I'm not worried about your father." She pushed him again, a little harder. "I'm not *worried* about anything. We have a plane to catch."

"If you're not worried—"

"Hush. Wait until we're on the plane."

He hushed, reluctantly. They boarded, Caroline prodding him from behind as if the plane might leave without them, even though there were plenty of people in the line ahead of and behind them. She counted the rows aloud and cried, "Here's ours!" in a strained, artificially bright way that made him nervous. *Was* she angry with him? He put their suitcases in the bins over their seats and they sat down, Caroline wedging her big purse (stuffed with the copies of *The New Yorker* and *The Atlantic Monthly* and *Harper's* and all the gum and candy she'd bought in the airport as he watched and asked, "Um, are you getting ready for a flight to China? We're in the air for like an hour and a half") under the seat in front of her. He watched her carefully fasten her seat belt and pull it tight. Then she turned to him and said, "Okay, here it is: I want to wait till after graduation."

"What? No." He did his best not to sound panicked. "Why do we have to wait that long?"

"It's not that long. It's not much more than a year away. And even then it'll still be awfully young to get married, you know that."

"So you think we're too young?"

"I'm just stating a fact, Jacob. Do you know anybody who gets married at twenty-one?"

"Lots of your high school friends. You've told me so."

"Not my friends. People I know—*knew*, in high school. Sure, there are people who still do that here. There are also people who get pregnant when they're still in high school, or even in middle school, and then have the baby."

"Come on, that's another thing altogether."

"I'm not my mother, Jacob. Or my grandmother."

"You're right. You're not. And I'm not my father. Is this news?"

He wasn't crazy about the look she was giving him.

"What?"

"We don't have to rush, Jake."

He was silent for a moment. "I'll be twenty-two by then."

"Just barely."

"And you'll be almost twenty-two."

"And what, that's too old to get married?" She took his hand and squeezed it. "We're going to wait until we finish school. We're going to be grown up and sensible."

"What's more grown up and sensible than *married*?"

She laughed. So she wasn't angry.

"Okay, I didn't mean that to be funny," he said. "But I have an idea. While we're waiting to be grown up and *sensible*, I mean."

"I'm all ears."

"What if, in the meantime, you move in with me?" He didn't even give her a chance to answer before barreling ahead: "We could be a *little* bit sensible right now and wait till the end of spring quarter, when you have to move out of your dorm room anyhow. And I know you just moved into it, so I don't want to rush you into anything, but my apartment is definitely better than a dorm room and way better than moving back home for the summer, right?" He was talking too fast, he knew—a habit he'd worked hard to break himself of when people kept saying, his whole first year here, "Whoa, slow down, I can hardly understand you"—but he didn't want her to interrupt, didn't want to give her the chance to say no. "You know you'd probably be staying with me most of the time anyway. So all we'd be doing is making it official. And it would be very practical. Financially, I mean, once school starts up again, because the dorms are crazy overpriced. And over the summer, we could—"

"Yes! Stop talking!" She took his face in both her hands and kissed him, hard. "It's a marvelous idea."

"It is?"

"It is." The plane was taxiing. Caroline looked out the window. "We're *moving*, Jacob." She was squeezing his hand again. She wasn't looking at him.

"And Natalie?" he said.

"Natalie what?"

"How seriously have you two talked about rooming together next year? Caroline, would you look at me?"

Without turning, she said, "You weren't worried about my plans with Nat when you wanted to get married in like a week."

"Because marriage is hard to argue with. Even for Natalie. Marriage wins arguments. Moving into some guy's one-room, partially furnished apartment? Not as good a case."

She still hadn't turned to face him. "First of all, you are not some guy. Second, Nat doesn't get a vote about our lives, so we don't have to make a *case*. But it doesn't matter because Nat isn't going anywhere. She talks about moving out of her parents' house, but she talked about doing it for this year too, right up until she said she'd changed her mind. I was lucky to *get* a dorm room. I think she'll be relieved that she doesn't have to think about it for next year, that I'll stop bugging her about it. She's perfectly happy at her parents' house now that they've fixed up that room for her in the basement. She has her own *entrance*."

The plane had picked up speed. In seconds, they'd be in the air.

"Man," he said. "You know what? I think I can't believe we're going to do this."

"It was your idea!" Now she turned to him. "Wait. Are you talking about moving in together? Or about getting married after graduation?"

"I'm talking about flying to New York to see my father."

"Oh, Jake," she said. "Oh, sweetie. Don't worry. It'll be all right."

"I don't know how you can know that."

"I don't know how, either," she said. "But I know it anyway."

And then they were off the ground. Caroline squeezed his hand tighter—squeezed it so hard he said, "Hey. Pain."

"Sorry," she said. But she didn't stop. Was she worried too?

"You know *you* have nothing to worry about, right? He's going to love you. Just like your mother loves me. Maybe even more, although that's hard to imagine, isn't it?"

She smiled but she still held on tight. She closed her eyes.

"And we're engaged, which is amazing, right?" She nodded, eyes closed. "What's going on, then? Because you're starting to make me nervous. Are you having second thoughts?"

She opened her eyes. "What? *No.* I'm really happy, Jake." But she looked terrified.

She didn't tell him until after they were married—until after they were married *and* after their son was born—that this had been her first flight. That she had been terrified when the plane left the ground. That she had been pretending she was more experienced and knew more than she really did because she was embarrassed to tell him the truth. That the only reason she even knew what a "boarding pass" was was that she'd looked it up. That everything she knew, she knew only because she'd read it somewhere.

And what Jacob thought, then, was, *Thank God*—she'd had secrets too. She'd claimed to be an open book, but everyone kept some things secret, didn't they? This just meant that they were even.

SIGNS THAT MIGHT BE OMENS

Driving Wheel	*I'll Be With Thee*	*Never Say*
Fountain of Sorrow	*Not Enough Time*	*To Be Alone With You*
Whose Son	*And When I Die*	*Your Mother*
Anybody's Girl	*Good Girls Don't*	*Should Know*
The Circle is Small	*Why Not Then*	*Nothing But Time*
Where Is She	*Morning Glory*	*Time Passes Slowly*
Come on, Child	*Spinning Wheel*	*Cold Blue Steel*
Steam Roller	*Bird on the Wire*	*and Sweet Fire*
Does Your Mother Know	*I Know Where*	*He's A Runner*
Father and Son	*I'm Going*	*Desperado*
Hard Headed Woman	*Stories We Could Tell*	*Wild World*
Hard Lovin' Loser	*Hey, That's No Way*	*Love Needs A Heart*
Hymn to Her	*to Say Goodbye*	*Carolina In My Mind*

—*Little Mama's, Kokosing, OH, 11/17/79*

L *ook around,* Jeanie Forester liked to tell her daughter, Carrie, who believed that her mother's life amounted to a series of mistakes and bad decisions and half-baked ideas. *Everybody's* life was made up of accidents and snap decisions—good and bad ones both—and ideas (good, bad, half-baked or unbaked—and who could tell which not-yet fully baked idea was a good one until later—until after it was, you know, baked? "The word is *realized*," her daughter said coolly).

Jeanie was on the bus, stopped dead in traffic, on her way home from her new job, which her daughter disapproved of. (She'd disapproved of her old job, too. And also the job before that.) But she liked her job. She liked the clothes she wore to *do* her job—the skirt and blouse and hose and good shoes that made a glamorous, efficient clicking sound as she passed the main receptionist and made her way to her desk each morning. She liked that walk. Maybe it was silly—and maybe she'd get over it, because it hadn't even been four months since she'd started here, but so far, so good.

As a child her daughter had posted lists on the refrigerator of what needed to be done in the coming days or weeks. "So you're the adult and I'm the child?" Jeanie would ask her as she examined one of her lists, painstakingly printed on lined paper and stuck to the fridge with a Curious George magnet:

> *we need appels bred penut buter sereal eggs*
> *libry books go bak 8-15*
> *skool supplys—see list techer sent!!*

"No, I'm the child," her daughter would say, so patiently and seriously it was unnerving. "I just like *knowing*."

She still liked knowing. It was what Carrie—*oh, excuse me, Caroline,* Jeanie had to remind herself—it was what *Caroline* liked best.

"I've been Caroline for years, Mom," her daughter was always saying. "You'd think you could remember that."

Well, Jeanie couldn't. Not reliably. Not when *Caroline* had been born Carolina and had variously been Lynne, Lynnie, C.J., Cara, Caro, and repeatedly—most often—Carrie. Now she wanted to be Caroline, but who knew who she might want to be next year, or even tomorrow? Maybe she'd pick an entirely new name—what was to stop her? Maybe she'd be Madeline or Jacqueline or Adeline. At *Adeline,* Jeanie snorted and the woman next to her, dressed just like her, she noticed only then (as if they were friends who'd shopped together and, for fun, picked out the same outfit to wear to work), turned to her and frowned, then quickly looked away.

Was her life so bad? Jeanie wanted to ask her daughter. Dressing up, riding the bus, having her own desk waiting for her when she got off the elevator at the sixteenth floor? The work itself wasn't all that interesting—answering the phone, greeting people who showed up in person, answering the same questions again and again, filing and photocopying and typing up invoices and agendas and smiling smiling smiling all day long (sometimes she had to be reminded to smile, reminded by her boss that it was part of her job). It was no better or worse, really, than waiting tables or selling blue jeans or almost any of the other things she'd ever done (though definitely better than housecleaning, which she had hated and was terrible at). But this was the only job she'd ever had where she had the sense that she was doing anything of consequence. Of consequence to *someone*. Even if she didn't always understand what the importance was of any given task, it was made clear to her that getting it done mattered. That if *she* didn't do it, and if she didn't do it well, it mattered. She liked that. She liked her new boss, too, liked her even when she was instructing her to smile (it was just part of *her* job to do that, and something in the way she said it—as if she were a little bit embarrassed—made it seem like the reminder was no less obligatory, even ceremonial, than the smiling was).

Even taking the bus was a kind of pleasure, she thought as she looked out the window at the people streaming out of buildings in clusters that split and scattered like they'd been hit by a cue ball. The ride downtown in the morning at the same time everybody else who worked downtown rode it, then the ride home every evening with the same crowd, made her feel like she was part of something even when all she was doing was sitting stuck in traffic, gazing out the window. She had tried to explain all of this to her daughter, but it was impossible to explain. Or else it was just impossible for *Caroline* to understand her explanation.

Now she watched as a balding man in a suit and tie and aviator sunglasses broke free of his pack and greeted a pretty woman in a striped sundress and high-heeled white sandals, then took her hand as they walked together to the corner and waited to cross the street. She watched a fat man in a pale gray suit carrying a tiny dog. A girl in a long flowered dress and combat boots, a portfolio tucked under her arm. Two old women—one old, one very old—walking slowly, their arms linked, heads tipped toward each other. They might be mother and daughter. Jeanie tried to picture herself and her daughter, both of them old (Carrie old, herself ancient), walking this way. Not arguing anymore.

Ha. They'd argue until she was dead. Maybe even after. Maybe *Caroline* would be picking a fight with her even as she laid her to rest.

When she got home, the kitchen phone was ringing.

"Aloha," Jeanie said. "It's you?"

"It's me," her daughter said.

"Like clockwork, huh?" Jeanie tucked the receiver between her shoulder and her chin as she sat down at the kitchen table and shook off her pumps, which somersaulted over her feet and smacked her insteps as they landed. "Ow," she said. "Jesus." She started digging in her purse for cigarettes and kicked her shoes back toward the hallway so she'd remember to bring them upstairs later. "Hi, you."

"Mom, are you sitting down?"

"What? Why?" She stopped rummaging and tipped her chair back to reach for the drawer behind her, where there was a carton.

"Just sit down, okay? And get a cigarette."

"I'm sitting. I'm getting. Why so much drama?"

"No drama, Mama. I have news."

"*Mama?* Now you're scaring me." But she didn't mean it. She wiggled her toes, hot and cramped and *ugh*, the nylon over them stained navy from the pumps, and opened a fresh pack of Marlboros. The kid had a flair—a weakness was more like it—for the dramatic. She should have been a theater major. (Actually, that wasn't such a bad idea. At least an actress stood a chance of making real money someday. Her daughter the

English major had assured her only last week that *she* never would. This had followed her announcement that she had been offered a teaching job in the fall at a dinky little private school on the northside, and that she'd already accepted it. Jeanie had been naïve enough to say, "I thought you were going to be a poet—I thought that was the whole plan." And Carrie said, "Oh, Mom. No one makes money writing poetry. It's not even a possibility"—saying it as if this were something to be proud of.)

She was waiting, Jeanie knew, to hear the click of the lighter, the first drag exhaled, before she spoke. Jeanie tipped her chair backwards again, balancing it on its two back legs the way she'd always told her daughter not to, and lit her cigarette. Inhaled, exhaled.

"All right, Mom. Are you ready?"

"I am ever-ready."

"Jacob and I got married today."

Jeanie slammed forward in the chair—it was like something out of a cartoon—coming down hard enough so that her teeth rattled when the chair's front legs hit the floor. She dropped her cigarette and scrambled for it before it burned the linoleum. "Jesus, Carrie."

"This is *good* news. Happy news. Don't sound like that. Don't make this a crisis."

"I'm not making it anything. Tell me again. Tell me slowly."

"We went down to the courthouse and we got married. I can't tell it any more slowly than that." There was a pause, a small sucking sound. She'd put her hand over the mouthpiece. Then she was back, to say, "We're very happy."

"You have to check with Jacob before you issue the verdict?"

"Mom, look. I know you don't—"

But Jeanie didn't want to hear what it was she *didn't*. "Where's the courthouse?" "Come on, I know—"

"Right now I don't care what you think you know. Where's the fucking courthouse?"

"What do you mean, where is it?"

Jeanie was trying—she really was—to stay calm. "I mean *where is it*? What's the address?"

"I don't know the *address*. It's downtown. It's on High Street. Not far from Main."

Exactly where Jeanie thought. Two blocks from where she worked. "Who else was there?"

"Who else was there? Nobody else was there. Why?"

"Just you and Jacob. And the judge who married you."

"That's right."

Jeanie lit another cigarette before she remembered that the first one was still burning in the ashtray. She picked up that one with her left hand and took a last drag on it before crushing it out. "So you two went downtown. And since you didn't ask to borrow the car—and I'm assuming you didn't just come and take it without asking and then put it back?—I'm guessing you took the bus, the number 2, *my* bus. And you got married, all by yourselves, two blocks from the Citywide building. Is that right? While I was, what, typing a letter? Photocopying a fucking claim form? What *time* did you do this?"

"We took the bus, yes. You know I'd never take your car without asking. I don't *know* the number of the bus. The one that goes down High, the one I used to take with my friends sometimes." *She* sounded calm. Improbably, insanely calm.

Jeanie tapped her cigarette over the ashtray that Caroline had made for her in ceramics camp at the Rec Center when she was eight years old—a large, low-sided, rainbow-colored bowl she'd told the camp counselors was "for jewelry" because she knew they wouldn't let her make an ashtray. "What time was it?" Jeanie asked her. "What time was it when you got on the bus?"

"I don't know. Maybe just past nine? We got down there around nine-thirty, maybe nine-forty-five."

So they'd made sure to miss her by at least half an hour. Well, of course they had: they had a secret.

"Then afterwards we took the bus back up to campus. We both had class."

"You got married and right afterwards you *went to class?*" And this was life with Carrie: first a secret wedding, then everything was meant to get right back to normal. "What class was that, that was so important?"

"I had my poetry workshop"—naturally, Jeanie thought (what else could it have been?)—"and Jake had his Kierkegaard seminar. It's the last week of the quarter. It was my last workshop, ever, with Professor Rosen, and it was Jake's last seminar. Neither one of us wanted to miss class."

"Oh, well, then, that makes perfect sense."

"You don't have to be sarcastic."

"And you don't have to be defensive. I'm just asking."

"You're not just asking."

"That's enough," Jeanie said.

And there they were, as usual. But Jeanie did not say, as she wanted to, I'm entitled to be sarcastic, I'm entitled to be hurt and angry, I'm a mother who was purposely excluded from her daughter's wedding.

She wondered what it was that Carrie—Caroline—wanted to say, but didn't.

"All I mean is that we both really needed to be in class today. Jake's one of just seven people in his seminar, and four of them are grad students—you don't just skip something like that. Plus he'd already had to miss two classes because of his traveling schedule."

Jeanie couldn't help herself. "I'm so glad he's got his priorities straight. Magic show? Skip class. Wedding? Why bother?"

"Mom." There was a pleading, hopeful note in her voice that gave Jeanie pause. "It's not as if we didn't celebrate. We went out for a late lunch after our eleven-thirty classes. We went to that new Indian place and Jake even got a little drunk. Drunk in the middle of the day—come on, that's a celebration, right? And then afterwards we stopped and bought ourselves flowers, and now we're home and we're calling you, okay?"

"Okay," Jeanie said. She matched her daughter's placating tone. Her daughter, she thought, who would get worked up over the most trivial things, and over things that had nothing to do with her, things that weren't any of her business—things that were so far in the past there was no point talking about them, much less getting worked up about them—and who was talking now about her wedding day as if it were no big deal. "You got married," Jeanie said. She said it cautiously—quietly, agreeably. "And then you went to class. And then you went out for tandoori chicken and got drunk."

"We didn't have tandoori chicken, we had saag paneer. And this incredible naan stuffed with coconut and dried fruit and almonds. And I didn't drink at all, Jake did. And we had to go to class, Mom. It's our last week of college. Please don't be angry."

"Why would I be angry?" Jeanie took a breath. "Now I suppose you have to go. Surely you have homework you need to do."

"No, Mom, no homework. School's done. I defended my honor's thesis last week, you know that. I don't even have any finals—just one paper to turn in, and I've already written it. I'm in no hurry."

"That's great. So what else do you want to talk about?"

"We didn't tell anyone, you know. We didn't even tell Nat."

"Oh, well, then, that makes me feel much better."

"I actually thought you'd be happy. I thought you loved Jake."

"I do."

"But you're mad anyway? Because we didn't make a big enough deal of it? Or just because we didn't tell you?"

"Just because you didn't tell me? Are you listening to yourself?"

"Seriously, Mom, that's what matters most to you? Because apparently that's what matters most to Jacob's dad."

"Jacob's dad? I didn't even get the first phone call? Jacob's *dad* got the first call?"

"*Mom.* Don't yell at me."

"I'm not yelling."

"You are. Look, Jacob called him first, yes. But only because we wanted to get it over with, we were both dreading it so much. He hit the roof when we moved in together, remember? And you were so, you know, so sweet about it. We thought you'd be even happier about *this*. And Martin, it turned out, was even madder about this than he was when I moved in with Jake. As far as he's concerned, we're too young to know what we're doing *and* he's outraged that we did this without him—without consulting him, as if we have to ask for his permission, and *also* without his being there. It's hard to tell which thing he's angrier about. I think he's just angry. I'm not even sure it has much of anything to do with us. He's acting like we pulled off some kind of *heist* that we're going to go to prison for when he ought to be happy for us."

She was still talking but Jeanie had stopped listening. An alarm had gone off in her head, as if it had been set on a timer. Jake even got a little drunk. *I didn't drink at all.*

"Oh, no, Carrie," she said. "Tell me you're not pregnant."

Her daughter went silent.

"You're not. You can't be."

Of course she could be.

"*Caroline.* You're pregnant? Just tell me."

"Yes."

"You're pregnant."

"Stop saying that."

"Why? Will that make it unhappen?"

"I don't want it to unhappen. I'm glad about it."

"So glad you weren't going to tell me?"

"I was going to tell you. I was just going to wait a couple of days. I didn't want to hit you with both things at once."

"I'd say these two things aren't entirely separate."

"They *are* separate. We were planning on getting married anyway. We've been planning it for a long time. We've been *engaged*. We just didn't tell anyone. We thought we'd tell you—you, and Jacob's dad, too, and all our friends—after we graduated, and then we'd have a small wedding. That was the plan."

"And then you got pregnant."

"Then I got pregnant. Don't be angry—please don't. I'm *happy*."

"You don't sound happy." Jeanie stabbed out her cigarette. She pushed the lopsided ashtray toward the center of the table, away from her. "How pregnant are you?"

"Totally pregnant."

"You know what I mean."

"Eleven weeks."

Jeanie closed her eyes. She let herself consider all the conversations they had had—conversations, arguments, debates, whatever they were—in the last eleven weeks. They talked nearly every single night, and there were some days, days when Caroline's first class was in the afternoon, when they talked in the daytime too. When she would call Jeanie at work, just to ask how it was going. So many conversations.

"How long have you've known? When did you figure it out?"

"I didn't 'figure it out.' I took a pregnancy test, like a normal person."

Jeanie let that go. Maybe she'd have to start letting a lot of things go. "When was that?" she asked her daughter. She said it as gently as she could.

"You want to know how long I've been keeping this a secret?"

"I want to know how long you've known." Jeanie paused. "And, yeah, sure, also how long you've been keeping it a secret from me."

Two months. She tried to remember what their conversations had been like *before* two months ago—if they had changed once Carrie knew that she was pregnant. Or before she'd known for sure but maybe had a feeling about it, the way Jeanie had when she was nineteen and pregnant and figured out that she was never going to see the guy again—and that she should not have slept with him after all, though she had been so pleased with herself at the time, so proud that she had managed to get drunk enough to gather up the nerve to talk to him after he'd played his last set. And then he'd left town the next day, off to his next gig, and she didn't even know where he lived—she hadn't thought to ask him. She'd been too busy asking him to play his songs for her again once they were alone together, passing the bottle of tequila back and forth. She knew that was the way to get him to love her. At nineteen she had truly thought that that one night *was* love. And he'd asked her for her number, hadn't he? Why would he have asked if he didn't plan to call her the next time he passed through town?

"You're so young," Jeanie said.

"I'm not that young. I'm almost three years older than you were when you had me. I'm almost twenty-two. And I'm married."

"You're married *now*."

"That's better than married never."

"Is it?" Jeanie said.

Suddenly her daughter was crying. "I didn't mean that."

"I know."

"I don't know why I'm crying."

"It's hormones," Jeanie told her, instead of, *Because you got married today without your mother there with you. Because you're twenty-one and pregnant and you got married in a place where people get put on trial and then go to jail. And because you said something mean to your mother and you feel bad about it—and maybe you feel bad now about all the mean things you've ever said to your mother. And because you're scared to death.* Jeanie was silent for a moment and then she said, "Would you tell me something? If you were going to get married soon anyway, why didn't you wait a little longer and do it right?"

"Because I'm starting to show," she said. She was still crying. "It's like it happened overnight. Just in the last couple of days, I turned into this pregnant person. I mean, no one else could tell, probably, just to look at me—I look like I've maybe eaten too much is all, I've got this little pot belly, you know?—but in another week or two, we figured, it would be obvious to everybody. So we decided not to wait any longer. We decided we didn't *want* to wait any longer. And today—you're going to think I'm stupid, but today—"

"Stupid?" Jeanie said. "You've been a lot of things, sweet pea, since the day you were born, but you've never been even a little stupid."

"Today is Jacob's birthday."

"Ah," Jeanie said. "Well, then. That *is* a little stupid."

"*Mom.*"

"No, I mean, that's quite a present. Happy birthday—I'm yours forever."

She'd meant it as a joke—a little joke—but Caroline was sobbing now.

"Oh, honey, listen," Jeanie said. "I was kidding. That's very sweet. It's *sweet* that you got married on his birthday. And you're going to have a baby! That's good news—it's *all* good news. Hey, I'm going to be a grandmother. You should congratulate *me*."

Caroline was crying too hard to talk. Jeanie couldn't remember the last time she had heard her cry. As a baby she'd cried all the time and Jeanie had thought she would go mad—there was nothing she could do to settle her (sometimes she wondered if her baby had been born grief-stricken—*that* was how bad it had been)—and then even when the constant crying ceased as she grew out of babyhood, for a long time she still cried more than it seemed to Jeanie other children did. She cried too easily, cried over nothing, could not be persuaded to *stop* crying once she'd started. But then all at once she did stop—stopped for good. So it had seemed to Jeanie, until now.

"Carrie. Caroline. Sweetheart. Do you want me to come over?"

"Oh, no," she sobbed. "You can't. We just got *married*. It's our wedding night."

"Oh, babe. Oh, doll. You poor thing. You've been living together for almost a year and now you're making me a grandma. And you went to Professor Rosen's *class* today after your little wedding."

"It just doesn't seem right," she wept.

"But it sounds like maybe you want me to."

"Maybe I do. But you shouldn't."

"Why don't you ask your husband? Tell him his mother-in-law wants to come over and say congratulations in person."

This time she didn't put her hand over the phone. Jeanie could hear her, talking and weeping at the same time, asking Jacob, "What would you think if my mother came over for a little while?" and the murmur of Jacob's response and then Carrie again, saying, "No, I'm sure she won't." Then Jacob again. Jacob her son-in-law, Jeanie thought—Jacob the father of her grandbaby. Jacob *the father*. It blew her mind.

And now Carrie—*the mother*—was back on the phone. "He says okay, sure. As long as you promise you won't start yelling at us like his father did—and we haven't even told him about the baby yet. He's going to lose his mind. Jake says he's tempted to just *not* tell him, to just show up with the baby later. Or maybe just never tell him. If we don't ever visit him again, Jake says, maybe Martin doesn't ever have to know." She dropped her voice down to a whisper. "I think he's losing his mind."

"He'll be okay," Jeanie said. "Not right now—I get that, it's a lot to take in—but in the end. He'll be just fine."

"Are you talking about Jake's father? Or about Jake?"

Jeanie laughed. "I meant his father. But now that you mention it—sure, both of them."

"Do you really think so? Jacob seems like his head is about to explode."

"His head is not going to explode," Jeanie said firmly. "And neither is his father's. The two of them are quite a pair, aren't they?"

But instead of agreeing—or for that matter not agreeing, for the sake of her brand new husband, who would so hate being compared to his father—Carrie said, distractedly, "Oh, um, also…Mom…"

What now? What else could there be? (What on earth was left?)

"I hate to ask you this. But…do you think you could pick up some food on your way over? We had that big lunch at like three o'clock, but I'm hungry—like, really hungry—again."

Jeanie exhaled. She hadn't even realized she'd been holding her breath. "Oh, yes. I remember that part. Of course I can. Anything in particular? Pizza? Chinese? Middle Eastern?"

"Middle Eastern would be great." Her daughter sniffled into the phone. "Stuffed grape leaves? Maybe a falafel sandwich? Some baba ghanoush?"

"I'll get a little of everything. Give me twenty minutes, half an hour tops. I'll call and put in an order and then I'm going to change out of my work clothes and head out. See you in a little bit."

The receiver was halfway to its cradle on the wall when she heard her daughter's voice again. "Also? Mom?"

Jeanie brought the phone back to her ear. "What is it, honey?"

"I just wanted to say...well, you know. I'm sorry."

And maybe she shouldn't have, but Jeanie asked—she couldn't help it—"For which thing, doll?"

"For lots of things. I've been hard on you."

File under: wonders never ceasing, Jeanie thought. "Yes, you have, a little."

"And I should have included you today. Or, I mean, I can understand why you'd feel bad that I didn't. But the thing is, we just kind of wanted it to be just us today. Just the two of us, nobody else. Not even you."

Ah. The *not even* got to her. And *she* was no crier, but she felt her eyes moisten. "Well, thank you," Jeanie said. And then: "Not the two. The three of you."

"The three—?" She paused. "Oh, right. The three of us."

"I'm sorry too, kiddo. You know that, don't you? Also for lots of things."

"I do know," her daughter said. She had stopped crying. "Love you." Something she never said. *They* never said. They weren't sentimental. They weren't that kind of mother and daughter.

The whole world had tilted, Jeanie thought. "Love *you*," she said, too late. Caroline—Carrie, Carolina—had already hung up the phone.

PART 3

DELIRIOUS

Is this your card? I'd ask. Is this? What's gone is gone,
I'd say. What's left is you and I. What's done is done.

— *Caroline Lieb, "Seen and Called"*

Jacob was practicing a new trick: the flap and flutter like wings as the deck of cards bridged his hands and then snapped shut, then fanned open again, so slowly that the cards appeared to be suspended in midair.

Caroline watched him from across the room they had begun, self-consciously, to call the "family room" after Harry's birth. The bird, renamed Delirious—which suited her much better than Dolores—was perched on her shoulder, probably asleep; the baby was awake, on a blanket at her feet. Caroline held an embroidery needle in one hand, a length of blue embroidery thread in the other. Five unopened skeins of thread—red, purple, green, black, yellow—and the blue one were in her lap, along with a brand new pair of sewing scissors, an embroidery hoop, and a pair of nine-month-size white denim overalls (on which she'd drawn a half moon and two stars and written Harry's name in careful script using the fabric marker she'd picked up yesterday at Jo Ann Fabrics along with everything else). On the little table next to her was the book she'd checked out of the public library that was supposed to teach her *how* to embroider, open to a page that explained the split stitch, but so far she had not even been able to thread the needle. It was possible she'd bought needles with too small an eye.

Jacob shut the deck of cards again—the many turning into one so suddenly it was as if they'd actually vanished, and an instant later the *one* was gone, too: his hands—palms up, then out—were empty. She'd seen him work a deck of cards so many times by now, it made no sense that this illusion was so potent, still—and yet there it was. Jacob had taught her to see many things as they occurred, things almost no one else could see, but somehow, no matter how he talked her through it and how much he slowed things down for her, she could never manage to see *this*: the place between there and not there, the instant of becoming gone—of something turning into nothing.

She watched him from her corner in the room that was surely meant to be a dining room—a hundred-year-old metal chandelier hung from the center of the ceiling—where she sat in the big, thick-cushioned glider chair that had been a present from his father. *One* of the presents from his father. Martin had showered them with gifts when Harry was born: expensive baby clothes and big stuffed animals and books and wooden toys for which his grandson would have no use for a long time, and all sorts of equipment—a stroller, a car seat (for the car they didn't even have), a swing, a crib, a changing table, and this chair. "It's too much," Caroline had told him. "You don't have to do all this." But Martin couldn't seem to help himself. "He has no self-control," Jacob observed. (But that made Caroline want to defend him—which was how it always went. "He means well," she told Jacob. "He's just excited. He wants to help us with the baby and he can't think of any other way to. It's really very sweet." Jacob said, "Yeah, right.")

The baby lay on a pale blue square of satin-trimmed monogrammed blanket—yet another gift from Martin—under the floor gym, a bright blue-and-yellow checked cloth-covered arch from which various toys dangled. Harry was studying it as if he'd be tested on it later, muttering a steady stream of syllables to himself and from time to time letting out a piercing shriek his grandfather referred to as his "excellent James Brown impersonation."

Jacob sat in the straight-backed wooden chair he liked to use when he practiced. There was a sofa, too—a brand new many-colored striped convertible that fit neatly between Jacob's chair and the sturdy cabinet they'd found at Volunteers of America to house their stereo and CDs and that was topped by the birdcage. Martin had insisted on buying them the sofa ("It's not for you, it's for me, okay?") during his third visit in six weeks, to replace the sagging Goodwill fold-out couch from Jacob's first apartment, upon which he declared he could not spend another night (Caroline had to give Jacob a stern warning glance to keep him from speaking up then) but, oddly enough, he had not slept on the new sofabed on his last visit but had booked a hotel room instead. He didn't want to put them out again, he said (Jacob noted that this was a lifetime first). He made himself scarce too, this time, which was unlike him. "Maybe he's changing," Caroline said. "Maybe he's becoming more thoughtful, more sensitive." Jacob snorted.

His father had last visited two weeks ago, just before Jacob had left on his most recent trip, and he'd brought more gifts—ten new picture books and two tiny hooded sweatshirts (a dark blue one imprinted with a Yankees insignia and a lighter blue one for the Mets: "to be fair," he said, winking at Jacob, "because we really do have to let the kid decide for himself")—proclaiming that a celebration was in order for the baby's "thirteen-week birthday" and taking them to dinner at the restaurant he had decided was the best in town, where the three of them took turns holding the baby while they ate their rack of lamb and mashed potatoes with fried leeks and drank a bottle of red wine that cost as much as the meal. Afterwards he didn't come in and keep them up too late, as he usually did. He kissed Caroline and the baby, shook Jacob's hand, and took off for his hotel. They didn't see him again until noon the next day, when he drove Jacob to the airport in his rental car.

Caroline was glad that Martin took so great an interest in the baby, and she didn't mind his frequent visits. He'd been angry when they told him they'd moved in together and he had been even angrier about their marriage, but her pregnancy seemed to have changed everything. He was madly in love with Harry (though Jacob had remarked that he treated him more like an *objet d'art* than a small human being in need of care—exclaiming over his great beauty, his perfection).

Jacob had one eye on the television, which was muted, as he opened up the deck again (and now the cards—imprinted with his name and RIGHT BEFORE YOUR VERY EYES on a scroll below it and, below that, his own gently caricatured likeness in top hat and tails—appeared to be spread flat across an invisible tabletop), then quickly swiped it shut, this time with a snap like a sprung mousetrap. The baby paused momentarily in his monologue of *ooh gah ah la*s to spit out a laugh, which at fifteen weeks wasn't much more than a clicking sound, as if he were stammering over a word that began with a \k\—*cards*, for example (it would not surprise her if *cards* turned out to be her son's first word). The bird woke up and shivered, fluffing her wings and ducking her head against Caroline's neck. Her stick-figure feet dug in a little harder through both the cloth diaper on her shoulder and the fabric of the two shirts she was wearing—a tee shirt and a flannel button-down, both Jacob's.

"Easy now."

Jacob glanced over at them, but only for a second. His attention was divided between the cards in his hands and the baseball game, which played out like a silent movie, complete with accompanying piano music (Caroline had stacked the CD changer with it). Right now it was Alexander Brailowsky playing Chopin's waltzes, music she had loved since high school—since Clifford Delgrange had introduced her to it along with bands like Cake and Third Eye Blind, as well as jazz— and which she believed would be good for Harry. Chopin was less demanding than the Mozart she had read could make a baby smarter, but still beautiful enough, she had decided, to give him a gentle nudge in that direction—because of course she wanted Harry to be smart, but she also wanted to be careful not to turn into one of those type-A mothers she had also read about, always pushing their children hard in one direction or another.

Brailowsky played Waltz No. 10 in B minor, Op. 69, No. 2, and the miniature baseball players on their sharply green field ran around after the ball. Jacob shuffled, fluttered, fanned, swiped, snapped. Harry babbled, laughed—*kuh kuh kuh*—gazed up at his dangling toys, shrieked. Delirious shrieked back, puffed herself up, bobbed her head. Caroline said, "Shh" and the bird pecked lightly at her ear. "Hey," Caroline said and tilted her head away—too quickly to suit Delirious, who squawked once, loudly, scoldingly, then followed up with a sound like a laugh of her own. The baby laughed back.

The bird had been with them for going on a year and a half now, ever since the second trip they'd made to New York, the one for which they'd borrowed Caroline's mother's car so that they could bring the bird home with them. Caroline had been glad to drive instead of flying, though she had not told Jacob that. She'd even let him drive part of the way back, which she'd thought would please him because he hardly ever had a chance to practice driving—a skill he'd learned at Caroline's behest soon after they had met, and which he had pronounced "a lot of fun, as it turns out—who knew?" and Caroline kept quiet, though she thought, *Everyone I grew up with? Every teenage boy ever?*—and perhaps it *had* pleased him, but not enough. She'd hoped they'd make their future trips to New York City by car, too, but that hope was dashed when Jacob pulled up in front of the building where they'd lived then and—as if he knew what she was thinking—he looked at his watch and said, "Come on, are you kidding me? Twelve hours going and ten and a half coming? That's a whole day of my life I'll never get back. Next time we fly."

The bird, however, had seemed to enjoy the drive. She'd sat calmly on the highest perch in her cage in the backseat of Caroline's mother's wheezing, rattling, rust-specked red Dodge Spirit, whistling quietly to herself and, until the sun went down nine hours into the trip, looking out the window with what certainly appeared to be great interest.

It was after the long drive, the settling into her new home, the trip to the bird vet for a checkup and a wing-clipping that was more than three years overdue, that Caroline had remarked that the name sixteen-year-old Jacob had bestowed upon his bird did not suit her at all. "Honestly, Jacob, if she had a dolorous temperament, you'd think that being neglected for years would have left her a lost cause. But just look at her."

They both did. She was perched on Caroline's outstretched index finger, making ecstatic chirping sounds and lifting her wings dramatically, then dropping them—it seemed like theatrics, like a dancer imitating a bird—and looking from her to Jacob and then back again. "She loves us. She loves being here. She's deliriously happy. *Dolores* doesn't suit her."

"It used to," Jacob said. "I swear it did. I think it's you. I mean, she likes me fine—don't you, Dolores?" He brought his face close to her tiny gray-and-white head; she rubbed her beak against his nose. Jacob laughed. "Okay, maybe she loves me *now*, but it's only an extension of how much she loves you. She loves you, and you love me, so she's come to the conclusion that I must be lovable after all, despite all evidence to the contrary. With you, it was love at first sight."

It was quite true that the bird had taken to Caroline at once, bursting into what sounded like a song when Caroline, on her first evening—her first hour—in New York City, bent to her cage and spoke to her. "Dolores," she'd said, "I'm so very glad to meet you." Caroline had no idea how, or even if, she was supposed to speak to the bird. Jacob had kept silent (indeed, he looked a little frightened, as if he thought the bird might scold him for leaving her behind); Martin hadn't even come into the room with them. Thus she decided in the instant to speak to Dolores as she would to anyone. "I've heard so much about you. I'm sorry it's taken so long for us to meet." At that, the bird began to sing.

"Jesus," Jacob said. "I'm pretty sure she's never done that before."

Caroline had hated leaving the poor bird behind at the end of that first visit. She made Jacob promise that they'd come back with a car as soon as possible—she figured her mother would lend them the Dodge (anything for Jacob, as far as her mother was concerned)—and she made Martin promise to take better care of the bird in the meantime, to visit with her for a little while each day. "You could talk to her for a minute. Just go in and say hello." Or, better yet, she told him, he could move the cage into his study or the kitchen, somewhere where she could *see* him sometimes, even if he didn't want to talk to her.

He did not do any of those things. It had been naïve of her to think he would, even as he smiled and nodded, promising ("Yes, of course, why not? Birds are people, too!"). It seemed he had been humoring—patronizing—her. So Jacob had pointed out. But it didn't matter. Even though when they came back for her she was still in the same spot in the same room, she seemed to have been waiting patiently for Caroline's return, confident she *would* return. For as soon as she saw her in the doorway to Jacob's old room, she began to sway and sing, and as Caroline approached the cage, calling to her, practically singing herself ("Dolores, Dolores, Dolores, how wonderful it is to see you again"), Dolores stretched out her wings and *bowed*.

She had proposed renaming her Delirious not just because it suited her but also for its sound. "Her new name should sound like her old one, don't you think? We don't want to confuse her."

"She's a bird, she's not a dog. Or a human. You don't really think she knows her name?"

Maybe not, Caroline told him, but why take a chance, when poor Dolores had been through so much already? (In fact she was confident Dolores knew her name. But this did not seem worth debating. Anything that had to do with her fiancé's former life—his childhood, the New York apartment, the city itself, his parents, and, it seemed, even the bird—had to be tread over carefully, she had learned by then.)

"Fine. In that case, why not Doris? That wouldn't confuse her very much, would it? Or Cloris. Or—since I don't suppose she'd care—Boris, or Horace. Morris."

"Now you're just trying to be funny. I *want* to call her Delirious." She would tread carefully, yes, but that didn't mean she had to give in to him. She hardly ever gave in to him. She was sure this was why—part of why—he loved her.

And so, to the bird, she said: "Hello, there, Delirious."

Delirious made a sound that was half song, half chortle.

"You see?" Caroline said. But she said it gently. Sweetly.

Jacob said, "I do."

After they were married, many months after that first visit, Caroline woke up one morning disconcerted by the thought that now all three of them—she, Jacob, and Delirious—had names that were different from the ones they had been given to begin with.

Her own, of course, was the one that had been most changed: both first *and* last—and she had even dropped the middle name, Joni, that she had always hated and had never once used willingly (and which had irritated her each time she pulled out her student ID or her driver's license). But like Jacob—like Delirious—she had retained something of the name she had originally been assigned (this was no consolation to her mother, who had objected strenuously, and who was furious when she reported that she'd made her name change legal).

Caroline loved her new name. It had gravity, she thought, and as Professor Rosen—who wanted to be called Jill now, but Caroline had so far not been able to do that—had noted, *Caroline Lieb* was a choriamb, a metrical foot derived from Latin and Greek poetry, *and* it contained "exactly the right amount of alliteration—admirably restrained alliteration."

When she and Jacob settled on Harry's name—his full name was Harrison Bishop Forester Lieb—it did not escape Caroline's notice that the two names to which this string of names would no doubt be reduced once he started school would make a *matching* choriamb. (She did not point this out to Jill Rosen, however, as there was a chance she would think Caroline was being silly—embarrassingly sentimental. It was hard to predict, with her.)

But it struck Caroline now, as she watched Harry swipe at a wooden half-moon that hung below a calico fabric cow, that in this family of renamers, her son too might want to change his name someday. Perhaps he would hate Harrison and would come to feel about Harry the way his mother felt about Carrie—that it was a remnant of childhood, insufficiently serious, insufficiently interesting. It was possible (oh, it was almost certain, wasn't it?) that he would be unmoved by the careful thought that had gone into his name—into, indeed, his string of names: the dactylic, non-nickname Harrison (a suffixation of the name Jacob had wanted for him, and which, when Caroline suggested it, he declared "a nice touch, actually"—he *liked* the added –son—"and besides," he told her, "Harry wasn't Houdini's real name anyway. *Houdini* wasn't even his real name, his real name, his original name, was Ehrich Weisz"); the Bishop after Elizabeth Bishop—"one name for one of your heroes, one for one of mine," Caroline told Jacob, who said he was just glad she hadn't wanted Dickinson ("Harrison Dickinson would just be begging trouble"); the Forester because, while Caroline's mother didn't seem to care (dropping *it* was the one part of Caroline's name-change to which she had not raised an objection), and Caroline herself had no particular attachment to the last name she had borne all of her life, Jacob was insistent. "It's only right," he said. For someone who insisted he would have been glad to put his past behind him, if only she were not insistent that he couldn't, he was surprisingly determined that she hold on to her own.

Harry kicked at a heart-shaped, quilt-backed mirror—the string of miniature cowbells from which it hung made a quiet, lonely-sounding clang—and she thought of something else: of how, when she was a little girl (changing her first name every which way, trying to settle on the right version of it), she had nursed a fantasy of changing her last name too. It had been a daydream that was all about her father—for years her daydreams had been all about her father—about how she would meet him finally, and he would tell her he'd been searching for her all her life. He was so glad he had found her at last! And because he was so happy to have found her, she would make the grand gesture of changing her last name—her mother's name, her grandfather she had never known's name, her grandmother who had appeared only to disappear again soon after's name—to *his*, whatever it turned out to be. And he would be so deeply moved and honored by this, he would ask her to come live with him.

But she wouldn't go—that was part of her daydream, too. Her sacrifice, her nobility. She would thank him and say no. How could she leave her mother? she would say. Without *her*, she would remind him, her mother would be all alone.

How disappointed he would be! And how impressed by her goodness. She would visit him each summer, she would promise then. Perhaps they would take trips together—they would go to New York City or to Paris or to Mexico.

It was a beautiful fantasy when she was a little girl—and then one day, just like that, she was done with it.

It was the last day of seventh grade, nine weeks to the day before her thirteenth birthday—she knew that because she had been counting down to becoming a teenager since mid-May, when Natalie turned thirteen and *she* had reached the twelve and three-quarters mark. She and Natalie were walking home together after school, and Natalie was talking about the summer ahead, the Olympic-size pool they were going to be able to swim in anytime they wanted at the apartment complex Natalie's Aunt Blanche had just moved into, and the two-week-long Rec Center teen camp in July for which they were finally old enough…and about some boy Natalie was wild about (and some other boy she *might* be wild about) and wouldn't it be so amazing if both boys turned up on the first day of teen camp too? And right in the middle of Natalie's chatter it came to her suddenly that even in the unlikely event that she ever met her father, she wouldn't want to *honor* him. That there were plenty of ways she could imagine herself reacting if he ever did show up, but changing her last name to his wasn't one of them.

At home, she did something she'd never done before. She looked in the phonebook for her mother's name. And there it was: the only Jeanie Forester in the book. She stood there trembling, her finger on the page, pointing to her mother's name. She told herself that even though her mother was the only *Jeanie* Forester, there were ten J Foresters and two JS Foresters, and it was possible, wasn't it, that some of them had the same first name as her mother? But even so, even if he'd called them all, how long would it have taken him to find the right one? An hour? Two hours?

He didn't want to find her mother. He didn't want to know he had a daughter.

She was eighteen—five whole years had passed!—before she understood that it was possible her father hadn't ever even known her mother's name. That her mother might not have known his. That all the times she'd claimed not to remember anything about him, it might have been meant to shield her from a certain kind of knowledge that her mother thought she wasn't old enough to be in possession of. But did her mother think she could shield her forever? By eighteen she knew about all kinds of brief encounters—sweet, romantic ones like Jesse and Celine's in *Before Sunrise* and grim, joyless ones like the weary typist and the young man carbuncular in *The Waste Land*. But by then it made no difference because she'd stopped wondering about her father.

That was what she told herself.

But it wasn't true, she thought now. It would never be true, would it?

She looked at Harry on his blanket, so serious and contemplative as he gazed up at the cow jumping over the moon. She thought of the secret she was keeping from Jacob: that she'd written a letter to his mother, at the last address they had for her, from so long ago—that address in California from the postcard she had sent him, freshman year. It had probably not reached her—but it hadn't come back, either, so it *might* have been the right address or else the letter had been forwarded. Still, if it had reached her, she had not bothered to answer. And nine weeks had passed since Caroline had sent it.

She'd written to Gloria Lieberman because it seemed wrong for her not to know she had a grandson. It seemed wrong that she didn't know she had a daughter-in-law, that Jacob had graduated with honors, that he'd majored in philosophy, that his career as a magician was going so well. It *all* seemed wrong.

But it was wrong too, she knew, that she'd written the letter in secret. It was wrong that she still hadn't told him.

The deck of cards in his hands rustled open again, the cards snaking between them, then collapsing back into the deck with a soft hiss. Then they fanned open and rose between his hands to form a spiral staircase in the air. When he snapped the staircase shut with a sharp single clap, Harry stuttered out his baby laugh and the bird shivered and fluffed out her feathers.

Now the cards were doing something new: coiling and bouncing between Jacob's hands—a Slinky traveling downstairs. His hands moved swiftly—two steps here, two steps below that, then the next two—and then the Slinky vanished, silently. The cards were only cards again in his left hand as his right hand tapped and straightened them. He looked up at her and smiled.

"Look," she said. She held up the needle and the length of thread. "I can't do this."

"Then don't do it."

"I want to, though."

He laughed. "But do you, though?"

"I don't know. I want to do *something*."

"You do plenty of things."

"You know what I mean." But she wasn't sure he did. She wasn't sure *she* did. She was pretty sure she didn't want to be embroidering, though. She sighed. The baby chuckled. "So, who's winning, anyway?"

"Who's winning?" Jacob said, and laughed. "Who's playing?" Teasing her. When they were first dating she'd listened patiently, even willingly—even ardently—while he explained baseball to her. She'd learned all about designated hitters (now she remembered only that they were bad) and stealing bases (good) and grounders and line drives and different kinds of pitches that all looked the same to her.

"The Padres are ahead by two runs, top of the fourth," he said. "Just so you know."

"Sorry," Caroline said. "Well, have faith. We'll catch up."

He smiled at the "we'll." It wasn't hard to make Jacob smile, but even so it felt like a triumph every time. You wouldn't think it would—you'd think by now she would be used to it. Her mother, she knew, would say, *Enjoy it while you can. It won't last much longer.* But her mother didn't know everything. (Her mother, it sometimes seemed to her, didn't know anything.)

Months ago she had made the mistake of telling her mother she was happy to sit in the same room with Jacob and watch him do whatever he was doing, and her mother had said, *Sure, for now,* and, *Things change, you know that—right, babe?*

"Bear with me for a second," Jacob said. "I have a thought." He glanced at her and glanced away, back to the game. "I'm just wondering if maybe you'd want to start thinking about writing again."

"Please, you sound—"

"And maybe not just thinking about it but actually doing it."

"—*exactly* like Professor Rosen."

"That's because she and I are like this." He set his cards in his lap and held up both his index fingers, a good ten inches apart.

"Very funny."

He picked up the cards. As he started shuffling them again, his eyes on the Mets game, he said, "No, really. It's because she's right."

"She isn't *right*. I can't do anything these days that requires concentration and you know it. It's one thing for…for *her* to lecture me about it, because she has no idea what this is like"—she inclined her head toward Harry; she stabbed her thumb in the direction of the baby clothes and diapers and the box of wipes and what her mother inelegantly called "burp cloths" and the clean unfolded clothes of hers and Jacob's, twisted up with towels and sheets, all piled up on the brand new sofa—"but you? You saw how it went when I tried to teach myself a new language."

"An old language, you mean. And that was a crazy idea."

"It wasn't crazy. I just couldn't do it. It was too hard for me. I didn't have the attention span and I didn't have the time. And my brain is like *soup*."

"Your brain is not like soup."

"You don't know that. You don't know anything about my brain."

He glanced at her, but he didn't say anything—he knew when to quit.

And okay, she thought, Yiddish *had* been a crazy idea. Why had she supposed that she could teach herself a new language (a new *old* language) via audiotape while taking care of a baby? But after one of Martin's visits she'd gotten caught up with the idea of learning the language he would sometimes switch to when he was upset or agitated, though he claimed not to understand *himself* when he did this. He swore he knew no more than a few words of Yiddish. "It was my old man's language," he told Caroline. "He spoke Yiddish before he spoke English, and he'd slip back into it whenever he was mad at me—which was all the time—or when he was feeling gloomy. Also all the time. I'm not sure he even noticed he was doing it. It was like a switch flipped and he was back on Orchard Street. I never had fuck-all of a clue what he was talking about."

She couldn't even remember what he had been so upset about, why he'd lapsed into Yiddish that particular morning.

She'd managed just three days of *git mir a lefl, repeat after me, vu iz der tate? repeat after me, nat aykh a gopl un a meser, repeat after me* before she put the tapes in a drawer. That was one day more than Indian cooking and two days more than calligraphy or watercolor painting (and, it was beginning to look like, *three* days more than embroidery). The flock-of-birds mobile she'd been determined to make for Harry never got off the ground at all: she'd brought home the instructions and supplies and given up as soon as she saw how many steps it would take, how many fussy bits of work. She liked to fuss over words—she liked to fuss over Harry. Otherwise, she was fuss-free. (So why had she thought making a bird mobile from a kit was a good idea in the first place?)

All those projects—all the *hobbies*—she had tried to take up in the last couple of months! She hadn't the talent for painting or the patience for calligraphy, and Indian cooking had been the worst fit of all. She hated everything about cooking: assembling ingredients and reading recipes and measuring and stirring and one step after another and *waiting*, and she didn't know why she had supposed that koyamboo would be more fun than lasagna or roast chicken. Because she liked *eating* Indian food? That was what restaurants were for, Jacob said. *He* made excellent lasagna and roast chicken—and soups, stews, omelettes. He liked to cook. And when he was on the road, she was content to eat sardines and crackers or Campbell's tomato soup with cheddar cheese melted into it, or else pick up take-out. And she'd teach Harry, when he wasn't a baby anymore, to be perfectly happy eating that way too when his daddy wasn't around to cook for them because he was off in some other city astounding people by making slotted coins slip out of the center of a piece of a string and then appear in what had just been his empty hand, or brandishing at chest-height a torn and miraculously restored card.

"I told my father you'd quit writing," Jacob said.

"*Jacob.* Why in God's name would you do that?"

"Because I got tired of his asking me how your writing was going. I got tired of lying to him, saying, 'Oh, fine, fine.' I suppose I could have said, 'Not very well, I'm afraid.'"

"You could have said, 'None of your business.'"

"But you've spent so much time over the last two years telling me *not* to say that to him, when I always want to."

"You could have said it nicely, just this once." She hesitated. "So, what did he say?"

"He said, 'Oh, that's terrible. What a pity.'"

"He did not."

"He did. He seemed very disappointed. He seemed upset. He might have lapsed into a little Yiddish."

"He did not." She was angrier than she thought it made sense to be. "He's never read a word I've written. Why should he care?"

"I don't know. Because Jill Rosen thinks you're talented, and he cares what she thinks? Because he likes the idea of you becoming a great poet? Or at least a famous one?" He shrugged. "Honestly, Car, are you asking me to explain Martin Lieberman to you?"

"No," she said. "I'm sorry. I'm not."

"Because while he imagines that he knows me better than I know myself, I have never deluded myself into thinking *I* understood him. Why does he make such a big deal over you being a poet? Fuck if I know."

"Oh," Caroline said. "I know why you told him."

"I just told you why I told him."

"But that's not the reason. You told him because you're sick of his making such a big deal over it. He's so dismissive of what *you* do. It isn't fair. And I'm *not* a poet. I'm just trying to be one. And I'm not even trying anymore."

"Oh, come on, that's not true."

"No, it is. And that's not even the point. I don't blame you for being sick of it. *I'm* sick of it. I'm glad you told him. I hate the way he's always asking me how my 'work' is going, I hate how when he's about to hang up the phone he says, 'Well, I'll let you get back to work'—as if he doesn't know or doesn't want to know or doesn't *care* that what he's letting me get back to is taking care of Harry. It makes me feel awful. It makes me feel like a fraud, and it makes me feel like taking care of Harry isn't good enough."

"So you're glad I told him that his daughter-in-law the poet is not in fact writing any poetry."

"I am."

"You don't look like you're glad. You look like you're about to cry."

"I am not about to cry."

"I know why, too. You don't *want* him to stop thinking of you as the poet his son married and start thinking of you as just, you know, his grandson's mother. His son's wife." His voice softened. "I get it, Car," he said. "Nobody wants the great Martin Lieberman to think less of them."

"He's not so great," she said. Jacob was right—she *was* near tears. She'd cried more in the last year than she had in the whole ten or twelve or maybe even fifteen years before that. Jacob raised his eyebrows. "Okay, he's a little great. As a writer, I mean. As a father, maybe not so much. He's trying, though. I think he's trying."

"He's trying to be a good grandfather, Car. That's not the same thing."

She wondered when he had started calling her *Car*. He pronounced it *Care*. She wondered if she liked it, if she should let him keep on doing it. If she should tell him to stop.

"I should never have quit teaching" was what she said instead.

It was hard to tell which one of them was more surprised. "You're kidding," Jacob said, at the same time she said, "I don't know why I said that."

She wasn't sorry she'd quit teaching. If she'd known Harry was coming she never would have started in the first place.

No. That wasn't true. She hadn't known when she was pregnant that she wouldn't want to be away from Harry. Even after he was born, she hadn't known. Right up until it was time to go back to work, she had thought she *would* go back to work. And then she found she couldn't bear to.

Jacob and her mother had been united in the belief that she was making a mistake, quitting her job, even though they both had been upset with her for taking it. Her mother had insisted that it was a "crappy job"—as if she were one to talk! She'd laughed when Caroline told her how hard it was to get a teaching job in language arts (and without state certification—it was practically impossible). Her mother had said, "No, sweet pea, not when you're willing to work for eighteen thousand bucks a year and no benefits it isn't." And when she'd told Jacob that she'd been offered the job right in the middle of her interview, that she'd already accepted it, he had been worried. "It doesn't sound like it'll leave you much time for yourself," he'd said—and she had snapped at him, which wasn't like her. "By 'time for myself' do you mean 'time for you'? Because you're the one who's always leaving. I'm right here, all the time," and Jacob had said, very quietly, "No, I meant time to *write*. Wasn't that the plan?" Which in fact her mother had asked too. Did neither of them understand that writing poetry was not a job?

Yet when she told them she was quitting, her mother hit the roof—"You're going to *quit*? Just because you've had a baby? What if everybody quit their jobs when they had babies?"—and Jacob looked worried all over again and she knew that he thought she'd made a bad decision (another bad decision). All he said, though, was, "I thought you liked teaching."

She *had* liked it. She hadn't planned on quitting any more than she had planned on teaching to begin with. She'd applied for the job at Miltonville Academy just as she had applied for a job at the *Herald-Tidings-Messenger* and every job on campus that had anything to do with writing, and then she didn't land a single interview for anything *except* the teaching job.

When she turned up five months pregnant at the start of the school year, the school's Director, Hallie Linsel, said, "Oh, my. You're not going to up and leave us, are you?" and Caroline assured her that she wasn't—and assured her again in mid-September and again in late October and then one more time at the start of winter break, the baby due any day.

Hallie was frosty with her when she gave her notice, but that didn't bother Caroline, or at least it didn't bother her as much as Jacob's bafflement or her mother's telling her how sorry she would be to be financially dependent on her husband and how bored she'd be at home.

She'd expected a more sympathetic response from Jill Rosen, who'd made it plain she wasn't happy about Caroline's having taken a full time job teaching middle school English "at that little private school that looks like a Howard Johnson Motor Lodge—that's the one, isn't it?" (Caroline had nodded miserably; she'd counted on Professor Rosen being proud of her, especially since Hallie Linsel had told her that she'd had an edge in the fierce competition for the job *because* she was a poet, because the parents had been clamoring for more creative writing in the classroom, and Hallie wanted her to start a literary magazine and a poetry club, too.) But Jill Rosen wasn't pleased about her quitting either. "So you've decided, then, to be a full-time mother?" she said coolly when Caroline stopped in with the baby during her office hours on campus to tell her the news. "It's not that," Caroline said. "It's not that I've *decided* anything. I just don't want to be away from him." "Oh, yes," Jill Rosen said. "I can see the difference."

She wasn't bored. It was hard to put her finger on exactly what she was. It wasn't boredom, but it *was* a kind of restlessness. A feeling that she was waiting for something, but she didn't know what.

She glanced at Jacob, who was snatching cards out of the air and studiously, she thought, not looking her way.

It wasn't even waiting—it just *felt* like waiting.

The trouble, she thought, was that she had never in her life before spent so much time sitting around at home. Not unless she was grading tests and papers, as she'd done almost right up to Harry's birth—or writing or reading, as she had before she'd started teaching (in what she now thought of as "the old days"). But that wasn't the same, because all of that had required concentration. Being a mother, so far, required only *attention*. She tried to think of whether she'd ever done anything before that entailed paying attention without having to concentrate on what she was doing. Not housework—at least not the way she did it (which was one reason Jacob did much more of it than she did).

Driving, she thought.

Sex.

Being on recess or lunch duty at Miltonville Academy. Sitting at the desk in the school library on Monday and Thursday afternoons. Sitting at her *own* desk in her classroom while the kids took a test on *Of Mice and Men* or *To Kill A Mockingbird*. Or wrote poems that began "I used to _____, but now I _____."

She watched Harry reach for a ring of plastic keys that hung from a plastic chain. *The yellow one's the key to the sun*, she liked to tell him, singsong. *The blue one is the key to the sky.*

There were lots of things, in fact, about being a middle school language arts teacher and part-time school librarian (she had never gotten around to starting the literary magazine or the poetry club she'd promised Hallie) that demanded that she stay alert and watchful but did not demand intellectual engagement. Really, if she looked at it that way, her teaching job had been good preparation for the life she was living now.

She thought of saying this to Jacob. But she didn't.

What she wanted to say to him was that some of the trouble—a lot of the trouble, maybe even all of the trouble—was that he was gone so much. But she was definitely not going to say that.

She needed a *friend*, she thought.

She considered this. Could it be as simple as that?

It could be, she thought.

Because she had no one, really—no one but Jake and Harry and Delirious. And her mother (her mother!). And Jake kept leaving and her mother was impossible and Harry and Delirious adored her but they were not exactly company in the way Natalie had once been. *Natalie* wasn't company in the way she had once been. She loved Natalie—still loved her, would always love her—but she could no longer really talk to her. Just finding a subject of conversation that was interesting to both of them took all the time they *had* to talk. Nat had switched her major to psychology late junior year, and had stayed at State for grad school and finally moved into her own apartment—but she still wanted to talk about boys. Or else she tossed out tidbits from what she was reading for her courses, most of which sounded as if she'd made them up—about what Harry would and would not remember from his babyhood, about attachment and developmental stages. Probably she mixed up what she'd learned and what she made up on the fly—that was Natalie.

She and Jacob had had other friends at college, but they'd scattered upon graduation. All the people she'd known from her writing workshops had gone off to New York to write and starve in garrets or to work in publishing (and *half*-starve in garrets, Professor Rosen noted), or else they'd gone right to graduate school to get their MFAs or PhDs, or to law school after all. And now she was married and she had a baby, and nobody had a baby. Her old friends, when she talked to them, seemed to assiduously avoid asking her about her life, and they didn't understand when she was in the middle of a phone conversation that she was doing her best to follow (boyfriends who hadn't called, galleys and page proofs piled up to *here*, PhD lit types who had it in for the MFAs, case law) and she had to hang up, fast, because Harry had begun to wail. *Can't he do without you for a single hour?* her friend Maureen had said the last time they had talked. Maureen was in Boston, studying with Robert Pinsky. She had no idea what Caroline's life was like.

There were her friends from *before* college, the girls she and Nat had both been friendly with. But the two she'd thought of as her second-closest friends in high school, Angela and Molly, had left town for college and never looked back, and while the two other girls she had been sort-of friends with, Erin and Amanda, had stayed here for school—like her, like Natalie—one had gone pre-med and one pre-vet, and she'd lost track of both of them by sophomore year, before she'd even met Jacob. And all the other girls she'd known from the neighborhood but hadn't ever really been friends with at all had vanished into their own lives, the lives her mother would sometimes mention after she'd run into their mothers: they were working at the corporate headquarters of a fast food chain or a clothing conglomerate (those were the ones her mother told her about; Caroline knew for a fact that not all of them had "good jobs," as her mother called them—that Amelia Davidson was working as a stripper at a club on the West Side, that Jen Cornell was tending bar across the street from campus and Jen Hirsch was working at a Starbucks in one of the new malls that had sprung up a year or two ago).

Jacob had a new friend, Ben—a juggler (it turned out that this was a legitimate profession too, just as magic was, and that there was such a thing as esoteric juggling, the *art* of juggling). Jacob had gone with Ben several times now to juggling club meetings and come home full of new ideas, and a month ago he had invited Ben and his girlfriend, Anya, to dinner. The dinner hadn't gone very well—Anya had seemed bored and Caroline was distracted by Harry, who as luck would have it was fretful and impossible to soothe that night—and there was no talk of trying again.

Embroidery. Yiddish. Watercolors. What was the point of any of that?

Really, she thought, it wasn't that she minded the work of taking care of Harry. She'd been surprised from the beginning by how little she minded even the most mundane parts of caring for him—changing his diapers, patting his back to make him burp. There was something wonderful about being so necessary to someone—something wonderful about how significant every small thing was.

It was not so unlike writing poetry, when every syllable and sound, each word, each line break mattered so much—except that the consequences of getting each thing right or wrong mattered *more* now, and it mattered right away. If Harry needed to be changed, he needed it at once. When he had to be nursed, there was nothing in the world that was more important to him. And therefore to her.

If you thought of it that way, then her life was immensely satisfying. All day long she was doing things that mattered.

She looked over at Jacob and she must have sighed because he looked at her too. His hands were still moving as he watched her. "It'll get easier, I think," he said gently.

"Which part?" she said. And then, "Anyway, it isn't all that hard."

"All the parts," he said. "And if it isn't hard, what is it?"

"I don't know."

"Oh, Caroline. Oh, Car."

She thought then that if she ever wrote a poem again, it would be about this. About the way he had just said, "Oh, Caroline. Oh, Car," and also about it—everything—not being hard, but how she didn't know *what* it was, then.

And about the secret she was keeping from him, the letter that would never, after all—she knew this in her heart of hearts—be answered. And about the cards in Jacob's hands. His hands like wings.

The bird's wings beating softly at her neck. The baby's laugh.

The blue satin blanket on the floor.

The four corners of this room.

The silent baseball game, the piano music just under the surface of everything else.

"Watching for it?" Jacob asked her.

"Sure," she told him. She hadn't been, but she was now.

Flap, flutter, ruffle, snap. The bird's shake and squawk, Harry's *kuh kuh kuh*. And here it came—she leaned forward slightly to make sure she caught it. The delicate injog of the force card.

"Yes," she said. "Got it."

"Good. Good eye."

"Ha," Caroline said. Jacob had *trained* her eye. She would never have been able to see it if he hadn't slowed the move down for her, talked her through it, showed it to her a thousand times. Most people would never have been able to see it. Most people would never be aware of *most* of what Jacob did onstage. They'd never see anything he did that actually mattered, that wasn't decoration, distraction, *show*.

Jacob liked to say, "It's *all* a show. What people see and what they don't, what they know and what they don't. What they think they know. What they think nobody knows. That's all part of it."

But there was something real at the core of that show, Caroline thought. Something *he* did. Something he did that no one but she could see, could know.

That was what her poem would be about—the poem she'd write if she ever wrote another poem. Because everything—the sweet way he talked to her, the nothing that was something but not something *hard*, the secret letter she had written, the deck of cards in his hands, their son, their bird, this room—came down, somehow, to this: to how even when Jacob was far away, and she was here alone with Harry, only *she* knew what was really happening.

She looked at the needle and thread in her hands. What was she doing? "Stupid," she said. "So, so stupid." She must have said it loudly, because the sound of her voice startled Delirious—who flapped off her shoulder with a squawk and down to the floor. Harry screwed up his face to cry, but then he didn't—Caroline saw him notice the bird beside him, doing her jittery walk-jump step on the blanket's satin edge. The baby's face changed. He spit out his sound that was just like a laugh— that *kuh kuh kuh kuh*—and Caroline said, "I'm sorry to break this up, you guys," as she dropped the needle and thread on the table and reached down to scoop up the bird. She put Delirious back on her shoulder. She closed the library book. *Enough.*

Harry looked up at her, aggrieved. If it were left to him, the bird would be at close hand at all times. She thought about how the first few days after he was born, she had been afraid to take Delirious out of her cage—afraid to let the bird sit on her shoulder or atop her head the way she had since they'd first brought her home from New York, from her exile in Jacob's old bedroom. She'd kept her in her cage for almost a whole week, because what if Delirious were jealous or anxious or angry enough about the baby to fly *at* him? Jacob said, "She won't hurt the baby. She loves you. She wouldn't do anything that would upset you, and she can see how attached you are to Harry." But he didn't tell her she was being silly, the bird could not be jealous, a bird could not *be* jealous. They both knew that wasn't true. And in the end she had decided that keeping the bird locked up was likely only to make matters worse. Delirious would figure out, if she had not already, that it was the baby's entrance into their lives that had led to her imprisonment.

And when Harry was six days old and Caroline let the bird out of her cage for the first time, she saw that she'd worried for nothing: Delirious would not attack the baby—Delirious was *afraid* of the baby. You could see it in the way she kept her gaze averted—her whole head tilted—away from him, and in the way her crest remained at least half raised until Caroline returned her to her cage. You could see it in the way she trembled, in the cage or out of it, whenever Harry cried.

If Delirious was angry in those early days, it was not with Harry but with Caroline, who no longer sat still with a book for hours, absently petting her with one hand as she turned pages with the other. Instead, in those first days and weeks, she had the baby in her arms and she was constantly resettling both him and herself into a more comfortable position. Or else, when the baby was on the floor on his blanket or in the cradle in their bedroom or in his bouncy seat or wind-up swing, or any other place where he had been content for a time but had suddenly begun to cry, she was forever jumping up to do something for him. Delirious would turn her tiny head away from Caroline even as she tightened her grip on her shoulder so that she would remain there no matter how much or how quickly Caroline moved around.

It was astonishing how much emotion—complex, big emotion, a whole range of emotions—seemed to reside in such a small handful of soft bones and feathers and pinpricked naked skin, which was exposed whenever Caroline gave her a neck rub with her thumb and index finger.

Lately all of that emotion had swirled into something else. As Harry had grown more and more aware of his surroundings, the bird had grown less and less afraid: now the bird seemed to love the baby as much as the baby loved the bird. At this very moment, even as he batted at his ring of keys, Harry's eyes were fixed on her. It would not be long before he would be able to reach for her if she were nearby. It was possible, Caroline thought, that of the two small creatures under her care, she had been worrying about the wrong one getting hurt.

As if he had been listening to what was on her mind, Harry smacked the ring of keys so hard it flew up and over the arch of the floor gym.

"Whoa," Jacob said. "Good arm."

So he'd been watching too. So often when she thought his mind was elsewhere, he turned out to be paying attention (but then just as often when she thought he *was* paying attention, she would realize that he wasn't—he was tricky that way).

"He's getting dangerously active, don't you think?" she said.

"You asked me the same question this morning." Jacob said it lightly. But he'd been gone for ten days this last time, his longest trip since Harry's birth, and she'd hated it, he knew—and *he* hated it when she so much as hinted at how much she hated it. So it was possible he was chastising her, if gently.

"All I meant was that we might have to start watching him more closely."

"*Caroline*," he said. Less gently. "I can't be here every single minute of every single day, you know that. I don't like to be away from you and Harry any more than you like me to *be* away. But this is my job."

"I know. That's not what I was talking about." She felt her face get hot. "It's *not*."

"Okay," Jacob said.

"I meant we need to keep an eye on him. He might use that 'good arm' of his for evil."

"You think our baby's evil?"

"I think he might accidentally do something evil."

"Then it wouldn't be evil," Jacob said, "would it?" He stood up and stretched. He put his cards down on top of the bookcase and crossed the room to her, bent and kissed her. Delirious chirped a protest. "Don't worry, okay?" he said. "Harry isn't going to hurt the bird. Nobody's going to hurt anybody."

From the kitchen, then, the shrill jangling of the telephone. Harry began to cry.

"I'll get it," Jacob said. "It's probably my dad. It's about time for his daily meddling." He disappeared into the kitchen as she rose from her chair, bending to pick up the baby, Delirious tightening her grip, beating her wings. "You can stay there if you promise not to move," Caroline told her as she sat back down with Harry in her arms. "Shh," she told the baby. "Mama's here." She undid the bottom buttons of her flannel shirt, lifted the too-big tee shirt underneath it. She could hear Jacob over the music on the stereo—Alicia de Larrocha and "Nights in the Gardens of Spain" now. "You're kidding me," she heard him say. "You *are* kidding, Dad, right? Tell me you're kidding."

"Is he all right?" she called to Jacob.

To his father, he was saying, "No, I'm sorry," and, "Of course. You're right. I will—I didn't mean to shout at you." Then his voice grew softer and all Caroline could hear was "Nights in the Gardens of Spain." She closed her eyes as she nursed Harry. On her shoulder, Delirious was motionless and silent.

"Okay, you won't believe it."

She opened her eyes. Jacob looked stricken.

"What's wrong? What happened?" Jacob shook his head. "*Jake*. Did something happen?"

"Oh, something happened all right." Jacob sat down on the floor at Caroline's feet. He rested his head against her legs. "He's fine. He's happy. He's *excited*. He's been offered a teaching job."

"A teaching job? Martin?" She started to laugh but Jacob lifted his head and looked up at her. "What?" she said.

"A teaching job *here*."

"What do you mean 'here'?"

"*Here*. In the English department. With your Professor Rosen."

"What are you talking about?"

"I'm *telling* you," he said. "That last visit of his? That was what he was here for. That Friday afternoon when he disappeared? He was giving a 'job talk,' he says, on campus. And meeting with a bunch of Deans and whatnot. It seems this has been in the works since February. He wanted to be sure it was a 'done deal' before he told us."

"A done deal," she echoed. How many times had she talked to Jill Rosen in the last couple of months? How could she have kept this secret?

"He signed the contract today. He hasn't just been offered the job. He's taking it. He's already taken it. He starts teaching in the fall. He's *moving* here. In August, maybe even sooner." Jacob groaned and laid his head down on her lap, nudging Harry over a few inches. "Sorry, kid, but this is an emergency."

"Martin's moving here?"

"Oh, yes," Jacob said. He didn't lift his head. It felt heavy in her lap. He wrapped his arms around her legs. "I can't believe it."

"And Professor Rosen knew about this."

"Sounds like she was the engineer of it."

"I can't believe she didn't say anything to me."

Jacob raised his head and turned to face her. "That's what you can't believe?"

"It's one of the things, yes."

"Well, it seems they wanted to surprise us."

"They did a good job, then."

"They did, didn't they?"

The sat looking at each other. Jacob's chin propped on her left knee, his arms encircling both her legs. The baby in her arms nursing so slowly, so desultorily, she could tell he was halfway toward sleep. The bird so still she must have been asleep already.

"It's a whole new ballgame, isn't it?" said Jacob. For a minute, stupidly, she thought he was talking about what was on the TV, and she glanced over at it. It seemed to be the same old game, but she couldn't tell for sure. Not when she wasn't even sure which team was which.

But of course he wasn't talking about baseball. For some reason, then, just as the idiom clicked into place (oh, how out of practice she was when it came to thinking about words, or ideas—how out of practice she was when it came to *thinking*), what came into her mind was her own father and not Jacob's. Her own father, who seemed always to be just below the surface—invisible and unimaginable. It occurred to her now for the first time that when she'd stopped hoping he would find her, she'd conflated his search for her mother with his search for her. How in the decade since she'd let go of that fantasy she'd never stopped to think that if her mother had been telling her the truth—that he hadn't known that Caroline was "on the way" when he left town— then if he ever *had* sought out and found the only Jeanie Forester in the Kokosing phonebook (if he'd ever even known her name to look it up—if he'd known it and remembered it, and remembered where they'd met, where they had made her), he most likely would have turned and run as soon as he learned that he had a daughter. He didn't know that she existed.

And if he did know—if her mother had been lying to her; if he *had* known she was pregnant—why would he have come back after he had run off in the first place?

So it didn't matter if her mother had been lying to her all these years, or if she had been telling her the truth. No good would have come from knowing one way or the other.

Was there a baseball idiom for *either way, it's too sad to consider?* For *the only certainty is that it doesn't matter what the truth is?*

She freed one hand from under Harry—he was asleep for sure now, still half nursing in his sleep—and stroked her husband's hair. She couldn't see his face—he had turned it away from her again.

Eventually, she thought, she would have to tell him about having written to his mother. He would be unhappy. Maybe angry. But she wanted to tell him. She wanted to get it over with, but more than that, she wanted him to *know*. She wanted him to know not only that she'd written, but that she was sorry that she had, and sorry too for keeping it a secret. She was sorry that his mother hadn't answered, sorry that she'd left, sorry that she hadn't been the sort of mother he deserved. The sort of mother everyone deserved. The sort of mother *she* wanted to be. Was going to be.

And the sort of wife, too. And even—yes, why not?—the sort of daughter-in-law. Even Martin deserved better, didn't he? Of course he did. Like everyone.

ONE OF EACH

The chaos and squalor of her childhood home, hardly a home at all if home meant something more than a hard place to lay one's head beside the head of another, whose head lay beside yet another—four children in each bed, the two beds in one room just wide enough to hold them—gave way before she was sixteen to the home of a husband. Older, a butcher. A tyrant. Only two in the bed now—and then, after a time, came two sons, twins, each of whom lay his lovely head on a bed of his lovely own. A luxury they would never, got tsu danken, know as one.

—*Martin Lieberman, The Greater Delilah*

"I**t's** remarkable, really, isn't it?" Martin said as he sat down across from Jeanie. He had an ice cream cone in one hand and had just set down the shopping bag that had been in the other—a bag full of fancy cheese and overpriced vegetables and bread and jars of expensive jam and mustard and who knew what-all else he'd bought when she wasn't looking. Carrot greens stuck out of the top of the shopping bag and drooped over its side like the world's ugliest bunch of flowers. He had wanted to buy flowers, too, for Caroline—a big bouquet of hot pink roses and white lilies and red gerbera daisies—but Jeanie had discouraged him. "If you want to pick up something for the kids, don't make it something that'll *die*," she'd said. "That's just throwing money out the window." Which she was beginning to understand was what he did, automatically—they'd walked into the North Market and it was like he'd taken out his wallet and just started shaking twenties out of it, leaving bills strewn everywhere they passed. It was some kind of disorder, Jeanie thought when he shelled out forty bucks on a couple of small blocks of cheese for himself.

He hadn't bought the flowers. He settled on "a good bottle of wine" instead (Caroline would pass out if she knew how much it had cost) plus two fat loaves of too-expensive bread. "One is plenty," Jeanie told him, standing next to him, the baby in her arms, at the baker's stand downstairs. "The other one will go stale long before they can eat it."

He ignored her. She had discovered, in the space of the less than two hours they had spent together today, that he responded only when he wanted to. The rest of the time, he felt free to pretend he hadn't heard or wasn't listening to her at all, which was even worse.

She, meanwhile, was determined to be polite no matter how he treated her. Thus, as he sat lapping at his ice cream, she said, "Oh, yes, it *is* good. Thanks for treating us" as she dipped her spoon and raised it, only half full, daintily—because someone had to model good behavior for him. She had already seen, in the brief interactions she'd observed between him and his son—last Sunday night at dinner at the kids' apartment, then again when they collected Harry for this outing— that it wasn't going to be Jacob. With his father around, her son-in-law, normally so sweet—a gentleman, a charmer!—turned into a sulky adolescent, and when he addressed his father (which mostly, Jeanie noticed, he did not) he was flat-out rude: when Martin looked around the table Sunday night and asked if someone would please pass the salt, Jacob stuck his thumb out like a hitchhiker and grunted, "In the kitchen." Jeanie was shocked.

"No, not the ice cream," Martin said. "Though the ice cream is very good. Caroline was right about that. Maybe not the best in the *world*, as your lovely daughter promised, but it's damn good ice cream." He grinned; he licked—one lick from the top scoop, then one from the bottom. "No, what I meant was that it's remarkable that you and I are here together after our two clever children did their level best to keep us apart for such a long time. Do you suppose they were afraid of our colluding, Jean?"

Jeanie, she wanted to tell him, but didn't. She would pick her battles with this one (if she corrected him, she thought, he wouldn't call her

Jean again—but he wouldn't call her Jeanie either; he'd call her Jan, Jen, Janie, Joan—anything other than her own name, either because he wasn't really listening or didn't care enough to bother remembering, and it would ruin the afternoon she had been looking forward to all week). And she didn't know what *colluding* meant but she was not about to ask him. So she said only, "I don't think they were purposely keeping us apart," even though, if truth be told, it had crossed her mind too that it was strange they hadn't met before last Sunday—but she hadn't blamed Jacob and Carrie for this, she'd blamed Martin. She had complained to friends at work: "You'd think he'd have the decency to include the baby's other grandparent when he comes to visit and takes 'the whole family' to dinner, wouldn't you?" But then when her friend Cheri *tsk tsk*ed and said, "So what's his problem, anyway? Is he super-cheap or just a jerk?" and Aileen said, "Maybe he wants to pretend like he's the only grandparent that Harry's got. Maybe he's starved for love and doesn't want to share"—which was Aileen's diagnosis of every guy—she realized that she didn't want to have to talk about how Jacob's father was a famous writer, how he most likely didn't feel he had to socialize with someone like her.

"Nonsense," Martin said. "Whenever I asked them about you, they'd engineer a change of subject—they'd get positively *shifty*, as if the very mention of the other parent in this family equation were a dangerous proposition. I had begun to think you were in prison for murder. Or bank fraud. Or that you worked as an exotic dancer. I pictured you in prison stripes, with feathers and high heels."

Did he talk this way all the time?

"Well, my kid has been more than willing to talk about you. No prison stripes or pasties necessary."

Martin laughed; he licked his ice cream cone. "And?"

"Oh, it was all, 'Martin took us out to that new restaurant on Main and Fourth and he told *such* a funny story about such-and-such big deal important writer that I never heard of,' or, 'Martin brought the baby the most *wonderful* stuffed elephant ! It was so big he had to check it through as luggage.'"

"It wouldn't fit into the overhead," Martin said. "The woman in the seat beside mine said, 'They sell toys in Ohio, too, you know.' That seemed mean, unsympathetic. I said, 'No doubt they do, but I felt my grandson deserved a Steiff elephant big enough for him to sit on from F.A.O. Schwarz.' And she said, 'Oh, we have Jewish folks there, too.'" Another slurp of his two-scoop cone (a scoop of buttermint, a scoop of Mexican hot chocolate). "I'd hazard a bet my son was not so voluble."

Voluble. "Your grandpa's a funny man, isn't he, Harry?" she said, turning to the baby in the highchair she'd pulled up to the table. She was dismayed to see that in the few seconds she had taken her eyes off him, his chin had become fully bearded in chocolate ice cream. "Oh, Harry." She took the plastic spoon out of his hand and swabbed his face with a napkin. He twisted his head away and she saw that he had ice cream in his hair, too. He had ice cream in his *ear.* Probably in both ears. "Shit," she said. "I shouldn't have let him hold the spoon himself."

"Don't be silly," Martin said.

"Mama warned me," she said to the baby. "Didn't Mama warn me? She said, 'He always wants the spoon, but don't give him a spoon, he can't *manage* a spoon.' But did Grandma listen? No, she did not." She dipped a folded wad of napkins into the Dixie cup of water she'd at least been smart enough to request before leaving Martin to ponder the many ice cream flavors while she and her grandson went upstairs to settle themselves at a table with their own ice cream—plain chocolate for him, plain vanilla for herself. She didn't remember much about babies, but she remembered this: the need for many napkins and a cup of water. That, and the crying.

But Harry wasn't crying; he was chortling—chortling, and banging his hands on the table, leaning precipitously far forward in the wooden highchair, his mouth open like a baby bird's. Unlike his mother, he was a cheerful baby, even when he wanted something.

Jeanie filled the spoon she'd taken from him—"All right, sweet pea, here you go"—but as soon as it got near his open mouth, he tried to grab it from her. "No, baby," she said. "Let Grandma do it."

"Oh, let him have the spoon. It's good even for babies to have some autonomy."

No wonder Jacob was so rude to him—the man was insufferable. "Is it good for him to have ice cream in his eyebrows and all over his clothes?"

"It isn't bad for him. He'll have a bath when he gets home." To the baby he said, "We can dump you in the bathtub *in* your clothes, right, Harry?" And to Jeanie: "Were you this fussy and flustered when your daughter was a child?"

"I don't get flustered," Jeanie said, bringing the spoon to the baby's mouth again and fending off his hands with her free one. "And it's not fussy to prefer not to return my grandson to his parents dipped in chocolate."

"Our grandson."

"Yes, of course." Harry seemed to have decided that he wanted the ice cream more than he wanted the spoon. He allowed Jeanie to feed him two spoonfuls in a row. "There you go," she said. "Good boy."

"It might be nicer if you didn't talk to the child as if he were a dog."

"It might be nicer if you weren't such an asshole."

She hadn't meant to say it—it had just come out.

Martin laughed. "Everything might be, yes. I suppose I could give it a try."

"Sure, if you're capable."

"Look, Jean," he said. "We have been entrusted with the care and feeding, for a single afternoon, of the heir apparent. I don't know if our two children have concluded that we won't after all put our aging heads together to conspire against them"—*Ah*, Jeanie thought: *collude*—"or if they've simply come to the conclusion that they couldn't pull off keeping us apart indefinitely now that I've moved myself here lock, stock, and barrel. Either way, here we are. So let's try to play nicely together. Perhaps we could start by not calling each other names."

"You're right," she said. "I shouldn't have called you an asshole."

"All right then," Martin said. He smiled. "Shall I confess to something?"

"Knock yourself out." She held both of Harry's hands in one of hers as she spooned ice cream into his mouth.

"I've been jealous of you for months. Jacob, when he deigns to speak to me at all, talks incessantly about what a 'godsend' you have been, how with all the traveling he's doing, it's made him feel so much better knowing you were here to help with the baby."

Now, this was interesting. Did Jacob not know—or had he lied to his father about—how little her daughter had allowed her to "help out"? Not that Jeanie hadn't offered—she offered all the time, and Carrie would decline politely: "We're okay, Mom. Don't you worry about us." She wasn't *worried*. She wanted the baby for her own sake—but Caroline must know that.

It didn't matter if she knew it or she didn't. Jeanie could not bring herself to say it.

"I've been dying to meet you—Jacob knew that. So perhaps he only put off a meeting between us as a way to withhold something from me that he knew I wanted. He'll take any opportunity to do that. Did you know that?" Jeanie shrugged. She had not known *that*, but she was not exactly surprised to hear it. "And perhaps it was your daughter who prevailed, who insisted on inviting both of us to dinner last weekend."

"Perhaps," Jeanie echoed him. But she did not believe it for an instant.

"Though who can explain why they decreed us fit to care for this fine young gentleman today? Perhaps they thought it would be safe to send him off with me as long as you were there to supervise."

Jeanie didn't mean to say it but she did: "I was thinking the opposite was true."

He didn't ask her what she meant. He said, "Perhaps it was simply a matter of safety in numbers, then."

"One of each bad parent," Jeanie said.

Martin looked surprised and then he laughed again. "Exactly."

Jeanie was silent, spooning ice cream into Harry's mouth until the cup was empty. "You want to know something?" she asked Martin. She dropped the spoon into the cup.

"Always," he said.

She lowered her voice—as if they were *colluding*, she thought— and said, "I don't even know if Harry's allowed to have ice cream. I think maybe there's a good chance that he isn't. I think it's possible that Carrie—Caroline—once said something about 'no sweets until he's a year old.'"

"But wasn't it Caroline who said, 'Oh, you must take Harry to the North Market. It's wonderful! It's just like a European market—"

"Yes. But she's never been to Europe, has she."

"You tell me," he said.

"I'm telling you."

"And wasn't it she who said, 'and you must get the ice cream when you're there! It's the best ice cream in the world.'"

"It was she, yes. It's a big world, though, isn't it?"

"Yes, indeed it is."

"And also, I think maybe when she said that—when she said 'you must'—she meant the two of us. Not Harry."

"Now you tell me."

"I'm the one who ordered chocolate ice cream for him."

"Yes. You're a bad grandmother."

"No. Only a bad mother."

"Maybe. You're a better judge of that than I. But not because you didn't remember something your daughter once mentioned in passing. And if it's any consolation to you, you don't hold a candle to your daughter's husband's mother in the bad mother department."

They were both silent then for a little while. Jeanie fed Harry what remained of her scoop of vanilla. Then Jeanie said, "Speaking of badness. Do you think it would be completely horrible if I went and had a smoke somewhere? I think I might die if I don't."

"Dying would be bad for the baby. Much better to smoke. Go. I'll wait here and I promise not to break him."

"You won't tell Caroline?"

"Of course not."

"I'd smell of smoke, though. There'd be no keeping it from her."

"She would scold you."

"She would, yeah."

Jeanie thought about it. She didn't even have a pack with her. She was trying to quit—she really was. She'd have to either buy a pack or bum a cigarette from somebody.

"Never mind," she said. "I shouldn't. I'm trying to quit. I've been trying since the baby was born."

"Well, good for you. I quit years ago myself. I remember very well how hard it was."

"What made you?"

"Jacob." Martin smiled. "Our children make all the rules, don't they?"

"They do."

"We can only take our grandson out if we do it together."

"Yes. And even then, they tell us where to go. And what to do when we get there."

"'Get the ice cream,' they say."

"'But don't feed it to the baby!'"

"Even though it's the best ice cream in the world."

"The best ice cream in the solar system," Jeanie said.

"In the universe."

"In the galaxy." Jeanie paused. "Wait. Is the galaxy bigger than the universe?"

"No, the universe is made up of all the galaxies."

"You're sure?" He nodded. "How many galaxies are there?"

"Billions."

"That's a lot of galaxies," Jeanie said. She sighed. "You realize we were probably supposed to have gotten Harry a fruit smoothie. Or just a *piece* of fruit."

"Or a head of lettuce."

They grinned at each other. And what was left of Martin's ice cream cone was still in his hand—melting buttermint and Mexican hot chocolate ice cream swirled together now—and his hand was resting on the table near enough for Harry, who must have been waiting for his chance, to reach for it, because he plucked the cone out of his grandfather's hand and lifted it, turning it upside down as he swiftly brought it down on top of his head.

Harry looked astonished. Then he started laughing—not just laughing but shrieking with laughter, laughing as if this were the funniest thing in the world. In the galaxy, thought Jeanie. In billions of galaxies.

The baby had been almost nine months old when Martin moved to town, too young to really know him despite his many visits, though he seemed glad enough to see him each time he turned up. "But he's like that guy you see at every party who smiles and says, 'Good to meet you' even though you've introduced yourself to him a hundred times," Martin told his daughter-in-law. He made sure to sound amused and not aggrieved. And—more important still—he made himself be patient. A skill he'd never bothered to employ before outside of his writing.

Now the baby was nineteen months old—no longer a baby. His patience had paid off (which caused him to wonder, fleetingly, if his whole life would have gone differently if he had been as patient in *it* as in his work all along). Now when he walked into Jake and Caroline's apartment, the boy jumped up from the floor where he'd been playing and ran to his grandfather, ecstatically shouting, "Pop Pop! Pop Pop is here! Hello, Pop Pop!" The child flung himself at him, wrapped his arms around his legs. As if he were a *landsman* from the old country, or a long-lost lover.

Martin's own heart beat a little faster when he set eyes on the boy. It was extraordinary, the stirring of emotions within him each time he and his small *landsman* met again. "And how is my young man today?" Martin would ask him. "What pleasures is the gentleman newly discovering?" And somehow his formality, the third person address, the small bow that accompanied the greeting, was a joke the child appreciated, for Harry would cackle and cry, "He is *me*, Pop Pop! Me's playing dinos" as he dragged his grandfather by the hand to see for himself.

How could one not be enchanted?

"Why Pop Pop, though?" Martin asked his daughter-in-law. "Can this be any easier to say than Papa? I cannot imagine why."

"I don't think it's easier. I think he just likes the sound of it."

He and Harry were on the sofa, as were two dozen multicolored model dinosaurs the child had arranged on the cushion between himself and his grandfather; there was also a parade of dinosaurs, carefully sorted according to a system only Harry understood, on the floor. Periodically—thoughtfully—the child would clamber down from the sofa and make a rearrangement of the line of them that led to the couch, remove or add one, speak to or for one ("You need to come up to here now," or "I am to go there"). Now that he was talking, forming complete sentences, the child talked all the time. "Just like his Pop Pop," Jeanie would say. "Can't get a word in edgewise."

Caroline was in the padded glider chair he'd bought for her, the bird on her shoulder. Jacob was, as he so often was these days, out of town, performing: Washington, D.C. tonight, midtown Manhattan tomorrow, then a day off in the city—and would he see old friends while he was there? Martin wondered but hadn't asked when he drove him to the airport (one of the few things Jacob would let him do for him) but he did allow himself to say that "Auntie" Claire would be thrilled beyond words to see him if he had a minute free, and Jacob responded with a noncommittal nod—then Boston on Friday, and back home at noon on Saturday. Martin kept to himself his fear that he and Jeanie would be denied their now-customary Saturday afternoon with Harry, that Jacob would object to the boy's being carted off by his grandparents after he'd been separated from him for nearly a week. *And whose fault is that?* Martin would want to say, but wouldn't.

And he did not bring it up now either. He was teaching himself to be smarter about such things. Instead he said, "I keep calling myself Papa, so you'd think he'd parrot it right back at me. He imitates everything else he hears."

"Not everything," said Caroline. "Only what he wants to."

"He wants to," Harry said obligingly.

"And even then, often enough, haven't you noticed that he gives things his own special twist?"

Indeed Martin had. Jeanie liked to call the child "sweet pea," which Harry echoed back as "sweet please"—which came out as *sweet pwease* and left one wondering why he had not simply repeated the simpler *pea.* Martin's theory was that "sweet pea" made no sense to him, that he was trying to find meaning in the phrase, and since his mother was forever saying, "Say please when you ask for something, Harry," he knew what *please* meant. But when he had shared this observation, Caroline had laughed and told him he was overthinking it, that it was just Harry's way of making words his own (but was that not also overthinking it? thought Martin—yet another thought he knew to keep to himself). Jeanie, perfectly predictably, rolled her eyes. Jacob pretended Martin hadn't spoken.

He did his best now to keep observations of this kind to himself. But he was fascinated by his grandson's acquisition and deployment of language. The child's intelligent mistakes—the grasp of grammar that anteceded the memorization of rules and their exceptions—delighted him. "I finded it," Harry would tell him, "so I bringed it to you." Or he "bringed" an armful of his various stuffed animals to Martin for him to admire: "I have two cows and two sheeps and one blue whales."

Just today, upon Martin's arrival, the child had proclaimed, "I have two new tooths" and opened his mouth wide to show him where two molars had begun to come through. "They *hurts*," he complained.

If Jacob had passed through this stage, he had missed it entirely. In his memory, his son had swiftly moved from infant wordlessness to fully correct sentences, then back to wordlessness again as a balky teenager. At some point, of course, he'd started forming complete sentences again. Martin could not recall when—only that by then he'd had one foot out the door.

He might have lingered over this sort of non-memory—prodding it and poking at it the way Harry couldn't keep his fingers off the sore spots where new teeth were poking through his gums—but he knew better than to touch what might turn out to be tender. Best to let things lie exactly where they were.

"Pop Pop, look," his grandson said and handed him a stegosaurus to admire, then snatched it up again and set it on the sofa's arm, far from all the other dinosaurs.

This was the way the boy played. He'd spend three quarters of an hour arranging his toys, contemplate the world he had created, shake his head, then move an orange three-inch-long dump truck from its spot behind a yellow taxi into a new, mysteriously better place behind a red convertible, and the black Volkswagon Bug it had displaced would be carefully inserted elsewhere. It was uncannily like the hours *he* spent at work: lifting out a comma, putting it back in, switching a dash to a colon, swapping this word out for that. Turning sentences around according to a method that made sense only to him.

"He's his own man," Caroline said. "I guess he'll call you what he feels like calling you."

"Own man," Harry repeated solemnly. He handed his grandfather an eight-inch tall, realistic-looking tyrannosaurus Martin had brought home for him from his last trip to New York. He'd stopped in at the Museum of Natural History for the first time since Jacob's childhood just to buy it (along with a velociraptor and a hadrosaurus, to replace the lurid-colored, much too lightweight plastic ones Harry already had). "I am calling *you*," said Harry. "Put *there*." He pointed to the sofa's arm beside Martin, where the lone stegosaurus waited for some company.

"Say please to Pop Pop," Caroline said.

"*Pwease* put there."

Martin obliged. "You're a take-charge fellow, Harry," he said. "Like your dad and your papa."

"Pop Pop," Harry said.

"There you go," said Caroline. "Get used to it, Pop Pop. It seems to be a done deal."

Jeanie had opted for Grandma and the child did a pretty god job with it—*Gammaw*. Their names had been among his first words. (The very first, right after *Mama* and *Dada* had been, perhaps predictably enough, *bird*.) The three of them—Jeanie and Martin and Harry—had been out on one of their earliest Saturday excursions, an early autumn afternoon at the zoo, when Harry had surprised them with both *Gammaw* and *Pop Pop* in the same sentence (albeit a sentence that was a request for a particular toy from the gift shop, absent both the nominative pronoun and the definite article, and yet still—his grandfather marveled—making himself absolutely clear). Jeanie was so elated she'd kissed both of them.

The Saturdays with his grandson and his *machateynes*—the Yiddish word that captured their relationship in a way the cumbersome English phrases (*my daughter-in-law's mother, my son's mother-in-law*) failed to do—had emerged as one of the great pleasures of his new life. Sometimes on a Saturday afternoon in his condo, when Harry played on the floor, a plate of animal crackers and a sliced orange beside him, and he and Jeanie sat talking over tea and their own slices of oranges as they watched him rearrange and mutter to his toys, Martin wondered at his own contentment. He could never have imagined such a thing.

Another tender place to leave untouched.

Now that it was summer and he had no teaching duties, he had started lobbying his daughter-in-law for a second standing date with Harry. He had proposed that, once a week, after his morning's writing, he pick up the child after his nap, take him to the playground or the pool—or perhaps they'd spend a few hours just knocking around at Martin's place, where he had given over an entire corner of his living room to toys—and afterwards meet Jeanie for an early dinner. "We could pick her up at work and go out or just get takeout and have dinner at my place or your mom's. We'd get him home in plenty of time for his bath, well before his bedtime. And you'd get another afternoon besides Saturday all to yourself, and you and Jake could have an early dinner too, just the two of you one night a week. That would be nice for you, wouldn't it?"

But Caroline had said, "You mean, like a date? What makes you think Jacob would be interested in that? What makes you think he'd even *be* here?"

Now Martin brought it up again, since she had not. "My dear, you know I don't mean to bug you. But have you given any more thought to what I proposed last week?"

"In fact I have," she said. "What would you think of Wednesdays? We could start tomorrow."

"Tomorrow!"

"Unless you've you changed your mind?"

"Of course I haven't changed my mind. I'm just surprised. But glad. That's terrific. Thank you."

"Don't thank me," she said. "You're doing me a favor. I'm sorry I didn't see it that way right away."

"And I'm sorry if I seemed overeager. We both are, I suppose—your mother and I."

Your mother and I—a phrase he hadn't used in years.

"Jill says if I use the time to write, she'll read whatever I come up with. That's incredibly generous of her, isn't it?"

"You're writing again," Martin said. "That's good news."

"I'm not, no—not yet, anyway. But I'm going to try. I promised Jill I would."

"Really," Martin said. He and Jill had lunch together once a month, but even during their most recent lunch he had heard nothing from her about any promises his daughter-in-law might have made. Indeed, any efforts he exerted toward real conversation with her were quickly subverted. She would change the subject to an interesting essay she had read in *The London Review of Books*, a problem student in one of her classes, an inept administrator, a new course she was developing. "Are you seeing much of her—of Jill?" he asked Caroline.

She was. It would seem that they were friends now. They'd had "the most marvelous picnic lunch in the park" last Thursday when Jacob had been in Chicago, and this morning, after Martin had picked Jacob up to take him to the airport, she'd met Jill for coffee "and she gave me the new Mark Strand *and* the new Alice Fulton *Selected*. Just like that," she said, "for no reason at all."

"But who have you been leaving Harry with? You know you could have called me."

"Oh, I don't leave him. I take him with me. The three of us have a lovely time together. Jill's picking us up on Friday afternoon and taking us to the topiary garden and then out to dinner—there's a new place on Hillview, she says, that's child-friendly. Harry likes spending time with Jill—don't you, Harry?"

Harry nodded, but Martin was sure he hadn't heard the question. He'd already mastered the agreeable nod—a precocious child, to be sure.

"She always brings him some amazing picture book she's found, or a sweet toy—this morning it was a set of plastic buckets with various combinations of holes in them. He's going to have lots of fun with them in the bath tonight. Right, mister?" This time Harry didn't even bother to pretend that he was listening.

"Let's go *there* now," the child ventriloquized through a turquoise triceratops, addressing a hot pink apatosaurus, and the apatosaurus said, "But I don't want to. I want to go *there*," as Harry marched him in the opposite direction.

Martin tried to conjure up an image of Jill Rosen shopping for toys—no, it was impossible. And did she actually speak to Harry when she was around him? (About what? The latest issue of *The New York Review of Picture Books*?) He retained a blurry memory of an afternoon he'd spent with her many years ago in the company of Jacob when he was a small boy—but he could not recall if Jill had interacted with his son. Certainly she did not seem—had never seemed—to be the sort of woman who had any interest in children.

But who would have supposed that he would turn out to be the sort of man who did? He had tried to talk to Jill about this very thing at their last lunch, during finals week. He began to talk about the pleasure he took in his grandson's company, but she interrupted him: "Oh, before I forget! What did you make of Coetzee's review of the Library of America edition of Bellow's first three novels? You saw it, yes?"

He'd seen it, yes. And so that was what they'd talked about, though he would have liked to talk to his old friend—he would have liked to talk to someone—about his relationship with the child. About the joyous surprise of it. He had spoken of this only once, to Caroline, too clumsily, and she had responded with what he supposed was purposeful ingenuousness, asking innocently if he'd forgotten Jacob's early childhood ("He must have brought you great joy too"). And what was there to say to that but to agree that he'd forgotten ("It was a long time ago").

He would have liked to speak of this to Jacob himself, if only he could find a way to do so without irritating or, worse, angering him. His own response to Jacob's irritation with him was, unfortunately, to be irritated in return—which made further conversation useless. And when his son was angry, Martin felt cowed; he felt obscurely ashamed. (He had told Jeanie this, apropos of a disastrous exchange with Jacob about his career, and Jeanie had shrugged. "Cowed? Like, intimidated? So what? Be *cowed*. Be ashamed. Let him have his say. You'll get over it." But he was not accustomed to feeling cowed, to feeling shame. He wasn't sure he would get over it.)

But if he could be sure his son would listen, and would take what he said in the spirit with which it was meant, he would tell Jacob that the pleasure he took in his grandson's company—his attentiveness and his availability, his eagerness to please the child—was not the result of greater interest in him but was attributable to his having more time, more attention to give. More capacity to *take* such pleasure.

Would Jacob understand this? Or would he refuse to? On the face of it, Martin knew that he had *less* time now than he'd had twentysome odd years ago. Arithmetically, this could not be disputed (from September until June he now had his students' work as well as his own to manage—and not only their work, but the students themselves, whose need for his time and attention seemed to be inexhaustible). What he meant—what he would explain if given even half a chance—was that he now experienced time (time, attention, life) differently, that he now recognized that it was finite in a way that he had been unwilling, or unable, to perceive when he was younger. When his son was a child. He had loved his son—he had loved his wife! (he had! did they both believe he hadn't?)—but wife and son were not the center of his life. They were not his life's work. It had been understood (how sure he had been that it had been understood!) that they had to make way for the work, the main thing. They lived on the edges of the main thing—but there was room enough for them around those edges.

Wasn't there?

Was there?

A tender spot he couldn't seem to keep away from.

Yes, of course, he wondered now if he'd been wrong. He wondered now because of Harry, but not only because of Harry. Because of

Caroline. Because of Jeanie, his *machateynes*. Because of his students, his teaching. Because the center, somehow, now held everything. It held his work and his grandson and his daughter-in-law and her mother and his students, and it would hold Jacob too if Jacob would let himself be held. It would hold Jill if she would let herself be held. So much, it turned out, could be crowded at the center.

He had not imagined this, had not imagined any of it. From his place on the sofa in his grown son's home, he thought of this, the paucity of his imagination when it turned on his own life (and oh, the irony of this!). He could not have imagined Caroline, her legs folded under her as she sat in the padded glider, the bird that had once been Jacob's perched now on her index finger as she crooned to it, her face so close to the bird's that it rubbed its minute beak against her nose—or Harry, now at his mother's feet, his dinosaurs reassembled in concentric circles on the floor.

Had he had some inkling of the happiness that was in store for him? Was that why he'd asked Jill about the possibility of a position at the university? No—none, absolutely not. He'd asked Jill about a faculty position because he could think of nothing else to do. By then he had already given up the place where he had lived with Gloria and Jacob. He had moved downtown, had given away most of what he owned. He'd started his book again—all over again, from the beginning, discarding most of what he he'd written. *Rearranging the deck chairs*, he'd thought one morning when he woke before dawn in his overpriced East Village sublet. He had failed to change his life. But he still *meant* to. He called Jill because it was the only thing he could think of.

Perhaps because it *was* the only thing. The only thing, the right thing. And he'd done it after all—he had changed his life.

"So where is he this time?" Jeanie asked her daughter. It was late October, a Sunday evening. They were on their way to a Japanese restaurant they both liked but which Jacob thought was nothing special—and which Martin wouldn't even try, since Jacob had told him he shouldn't bother.

"LA tonight. San Diego tomorrow. Back on Tuesday."

"He'll be jet-lagged."

"Not my problem, is it?" Caroline was driving Jeanie's car—she'd asked to; she missed driving, she'd said—and it felt weirdly like collusion, as if they were teaming up against the boys: going to a restaurant Jacob disdained, with Caroline behind the wheel though Jacob always said the two of them had no need for a car—plus leaving Martin home alone, not even telling him that they were going. When Caroline had called to ask if she wanted to go to dinner, "just the three of us," Jeanie had asked her, "Which three?" She was genuinely confused; it was so unlike Caroline to exclude her father-in-law. (*Thick as thieves, you two*, Jeanie had remarked once, and Caroline had said, "What have we stolen?")

Harry, strapped into his car seat in the back, was having a conversation with himself. Just like his grandfather, he didn't need anyone else to say a thing. "If you have a hat," he was muttering, "then you can have a house." Or something like that. (Also like his grandfather: sometimes it was impossible to understand what the hell he was talking about.)

"Thanks for letting me drive, Mom," Caroline said.

"And if you have a *cat*, then you might have a mouse," said Harry.

Jeanie turned around in her seat. "But probably you wouldn't, right?" she said to her grandson, who smiled radiantly at her but went on talking: "But if you have *no* hat...." Jeanie turned to face front again. "No problem," she said. "Anytime. But also, you know, you can borrow the car anytime you need it. I mean, it just sits there all day long while I'm at work, no use to anybody."

"You sound just like Martin," Caroline said. "Though *first* Martin says, 'How on earth are you two managing without a car in this godforsaken town?'"

It was only once they were settled in a booth at the restaurant, Harry on a booster seat beside his mother and drinks ordered all around—tea for Caroline, a Kirin for Jeanie, ice water for Harry, which Caroline poured into his sippy cup—and Caroline was examining the sushi menu with the rapt attention she had once trained on her schoolbooks, that Jeanie asked her casually—as if she hadn't been wondering about it all day—why Martin wasn't with them.

Caroline looked up. "Did you want him to be?"

"I didn't say that," Jeanie said.

"I thought you'd be happy that for once it was just us."

"Sure," Jeanie said. "I am. I'm only asking."

"And I'm only telling you. I thought it might be nice, that's all."

But she sounded like there was a secret she was keeping from her. Jeanie said, "So, what is it? Is he out on a date?"

She'd meant it as a joke, but Carrie said, "What? *No.* God, Mom."

Her dismay made Jeanie want to tease her. "What makes you so sure? For all you know he's dating that friend of yours, the poetry teacher you're both always going on about."

"He and Jill are old friends. They've known each other forever. And I do *not* 'go on' about her. Neither does Martin."

"Maybe not to you."

"They're not dating, Mom." The waitress had returned with edamame and a bowl of rice, and Caroline spread a napkin out in front of Harry and put the bowl of rice on it. She handed him a spoon. "Use this nicely," she told him. Grudgingly, to Jeanie, as she began opening edamame pods and making a little pile of beans for him on the napkin, she said, "They *might* have dated long ago. It's possible. It's crossed my mind." She lowered her voice—although there was no one around who could possibly have cared what she had to say—and added, "You know, from the way she talks about him, sometimes."

Jeanie took a long swallow of beer. "That's interesting. Because you'd never guess it from the way he talks about her."

"Mom. You are so infuriating. You just *did* guess."

"Well," Jeanie said. "Seems like he's faking, that's why. I ask if he's seen her and he's all, 'Oh, yes, my colleague Jill Rosen and I did have a lovely lunch not long ago at the Faculty Club. I believe it was last Tuesday'"—she pronounced it *Chuse*day—"or, 'Why, yes indeed, I did meet my esteemed colleague *Professor* Jill Rosen for a drink after my late class only yesterday. She was so very helpful with the honors seminar I'm planning for next term on the fourteen most important writers that no one but I have ever heard of.'" Jeanie cracked open an edamame pod herself. "Stick up his ass about her. Makes me wonder."

"You can stop wondering," Caroline said. "I know for a fact that they're not dating."

"You know 'for a fact'?"

The waitress returned with their food and Caroline spoke sweetly to her as she set the plates down. "Thank you *so* much. This looks wonderful."

Jeanie thought, *Fine, right, I get the message.* "I don't know what's wrong with me," she told her daughter. And she meant it. "Sorry."

"We have bad habits, don't we. Both of us."

"I guess." Jeanie watched her pick up a piece of gleaming pink raw fish with her chopsticks. "I'm not trying to be combative, I'm really not. It just comes out that way somehow."

"I know. Me too."

"Okay, then. Let's both make an effort to do better," Jeanie said. She picked up a tempura green bean. "Is it okay if I give Harry one of these? Maybe a slice of sweet potato?"

"One or the other, and make sure it's not too hot."

Jeanie bit one end of the green bean to check, then handed it to her grandson. She used one chopstick to spear a shrimp, in that way she knew made Carrie crazy—she couldn't help it. She said, "So tell me about Martin and your favorite professor."

Her daughter sighed. "I don't know, maybe they dated once, when they were both, like, twenty-two or something, before he met...you know, Jacob's mother."

"You can say her name."

"I know. I don't like to. I don't like to talk about her at all. It makes Jacob too…well, I don't know what it makes him. I was going to say *sad* but that's not it. And not exactly angry. Upset, frustrated, weird." She ate another piece of sushi. Took a sip of tea.

Jeanie ate her shrimp. "Delicious as ever," she said. "Jacob's out of his mind to think this place is no good." She set down the chopstick (what was the point?) and used her fingers to pick up another piece of shrimp. "And the romance between Martin and your teacher?"

"Oh, Mom. I don't know that it was a romance. I don't know that it was anything. But I can tell you for sure that the two of them are just friends now. Friends and colleagues. Period." Then: "I wish you would at least try to use your chopsticks properly."

"I wish you weren't such a snob. Would you like me to ask for a fork?"

"Suit yourself."

"That's what I'm *trying* to do."

"Look," Harry said.

They both looked. He had dumped his bowl of rice out on the napkin and was using his hands to mash the shelled beans and rice together.

"I cooking," he said.

Caroline didn't react other than to scoop the rice and edamame back into the bowl with her own hand. "Eat, don't play," she said. "And use the spoon."

"So what's the deal, then?" Jeanie said.

"What *deal*, Mom?"

Patient with her son, no patience whatsoever with her mother. You'd think she was the most exasperating mother in America.

"I think you know what *deal* I mean, babe. Martin's a good looking man. He's very successful. He obviously has plenty of money. He talks too much, but not everyone is bothered by that. Everyone I know who has a husband or a boyfriend complains that he doesn't talk *enough*. And everyone I know who *doesn't* have a husband or a boyfriend says she never meets anybody. I hear it all the time—there's nobody out there to meet. And some of the women in my office who *are* married say, 'If only there was something better out there, I'd leave my asshole husband in a New York minute.'"

Caroline inclined her head toward Harry.

"Sorry," Jeanie said. "I meant 'leave my *not-very-nice* husband.'" But Harry wasn't even listening. He was busy grabbing handfuls of rice out of his bowl, only a small portion reaching his mouth.

"So you think all your friends should line up to meet my rich, handsome father-in-law?"

"They're not my friends," Jeanie said. She picked up the slice of fried sweet potato on her plate and put it in front of Harry. "They're just women I know from the office. And I didn't mean he should meet them. I was just trying to make a point."

"But what *is* the point, Mom? If you mean, 'Why is Martin not dating anyone?' I think you of all people would understand. He's been disappointed and he's had it. He's done with all that. Just like you always say you are. And I asked you not to give Harry two pieces of tempura."

Jeanie paused, her beer bottle midway to her mouth. "You think I'm disappointed? *That's* what you think? And two small pieces of vegetable tempura are not going to hurt that child."

"Yes. That's exactly what I think. And also, I'm the one who decides what's going to hurt him and what isn't. Plus, you ought to eat some of those vegetables yourself."

"I'm not disappointed," Jeanie said. She didn't have the energy to argue about the tempura she was sharing with her grandson. Or her own dietary needs. But she did find herself thinking, as if Caroline had asked, what she *was* then, if not disappointed. And also what people thought she was. Like, if someone said, "What's Jeanie Forester's deal, anyway?" what would the answer be? If it was, "Oh, she's just disappointed," that meant that she hadn't made herself clear, didn't it? Because *disappointed* was too simple and too small.

But what was the more complicated, bigger, true thing that she was? And what was Martin Lieberman, then, really? Because if this was too small to explain her, she'd bet anything that it was too small for him, too.

She decided not to say this to her daughter.

And Caroline must have decided not to say what she was thinking, either. So they ate in silence for a while, Harry squashing mounds of rice flat against the napkin and accepting every battered crispy vegetable that Jeanie passed his way, chewing meditatively on a stalk of broccoli, a thick slice of carrot, a lettuce leaf. Caroline surprised her by not objecting.

When the waitress came around to check on them, Jeanie ordered a second beer and Caroline surprised her once more by ordering tempura ice cream for herself and Harry "and one for you too, Mom, if you want." Jeanie said no, thanked her for asking, and everything seemed okay again—and over her second Kirin and the kids' ice cream, Caroline told her a story about the poetry professor that was more interesting than Jeanie would have guessed (although she'd never met the woman, she'd always sound like a bore, and Caroline's complete enthrallment with her all these years had been bad enough; the way Martin talked about her was just icing on a bad cake)—punctuated with periodic interjections from Harry, echoing something his mother had just said ("Five years!" "Goats and chickens!") or embroidering on it ("Sheep say baaa but goats say maaa") or offering up some piece of inscrutable Harry-specific information ("Flowers are not food but flowers smell"). He liked the green tea ice cream hidden in the ball of hot fried batter, too, and Jeanie, tasting it, made a mental note to report to Martin that Jacob was definitely and preposterously wrong about this restaurant—forgetting for the moment that she'd planned not to tell him about her evening out with Caroline and Harry, to spare his feelings; and then, when she remembered, deciding she would tell him anyway, because they were friends, and there should be no secrets between friends. (And because according to his very own daughter-in-law, whom he loved almost as much as he loved his grandson, he and she were two of a kind—people who were *disappointed*. They had to stick together, didn't they?)

Which was why, when Jeanie saw Martin on Wednesday night as usual for dinner—just the two of them and their grandson, after Martin and Harry spent the afternoon at the art museum and then picked her up at work—she told him what Caroline had told her over dinner (and she hadn't told her *not* to tell him, had she?), all about the poetry professor's romantic correspondence with her long-ago old boyfriend. "Over twenty-five years later," Jeanie told him, "and they're writing to each other almost every day! Can you believe it?" The question was rhetorical—it was meant to be a flourish—but Martin seemed to take it literally. He said, "No, I can't believe it" and "Come on, you're got to be kidding me" so many times as she told him what Caroline had told her, she had to scold him: "I can't tell it to you if you keep on interrupting."

"Sorry," he said. "Go on—do."

But seconds later he was smacking the table and declaring, "No, that's just—I'm sorry, that's impossible," and, "Wait, go back. Say that again." Harry smacked the table, too, delighted. Jeanie felt uneasy. She knew Martin would be interested—more interested than she had been when Caroline first started talking, for sure—but she had not expected him to be so agitated.

She said, "Martin, why is this making you so agitated?"

Martin was indignant. "I am not agitated in the least. I'm... fascinated. I'm engaging with what you're saying."

"Indeed," Jeanie said dryly. Did he notice that this was her imitation of him?

"I knew something was up with her," he said. "She's been so different."

"Different from what? Different since when?"

But he wasn't even listening. So much for "engaging."

"I knew that guy would turn up again someday. I did, I knew it. What's his name? I can't remember." He was frowning, concentrating. "Ivan? Vaclav?" He shook his head. "A farm," he said. "Jesus. A farm. With sheep. Janos? Bogdan?"

"No, nothing like that. Tim, maybe? Tom? No, Thomas."

"Tomas!" Martin said, smacking the table again. "I knew it!"

"Tomas!" Harry shouted. He slapped both hands on the table. "Tomas! French fries! Coke!"

"We'll get you some French fries," Jeanie told him. "Just hang on. Calm down." She narrowed her eyes at Martin, "You too, bud." And to Harry: "No Coke, for godsakes. Where the hell did you hear about Coke?"

"Hell!" said Harry. "Godsakes! Coke! French fries."

"Tomas," Martin said. "Goddamn. Who got in touch with whom, the first time, do you know? I'm betting he tracked her down."

"I don't know who got in touch with *whom*, Martin. Carrie might have told me, but I don't remember. Why don't you ask her yourself?"

"Caroline?"

"The professor."

"Jill," Martin said. "She has a name. Just like everybody else."

"Ask *Jill* then," Jeanie said. "Your good friend Jill. Your colleague."

"I bet he's married, too."

"He's married, yeah." That much Jeanie remembered. "He has—I don't know, six or seven or eight kids? Nine kids? A lot of kids."

"Right. That makes sense."

"That makes *sense*? Have you lost your marbles?"

"For him, I mean. Are they only writing, or do they talk on the phone?" But without waiting for an answer, he asked her another question, then another—and he never waited for an answer, which was fine with her. She could not have answered any of them anyway.

For someone she didn't know, and was sure she wouldn't like if she did know, the professor—*Jill*—was taking up an awful lot of her brain real estate. Not to mention all her dinner table conversation. And all she'd wanted tonight was to tell Martin something that would interest him. Just like with her daughter, it was hard to find something to talk to him about that she both knew more about than he did *and* that wouldn't bore him. Tonight she had imagined she'd struck gold, but she hadn't known that he would be *this* interested. It put her in a bad mood as she ate her spanakopita and salad, drank her glass of wine, helped Harry with his French fries and his hummus, persuaded him to give up on the Coke and drink his water. And the fact that she had let this put her in a bad mood put her in a worse mood. And then in the car, on the way home, Martin baited her. He took advantage of the opportunity to compare her to his friend, his *colleague*, suddenly asking about *her* old boyfriends, asking if there hadn't been one she'd be glad to hear from after all these years the way his dear friend the professor, the *estimable* Jill Rosen Herself, was evidently glad to hear from Tomas—a name he pronounced as if it were as idiotic, as pretentious, as *estimable*—and then he was asking, as if he'd been waiting all this time just for the chance to ask, about her daughter's father, and she said, "That's not something I talk about."

It was the answer she had given all her daughter's life when people had the gall to ask, as if it were any of their business. But he pressed her the way Carrie used to, asking her too many questions, one after another. And so finally she snapped at him. She told him he had one hell of a nerve. She never asked him anything about his wife who'd left him, did she? *Did she?* And then she began to cry, and she was horrified—and then (and this was even worse, although it was already bad) *he* began to cry, and his crying was a terrible thing to see.

You'd think he didn't know how to do it—you'd think he never had before. Even she, who hadn't cried in years, in decades, knew more about it than he did. (At last, she caught herself thinking—and it almost made her laugh even though she was still crying—something she knew more about than he did.) Her face was wet, yes, that was true (her eyes were producing a truly surprising quantity of tears) but she was managing to be a little *quiet* about it. *She* was trying to contain herself. Her small gasping sobs were nothing to his wheezing, racking ones. He cried wildly, his shoulders heaving.

They were at a standstill by then, thank God. He had just pulled up to her house. He laid his head down on his forearms on the steering wheel and Jeanie didn't know what to do.

And now, from the backseat, she heard her grandson, also crying. "It's all right," she tried to say. "We're all right, sweetheart." But she could hardly get the words out. And it didn't matter, did it? He would not have been able to hear her over his grandfather's sobs.

So all three of them sat crying in the idling car in front of Jeanie's house, and not one of them could do anything to comfort anyone.

Martin, home at last, a good glass in his hand, two ounces of good Scotch in it, the TV on across from him (but he wasn't watching it; he had turned it on only for company, the way his mother used to), was shaken—humiliated. What must Jeanie be thinking of him now? He resisted the impulse to call her—to demand that she believe him when he told her that he'd kept himself together through blows that would have laid him flat if he were less resilient, less *himself*. He was holding himself together *now*—or he had been, until driving Jeanie home tonight. She had no idea.

Well, that was his own doing. He could not fault her for it.

He had a secret. He had told no one but Caroline, and he had made her promise to tell no one. "And I mean *no* one," he'd insisted. "Not your mother, not Jill, and absolutely not your husband." And she had agreed. Until he knew more, there was no reason to tell anyone—and once he did know more, if there was anything to tell, he would tell them all himself. Why upset them if it turned out to be nothing?

To her credit, Caroline did not ask why he was unconcerned about upsetting *her*. Perhaps she understood, without his saying it, that he needed to talk to someone and knew she could be counted on not to be histrionic, as her mother would have been (consider tonight's tears when all he'd done was ask too many questions about Jill's supposed long-lost love and a few unremarkable ones about her own, if such existed), or to make painful jokes in a misguided effort to cheer him up (again, his *machateynes*). Or to purposefully *under*react, as Jill would have done—so coolly insistent had she been since his arrival that nothing he said, nothing he was, could have an effect on her—which would have made him feel a *schmendrick* (he could easily imagine the look she would give him, one that said, *Ah, so this frightens you? Are you so weak, so small?*). And then there was Jacob, whose reaction was wholly unpredictable, except that it could be relied upon to leave him feeling worse. He had considered calling Claire on Friday, and fleetingly, on Monday, he had thought of his sister— but when he thought of talking about this to anyone but Caroline he was paralyzed with dread. Better to wait, as he'd told Caroline so firmly one would think he had it all under control—so calm, so sure of himself—until he knew something.

In any case, it had been Caroline's idea for him to see a doctor for a routine checkup. "So really this is all your fault," he'd said on Friday, on the phone—he meant it as a joke, and she tried gamely to accept it in that spirit, but he heard the strain in her voice when she said, "See, then? You *should* tell Mom. She'd jump on the it's-all-Caroline's-fault bandwagon for sure."

"I didn't mean it," he said, "and you know that."

"Yeah," she said. "Except you sort of did."

When she'd first started in with him about a checkup, he had batted her away. She persisted; he pushed back. Eventually she had played her trump card: "Harry needs you alive and well for a long time. You're the only grandfather he'll ever have."

And so he saw a doctor. *All your fault.* It wasn't a joke, really, was it?

He had made the appointment with someone whose name he'd liked the sound of—a Dr. Beatrice Bloom—from the university's list of "approved primary care providers." She was not much older than Caroline and charming in a blunt, no-nonsense way, laughing efficiently at his jokes.

When she called with his lab results on Friday, cutting straight to the chase—"Your PSA level is extremely elevated"—he was not immediately alarmed. He'd said, "And how's the cholesterol? Extremely or only slightly elevated?" But she didn't answer his question. She said, "I'm making an appointment for you with a urologist. I want you to see him first thing Monday morning."

"You make this sound somewhat urgent," he said.

"Why don't we see what Dr. Starker has to say on Monday?"

Even then he was not sufficiently alarmed—he had to fight off the instinct to say, "*Starker*? You couldn't send me to someone a bit more ambiguous? Just to soften the blow?" Instead he asked what she believed the urologist *might* have to say on Monday morning. "Go out on a limb, Dr. Bloom—why not give me a little preview of coming attractions?" When he hung up the phone, he found that he was trembling. Sufficiency of alarm, at last, had been attained. He picked up the phone again and called his son's wife.

And it was a good thing he had, because on Monday, when he saw the urologist (who, like Dr. Bloom, could not have been much more than thirty), he was told he would need someone to drive him four days hence when he returned for his "procedure"—this was the word the doctor used (as did his nurse, as did the scheduler at the front desk). But Martin wanted spades called spades, he told them all (without raising his voice, without offering a treatise on the use of euphemisms, without commenting on the irony of the doctor's name after all—all of which he saved for his next phone call to Caroline). He asked both the doctor and his nurse if the *biopsy* was likely to be painful. Dr. Starker looked thoughtful. "I wouldn't say so. I would say, instead, somewhat uncomfortable." The nurse was more forthright once she was alone with him (*she* was the starker one, he thought but didn't say). "It's going to be unpleasant, I can tell you that. It's no walk in the park."

But it would soon be over with. It would no doubt be painful—even the nurse was only starker, not starkest—but then it would be finished. And certainly there was a chance they would find nothing. A good chance, he told himself. He'd had the time by now to do some research. Elevated PSAs were fairly common. For all he knew, the young doctors were overzealous, votaries of better safe than sorry.

On the television, *The West Wing* was on. The President stood at his desk looking grave. A helicopter hovered, landed. Martin glanced at the clock that Caroline had picked out and hung for him over the gas fireplace (she had also framed, and arranged all along the mantel, an assortment of photographs of Harry at various ages—and one, which she had taken the first time she and Jacob came to see him in New York, of father and son standing side by side in front of the old building on West End).

Just under thirty-six hours now until his "procedure." Then, ten minutes (he had asked) and it would be over.

Caroline had kept his secret, he was reasonably sure. If Jeanie had known, she would not have kept it to herself, not even if Caroline had made her promise to. And her tears tonight? Not for him, he thought. It seemed rather more likely that he had stepped into a minefield, asking her about the man who'd fathered Caroline. Or that he'd asked too many questions about Jill, toward whom Jeanie had developed a strangely strong antipathy—jealous, he supposed, of her relationship with Caroline. Or jealous of what she imagined as Jill's relationship with *him?* Or what she thought he hoped for from it. More than once she'd accused him of being "interested" in her. If he'd said what occurred to him at such moments—*Why should you care?*—it would be tantamount to a confession. And he was *not* "interested." Instead, the last time she had said this, "teasingly," he had responded with, "Just what exactly do you think you are accusing me of, Jeanie?" And she laughed. She said, "It's not an accusation, it's an observation," and when he reminded her that she hadn't *observed* anything, she said, "Sometimes you don't have to see it to believe it."

It was true—ah, but this was a confession he would never make to Jeanie—that when Jill had first agreed to put forward the idea of his joining her department, he'd experienced a mild flutter of hope that they might consummate what it seemed to him they'd started all those years ago. Her coolness toward him when he visited the campus for a formal set of conversations and meals out with faculty, meetings with Deans, a reading and Q & A that wasn't nearly as much fun as his first visit to KS had been, he had assumed was attributable to her desire to be wholly professional in the company of so many of her colleagues and her Chair. But she remained aloof, even after he arrived and settled in, even when they were alone together. She had made it clear she had no interest in him in that way, not anymore. It sometimes seemed to him that he'd imagined what there once had been between them. There was no proof of it; they never talked about it.

Had he been disappointed that she seemed to have so cooled to him? Of course—both disappointed and rather insulted. But the insult to his ego was a glancing blow (and he'd survived much worse, had he not?) and the disappointment, he found, was a mild one. A whisper of a disappointment after a whisper of almost-hope. A breath, a sigh, of hope.

Because—here was another truth about which he would never speak (not to Jeanie; not even to Caroline, who seemed to have become his confidante)—although he would not describe himself as "glad," as Jeanie insisted that she was, to be done with "all that," he was in fact relieved to be.

Relieved, and yet ashamed (ah, how he was growing used to feeling shame) of this relief. He thought of Bellow and his many wives and lovers, of Roth. Updike. Chekhov, of course. Of how baffled, how contemptuous, such men—such writers, the writers who had shaped his writing, his way of making sense of the world using words; the writers among whom he'd dreamed, as a young man, of walking alongside in history—would be by his willingness to be released from what he thought of now as the tyranny of love. The tyranny of women and what they might want or need from him.

And so when young Dr. Beatrice Bloom had told him she was sending him to Dr. Starker to discuss the possibility of further testing, and that, yes, this meant he might "and only *might*, so let's stay positive then, shall we, Mr. Lieberman?" have cancer of the prostate, and confirmed (reluctantly) that, yes, if it should be determined that if he did have this cancer, the usual treatment was surgery, a "radical prostatectomy," and that, yes ("but this conversation is drastically premature, Mr. Lieberman"), what he'd heard/read/otherwise had gathered somehow was correct, this type of surgery did sometimes ("no, I would not say 'often,' Mr. Lieberman") result in incontinence and impotence (more sternly now: "Mr. Lieberman, I'm afraid you're getting way ahead of yourself. Perhaps it would be helpful if I prescribed just a few Ativan to get you through the next few days?"), he thought: *At least it will be only me—at least there will be no witness to this humiliation.*

He would live through this alone—that was a relief about which he had no shame.

He had not yet thought: *And what if I don't live through it?*

The boy-urologist, on Monday, had told him: "If it turns out that you do have prostate cancer—and I'll just say one more time that this is by no means a foregone conclusion, that this is what this procedure we are scheduling is meant to discern—the fact is that prostate cancer is among the very best cancers to have." *Among the very best*—for an instant, Martin felt as if he'd won a prize (a small one, or not even a real prize but one of those momentary flatteries, inclusion in the *Times*'s Ten Best Books of the Year list).

He had not accepted Dr. Bloom's offer of anti-anxiety medication. By Monday night, after he had had his consultation, and the biopsy— *excuse me: procedure*—appointment had been made; after he had called Caroline to tell her what the urologist had said and to ask if she and Harry would accompany him on Friday ("and you can keep the car for a few days afterwards—I'm supposed to engage in only 'light activities' for forty-eight hours, which I shall interpret as 'lie in bed with a book and a large glass of Scotch whisky'"), and thank goodness Jacob was in San Diego, because she had cried; after he had given up his half-hearted attempt to heed Dr. Bloom's advice not to *get too far ahead* of himself; after he'd begun to think, incessantly, *And what if I don't live through it?* he'd realized that he should have let her write the prescription for Ativan, because he couldn't sleep.

His *life*. He'd lain awake on Monday night and Tuesday night, and he dreaded tonight—for he would lie awake again, he knew—the phrase repeating itself in his mind, like a fragment of a song. *My life, my life, my life.*

The West Wing had given way to *Law and Order*, which he could not bear to look at, not even as background. He turned the television off and rose and went into the kitchen with his empty glass, filled it with water. If this news had come before he'd left New York—if it had come before Jacob had called him, at Caroline's urging, after his long militant silence—he would have reacted differently to it. He would have thought, *Well, yes, of course*—not welcoming his fate but unsurprised by it. Resigned to it. *Why* not *this?* he would have thought: the inevitable unfolding of the plot, his life proceeding relentlessly toward its grim ending.

But it had not proceeded relentlessly. It had taken a turn.

He liked his life—there was joy in it every day. Who could have predicted that?

Had he ever felt this way before? Perhaps he had, he thought. He must have, no? Early in his marriage or in his career. Not in childhood, not in youth—his father casting his harsh shadow. But later—surely.

And yet he could not recall it—joy. He had had his moments of delight, pride, pleasure. Amusement. Gratification. But he could not recall experiencing happiness of the sort that filled him when he was with Harry. And when he sat talking with his daughter-in-law, both of them watching his grandson playing with his wooden trains or model dinosaurs, he often thought, in wonder, *Why, this must be what I had been waiting for.* Waiting, without knowing he'd been waiting. It was the way he felt, too, more often than not, in the classroom with his students. It was the way he felt with Jeanie—not tonight, no, but so very often.

Someday, perhaps, when he was with Jacob.

He drank the glass of water he had poured. He thought about the book he'd started working on when classes let out in the spring. He'd worked on it all summer, and while it was still too early to tell what it would be—or whether it would be anything at all—he'd been working steadily, keeping up a daily writing schedule even after school had started up again this fall. The setting was the Midwest, in a city like but not exactly this one. The protagonist, he was aware, resembled Gloria—Gloria as she might have been had she been born and reared and educated (or not educated) in a place like Kokosing. Gloria as she might have been if her life had been Jeanie's.

It was not a generous portrayal, but who could fault him for this? And perhaps the book would come to nothing, perhaps he would set it aside. The important thing was to be working, whether the work came to anything or not. This was what he told his students. It was what he'd always told himself.

And the book he'd finished during his first year in Kokosing, the one he'd started after Gloria had left and worked on for two years in the East Village rental before leaving the city, would be out soon. The early reviews, from *Kirkus* and *Publishers Weekly*, were good—not great, but good enough.

That "good enough" did not depress him was itself a sign that there had been a turn.

There was a *Times* review, he had been told, scheduled for Thanksgiving weekend. But he had not been counting off the weeks till then, as he would have done before. (Gloria, if she knew this, would disbelieve it.) What he counted off now were the days, the hours, between his outings with his grandson. The new words in the child's vocabulary, and the ever-more complex arrangements of them. He counted too the words his son directed kindly (even neutrally) toward him, and the sentences he willingly exchanged with him.

He counted, and he waited. He accepted Caroline's and Jeanie's coaching: he didn't pry, he didn't lose his temper, he avoided making jokes or indulging in long lectures—or long anecdotes (*monologues of any kind*, as Caroline said warningly)—in the presence of his son. He had nothing to lose by exercising this restraint. Nothing to lose by being patient.

Until now. Now he had everything to lose.

Let's stay positive, shall we, Mr. Lieberman?

He set his glass down in the sink and noted the tidy, man-alone sufficiency of the kitchen—the clean, uncluttered surfaces. Here was the legal pad and the ballpoint pen he kept beside the phone on the white countertop, on which resided nothing else but the new toaster he had bought when he'd decided to get rid of nearly everything he'd brought from "home." He'd kept his square-bottomed glasses, his Melitta one-cup, and the bare minimum of plates, pans, and utensils (two of each, like Noah). All of these were hidden in the tall white cabinets. He regarded them with satisfaction before switching off the kitchen light.

Who would have expected this small, satisfying life? He paused in the doorway to his bedroom and looked in at the darkness until his eyes adjusted and he could make out the two tall, narrow windows, the bureau, the one night table, the bed. The bed was a full, not a king or even a queen. He had discarded his old bed and all of the expensive linens that Gloria had organized by color on shelves in a closet in the hallway just outside their bedroom.

He had no such closet now, and he was grateful for this. Grateful not to have so many places to put things he didn't have, grateful not to have so many things—for in the end, he'd kept just half a dozen towels, white ones in three sizes, two of each, and kept all of them hanging in the bathroom. He'd bought a single set of sheets and pillowcases and a down-filled comforter, the softest one that he could find, for his new bed, and kept just two firm pillows, which he stacked to form the obtuse angle that allowed him to read comfortably before he went to sleep. There was a small reading lamp on the bedside table, a pile of books, a pair of drugstore reading glasses, a notepad, another ballpoint pen.

He'd bought only a small couch—a loveseat—and a television set. A single small end table, where he could lay a book. From the living room in the old apartment he had kept nothing but his rosso corsa colored chair and ottoman—the only furniture from his former life that he could not imagine doing without.

He had been lucky, he understood. Everything could have gone differently. But here he had everything he needed—and he had not even known, before this, what that might be.

PART 4

HOW TO LIVE

All wrongs forgiven, and all rights
not specifically enumerated—they're all yours,
my darling—the right to be
right, or to insist you are. The right to be left,
to stay behind, or just to stay. To stay
or go. To be or not to be.

—J. T. Rosen, "How to Live"

There were two things Jacob couldn't tell his wife, to whom he told everything. The first was how much he liked being on the road, and the second was how guilty he felt about it.

To enjoy being away from her—from Caroline, from their son, from the life they'd made together—was bad enough; that he continued to take pleasure in it might be unforgivable, and so how could he tell her?

But it was a principle between them to tell even what was hard to tell. She did not hide from him how she felt about his frequent travel or what she thought of his obduracy (what she called his *obduracy*; he saw it as simple self-defense) where his father was concerned. And he had never thought of keeping from her his unhappiness about her invitation to his father to come home with them after his surgery ("and stay as long as you need to—or just want to," he had been alarmed to hear her say as she held the old man's hand from the chair beside his bed) or how much he detested watching her wait on him hand and foot—*hand and foot and dick* was what he'd said, because it was she, those first weeks after the surgery, who cleaned the catheter they'd sent him home with;

she who walked backwards, just ahead of him, holding the tube and the bagful of urine steady as he shuffled, grimacing and cursing, to the bathroom for a shower.

And still he could not tell her *this*.

There had been a time—the whole time, in fact, before he'd met his wife—when he had hated traveling, when it was the necessary evil he pretended it was now. As he walked through unfamiliar streets, as he sat in his anonymous hotel room with the TV on for company, as he ate solitary meals in haste, his misery was thick. A bleak cloud of loneliness formed at the instant he set off on a trip, as he boarded the train or bus (or, later, plane, once he'd left home for good and could accept an invitation to perform halfway across the country—or the world—without consulting anyone). The cloud would lift as soon as he stepped onstage to perform; as soon as he stepped off, it would re-form itself.

He spoke of this to no one until he met Caroline. He believed, he told her—and it was true that he had tricked himself into believing—that it was unseemly to complain. He was afraid (but of course he couldn't tell her this, not then) of sounding like his father, grumbling about book tours and too many interview requests and invitations to give talks or readings from his work.

This was in the beginning, when he told her everything except whose son he was—when neither one of them, it seemed, could bear not to tell the other everything they'd ever done or thought or felt. And so he told her on the eve of a trip he had been dreading, the first since they had started dating. She didn't like him any less for it (indeed, she petted and pitied him and made him promise to call her as soon his plane landed in Seattle, then as often as he needed to over the weekend he would be away) and he understood the smaller, less attractive truth: that he'd been embarrassed—mortified—to speak of his loneliness before this. Before her.

But something unexpected and extraordinary happened after his confession. As if she'd cast a spell on him—or broken a bad one: that trip to Seattle, to perform and lecture at a conference for magicians, was the first one in his life that he enjoyed.

He'd marveled over it all weekend; he kept marveling on his return. You'd think, he told himself, that leaving would be easier when you were leaving nothing and no one behind. Or when what you were leaving were your crazy, inattentive parents. But it turned out that leaving something was much easier than leaving nothing, or leaving what was disagreeable. Not only easier but *easy*. With Caroline in his life, waiting for him to return and crying, "Oh, it's you! Hooray! Now tell me every single thing about your day" when he called her each night, it became a pleasure to go off alone for a few days, to walk on streets he knew only from previous short visits or on streets he didn't know at all. The cool impersonality of a hotel room, which had once depressed him, didn't faze him anymore: he'd lie on the bed after a show, still in his tuxedo, talking to his girlfriend on the phone. She had dispelled the cloud— she'd changed the weather.

And he couldn't tell her. How could he? *I'm so glad I found you— you're so easy to leave.*

He had never told her and as time had passed it had become more complicated. He'd gone from lonely to not lonely to *please God just give me five minutes alone*. Now what he marveled over were the days and nights when no one asked for anything from him except for magic; nights when no one woke him before dawn (not his son calling from his crib, not his father banging into something as he stumbled from the fold-out couch into the kitchen or the bathroom, not his wife saying, "Go check on him, would you? I'm too tired, I don't think I can"); nights in a room that had no clutter and no character—a room in which there was no object that had any meaning to him. At home, everything meant something: he was surrounded by his things and his wife's, by everything they had accumulated since they'd first moved in together, by their son's things (he was so small and already had so many things!), and now by his father's, too—for nearly every day he'd ask for something else to be brought over from his condo: a book or a record or a DVD of some grim foreign film or ancient screwball comedy that Jacob couldn't sit through but that Caroline would watch with him.

It was good, Jacob thought but did not tell his wife, to leave home knowing that while you were loosened for a little while from all that bound you, everything that mattered remained fixed, was *still*, was waiting for you to return. For a few days, he *liked* being loosened from his life. He liked being (no, not being—playing at, pretending to be) what he had so hated being, before Caroline: alone in the world.

Just himself. No one's husband, no one's father. Nobody's nice son-in-law.

No one's son.

No one in the world but *Jacob Lieb, Right Before Your Very Eyes.*

Her mother told her she was out of her mind when she said, over the phone, that she had made an appointment with a marriage counselor. "You know what those people do, don't you? They escort you—they *waltz* you—right to a divorce."

"Oh, that's nonsense. Where did you hear that?" Caroline kept one eye on Harry, edging ever closer to his grandfather, who was napping on the sofa. At least Martin had been willing to let her close *up* the sofa after breakfast. That was progress.

Harry would not be satisfied, however, until Pop Pop was awake and playing with him.

"I hear plenty," her mother said. "Girl in my office saw a marriage counselor with her husband for six months before, pow, game over. And she's not the only one."

"Mom," Caroline began, but Harry had set a large plastic model elephant on the sofa's arm, too close to his grandfather's head. "Wait—just a sec." In the whisper-shout she had perfected, she called, "Harrison B.F. Lieb. Let your Pop Pop sleep, please."

But Martin was awake. "It's all right, he's not bothering me." To Harry he said, "Would you like to know four exciting facts about elephants?"

"How *is* your father-in-law? His name is on the tip of my tongue."

"Don't start with me, Mom. Take it up with him."

"He won't even answer his phone."

"Well, don't take it personally. He doesn't want to talk to anyone but Harry. He doesn't want to *see* anyone but Harry."

"And you."

"He doesn't have much choice about that."

"Speaking of choice, are you *making* Jacob go to counseling or did you give him a choice about it? Does he even know about it yet?"

"He knows."

"But he has no choice. You gave him an ultimatum? What has he done that's so awful?"

"That's not the way this works. He hasn't done anything. I just think we could use some help. He's gone all the time and even when he's here it hardly seems like he's here. He has this whole life of his own and I have Harry. It's like we're living on parallel tracks."

"You're full of shit."

"Oh, that's great, Mom. Nice way to talk to me."

"When you're full of shit, who else is going to tell you?"

It was not until after she'd hung up the phone, made lunch for Harry and Martin (Jacob was out of town again, due back tonight), cleaned up, and settled Harry for his nap that she remembered that the reason she'd brought up the counseling appointment was that she wanted her mother to be Martin's backup. In case anything went wrong during the brief time (she had timed it: twenty minutes there, twenty minutes back, fifty minutes with the therapist—they'd be all right for an hour and a half, wouldn't they? But it made her very anxious), she wanted her mother to be ready to race over. She wanted her to take her car to work on Thursday, just in case. She'd forgotten that it would be impossible to ask her without first running through a gauntlet. Her mother's opinions. She had so many, whether she knew anything about the subject or not.

Well, at least she'd gotten the gauntlet over with. That one, anyway. There'd still be plenty to contend with. *Why can't you see the counselor at a time when you can leave my grandson with me? When am I going to see my grandson, anyway? How the hell am I going to come to the rescue if something goes wrong if Martin won't let me in to his place?*

Caroline sank into a chair at the kitchen table. Jesus. It was no wonder she was so exhausted.

From the family room, Martin called to her. "Caroline? Car? Could I possibly trouble you to bring me a cup of coffee?" And just then Harry cried out, "Mama! Mama, I need you! I *wet*."

"I'm coming," she called to Harry as she started toward his room.

"Thanks, dear," Martin said.

"Just give me a minute," she told him, pausing in the doorway to the family room, on her way to Harry.

"No minute, Mama," her son cried. "No minute. *Now*."

In the office of the marriage counselor, they'd been asked to close their eyes and picture what their lives would be like "if you'd never met, you'd never come to love each other and then made the choice to be together."

Caroline had closed her eyes obediently; Jacob balked. "I don't want to picture that," he told the therapist, whom Natalie had recommended. ("That's one strike against her," he'd told Caroline, who'd said, "Don't be an idiot, okay?" and told him Natalie had taken Dr. Derring's seminar on marriage and the family during her final year of coursework and swore she was a genius.)

Dr. Derring said—too gently—"I understand. But let's try anyway, shall we? It's just an exercise, a thought experiment," and Caroline, her eyes still closed, said, "Jacob, if you're not going to cooperate, then what's the point?" and Jacob said, "*Exactly*."

They had seen the therapist only twice before he had to leave for this last trip, to Miami. But now he was back and Caroline had reminded him twice since this morning that they hadn't done their "homework" yet—another exercise, this one with their eyes open. They were to look at each other without speaking, holding hands, for one fifteen-minute period each day. When Jacob pointed out that he would be away for three days of the seven before their next session, Dr. Derring laughed and said, "Yes, I can see how this would be hard to pull off from a distance. What about if you just do it on the days that you *are* here?"

It was ten PM—he'd been back for nearly twenty-four hours—before they got around to trying it, three days before their next appointment. Harry was asleep, and Martin seemed to be—or at least he wasn't calling out for Caroline, or bumping into things and calling out apologies. Jeanie had already phoned and Caroline had grown impatient with her, then hung up, abruptly. And the birdcage was covered for the night.

Jacob wanted to talk about the Miami shows, in which he'd tried out parts of what he hoped would eventually be an entirely new kind of show, and they'd gone over well enough that he thought he was on the right track. Telling her about it seemed a much better use of the little time they had alone together than what Dr. Derring had instructed them to do, but he didn't say that. Caroline was serious about these counseling sessions: she'd made it clear that they were not negotiable (and both times, when they'd left for them, she'd been a nervous wreck—and when he'd said, on the way there the first time, that he wouldn't hold it against her if she wanted to cancel, she jumped down his throat, telling him he wasn't funny and had damn well better take this seriously, that it was *important*).

He sat on the bed with her, cross-legged, facing her and holding both her hands as they "gazed silently into each other's eyes." He couldn't remember if he was supposed to (or allowed to) think while they were gazing. Was it meant to be like meditation, where the goal was to empty one's mind? Or were they supposed to be thinking about each other?

He knew better than to ask.

He gazed and kept silent, as instructed. But his thoughts were skittering all over the place. First there was the secret, guilty one that the weekend in Miami had been so great—the three shows successful, even with the new material (more talking, longer intervals between the tricks), and the rest of the time he'd eaten fantastic Cuban food and walked on the beach near his hotel. Then there was the also secret, guiltier thought that he was already looking forward to his next trip—a series of dates around New England and the chance to try out more of the new show. And he felt guilty too about how little time he'd spent today with Harry, because it was hard to avoid his father and not end up avoiding his son too. Caroline was constantly saying, "Honey, you have to let Pop Pop rest now. He'll play with you more later on," and his father would say, "No, no, let him be. I'll rest when I'm dead." Harry seemed to think this was hilarious, and this afternoon when Jacob said, "How about we lay off on the 'dead' jokes when my kid's around, okay?", Harry cried, "Dead jokes, dead jokes! Pop Pop tell dead joke." Did he know what "dead" meant? "Joke," he knew. He'd greeted Jacob when he had come home last night with a joke: *Where do cows go on Saturday night? To the moooovies.*

Maybe he should let his son write jokes for the new show. His son and his father both. Bad puns and morbid wisecracks—that would be just the ticket.

Caroline didn't even know there *was* a new show—the beginnings of a new show. He'd written a lot on the flight to Miami, written and revised and then revised some more until he couldn't see what he had written in the first place and he had to start a new page in his notebook, writing it out clean. Then he realized he was memorizing it as he recopied it and he made the decision, just like that, to go ahead and try it, at least on the first night. Otherwise how would he know if he was on to something? And if he wasn't, he could just forget the whole thing. Stick with what he knew, what worked.

But the new material *had* worked. It had gone better than he had allowed himself to hope it would. So he tried out more of it on the second and the third nights—telling stories, punctuating them with tricks, changing the balance of the act. And people laughed at what was funny and he felt the air shift in the room when they were moved—and then there'd be a trick, something he'd never done before onstage *or* an old familiar one he could do in his sleep, and either way it seemed to him that their applause was warmer than what he was used to. The longer intervals between illusions seemed to make each one more important, more impressive. Or he'd become more human to them, telling stories about his own life—so the magic was more surprising. So now he was thinking about moving ahead with it, talking to his manager about a whole new show that would be about half tricks and half…well, half *life*, he guessed he'd have to call it.

And he wanted to show Caroline what he'd written so far. She would be amazed, wouldn't she? She would be pleased, he hoped. She might want to help with it. That was what he was counting on—that she would want to work with him on it. She was the writer in the family, not him.

"Okay, time's up," she said and dropped his hands. He was about to speak—now he could tell her about the show, ask her opinion, ask if she'd mind reading some of what he'd written, ask—

But it was too late. She was up, off the bed, halfway across the room, telling him without turning around that she was beat, it had been a long day—a long *few* days, she said, and even though she didn't look at him when she said this he knew it had been pointed, aimed right at him—and she was going to go brush her teeth and wash her face and get right into bed. But he didn't have to feel obliged to go to bed yet if he wasn't tired, she said. It was all right if he wanted to sit up.

And then she was gone. She closed the door behind her.

He was still sitting in the middle of the bed, knees splayed, ankles crossed. He thought about the other homework they had been assigned—more of what they were paying Dr. Derring a hundred dollars a session for. They were supposed to start leaving Harry at home one night a week and have a "date night," which the therapist had suggested might be a time when they could talk about something other than Harry, other than their parents. "We can talk about this more, but in case you're eager to get started on it, for now I want to caution you that this is not meant to be time set aside for arguing, either. This is not the time for you, Caroline, to accuse Jacob of 'never being home' or for you, Jacob, to accuse your wife of pretending that this matters to her more than it does," she said. Jacob did not say, "We've seen you for a total of two hours and you think you can tell me what I 'tend' to do?"—mostly just because he was impressed that Caroline had not objected to their marriage counselor's characterization of her as "accusing" him (when he used the word, she always protested). Instead he asked Dr. Derring, jokingly, "Well, what's left, then?" but before she had a chance to break out her reassuring, gentle laugh, Caroline said, "Wait, we're supposed to leave Harry at home one night a week? With who—with Martin?"

"Why not?" Dr. Derring said.

"Because he's *sick*."

"In point of fact," Jacob said, "he isn't sick anymore."

In point of fact, it didn't seem as if he'd ever been sick—not until after the surgery that made him "well." But it made no difference because Caroline ignored him. She told Dr. Derring that it was impossible, that it was hard enough to leave Harry at home during his naptime for the hour and a half—"or longer, like last time when we hit traffic going home"—required to come here, but Martin wasn't strong enough for what she was proposing. He could not move fast enough.

"Jesus," Jacob said. "What exactly are you expecting the kid to do while we're gone?"

The therapist offered a list of suggestions: they could go out for an early dinner, something casual and quick—"It's not about the food, you understand. Go get a pizza, get a burger. The point is to spend at least an hour together, just the two of you, away from home, away from Martin and your son." Or they could go out after both Harry and Martin were asleep, for a drink or a walk ("That is, if you believe your father-in-law can be counted on to wake up if his grandson cries?"). Or they could hire a sitter to come and stay with Harry *and* his grandfather, so that someone would be there to "do the heavy lifting." They could ask Caroline's mother instead of a sitter. They could drop Harry off *with* Caroline's mother and let Martin rest at home, alone.

Caroline didn't like any of these ideas. "I *can't*," she said.

"You can't what?"

"I can't leave him anywhere. With anyone."

"What are you talking about?" Jacob looked at Dr. Derring for an explanation but she kept silent, her expression unreadable.

They'd only had five minutes of their session left and it was like a bomb had been dropped right into the middle of it. Suddenly Caroline was crying, and saying that she couldn't stand to leave Harry, that it wasn't fair to make her. Jacob was bewildered. He reminded her that she had let their parents take him out twice a week for the last *year*.

"And I *hated* it," she cried.

"But why?" To the therapist he said, "Do you know why? What am I missing here?"

By the time they left her office, Dr. Derring had persuaded Caroline that the date-night homework was just as important as the sessions. "Going out with your husband is not only something you need to do for your marriage, but also for Harry. He needs to know that you can leave and will be back," she said, leaning forward in her chair, locking eyes with Caroline just the way, Jacob thought, she wanted *him* to do. "You cannot be with him all the time. He needs to know that, too."

On the way home after the session Caroline had not wanted to talk about it. She was a wreck, her face so wet it was as if she had been swimming. "Are you sure this is going to help us?" he had asked her in the car. The look she gave him in return was so filled with fury he had ducked—as if there were a chance that she might take a swing at him.

And then he'd had to leave for Miami.

But now he was back and she still didn't want to talk—not about this, not about anything. She had returned to the bedroom, where she was pulling the curtains shut and turning away from him to change from her jeans and KS sweatshirt into a long nightgown. Then she flipped the switch for the overhead light and the room went black. "This is okay, isn't it? I need to sleep. You can turn on your lamp if you want to read."

"No, it's all right." He moved toward his side of the bed to make more room for her as she got in. After a moment, he stretched out too, beside her. His eyes adjusted to the dark and he turned on his side and reached for her—she had drawn the blanket over her, but one shoulder and arm were exposed as she lay with her back to him, as far away as she could be and still be in the bed with him. He moved closer, past the center, and took her free hand. It was balled into a fist in front of her mouth. "Sweetheart," he said.

She murmured something that he couldn't hear.

"Here's a thought. Why don't we go out tomorrow night? For dinner, just the two of us. Like we used to. Like Dr. Derring said we should."

She couldn't have fallen asleep already—could she have?

"She seemed to think it was important."

Silence. (But at least she wasn't saying no.)

"If you don't want to leave Harry alone with Martin—and I get that—let's call your mother. He'll just have to live with that. You don't even have to call her. I will. You don't have to do anything. I could even ask her to bring dinner over for them. She can feed them both and give Harry his bath and put him to bed and then she can keep an eye on Martin. You won't have to worry about either of them—any of them."

He listened to her breathing. He could feel her breathing, his chest pressed to her back, through the blanket that separated them. "You know Jeanie will be thrilled. She misses both of them so much. She misses *you*—she misses all of us."

It took too long for her to answer, but finally she said, in the smallest voice possible, "Okay."

"Okay," he said. He squeezed her hand. "And then we'll get an A when we go back to Dr. D on Thursday."

Ah—she laughed. Just a very small laugh—more like a sigh—but still, it was something. "That's good," she said. She sounded half-asleep. "You know how I hate getting anything less than an A."

"When did you ever get anything less than an A?"

But she had fallen asleep. And then before he knew it, he was asleep too—still in his clothes, on top of the blanket, his teeth unbrushed, his hand over hers. Both of them on her side of the bed, the other half empty beside them, as if someone were missing.

In the morning, before Caroline or Martin were awake, he changed Harry's diaper and got him fed and dressed. He was zipping him into his snowsuit—it had snowed all night, the first big snow of the year— when Caroline emerged from the bedroom in her long pink and white striped nightgown. "You're going out? It's still so early."

Jacob held a finger up to his mouth—*don't wake Martin*—and whispered, "We're going to make our first snowman." To Harry, as he tugged a hat on his head, he said, "Aren't we, buddy? We're going to go out in this beautiful snow and get out of Mama's hair for a bit."

"You're not in my hair," she said. As if to demonstrate, she raked her fingers through it. It had grown very long—she looked like Alice in Wonderland, Jacob thought. "It's not even eight o'clock. The sun's hardly up."

"It's been up for half an hour," Jacob said. He heard his father stirring in the family room. "I made a pot of coffee. We'll be back soon." And he kissed her, quickly, and ushered Harry out the door.

Outside, he demonstrated as he talked Harry through how to make a snowball big enough to serve as the foundation for a snowman. Harry said, "No, not snowman. Snow*boy*," and Jacob laughed and said, "All right—why not? I'll tell you what. Let's make a snowboy *and* a snowman."

"Snow Harry and Snow Dada?"

"Yes. Let's do it," Jacob said.

They worked side by side, Harry mostly clapping snow between his mittened hands and chortling as it dispersed, and sometimes patting the snow flat and then thumping it apart and eating it. Jacob as he rolled and packed snow thought about how he would tell Caroline about the show he had in mind, how he would ask her for her help with it, while they were out at dinner. He could not remember the last time it had really been just the two of them. He could not recall the last time they had really talked, except with Dr. Derring as their referee.

Caroline had once remarked—it must have been last summer (he'd been watching a Mets game on one of those evenings when their parents had their Harry)—that they seemed to have "skipped ahead" to middle age. "We never talk anymore," she had said. She'd sounded so sorrowful. How had he responded? *Had* he responded? He hoped so.

Tonight they would talk. He would tell her all about the show, about Miami, about everything he had already written about life as a young magician. He'd written something funny (at least in Miami they had laughed) about his mother trailing him on bookings upstate and to Jersey when he was underage and couldn't register for a hotel room on his own: he'd devised a couple of new tricks he performed in the persona of the humiliated teenager he'd been then. He'd even created a trick that made use of the workaround he'd come up with at sixteen, when he got his own credit card and carried a notarized letter of permission from his parents. It was more joke than illusion when he produced that letter (not *the* letter, of course, but a version he wrote just for the show) and read it aloud, but the applause was enthusiastic, and he *liked* that it was mixed with laughter.

He'd started writing about his first trick, too. Everything he could remember about learning it: school closed on a day just like today—a snow day—and his mother off somewhere; his father restless, bored, and showing him the trick, no doubt, because he couldn't think of a single other thing to do with him. He was trying to write it as a sort of skit—no, more than that: a little comic play. He would be both his young father showing off for him and his own seven-year-old self showing his father that he could not (would not) be mystified by him.

As Jacob patted and smoothed snow for the base of the snowboy, he considered how this might lead into another bit—one in which he conjured himself a few years hence, and Harry at the age that *he* had been when he'd watched his father do the phoenix trick. What if his son, instead of being mystified and fascinated, as he'd been, were bored? He would once again play both roles: desperate father, uncharmed son baffled and bored by each (ever-more elaborate and more desperate) trick his father trotted out for him?

This had comic potential, didn't it? And it would give him the chance to work up some new kinds of tricks, some over-the-top comic ones, to "illustrate" the story.

And maybe there was more to say about himself and Harry—Caroline could help him with that. And more to say about his father? About the way Martin had followed him halfway across the country?

Not about his getting sick, though—that was much too dark.

Unless he could devise a trick that would lighten the darkness. (That would be interesting, wouldn't it? It might be *very* interesting to go darkly comic partway through the show—to make that shift while the audience was laughing and amazed. They wouldn't know what had just hit them.)

He thought of Caroline kneeling on the bathroom floor, cleaning the catheter, cleaning *his father's penis.*

No, there was no comedy in that.

He rolled another snowball in the soft snow at his feet. *She* thought he was heartless, but he wasn't. He had sympathy for the old man. He was relieved—of course he was—that the prostatectomy had gotten all the cancer, that there was no evidence that it had spread. That Martin would be fine once he recovered from the surgery. But having him here with them had been a terrible idea. Especially for those first couple of weeks. The moaning and the sobbing, the threatening to rip the catheter out. Caroline kept calling the doctor's office, asking if there could be something wrong—a complication of the surgery, an infection. "Maybe they put it in the wrong place?" she whispered to Jacob as his father groaned in the next room. "There's only one place," Jacob told her. "Trust me on that." But she didn't trust him, no more than she trusted Martin's doctor or the nurses who kept telling her not to worry, that Martin was fine, that he "must just not have much tolerance for being uncomfortable." "Uncomfortable!" she'd said to Jacob. "No one screams like that because he's uncomfortable."

She didn't know his father. She only thought she did.

And even after they got through that part, after the wailing and the cursing and the screaming was behind them, he was still weak as a baby. Caroline was still fetching and carrying for him. And when she sent Jacob to the store, the last item on the shopping list she handed him was "adult diapers for men—generic brand OK," and that felt like the last straw.

"So he's pissing himself now? How is it no one told us this would happen?"

"No one told *us* anything. Martin says he knew it was a possibility."

"Excellent. How nice of him to keep that from us."

"What difference does it make? We'd still have to deal with it."

But why should he have to?—that was what he wanted to know.

He couldn't understand how she could stand it. It had been so much worse than he'd imagined—and he had imagined that it would be bad, having his father with them. What he'd dreaded was having to listen to him *talk*, the interminable lectures and supposedly amusing and/or edifying stories—nearly all of which he would have heard before, but when his father said, "I never told you about _____," one was never meant to say, "Oh, but you did." It would be his childhood all over again— as if he'd never managed to put hundreds of miles between them.

But it wasn't like that at all. Even now, it wasn't. He was both cancer- and pain-free, and his strength seemed to be returning—he no longer held on to the wall on both sides of him when he made his way down the hall—but still he was not himself. He spoke only to Caroline—and only to ask for things—or to Harry, who would climb up on the sofa next to him and put his arms around his neck. "There's my boy," Martin would say. "What a good boy." He napped, he read the local newspaper (since when did he do that?), he watched TV. He played with Harry if it did not require moving around or talking very much. He refused to see Jeanie (well, he would have to, now—it was no longer up to him). He didn't even want to talk on the phone.

The self-aggrandizing, the jokes, the bluster of the old days, his father's old self, were all gone. Gone for good, or just for now—who could tell? And you wouldn't think he'd miss it, would you? Well, he didn't miss it, Jacob told himself. It was just puzzling, strange. Confusing.

Oh. He paused, a snowball as big as his own head in his hands.

This was why he'd cut off contact with his father when his mother left. He hadn't understood it at the time. It had not seemed like enough, somehow, to be hundreds of miles away. He had to protect himself from *this*—this diminishment. He must have always known, without knowing he had known, how pathetic his father could become, just given the chance.

"Put snowdada head on!" Harry shouted. "Come on, Dada, do it!"

"I was just about to," Jacob told him. He set the taller snowman's head atop its belly and stepped back to look it over. "What do you think, son?"

Harry was flinging fistfuls of snow into the bushes. He stopped to cock his head thoughtfully. "Good," he said.

The two snowmen did look like father and son. The smaller one was less than two feet tall, the larger nearly twice that size, and they were standing too close to each other to be strangers. But they had no faces. "What do you say we find some sticks and stones to make our snowguys' eyes and mouths and noses?"

Harry abandoned his pelting of the bushes and flung himself toward his father. "Noses!" he cried. His face was flushed, or frozen.

"Oh, Har, you're so cold. We should go in. We can give them faces later."

"No!" Harry wailed. He let go of Jacob's legs and sat down in the snow. "Not *yet*." *Yet* was a new word. He looked up at Jacob, his hat askew. "We need snowmama, too." *Too* was also new.

"Ah, a snowmama—of course we do. And we'll make one, but later on, or else tomorrow. It's going to stay cold all week. These guys aren't going anywhere."

"*No*," Harry said again. "*Now*."

So together they made the base and rolled it toward the other two. The mother was a good three feet away from the two snowguys. More like the family he'd come from than the one he'd made himself, thought Jacob.

That observation gave him pause—but it was true, wasn't it? It had become true. He and his father were together; his mother was somewhere else.

He hardly ever thought about his mother anymore. He'd conjured her up as a comic figure in the bit he'd written about her traveling with him—but he never let himself really remember her. If he started to, he caught himself, and stopped. He never thought about the mystery of her decision to leave, not anymore. He could hold his father responsible—he *had* held his father responsible—but after all, he'd come to think, his mother had chosen his father, chosen to spend her life with him, just as he had chosen Caroline. Was she not paying attention to who he was? Or had she supposed that he would change? Or had *she* changed, and then woke up one day and thought, for the first time, *I don't have to put up with him. Why* should *I stay?*

At first he had spent too much time thinking about this. Trying to figure it out the way he'd always been able to figure things out—taking it apart the way he took apart a trick to see how it was done. At some point it struck him that his father must have been as unhappy with his mother as she'd been with him. But he would not have left—Jacob was sure of it. And that didn't make him "better" than his mother, he had once told Caroline. It just meant that he had more to lose.

"Or maybe he just has a greater tolerance for being unhappy," Caroline said.

He had supposed for a long time now that he would never hear from her again. That final letter—those few lines that told him nothing—seemed to him now to have landed in the life of someone else (that angry boy who had stopped speaking to his sad, bewildered father; the boy who had not yet met Caroline and started a new life—whose life had not yet changed as much as he had hoped it would, simply by leaving home). But as he and Harry rolled another snowball, he felt this supposition become knowledge, and the sorrow of this knowledge filled him. He *let* it fill him. Just for a moment, all the grief he hadn't even known was in him to feel.

She had left them both, for good.

She might not even know herself why she had left. Was it not possible that some things happened and there *was* no explanation, no real reason? It was only someone doing what seemed like the next thing to do.

There had been three of them, a family, and then there had been just three separate people, each doing whatever the next thing was. But now there were two of them again—two and the new family he'd made, with Caroline. And because of her, his father was a part of that one, too. She held them all together.

By now both he and Harry were cold and wet. "Let's give it a rest, buddy," he told his son. "Mama misses us, I bet. Maybe later she can help us make the snowmama."

Harry agreed. Either he was tired or he missed his mama, Jacob thought. Or else he understood: these guys weren't going anywhere.

Martin had fallen asleep again after breakfast. Caroline had insisted he come sit at the kitchen table—it was good for him, whether he wanted to or not, she told him, to get up and walk around and to sit up in a chair—and have some fruit and cheese and bread with her, but right afterwards he had gone back to the sofabed with the newspaper, and soon she could hear him snoring.

She glanced at the kitchen clock. Jacob and Harry had been outside much longer than she'd thought they would be. Harry must be soaked through, frozen stiff. But it was good that they were playing together outside—good that they were together anywhere, doing anything, just the two of them. She knew this, but she still had to remind herself of it. There was something wrong with her, she thought. She shouldn't have to work so hard at this. (And Dr. Derring was on to her, she knew. She'd say things like, "You let Harry spend time with his grandparents because you know it's the right thing to do." Or, "I can see that you know when to pay attention to your instincts and when to fight them off." It was a way of tricking her, a way to encourage her to resist wanting to keep Harry to herself.)

She decided to make a fresh pot of coffee. When Martin woke up, she'd make him get out of bed and walk again, come into the kitchen and sit upright in a chair. She would make cocoa, too, so that when Harry came in and she stripped him out of his wet snowsuit and his hat and mittens and put him in dry clothes, he could have "coffee" with his father and his grandfather.

Poor Martin, she thought as she heated milk for cocoa. Sometimes, as she helped him get comfortable with pillows stacked behind him, and she saw how tired and sad he looked, she said it aloud. But then he would say, "Poor *Caroline*. You're the one who's got it hard."

He might be coming back to himself. This morning at breakfast he had made a joke—his first since the morning of the biopsy, when his conversation on the drive there had been nothing but bad puns and stupid jokes ("so they tell me they'll be probing my rectitude this morning, searching for evidence of moral failings"). But at breakfast he'd suggested that it might be time for him to start thinking about going home: "That's where the heart is, is it not?" But she could not imagine him at home alone. He still seemed so fragile.

Jacob, she knew, would suggest hiring a nurse. It was what he'd argued for in the first place—sending Martin home instead of bringing him here, getting someone from a visiting nurse service to stay with him, "which might be covered by his university insurance and then even if it's not, he can afford to pay for it." They'd fought and she'd won. But if she told him now that it wasn't nursing that his father needed anymore, only company and someone to look out for him, he'd say they should hire a student, then (he'd say, "Get one of his own students— God, think how thrilled one of those kids would be"), but she knew Martin wouldn't want one of his students around—for godsakes, he didn't even want Jeanie, his *machateynes*, around. He wouldn't even talk to his agent on the phone.

She'd have to be firm with both of her husband and her father-in-law: he wasn't going anywhere. Not yet.

In the meantime, though, it was nice—she had to admit it—to be almost alone in the apartment, which for once was quiet. Not silent, but quiet enough. Martin was snoring softly, and on her shoulder Delirious was making her own soft noise, the *gritch gritch* of her beak-grinding, which she did when she was sleeping, a sign of bird-contentment. The last time she had actually been alone in the apartment was the last time Martin and her mother had taken Harry for the afternoon while Jacob was out of town—the weekend before Martin's biopsy—and she had been so anxious she could hardly catch her breath. Not even an hour into the afternoon, she had called Natalie and asked her to come over, hoping that her chattering about some man or another (there was always at least one) or her dissertation research (there was always a problem with it) would keep her distracted. But at some point while Natalie was telling her about a fellow grad student in social psychology who might have a crush on her, she had begun to cry, and because she was not permitted to tell her about Martin's urology appointment—and she damn well wasn't going to say anything about Harry (she'd once made the mistake of mentioning that it made her "just a little nervous to be away from him" and Natalie, whose dissertation project, improbably enough, was on "self and identity in the family," had started talking smugly about "separation anxiety" and "failure to differentiate")—she said the first thing that occurred to her, the sort of thing she used to talk about with Nat: that she'd had a fight with her mother. Which was when Natalie had given her the name of the marriage and family therapist she'd taken a course with. "You and your mom will love her," she said. "It's never too late to work on these relationships, you know."

She should have just said that she cried all the time since Harry was born. It wouldn't be that far from the truth.

As she measured cocoa and sugar into the mug with a blue dinosaur on it, pouring hot milk into the mug, stirring—she told herself to try to just enjoy the time alone. *Your son is with his father—he's fine, having a good time.*

For once, no one asking her for anything. No one reminding her of anything she promised she would do. No one wondering aloud. No one crying, flying, shrieking, whispering, asking her to keep a secret, proposing the hiring of a nurse or an adoring student. Demanding an evening out.

She was trying not to think about that—about going out and leaving Harry. About how angry Martin would be when he learned that Jacob had invited Jeanie over to keep him and Harry company. If Jacob was still planning that. If he had not thought better of it—or forgotten that he had suggested going out at all.

What would she and Jacob talk about tonight if they couldn't talk about their son or their parents? They had already told each other every story about themselves there was to tell.

She put animal crackers in a dish; she cut an orange into smile-shaped sections. She glanced at the clock once more, put napkins on the table, played a game with herself: What do you need more? Time alone—or time with someone you can talk to about anything? A new friend, or a way back into the old friendship with Natalie, when it was possible somehow to say everything you felt—or the guts to let Jill Rosen know that your life was not as perfect as you made it out to be?

Or what about this: Not having to part with Harry, or being able to be all right—calm, even happy—when you do?

Or this: Martin to get well and go home without your having to be worried about him, or Jacob making peace with Martin here?

It wasn't a very good game. The answer to every question was *I don't know.*

She took out the half-and-half and three more mugs. She thought of her mother, the only one of them who was at work. Her mother at the desk she was so proud of, reaching for her ringing phone as others jangled all around her, the receiver balanced on her shoulder as she typed, lit up by a patch of too-bright light from overhead as if each day were an interrogation. The constant hum and buzz of people talking. And then, after work, in her dark, silent house—a shock after the fluorescent glow, so many people, so much noise. What must that be like?

Caroline heard her husband and son coming up the stairs. They were making a lot of noise, laughing and possibly (but could that be?) singing. And now they were inside, stomping their feet and still laughing and—yes—singing. It was a made-up song, something about *stout snowmen and good snowboys and sweet, smart, nice snowwomen*, to the tune—mostly to the tune—of "The Happy Wanderer."

"*Tweedledee, Tweedledum,*" Jacob sang as Caroline came to meet them in the foyer. Delirious had awakened but remained on her shoulder, chirruping into her ear. "*Tweedledee, Tweedle*"—Harry joined in—"*dum dum dum dum dum dum,*" but then Harry stopped, his mouth wide, to stare at his mother as she sang along with Jacob on the next "*Tweedledee.*"

"How does Mama know our song?" he asked Jacob.

"Mama knows everything. I thought you knew that."

"I don't know the words, sweetiepie," she told Harry as she got on her knees to unzip his wet snowsuit. "I know the tune because it's an old one, but I don't know how your version goes. Sing the rest of it for me."

Jacob and Harry sang the end of their song together:

"*Tweedledee, Tweedledum*"—they shouted the last line—"*my snowfamily's all here.*" On "*here,*" they both grabbed her—Harry hugging her knees and Jacob hugging the rest of her—and now Delirious shrieked and flapped her wings and lifted off to swoop down the hall, back toward the kitchen. Harry yelled, "Hi, Leery. Bye, Leery," and Martin called from the family room, "What's going on?" and her husband and son were dripping snow on her and on the floor—and Caroline was laughing, the three of them were laughing, and she thought, *Why can't it always be this way*, and Jacob released her and they looked at each other as he stood there dripping and she felt as if she could see him thinking the same thing.

He unwound his scarf, one she'd made for him back when she was doing "projects"—knitting had lasted just long enough for her to make this one, long, lumpy, pale gray scarf—and steadied himself against the wall as he pried off his boots. "Where should we put all this wet stuff?" he asked, but what he was thinking was, *If I don't do something, fix something, figure out how I can make things right, she's going to leave me.* It came at him now with the force of a universal truth, a fact of life.

And if she left him, she wouldn't leave her son. She'd take his father, too. Her mother. Everyone.

"Let's hang everything that's hangable in the bathroom," she was saying, as if all were well. "I'll go get some hangers from our room. And we can put the gloves and hats and boots on the heat registers."

He tried to catch her eye, to communicate telepathically: *I'll do whatever I have to do. I love you. Don't go.*

But she wasn't looking at him. She was talking to Harry. "Let's get everything off you and get you into a warm bath, just a quick one, and then we can put you in dry clothes and have some cocoa, okay?"

And his father was calling, "Caroline? Jake? Harry? The bird is circling this room like a vulture. Do you think she's trying to tell me something?"

"It's okay," Caroline called back—she hoisted Harry onto her hip and headed to the family room—"I'll get her and put her back in her cage. She's just excited." And, without turning, "Don't just stand there, Jake. Come get warm. I made coffee. We'll have coffee and cocoa."

Harry sang, at the top of his lungs, "*Tweedledee, Tweedledum,*" and Martin said, "That old rhyme! *Tweedledum and Tweedledee/agreed to have a battle.*"

Harry said, "No! That's not our song."

And Caroline said, "You must be feeling better if you're quoting verse."

"Hardly verse," said Martin. "A nursery rhyme! Did you know that Kipling referenced it in one of the stories in *The Jungle Book*?"

"I didn't know that, no," Caroline said. She was coaxing Delirious down from a high shelf, her finger extended: "Come on, sweetheart, come to me. It's okay."

"Joyce once referred to Freud and Jung as Tweedledum and Tweedledee," Martin said. "Did you know that?"

Delirious leapt onto Caroline's finger. "Good girl. Sweet girl. Let's take a rest now," she cooed as she brought her to her cage.

"No rest," Harry said. "Cocoa."

"No rest for you. Only for Delirious. No rest for any of the rest of us." She said it cheerfully. "Martin, I want you up and walking around. We'll meet you in the kitchen."

"Meet you in the kitchen, meet you in the kitchen," Harry chanted as his mother carried him off to the bathroom.

"Okay, Dad, let's do as she says," Jacob told his father.

"We'd have to be fools not to," his father said.

I CAN SEE YOUR HOUSE
FROM HERE

What would it take, Jeanie had asked herself throughout her daughter's childhood, to make her turn her back on her? When she was a baby, when she was a wobbly thirteen-month-old and already nonstop-talking toddler (she said *I want* about a hundred times a day and only sometimes bothered finishing the sentence), when she was a mouthy, stubborn three-year-old full of her own opinions, when she was in kindergarten and changing her name without paying her mother the courtesy of mentioning it, Jeanie had looked at her and thought: *Could there be anything? Would there ever be?*

Because either you loved your kid just because she was yours and you would put up with her no matter what she did or didn't do (and it would not feel like *putting up with*, either; it wouldn't feel like something you could make a choice about) or you didn't. And if you didn't, didn't that mean you'd never loved her to begin with?

And didn't that mean her own mother never had?

She tried, she really did, for years, to think of whether there was anything—some argument that couldn't be retreated from, some bad behavior, lapse in judgment, lie—that would make her cut all ties with Carrie, as her mother had with her when she was nineteen and pregnant. Maybe like so many things about being a mother that it was impossible to prepare for (nursing, or how much you'd worry, or what it was like to go without any sleep for days on end), this was something that you couldn't know until it happened—she tried this idea out for a while. But every time and every way she thought it through, she came to the same conclusion: you were all in or you weren't. And she was and her mother hadn't been. Just as Jacob's hadn't been.

Her mother had come back—*come back for Carrie* was how Jeanie thought of it—but only for a little while. Carrie had just turned nine when Jeanie's mother showed up one day without warning, and when Jeanie said, "How did you find us?", her mother looked insulted (*that* was rich) and said, "What, you think I don't know how to use a phonebook?" And then Jeanie said what she should have said in the first place: "What are you doing here, Mother?" But her mother didn't answer that. She just said, "So, where's that grandchild? Girl or boy?" And, "I'm here, all right? Stop looking so surprised."

Carrie was surprised, too—more surprised than Jeanie was—and she was also furious, but not at "Grandma Gwen." (Grandma Gwen! Even now—oh, especially now—the thought of this enraged her. A person earned that title, she'd wanted to tell her mother. But she hadn't, because Carrie was so happy.)

They all sat in the living room and Jeanie's mother asked the nine-year-old she'd never met before about her friends and school and what their neighborhood was like and what kind of games she liked to play and what TV shows she watched and what she liked to eat and didn't ask her daughter *how have you been*, or *how have you managed all these years*, or even *are you all right?*

Carrie, all smiles, told her *Grandma Gwen* things she had never mentioned to her mother (she liked to play with a Ouija board? where had she even seen a Ouija board? oh, right—must be the same place she'd eaten the fettuccini Alfredo she said was her favorite food). But as soon as Jeanie closed the door behind her mother, who'd left them with a promise to return on Sunday to pick Carrie up "for a nice day out together, just the two of us," her daughter turned on her. "You told me she was *dead*," she shouted. "What's wrong with you? How could you have told me that?" And then she cried—of course she cried. At nine, she was always angry at her mother or else she was crying, or she was in a rage *and* crying.

"You're too young to understand," Jeanie assured her. It was true. The child was smart, but she was still a child, and so there were a lot of things she didn't understand. Sometimes Jeanie thought that it was this that really enraged her. That it was this that also made her cry.

Carrie gave her the cold shoulder for days after her "grandmother" showed up.

This itself was no big deal—Jeanie was used to it. Yes, already used to it, Jeanie told Martin, who pressed her when she told him this. ("By the time she was *nine?*" he asked her skeptically. "No," Jeanie said. "By the time she was six. Maybe five.") She knew she'd come around; she always did. And wasn't it a mother's job to let her kid ignore her sometimes? Or tell her she hated her? Or, you know, not to disappear because you disapproved of something she had done?

Grandma Gwen, it turned out, lived only half an hour away from them, in one of the new suburbs that had sprung up in a ring around the city. "It's a nice apartment. Just three rooms, but lovely. It even has a terrace," she'd informed them that first day. And how long had she been living there? Jeanie had asked her, squeezing in the question before the Q&A with the celebrity granddaughter resumed ("And which one is your *best* friend?" "What's better, chocolate or vanilla?"). *Oh, a while,* her mother said, as if the answer wasn't Jeanie's business. And was she still working? Her mother gave her a hard look. *I'm forty-six years old. Why wouldn't I be working? What else would I be doing?*

Fifteen years had passed now since the shock of her mother at the door—ten since she had disappeared again—and even so, as Jeanie told Martin about it, her eyes filled. Crying with Martin had become a regular occurrence. Martin said sometimes he wondered if they didn't *try* to make themselves sad in each other's company. "Ourselves and each other, both," Jeanie corrected him. "Some people like to make each other laugh. We like to make each other cry. Don't you think that makes us deeper than most people?"

Now Martin said, "She was still working downtown? Selling curtains?"

"Yeah." Jeanie poured herself another glass of wine. She'd brought over a bottle and a pizza (*cut like a pie,* she now knew to say, *not into little squares, please*). "And you know what? I'd figured that. All along, I'd assumed she was still there, still going about her life, the same life she'd had before, except without me in it. The only part that felt like news to me was that she'd moved out of our house. But really, once I thought about it, it was like, *well, yeah, of course she did.* What did she need a whole house for once it was just her?"

"You stayed in your house after your daughter moved out."

"That's different. I like knowing my kid has a room there if she ever wants it."

Martin raised an eyebrow.

"I'm not saying I expect it. But a kid should always know there's somewhere she can go back to if she needs to."

His eyes filled. She hadn't even meant to but she'd made him sad.

"I mean, sometimes that isn't possible, I know. But if it is—that's all I'm saying. For me, it was easy. It was the path of least resistance, honestly."

Martin shrugged and drank his wine.

Jeanie ate a slice of pizza the way he had taught her to, folded into a wad of napkins that caught the grease. Finally he said, "So what happened after that? Did she come back the next Sunday?"

Oh, yes—that Sunday and every Sunday after it for two or three months. There were trips to the zoo and the botanical gardens, movies, shopping expeditions, restaurants. Then it was more like once a month. Then maybe once every three months. Then twice a year— by then Carrie was twelve—and her grandmother would keep her only for an hour or so, just long enough to go out for ice cream. But Carrie never complained. All that mattered to her was that now she had a grandma, just like all the other girls. "And I apologized a million times for having lied to her," Jeanie told Martin. "I told her that really it wasn't even a lie because I'd had no way of knowing if she *was* alive."

"That must have gone over well."

"Don't you start in on me now."

"Didn't she ask you *why* you and your mother hadn't talked for almost a decade? Didn't she ask your mother?"

"She didn't want to know. She didn't want to ruin things between them. That's what she told me later, when I told her the truth."

"And when was that?"

"Much later. After she was grown up. After—you know."

"After she told you she was pregnant?"

Jeanie nodded. All her life, she'd thought it would be devastating to her daughter when she told her—*if* she told her. But by the time she did, Carrie had already guessed. She hadn't brought it up herself, she said, for Jeanie's sake: "Why would I dredge all that up again for you?"

"Your mother was out of the picture again by then, I'm guessing?"

"Oh, yes. When Carrie was fourteen, 'Grandma Gwen' met 'a very nice man' and married him."

"And was he? Nice?"

"Who knows?"

"You never met him?"

"Once. She brought him around, they stayed for maybe ten minutes, and he didn't have much to say. But it didn't matter, because, soon after that, he retired with a good pension and they moved six thousand miles away. For a few years, there'd be an occasional postcard with a hula girl on it. A card to Carrie—Caroline—I mean. Not to me."

"Did Caroline write back?"

"Ha. She couldn't. No return address. Just like—" But she stopped herself from finishing the sentence.

"It's all right. That's old news."

"It's all old news now, isn't it?"

It was—but somehow, old or not, she and Martin talked about it. Talked about it, cried about it. She couldn't get over the way she found herself telling Martin things she hadn't thought about in years, things she'd never talked about to anyone. Almost since the first of her visits with him, once he had left the kids' place and gone home to his condo, she'd been telling him things she hadn't even known she was still thinking about, things she had not remembered until she heard herself talking about them.

She talked instead of smoking cigarettes—that was what she told herself. She was drinking more and eating more since she'd quit smoking, and she'd expected this. Everyone at work who used to smoke had warned her about it. Martin had too. But nobody had warned her about talking.

Martin's theory was that she had got it backwards: that years ago she'd started smoking to *keep* herself from talking, and now she was free to talk. That this was a good thing.

"Free to talk only to *you*," she told him. "What the hell kind of freedom is that?" But she said this with affection.

Martin grinned. "Hey, I just happen to be here. Also free—to listen."

He knew as well as she did that she saw people all day long. People at work. Her daughter, plenty. Also Jacob. She wasn't tempted to tell any of them about the trips downtown to her mother's store (that was how her parents had referred to it, as *her* store, and when she was very young she'd thought her mother owned the place—thought the "G" in "A & G Department Store" stood in for Gwendolyn, and wondered who "A" was). Her happiest memories of the years before her father left them were of her and her mother in the store amid the Lionel trains and marionette shows, and the showboat in children's shoes on six; on five, the coin and stamp shops, the music center, the bookshop where she was allowed to sit on the floor and read while her mother talked to her friend Marilyn, who worked there; on four, the rooms full of furniture arranged as if people lived in them, and the hallway full of mannequins in Victorian dress posed around a Victorian store counter.

"Your happiest memories of life with your father are of when he wasn't with you?"

Put that way—by Martin, of course—it sounded strange, sure. But once her father left, her mother seemed to lose all interest in her. She never took her downtown again. And Jeanie never set foot in A & G again after the last time her mother took her. "You know," she told Martin—her *machatin*, he called himself—"when they closed the place down at last, I celebrated."

"When was that?"

"You remember. Last summer. It was front page news."

"No, I mean when was the last time your mother took you?"

"How could I possibly remember that? Let me tell you what I do remember, though, about the store. I remember that when Carrie came home from one of her Sunday outings and told me that she and her grandmother had gone downtown to see Grandma Gwen's store, I felt as if I'd seen a ghost. Needless to say, everything had changed. I mean, I asked. I wanted to know all about the trains, the pet shop, the showboat—but all of that was gone. It was just a regular store by then. And Carrie said, 'It was pretty boring, actually.' I remember how pleased I was. Isn't that awful?"

"Not so awful," Martin said. Then, gently: "But Jeanie, you do remember when the last time would have been if she stopped taking you once your father left."

"You know how old I was when he left. I've told you that story. I was nine. I'd just started fourth grade."

"Yes, that's what I thought. Isn't that how old Caroline was when your mother showed up at your door?"

Martin was always pointing out things like this—coincidences, repetitions "with slight variations," situations that "might as well be metaphorical." When she objected to his psychoanalyzing her, or treating her life as if it were one of his novels, he apologized. He called it an occupational hazard.

He had been back in his own place for over a month now. Caroline visited with Harry every day; she brought him groceries once a week. Jeanie went over to the condo straight from work most nights (it was right on the bus line—no big deal, she told both her daughter and her *machatin*). She'd bring dinner or else fix something with the groceries Caroline had brought. Once or twice a week she'd try to coax him *out* to dinner, but he didn't want to go anywhere and insisted that there was no reason to—"not with you and your daughter catering to my every need." She thought of saying, "Then maybe we should both stop catering," but she was afraid that the threat wouldn't work, that he'd just take her up on it. He'd already said it wasn't necessary for them to check on him so often. He'd told them both that that he could manage on his own "as long as I don't lift anything heavy"—that was what the doctor had said (and Jeanie snorted when he told her this; she said, "Right, like you ever have"). She and Caroline had agreed to ignore his assurances that he didn't need their help. Until he felt completely like himself again, Jeanie told him every time he protested that they were overdoing it, this was how things were going to be. He might as well get used to it, she said.

"I'm used to it," he said. "I'm grateful for it."

"Then stop complaining and just enjoy the attention. It won't last forever."

"I don't know," he said. "If you're waiting for me to feel 'like myself,' it might have to."

"Don't be silly," Jeanie said. But she knew what he meant. He had changed. He was quieter now. His personality seemed smaller. *He* seemed smaller. And Caroline had told her he was still incontinent. (Martin never spoke of it, but Caroline took him to all of his follow-up appointments, taking notes and asking questions. She'd told Jeanie that this might go on for the next year, or maybe two. There was even a chance it would be permanent.)

He wasn't frail, exactly, but he wasn't hardy, either. He had not gone back to teaching yet—he had taken a leave of absence, with a tentative plan to return to the classroom in March, for spring quarter—and he wasn't driving. He said he didn't trust himself to drive (he'd never been good at it in the first place, he confessed, and this too was new: pre-cancer Martin would never have admitted there was anything he wasn't good at). He wasn't even walking more than a few blocks, and then only when Jeanie dragged him out of the condo.

He had, however, started writing again.

He told Jeanie this on a Tuesday night, in the new Vietnamese place three blocks from his building that she had persuaded him to accompany her to, telling him she wanted to broaden her "gastronomic horizons, just like you've been badgering me to."

"I haven't said that in some time, haven't you noticed? I'm a new man. I don't badger anymore. What do I care what you eat?"

"Well, you've made me care. There's no going back now." She had managed to convince him to get dressed and was attempting to help him into his coat. He shook her off.

"I don't need help."

"You can't have it both ways, Mister," she told him. "You can't both not need help *and* stay in this stuffy condo seven days a week, twenty-four hours a day."

"Professor," he said. "I'm proud of that title."

"Fine," Jeanie said. "You can't have it both ways, Professor. Now let's go."

Over bowls of beef broth and noodles, he told her that he had begun a new novel. He'd abandoned the one he was working on before what he referred to only as *the ordeal* (never *cancer*—and when anyone else uttered the word, he'd scowl and tell them not to be so melodramatic); in its aftermath he'd written nothing and had wondered, he told Jeanie, if it was the end. "The last time I'd been this little interested in writing, it occurred to me, were those last months of

2001. When it seemed like the world was coming to an end."

"Because of 9/11 or because that was when the kids moved in together? And when they drove out there and took the bird?"

He stared at her. "You are a hard woman." He dipped his spoon into his bowl, then paused before he lifted it to his mouth. "But you're right. It was all those things."

"And now?"

"Well, it seems that the world, once more, isn't coming to an end—my world, at any rate. Because although it's too soon to tell if it's going to be anything, over the past week I've written what would appear to be the first draft of a first chapter of something I'm actually interested in."

"Well, then," Jeanie said, "it must be about me, then."

Martin said, "It sort of is."

He wasn't smiling. "That's a joke, right?" Jeanie said.

He shrugged.

It had to be a joke. She thought about it as she picked up several strands of noodles with her chopsticks—under Martin's tutelage, she'd became quite the expert—and deposited them on her spoon, set a piece of beef atop the noodles, dipped the spoon to collect broth (Martin had demonstrated), and brought the spoon to her mouth. The food was delicious—or so *she* thought. Martin had pronounced it only "far from inedible" after his first spoonful. ("See?" she'd said. "There's the judgmental prick, the snob, the nothing's-ever-good-enough-for-me complainer we all know and love. You're *remarkably* like yourself.") She tried to figure out if she should be worried.

"Can I read it?"

"Sure. As soon as it's finished."

"And that will be when?"

"A while."

"Come on, Martin."

"Come on what? It takes a long time to write a novel."

"Tell me the truth. Are you really writing about me?"

"Let's say it's been inspired by you. Its protagonist shares some of your qualities—"

"Like what?"

"—and some of your background."

"What the hell does that mean?" But she didn't wait for him to answer that. "What's my name?" she said.

Now he grinned at her. He leaned over the table and sang, softly—not too badly, either—"*And she feeds you tea and oranges.*"

"Suzanne? You named me *Suzanne*? From the Leonard Cohen song?"

"Not *you*," Martin said. "This is a novel, not a biography. And I thought you'd be pleased. You like the song, don't you? I would've thought you would. And the name—"

"I love the song. It's my *favorite* song. It's my favorite song of all time." She felt lightheaded, breathless. "But I've never told you that. Have I?"

"No," he agreed. "You never have."

"And I never told you that Suzanne was almost Caroline's name."

"No, you never did."

"That's good. Because I've never even told her."

"Why not? It's a sweet name from a beautiful song."

"She wouldn't think it was sweet. She'd think it was stupid. I've never told her she was named for a different song, either. She'd hate it if she knew I'd named her for a song."

Martin sang—louder this time—"*Look at the night and it don't seem so lonely/We filled it up with only two.*"

"Martin, hush. I did not name her after a Neil Diamond song. What do you take me for?"

"The Hollies' song, then? *You were always something special to me/ quite independent, never caring.*"

"Stop singing. What are you, a jukebox? I didn't *name* her Caroline *or* Carrie." But he was still singing "Carrie Anne."

"Please stop."

He stopped. "So I guess you didn't name her after the 'mean old daddy' in that great Joni Mitchell song on *Blue*, either?"

"No. What I *named* her was Carolina."

Martin thought this over. "Oh, I get it," he said. "From the James Taylor song. That was a great favorite of my sister's. That whole album was—James's first, right? I was the one who had a record-player—Anna was only twelve—and she'd beg me to play it, over and over again, every second that our father wasn't home."

"I didn't even hear the song till later, on his *Greatest Hits*," Jeanie told him. Then: "Wait. Since when do you have a sister?"

"Since I was two years old."

"But you've never mentioned her. Jacob's never mentioned that he has an *aunt*."

"He doesn't really know her. It's not as if we're close. Anna and I."

"Or Jacob and you."

"Jeanie." He looked surprised.

"I'm sorry. That was mean. I just—oh, I don't know. If I had a sister…." But she couldn't think of a single way to finish that sentence. "Why aren't you close?"

"Jacob and I or Anna and I?"

"I said I was sorry, Martin. Where does Anna live? When was the last time you talked?"

"She lives in Washington, D.C. We talk occasionally. Mostly we write letters. We're not enemies, we're not estranged. We just don't see much of each other."

"But when you got sick—"

"I didn't tell her. And I wasn't even ever *sick*. It was just—"

"An ordeal, I know. But it's over now. So why don't you call her? Let her know what happened."

"Why is this of any interest to you?"

"I'm not interested. I'm jealous. All the rest of us are only children— me, our kids, our grandson."

"So far, our grandson."

"Martin. Call your sister. Invite her for a visit. I'd like to meet her. We can talk about James Taylor. I was only eight when that first album came out, but I caught up quick."

"You're out of your mind."

"Maybe. But not about this. Come on—it's not like the kids have a lot of family. They could use an aunt. And cousins, maybe? Does Anna have children?"

"Two daughters."

"*Martin*. Call her."

"All right, all right," he said. "I will." He paused. "And you can call your mother. Maybe they could visit at the same time."

Jeanie narrowed her eyes. "Sure. Good idea. We could ask Gloria to join in, too."

"Low blow," Martin said.

"Tit for tat," said Jeanie.

They sat in silence then, their pho cooling and their beers warming on the table between them. She took a sip of beer, wondering if he was thinking about his vanished wife. He never talked about her. Did he think of her?

Or he might be thinking about Jeanie's mother, whom he had never seen—whom he almost certainly would never see—but was probably writing about anyway in this book that he was writing about *her*.

A book about her! Or—what was it he had said? Sort of about her. Inspired by her. It made her feel…well, she didn't know what the word for it was. There was a word, she was sure of it. Caroline would have been able to snatch it out of the air, Jeanie was sure.

He had not intended to tell Jeanie anything about what he was writing. Not until after the book (if it indeed turned out to be a book) was done. And perhaps not even then, because by then *Suzanne Takes You*

Down might have veered so far from the stories she had told him there would be no point in his confessing that she had inspired it. He'd found that you could not predict when people would "recognize" themselves in characters drawn, no matter how generously, from what one called *real life*: people often didn't see themselves in those who had the greatest likeness to them, and they were forever claiming as themselves characters that there was no earthly reason for them to imagine had anything to do with them. (Gloria in particular had always seen herself everywhere but where he'd consciously made use of her.) He'd figured that the reckoning with Jeanie was at least three years into the future—if it came at all. And that if it did, she would get over it. So there was no reason to tell her anything about it now.

And in fact he had not planned to tell her—he had not planned to tell anyone—that he was writing anything. Just today both Jill Rosen and Caroline had asked him. Jill had asked the question in a breezy P.S. to an email ("*Nu?* Getting any work done yet?") that he had not answered, and Caroline, when she'd stopped by with Harry in the afternoon, had asked, more earnestly, "Are you feeling ready yet to get back to writing? Is there anything you need?" and he had smiled and said, "You mean, like a quill and a scroll you might pick up at the Giant Eagle along with a dozen eggs, some English muffins, and a bag of oranges?" It was possible that they'd conspired, that they were making him a "project." But whether he was writing or not was no one's business but his own.

Of course, it was Claire's business, literally so, and when *she* had asked, he'd lied. She had been calling once or twice a week, but several days ago was the first time since the ordeal that she had asked how "the new book" was going. He'd made the mistake last summer of telling her about the vengeful novel he'd begun—and she had said, "Good! Aren't you the one who likes to quote Alison Lurie quoting Philip Roth? 'Nothing truly bad can happen to us—it's all material'?" But he wasn't sure that he believed this anymore. Or if he ever really had, no matter how often he had said it. The bad things still *happened*, didn't they? He would put it differently, himself. He'd say *Thank God we are sometimes able to make some use of the dreadful things that happens to us—small consolation though this may be, to make art from sorrow, from loss. Others are not so fortunate.* But most likely Roth had never said it either. The line was from a work of fiction, Lurie's marvelous *Real People*, a sharp, slender novel set at an artists' colony she called Illyria—recognizably Yaddo. He recalled that he had bought Jill Rosen a copy of it at the Eighth Street Bookshop right before it closed, eons ago. (But he could not remember what she'd thought of it, or even if she'd ever told him that she'd read it.)

Claire had exercised great restraint in not asking him about his writing before this. She had been restrained about *Delilah*, too. She had kept his publisher away from him after the book tour they had planned for him had to be canceled, she sent him only the most unambiguously good reviews (none raves, but still none with cavils or caveats), and she never once asked how he felt about the book once it was out, as she'd asked about the others. When he told her about the letter from his sister, thanking him for his "failure to provide Delilah with a daughter" and mentioning how much more she enjoyed his writing when she was not "obliged to be on the lookout for examples of slander" (which he believed to be a joke, but who could tell?), Claire said, "Don't let her get to you. Anna's a pain in the ass and always has been."

So when she asked about his progress on the manuscript he had jokingly told her in July he meant to call *No Guts, No Glory*, it was churlish for him to have said, "I trashed it, it was shit," and then, when she said, "Oh, too bad. I thought it sounded like a lot of spiteful fun," he should not have gotten angry. He certainly should not have been so hard on her when she asked if he had started something new.

These days, Jeanie was the only one he felt like telling anything to.

And she apparently felt the same way. For weeks she had been coming over almost every evening to sit on his loveseat or his leather chair, her feet up on the ottoman that was wide enough for many pairs of feet, or at the table in what she (just like the realtor who had found the condo for him) referred to always as his "eat-in" kitchen—or, more and more often, at her urging, in a restaurant—and tell him things. She told him about hearing her parents arguing and about how even now she remembered things her mother had said then, all the things that she disliked about him, all the reasons it had been a terrible mistake to marry him. "Well, at least she *told* him," Martin said, and Jeanie said, "Yeah, but don't you think that's why he left? How many times can you listen to a list of everything that someone thinks is wrong with you before you don't want to hear it anymore?"

And even so her mother had been shocked when they "woke up one Sunday morning and he was just *gone.*" He'd snuck out while they were sleeping.

She told him about how hard she'd tried to please her mother after that, and all the ways she'd failed ("before the big one, the final failure after ten years' worth of failures"), and how she'd sworn she'd be a different kind of mother but how difficult that had turned out to be—"half the time I'd hear myself picking at Carrie, criticizing her friends, and I'd think, *What are you doing? This is what you* weren't *going to do,* and the other half I'd be trying so hard not to push her around, to just let her *be* the way my mother never let me be, that she'd think I didn't care."

She told him about the "crappy fake-Mexican mall restaurant" she'd worked at for years when Caroline was little, where all the waitresses had to wear neon-colored low-cut peasant blouses and big ruffled short skirts "like toddlers at a 1950s birthday party" and how terrified she'd been that when she was as old as she was now—"you know, completely ancient"—she would still be in that outfit, saying, "*Hola, me llamo Juanita!*" as she set down bowls of chips and salsa. She told him about the six months before *that* that she'd spent cleaning houses, how by comparison the restaurant hadn't seemed so bad at first. She told him about the many disgusting things she'd seen in other people's houses; she told him about disgusting things she'd heard, too, because no one worried about what they said in front of "the cleaning lady." The cleaning lady was invisible. More than two decades later, she told him, she still remembered what it felt like to have been invisible.

It seemed to Martin that he listened to Jeanie's stories as he had not listened to anything—to anyone—for years. But was he listening so closely and so carefully, he asked himself, *because* he'd started writing about what she told him? Or had he started writing this new novel just because, for once, he had been listening?

She had been carrying these memories, old hurts and grievances and grief, around with her her whole life in a large and bulging suitcase she had zipped up with great difficulty and then padlocked—then dragged behind her all these years, he thought, banging it along the sidewalk, just waiting for somebody to stop her and suggest she put it down, open it up. Lighten her load a little.

Maybe that was why he'd told her about what he had been writing. Maybe telling her this was his way of saying, *Nothing truly bad can have happened to you—not if it's all material.* Or even only, *See? Some use can be made of this. Small consolation though it may be.*

Was it a consolation?

It was hard to tell. But knowing that he might be making use of what she told him had not stopped her from talking. Or it was what had *kept* her talking. She might not know herself. And did it matter? She kept talking; he kept writing. Both of them were doing what they had to do. The only thing, it seemed, there was to do.

They were back at the Vietnamese place for dinner. It was an easy walk and the food was "good enough," Martin allowed. His hated its name, though. *Friend or Pho* "only encourages mispronunciation," he complained, as well as offering a "plainly illogical" choice. "It's not a good pun if it makes no sense."

He was coming back to himself, Jeanie thought.

Friend or Pho's owners, a family, recognized the two of them by now—it was their fourth visit—and tonight the father had brought them a plate of spring rolls on the house before they ordered anything. "Special because you are nice couple!" he said, and while Jeanie was trying to decide if it would embarrass him if she corrected his assumption (but if she didn't correct him now, they would have to be a "couple" every time they came in from now on, wouldn't they?), Martin said, "The lady has the great good fortune not to be my wife. We both thank you very much for your kindness." Sometimes he could be counted on to say precisely the right thing, with no effort at all.

They ordered beers, the "33" Exports Martin insisted on, the only Vietnamese beer on the menu. The elder daughter, hugely pregnant, brought them and took their order for pho. Jeanie poured her beer into a glass and took a sip as she watched the girl—she couldn't have been more than twenty-one—return to the kitchen. "Did I ever tell you," she asked Martin, "what my mother said when I told her I was pregnant and was going to keep the baby?"

"She said, 'You are throwing your whole life away.'"

"Jesus," Jeanie said. "You're like my own personal external hard drive, aren't you? It's like I'm offloading my entire life onto you."

Martin took a sip of beer. "What can I say? I remember things. Tool of the trade."

"Another 'occupational hazard,' then."

He smiled. "Exactly."

"Well, do you know why that was such a lousy thing to say?"

"You mean, besides the obvious? The implication that raising your daughter would be a waste of your life?"

"Yes. Besides that."

"I'll bite. Why?"

"She was telling me that she had thrown *her* life away."

"What makes you think that?"

"Because she was pregnant with me when she married my dad. And I already knew that—I'd worked that out long before. Before he left us. I mean, I knew how to count. But what I didn't know, till then, was how she felt about it."

"Are you sure about that? She might just have been angry when she said it."

"Oh, she was angry, all right. But if she was *only* angry—if she wanted to provoke a fight—she would have come out with it. She would have told me that I'd ruined her life. No, the thing is, I don't think she meant to let me know she felt that way. Which is how I figured out it must have been the truth. Because she wasn't trying to fight with me. She was trying to convince me not to have the baby, and I couldn't be convinced. I *wanted* the baby. I kept telling her that. But she wasn't thinking about me. She was thinking about herself, about how much better her life would have been if I'd never been born."

Their pho came—the younger daughter brought it, the unpregnant, teenaged one. Jeanie wondered if the older one was married. Probably. She wondered which had come first, the marriage or the pregnancy. She wondered if she loved the father of the baby. If she even liked him.

Jeanie never let herself think of her mother as a girl, even younger than *she* had been when she'd gotten pregnant. But her mother had married the boy who had knocked her up. By the seventies, you didn't have to. Although Martin and Gloria had gotten married in the seventies when Gloria was pregnant. So they must have been in love, unlike her parents. In love like Caroline and Jacob. For the briefest flicker of an instant, she felt sorry for her mother. But not *that* sorry—and then it was gone.

She watched Martin eat for a few minutes. Then she said, "Would you tell me something? Were you happy when you found out Gloria was pregnant?"

"Honestly?"

"Of course honestly."

"I don't remember. That's pretty bad, right? Or pretty strange, at least."

"It's so strange, I don't believe you. We just established that you remember everything."

"Not everything. Not this."

"Do you remember if Gloria was happy?"

"I don't know. I don't trust my memories of Gloria anymore."

"But did you think she was happy at the time?"

"I did, yes."

"You remember that. So maybe she was. Maybe she got unhappy later."

"Maybe so. We'll never know, will we?"

She took up her own chopsticks and spoon at last. But she just held them in her hands—she didn't use them. "I don't think my mother was ever happy," she said. "But how could she have been? She married someone she didn't even like because she thought she had to. Then she wished she hadn't. She spent her days on her feet selling drapery and her nights telling the guy she'd married how much she hated him and why. And then he left and she was all alone with me—the one she'd thrown her life away for." She dipped her chopsticks into the bowl and pushed noodles and beef and vegetables around aimlessly. She wasn't hungry, really.

Martin noticed. He stopped eating too. He said, "Tell me something, Jeanie. Did she seem happy when she came back—when she showed up unannounced, all those years after she'd kicked you out?"

"I have no idea." She had to look away. He was studying her too intently. "I wasn't paying attention to whether she was happy or not. I wasn't paying attention to her at all. I was thinking about myself. And about Carrie. And I didn't *care* if my mother was happy." She picked up her beer and took a long sip, set it down, and picked it up again. Finally she said, "Later on—you know, before she disappeared again, before she broke her granddaughter's heart—she *said* she was happy. She announced it, like it was supposed to be a challenge to me. 'I'm happy now. I've met a nice man and I'm happy.' Well, good for you, I thought. Have a great life. Don't let the door hit you on the behind on your way out."

"Can I ask you something else?"

"About my mother? I have nothing else to say about her."

"No. About your father."

"I've already told you everything I know about him."

"I don't think you have. For instance, did you ever hear from him again after he left? Did your mother?"

"No. He died."

"He *died*? Right after he left you and your mother?"

"Not right after. Ten years after. But we didn't hear from him, not once, during those ten years."

"Wait—ten years? He died when you were nineteen?"

"November 1979. A week before Thanksgiving. Yeah, I was nineteen."

Martin was staring. "Caroline was born the following August."

"So?"

"So your father died and then you got pregnant?"

"Oh, Christ, Martin," Jeanie said. "You're not going to trick me into telling you there's some connection between my father I hadn't seen for ten years dropping dead and my going to a bar and getting drunk and doing something stupid."

"Something stupid that worked out so well. Something stupid with a happy ending."

"Stop it," she said. "Stop making a story out of my life. Real life doesn't work that way. Things just happen sometimes. Not everything means something."

"Everything does mean something," Martin said. "In fact"—he raised his glass—"let's drink to that. Let's drink to everything meaning something."

But Jeanie had finished her beer. She didn't want to drink to that, anyway.

Even so, Martin ordered two more "33"s. He drained what was left of his first one and said, "Why don't you tell me the story of that night—the one when you did something stupid and then, just by coincidence, nine months later our grandson's mother arrived on the scene?"

"That part wasn't a coincidence, obviously."

"Only the part where you went out and got drunk and slept with someone right after you heard that your old man was dead."

"It wasn't right after."

"Was it before?"

"It wasn't before."

Their beers arrived. It was the son who brought them, or perhaps the pregnant daughter's husband. Martin poured for both of them, then held up his glass and motioned for Jeanie to pick hers up too. They drank, at his insistence, to the meaning of everything. Jeanie said, "I'm crossing my fingers behind my back."

"It's not a promise, Jeanie, it's a toast. And I can see your fingers."

"It's a metaphorical promise. I'm crossing my metaphorical fingers."

"Very nice." He smiled. "Okay. Now tell the story."

"She said she'd never meant for it to be some great big secret," Caroline told Jill. "She said she'd always figured she'd tell me when I was 'old enough'—fourteen, maybe. Sixteen at the latest. It would be a cautionary tale. She'd know when the right time came."

"But then she didn't tell you."

"No, because I was such a good girl, I didn't need a cautionary tale. I *was* a cautionary tale. So then, she says, it began to seem like telling me would just make her look stupid by comparison to me—'and you already thought I was an idiot,' she says, which isn't true. I can't believe she thought that."

Jill made a sound that could either have been sympathy or disapproval. They were having coffee. Caroline had brought Jill two new poems; Jill had brought Harry a Matchbox car—a yellow taxi—even though Caroline had told her that she didn't have to keep bringing him presents, that it was too much. "I should be bringing *you* presents," she had told her the last time they'd met for coffee.

"You bring me poems to read," Jill said.

"That's why I should bring you presents."

"Oh, Caroline," Jill said. But what did that mean? She was so inscrutable—she was as hard to read as the most opaque, the most beautifully difficult, of poems. (And you could no more ask her to explain herself than you could ask a poem by, say, Hart Crane. Or Lyn Hejinian.) Today Jill had surprised her, though. When she took the Matchbox taxi from her purse and handed it to Harry, she'd said, "Caroline, please understand, I *like* to give him things. I like the look on his face when he sees me, when he knows there's going to be a little something. It gives me so much pleasure. It's splendid to be reminded how little it takes, really, to make someone happy."

Now Caroline said, "So, you know how she always told me he was nobody? My father? He was 'just some guy'?"

"The tequila drinker," Jill said. "Tall. Blond. Long hair. So who does he turn out to be?"

"That's the thing. He really *was* nobody—she wasn't lying to me. I mean, she didn't even know him. He was just some guy with a guitar passing through town. The whole story couldn't be more cliché. It's not even a *story*—it's just, like, an anecdote you can tell in about two minutes. That's how long it took her to tell me."

"What made her tell you at all? Surely she doesn't think you're in need of a cautionary tale *now*. Unless there's something you're keeping from me?" Jill tore open a sugar packet and shook it out into her cappuccino. "You aren't in danger of getting knocked up by some rocker on tour, are you?"

"The guy wasn't even that. He was just an aspiring folkie who sang covers, she says. And a few half-assed originals."

"And she slept with him anyway?"

"She said the covers were really good."

Jill laughed.

Caroline wanted to tell her it wasn't funny, but it *was* sort of funny—she started laughing too. And then Harry started. His laugh was so much like hers she was never sure if he was mimicking her or was actually amused.

"We shouldn't be laughing," Caroline said.

"What else are you going to do about a story like this? Cry?"

"My mother cried a little when she told me." Caroline had been afraid she might cry, too. That was why she was trying the story out on Jill, before she told Jacob. Or Nat. Anyone. Of everyone in the world, she was least likely to cry in front of Jill.

"Seriously, though, why did she tell you, after all this time? She must have had a reason." Jill took a sip of her cappuccino, frowned, then tore open a second sugar packet and stirred its contents in.

"She told me because two nights ago she told Martin. She felt guilty that he knew and I didn't."

Jill had brought her mug to her lips again but she set it down, hard, without drinking from it. "She told Martin about your father before she told you? Why would she tell him at all?"

"Apparently they tell each other everything."

Harry was banging his plastic cup—empty, luckily—on his highchair tray. "Don't bang, Harry," Caroline said.

"Jill banged."

"Well, there you go," Jill said. "I banged." She took a sip from her mug and made a face. "Too sweet."

"Eat your cookie," Caroline told Harry. "And no banging, no matter what Jill does."

"Sorry," Jill said. "So, what long-kept secrets do you suppose Martin is unburdening himself of, then?"

"Who knows? But whatever they are, at least he can be sure she isn't writing about them. I, on the other hand, can now look forward to reading a fictionalized account of my own conception."

"Do you think your mother realizes that?"

"I think my mother would be thrilled by it."

"*Vroom*," Harry said. "*Vroom vroom*." He was racing his taxi cab and two other Matchbox cars (also presents from Jill, from other coffee dates) around the highchair tray. He made one of them—the convertible that was the color of the big chair in his grandfather's condo—ride over his cookie, in the center of the tray.

"A little quieter, Harry, okay?" Caroline said. "I'm trying to talk to Jill. And remember what we said about public places?"

"We be very quiet!" Harry shouted. "Pubbic paces shhh." He put his finger to his lips.

"That's right," she said. "Listen to how quietly I am speaking to Jill." And to Jill, in hardly more than a whisper, she said, "So, here's what she remembers. He was playing at some club. She was out drinking with friends. He opened his second set with a cover of a song off a new album she loved, which wasn't a very well-known album, and she just—I don't know, it was just one of those moments, she says. She thought he was singing it *to* her. And here's the weirdest thing. She remembers hardly anything about the guy but she remembers the song, a song called 'Hymn to Her.' Not the Pretenders song that came later—she wanted to make sure I knew that, as if I care, as if it makes any difference to me which 'Hymn to Her' it was."

"*I Can See Your House from Here.*"

"You can what?" Caroline looked out the plate glass window they were sitting by. "We're like half a mile away. How is that even possible?"

"No. The name of the album that 'Hymn to Her' was on. It was Camel's *I Can See Your House from Here.*"

Caroline blinked at her. "Well, you certainly are full of surprises."

"Everyone is," Jill said. "I guess your mother and I listened to some of the same music in our youth. Camel was a good prog rock band."

"My mother listened to folk music."

"Well, it would seem, not *only* to folk music. Goodness, Caroline—don't look so shocked. So you don't know everything about her. Nobody knows everything about anybody. Seriously—is there anyone who knows *everything* about you?"

"I guess not," Caroline said. But she didn't mean it. Didn't Jacob? Wouldn't Harry, eventually? She wondered if she'd ever get to the point where it felt okay to disagree with Jill. Where it would not seem disrespectful or ungrateful or just…wrong.

"And that's it?" Jill said. "That's the whole story?"

"About the night my mother met my father? My 'so-called father,' as she says? I told you, it's not even a story. She stuck around after he finished playing. She talked to him. They went somewhere. They drank some more. They talked some more. He drank tequila. She drank beer. The rest, as my mother says, is history."

"It's kind of a sad story, isn't it?"

"More than kind of," Caroline said. She hadn't realized how much she had hoped Jill would see it that way, too. "She was nineteen and drunk. She was flunking out of college—she'd transferred that fall from Tech to State—and she was miserable. She hadn't wanted to go to college in the first place and she *really* hadn't wanted to transfer. But in those days she did whatever her mother told her to do. Well, you know, until she didn't." Caroline paused. She hadn't understood, until she'd heard herself say it, that the night she was conceived was the night of her mother's first rebellion. Her only rebellion, in a way, since everything else—deciding to keep the baby (to keep *her*) and giving up on school, living on her own, raising her child by herself—had flowed from that, from that one night. And now Caroline remembered something else. She said it out loud, to Jill: "*And* her father had just died. She hadn't seen him since he'd walked out on her and my grandmother years before. But she'd just heard the news that he'd died of a heart attack in Toledo. He was in the middle of selling somebody a life insurance policy. That's ironic, right?"

"Maybe only if he didn't have a life insurance policy himself."

"Apparently he didn't. Since he and my grandmother had never divorced, but Gwen got nothing. My mother got nothing."

Jill was silent for a moment. "She really never saw him again?"

"Her father?"

"*Your* father. The guy with the guitar."

"She never did. For a while, she says, even after I was born, she checked the listings for the clubs in town, looking for him, until it began to seem pathetic—the stupid lovestruck groupie. And she wasn't lovestruck. She wasn't even sure what she would do if she did find out he was playing somewhere around here. Go to his show, go up to him and say, 'Hey, remember me?' She figured he *wouldn't* remember. That this had just been something he did."

"He might have wanted to know that he had a daughter."

"A daughter—*God*. I don't feel like his daughter."

"Of course you don't," Jill said. "But it's odd, though, really, that he never came back through Kokosing if that was his life—traveling around to clubs, playing good covers and bad originals, sleeping with the local girls."

"For all she knows, my mother says, he gave up music."

"Or else she was wrong and his own songs *were* good. Maybe she just couldn't tell. Maybe he went on to be too big to play little clubs in the Midwest. Maybe he got famous. But if he did turn out to be famous, you'd never know—*she'd* never know—because, let's remind ourselves of this, she says she doesn't remember his name."

"That doesn't sound plausible, does it?"

"Her not remembering his name? No, it doesn't."

"I meant that he went on to be successful."

"That too," Jill said. "You know, if you knew his name, a quick Google search would tell you if he's out there making music after all these years."

"But I don't, because she doesn't."

"She looked for his name in the paper when you were a baby."

"She remembered it then, she said. She doesn't remember it now. I asked her how that was possible. She said, 'I might've gone out of my way to forget it.' She says his first name was a really common one, like Jack or Mike or Bill. And that he had some kind of nickname. Like 'Happy Jack' or 'Smilin' Bill.'"

"*Like* that?"

"She says she isn't sure."

"I understand that's what she says. What I'm wondering is whether you believe her."

"I don't know. Maybe. Maybe she remembers but doesn't want to tell me because she doesn't want me to do a Google search and find out that he's, I don't know, just some boring middle aged guy who sells refrigerators. Or life insurance. Or that he's a drug addict, or a criminal."

"Or dead," Jill said.

Caroline felt tears spring to her eyes. "Right," she said. "Or dead."

"Oh, God," Jill said. "I'm sorry. That was a dreadful thing to say."

"No, it's fine. It's nothing. My mother's right. He was just some guy. It doesn't matter what his name is. Was. It doesn't matter if he *is* dead. It didn't matter to my mother when her father died and she had *known* him." She picked up her mug and drank the rest of her coffee, quickly. It was bitter. And it was cold now, too. She'd been training herself to drink her coffee black, without sugar, like a grownup, the way Jacob and his father did. But she hated it. "Can we talk about something else?"

"All right," Jill said. She looked as if there might be something she wanted to say but then instead of saying it, she decided to say something else. "So, do you think Martin knows that we all know he's started a new book?"

That wasn't what she really wanted to know, Caroline felt sure. But since there was no way to know what her real question was, she answered the one she had been asked. "Probably," she told Jill, "since even his agent knows now. He was trying to keep it a secret from her until he felt ready to show her any of it, but after my mother told me and I told you and Jake, Jake told Claire Alter—that's Martin's agent. He didn't know she didn't know. I had told him not to tell his father that my mother had told me, but I didn't think to tell him not to tell anyone else. I forgot there *was* anyone else. So the last time he talked to Claire, he said something about Martin's new novel, which he assumed she knew about, and Claire said, '*What* new novel?' And Jake and I can't imagine that she wouldn't have said something to Martin about it. He didn't feel like he could tell her not to."

"You're making me dizzy. I don't understand why Jacob was talking to his father's agent in the first place."

"Oh, you know, she's his Auntie Claire."

"His aunt? Martin's agent is related to him?" Jill looked bewildered.

"No, not really. It's just that they were close when Jacob was growing up."

"And they still are?"

"Well, he hadn't talked to her in years, but she called him the day after Martin's surgery. Martin had promised her he'd call when it was over, and when a whole day passed and he still hadn't called her and he wasn't answering his cell phone, she got worried and tracked us down. And she and Jacob had a good conversation once they got past the prostatectomy and the pathology report. When he hung up he told me he hadn't known he'd missed her until she told him how much she'd missed him. Now they talk all the time. She's the closest thing to an aunt he has. Or, you know, an uncle or a cousin or anything."

"But doesn't Martin have an actual sister?"

How on earth did Jill know this when she hadn't? "He does, yes, as it turns out. But Jacob hasn't seen her since he was a child, since his grandfather's funeral. She and Martin have a 'difficult' relationship, apparently. But my mother says she made him call her."

"She did, did she? They really *are* tight, aren't they, then? I'm glad Martin has such a good friend. He seemed so lost when he first moved here." But she did not sound glad, or sympathetic. Caroline longed to ask her why, but she didn't dare. "Now Jacob will have two aunties," Jill said. "Which means you will, too."

It was possible she was being sarcastic. Still, Caroline said, "I will, yes. We all will—Harry too."

"And you're happy about this."

"I am. What can I tell you? I'm a sucker for family."

"That's only because you haven't had one," Jill said, and though Caroline would have sworn—she would have placed a big bet on it—that there was not a single chance that this would ever happen in Jill's presence, suddenly she found that she was crying.

She stood up so abruptly she banged into the little café table. The mugs and spoons jumped and all their crumpled napkins and Jill's empty sugar packets slid off the table onto the floor. Caroline scooped up the toy cars and Harry's plastic cup and dropped them into her big purse. "Come on, sweet pea," she told him through tears, "it's time to go home and make dinner."

Jill started to speak but Caroline said, "Really, we should go. It's late." She lifted Harry out of the highchair and set him on her hip. "Thanks for the coffee and the toy. Oh, and Harry's cookie. I'll get the coffee next time." She was almost to the door when Jill called out, "How's Wednesday? For next time?"

It was so unlike her that Caroline almost turned around. Jill wasn't *eager*—that was not her style. But she didn't turn. She called back, "Not Wednesday, sorry—I've got a doctor's appointment with Martin. Soon, though. I'll give you a call." And before Jill could say anything else, she fled.

Outside, as she hurried with him to the car, Harry reached for her face. "Mama crying," he said. "Why Mama crying?"

But she couldn't tell him. She didn't know.

The fatherless women. The motherless men.

The conversation with her young friend had set Jill spinning, had sent her to her desk. When her own father had died, she had made no attempt to write about the loss. What was there to write? Her grief had caught her by surprise. She was too young to have given any thought to how she'd feel about the death of either of her parents—and if she had thought about it, she was sure, she would not have supposed she would be so laid low. She was as much shaken by her grief as she was grieved by his sudden death.

But all these years later, the day after seeing Caroline and her sweet little boy, she was at her desk early in the morning, thinking—writing— about it. Not only her own loss but others. Her own mother's father—the grandfather she'd never known—had died just as suddenly as hers, when her mother was only seventeen. And Jill had heard about this all her life. How was it she had never spared a thought—a line—for it before?

(But she knew how, she thought: the same way she'd kept herself from worrying about her mother after her own father died—the way she avoided *any* thoughts that undermined her irritation with her.)

The fatherless women don't close/ranks, she wrote, they break them. One pulls/rank, and then another breaks/the bank. They brake for grief./They rank their losses.

No—*their wrank losses.*

No. That was too much.

But then it was all too much. Losses upon losses.

She thought of Jacob Lieb—his vanished mother. And Jacob's father, whose mother had already been gone for years when she'd first met him at Yaddo a quarter of a century ago. He had dedicated his first book to her: *to the memory of Lila Bernstein Lieberman, with love and sorrow.* And only pages into his most recent, *The Greater Delilah*, it was plain to Jill that he was still in mourning for her.

> *The butcher was in a fury always. Delilah bent to his will—what choice did she have? The sons grew up, grew tall. Handsome boys. Intelligent. "I'm sorry, Ma," they*

said, one after the other. They kissed her, whispered so the
butcher could not hear them: "I would take you with me if
I could."

If she had not remembered that Martin and his father's relationship had been at least as troubled as hers with her mother, the portrait of Delilah's husband—*a surprisingly old-fashioned villain in his nearly unrelenting viciousness as the titular character recalls her marriage and her sensitive twin sons their painful childhoods,* the Sunday *Times* reviewer said—would have reminded her. The novel's twins (*a signature move of Lieberman's,* the reviewer noted, which Jill thought was unfair: there was a pair of twins in just one other of his novels) had afforded him this time the opportunity to reimagine his life absent his long marriage—for while one sensitive twin married young and soon produced a daughter, Lila (named, in defiance of tradition, after the book's matriarch, still alive in her late nineties in this version of the story), the other son remained unmarried, happily so. Both twins were successful artists: the married one, a photorealist; the happily unmarried one, an abstract expressionist turned conceptual and installation artist in his middle age. Both artist-sons despised their father, whom Martin killed off young.

She could not think of Martin's fictional twins, Morty and Bart Stein, without thinking of Tomas's real-life ones—but she did not want to think of Tereza and Katerina Vítámvás now, and so she banished them for the moment. She thought instead of Martin's unforgiven father, turning the page of her legal pad and wrote half-lines, phrases, words—*sins of the father* and *you can lie back now (Plath)* and *mother, another, other.* She thought of Jacob's sternness toward Martin in the wake of his mother's desertion. She thought about—she wondered—what little Harry might someday be unable or unwilling to forgive *his* father for.

Curled up at her feet, her dog groaned in his sleep.

There was always something one could not forgive. Or that one *would* not forgive. What was it that enabled the forgiving of the unforgivable?

Grace, or mercy? Goodness? Or was there a trick to it—a way of making what was indefensible invisible? Not forgiving but forgetting.

Two hours later she had gone as far as she could. As she laid down her pen beside the yellow legal pad, she thought of something Caroline had said to her before Jacob had told her who his father was, when she knew only that he wasn't speaking to him—that her new boyfriend had purposefully estranged himself *from his own father—honestly, can you believe that?*

He doesn't know how lucky he is to have *a father.*

She remembered that *she* had said something like, "Give him time. Perhaps he'll work it out." It was the sort of thing one said to a student who has revealed too much during office hours. (She had not yet been introduced to Jacob. If she had been, in those early weeks of their romance, she wondered even now if she would have known him immediately as her old friend Martin's son.)

She picked up the pages Caroline had given her yesterday—typed drafts of two new poems. The one on top was called "Overwords" and began:

> *Let me ask you this—about those words you murmured.*
> *Was that prayer?*
> *They were like birds I want to know the names of, but I*
> *don't have a prayer.*

Jill glanced down the page. The word *prayer* was repeated often enough so that she could see the poem was meant to be a variation of a ghazal. It ended:

> *I try my best, on wing, on prayer—but even*

As I watch you, the same

Way I watch myself, I can't
Tell how ordinary

Slips free and takes
Flight. Poor me, I say—I cry, I rail—I never was
much of a prayer.

A difficult form, even when you let go of—as Caroline had let go of—
many of its strictures. She was glad to see her trying something new,
something hard.

She would call her, Jill thought, and make things right with her.
If indeed they weren't right. If Caroline did not call her. She'd give her
some time. The day after tomorrow, after Martin's doctor's appointment?
It provided an excuse, however slim, to make the call—she could ask
how it had gone.

There was something touching about Caroline's accompanying
him to all his doctor's visits, sitting with him when his blood was
drawn, taking her earnest notes when the urologist made his various
pronouncements. Was Martin sufficiently grateful? It would be quite
like him for him to take it as his due.

She looked at the second poem, a longer one—fifteen free verse
tercets. It was called "Any Which Way," and it began:

A deck of cards like a road you've sliced right
through the air, not long but winding—which
is the least I can say about it—and you,

with your invisible wings spread wide and so far
up above the earth so high, a diamond twinkling
in the inky night, leaving this earth now, again.

The dog, Phil, stretched and moaned under her desk. Dreaming. Jill set her bare feet on his back. Even in his sleep, now that he was getting older, it calmed him to be reminded of her presence. Or it calmed her, to imagine she was calming him.

Yes, a call after Wednesday's doctor's visit was a good idea. But she might hear from Caroline before then. And if she didn't—well, she might not be able to make herself wait until Wednesday evening. There was something she wanted to talk about, had planned to talk about when they'd met for coffee yesterday—it was why she had requested that they meet—but even before Caroline had begun to tell her story (the story that was a not a story), Jill had wondered, hesitated. The girl was young enough to be her daughter, and it was not so long ago that she had been her student. They were friends now, yes—but still. Did she really mean to ask her for advice?

Then the chance to ask was lost, once the story Jeanie Forester had told Martin—her new best friend, it seemed—then at long last told her daughter, who understandably could think of nothing else, was underway. But now Jill was resolved. Perhaps not to *ask*, but to talk things through. With whom else could she talk this through? Only with Tomas. But it was Tomas she needed to talk about.

Caroline was aware that she and Tomas had for years now been corresponding—and when they had begun, after the many emails that had passed between them, to talk on the phone as well, Jill had told Caroline that too. She told no one else but Phil—to whom, each time she hung up the phone after a long talk with Tomas, she would say, holding his face close to hers, "What do you make of that, my friend?" and he would lick her cheeks and nose, which made her laugh and feel a little less uneasy. And when Tomas's wife had left him and the children, she had been so distraught she had called Caroline at once.

No one else knew anything about him. She had somehow found herself, at this late stage of life, without friends her own age. Without friends among her colleagues. Only Martin, who was both her own age and a colleague. But it had never even crossed her mind to speak to him of Tomas—to speak to him of anything of consequence. She remembered speaking of Tomas to Martin all those many years ago. A painful memory. There was some consolation in her certainty that Martin had forgotten what she'd told him—that Martin had forgotten everything.

When he had first approached her with the notion of securing a position for him at KS, how afraid she had been that she would allow herself to be charmed by him once again. That she would not be able to *prevent* herself from being charmed. She had seen that this was possible four years before, when he had visited the campus for a reading at her invitation. She remembered that she had invited Caroline and one of her friends to join them for drinks after the reading *because* she was charmed—she wanted to break the spell.

(Oh, how very long ago this now seemed!)

But it was easier than she could have guessed to hold him at bay once he joined her department. She was always pleasant to him; she never refused an offer of lunch or a drink. It had been a coup for her department—for the university—to have brought the great Martin Lieberman onto the faculty, and her role in his hiring had caused her own stock to go up. He was doing good work, too. He'd surprised himself (he had surprised her, too), taking to teaching as he had. But neither her gratitude for the new appreciation shown her by her colleagues and her Chair and Dean, nor the hard work Martin put in in the classroom (which she could see for herself was paying off, as students who had taken one of Martin's classes came to hers better-prepared), had altered her resolve to keep him at arm's length. Nor had the crisis in his health.

Ah. She could not call Caroline—she could not use the excuse of asking about Martin's checkup.

She would simply have to wait for Caroline to call.

Monday afternoon and evening came and went. The phone rang

once late Monday night, but it was Tomas—who also emailed twice on Tuesday, once in the morning and once in the afternoon. She did not respond until that evening. It had been a busy day, teaching two classes of her own, meeting with students in her office, then observing a class taught by the Visiting Assistant Professor who'd taken over Martin's workshops—a kid just out of grad school with a very smart and funny first book, one he'd published as a second-year MFA student. (He was cocky and rather a know-it-all—and sometimes, of course, as she stood talking with him in the hallway of their building, she would think of Martin as he'd been when they had met at Yaddo. When everyone but she disliked him so. She wondered if this young man were as much despised as Martin had been—and if there was anyone who liked him anyway, who felt she saw the "real" him as his detractors didn't.)

She emailed Tomas, read a batch of student poems, and wrote up the teaching observation. The class had been fine, if uninspired (it was obvious the young professor was mimicking his own recent teachers— she remembered very well that sort of coolly detached teaching by bored, well-known writers). The students, who had registered believing that the course would be taught by the wildly popular Professor Lieberman, had seemed to Jill restless and inattentive (this had tempered her own judgment with a modicum of sympathy). She kept the observation letter vague, and noted graciously that the young man's task was, "as we all are aware, unenviable."

All the while, she waited for the phone to ring, but Caroline did not call. Tomas would not call tonight, either (not after he'd read her email, in which she had reminded him, in a gently worded postscript, that she'd asked him to give her some breathing room while she thought things through).

She had nearly wept while telling Caroline about Tomas's wife. She had left him for another man, his daughter Nina's soccer coach—a detail that seemed too banal to be true, and yet there it was. Tomas would run into his estranged (and soon enough ex-) wife whenever he went into town—their tiny Iowa town, where it was impossible *not* to run into everyone one knew. The soccer coach's arm would be around the mother of his children's shoulders; her arm would be around his waist. She had left her children. She had left her life.

"At least Tomas knows why she left him," Caroline had ventured. "I know it's not much, but it's something. At least he doesn't have to spend the rest of his life wondering."

Jill had responded sharply, "At least Martin's child was grown."

That had been unkind, she'd recognized as soon as she had said it. She *should* have wept—she should have allowed herself to weep.

But Caroline had understood. "I know you must be very sad for Tomas," she had said then, softly. "I know how deeply hurt you must be on his behalf."

How was it, Jill had wondered then—she had wondered often since—that her young friend understood so well how hard it was for her to express her sorrow in the usual way? Jill was well aware that many of her colleagues thought of her as lacking feeling, as remote, unsympathetic, cold. Well, her own mother had accused her of this. "You were always a hard-hearted girl." And her fourth grade teacher, Mrs. Greenman, had once annotated her report card—with its uniform column of *E*s for excellence in every subject—with a note: *Jill is very bright and reads/writes far above her grade level, but I am concerned by her indifference toward the other children and her overall demeanor (unfriendliness?).*

There had not been so many people in her life who understood her properly. Martin, once. Tomas, both then and now again. And—somehow—Caroline Lieb.

Who perhaps was not angry or hurt now. Perhaps she was only busy. She had her hands full with the baby, with her husband's father. With her husband, too. Were they still seeing the marriage counselor? She should have asked her. If Caroline called (*when* Caroline called), she would ask how she and Jacob were getting along. She would ask before she spoke of her own life.

The ex-wife had left the soccer coach soon after she and Tomas were divorced. Perhaps he was not the reason, after all, that she had left him. Perhaps he had been no more than a convenient excuse (perhaps she, like Gloria Lieberman, had her own reasons to which no one—or at least no one in her family—would ever be privy). It didn't matter. To Tomas and the children, it made no difference why she'd left, only that she had. She had relinquished her claim on the children. Tomas never saw her anymore at the post office, the bank. The children never heard from her. She had vanished from all of their lives.

And Caroline knew all of this. At each new turn of the unfolding story, Jill had confided in her. What Caroline did not know was that Tomas had invited her to visit, to come to the farm and see him "in real life, after all these years" and meet his children. And that she had gone. The invitation and the visit had both taken place during the aftermath of Martin's surgery, when Caroline had been preoccupied. Jill had told her only that she was going out of town for a few days and asked if she might leave Caroline's phone number with the student who was looking after Phil, in case of an emergency. She implied without saying that the trip was for a reading. Caroline had asked no questions—her mind was on her father-in-law.

But Jill had meant to tell her afterwards. Not only meant to—she had wanted to. Every time they got together, every time they spoke on the phone, she believed she would tell Caroline about the visit, about what had happened between her and Tomas.

She should have been prepared for the escalation of their relationship. Caroline would have said that. *After hundreds of thousands of written words between you, after so many hours on the telephone, didn't you know?* But how could she have known? She could not have known how she would feel about him more than twenty-five years after she'd last seen him. She could not have known how she would feel about his children.

Somehow she could never speak of any of it. She would tell herself that this time, each time, she would—and then she could not. She felt foolish. She felt shy. As the weeks and months passed, as she and Tomas grew still closer, talking several times a day, telling each other everything about their lives, planning another visit—planning a series of visits— she wanted to tell Caroline and she could not.

And now this.

As little as she'd been able to ready herself for what seeing him after so many years would stir in her, she was less prepared for the question he'd posed on the phone last Saturday. As soon as she'd hung up, she had called Caroline without giving herself time to change her mind. She asked if they could meet—was she free for dinner or perhaps a drink that evening? She was not. An old friend ("You remember Natalie, I'm sure," but Jill did not) was coming over. But she could meet for coffee the next day. Caroline was cheerful and distracted, glad to make the date—Jacob had left for the West Coast and would not be back until the middle of the week—and Jill, who had been certain her voice would betray her, certain Caroline would ask her what was wrong, agreed to wait. It would seem that she had spent too many years perfecting her mask of sangfroid. She had no idea how to unmask herself. Tomas had not waited for her to do so—he had unmasked her. For himself, and for his children.

On Wednesday, a non-teaching day, she was at home. She left the house only to walk the dog. If not for Phil, there were many days she would have remained indoors, would not have seen anyone or anything aside from what was hers—the contents of her house, her own face in the mirror. All day Wednesday she talked to the dog, she petted him. She worked on her new poem. She read her students' work and made notes for them. Too many days had passed, she thought, without a call from Caroline. Perhaps Caroline had not forgiven her. Perhaps she was tired of excusing her thoughtlessness, her unintended cruelty. Her mask of equanimity.

She answered emails from her students. She read a few pages of the novel, Coetzee's *Elizabeth Costello*, that she had been reading with pleasure before Tomas's call. She found it face down beside the phone in her bedroom.

At six-thirty—late enough so that she could be sure Harry had been fed, early enough so that he would not be in the bath yet—she dialed Caroline's number.

"I hope this isn't a bad time?"

"No, it's perfect. For a few minutes, anyway. Harry's fed and for the moment docile. I let him have a deck of cards and he's pretending to be Dada, who's due to land from Portland tonight. His friend Ben's going to fetch him from the airport, thank God."

She did not sound angry or hurt. But she did not acknowledge, either, that they hadn't spoken since their coffee date.

"How have you and Harry been?"

"We're good. Keeping busy. Natalie kept him for a little while today while I took Martin to the doctor. Something crazy happened, though."

"To Martin? Or to Harry?"

"Oh, no. Natalie's eccentric but she turns out to be very good with Harry. She likes having him all to herself when she has the time. And Martin's fine—his PSA is undetectable. To me, I meant. At the Med Center. I've told you about my high school boyfriend. Do you remember? The one who wrote songs and recited poetry from memory?"

"I believe I do remember," Jill said. "It's not every day I hear about a teenaged boy who can quote Dickinson."

"Well, I saw him. Clifford Delgrange. At the hospital. It was the strangest thing. After all this time! I would never have guessed it but he's in med school."

"Ah—no more Emily Dickinson, then."

"Actually, he told me he still reads poetry. And still plays the guitar—I asked. He'll be a poetry-reading, guitar-playing doctor, I guess. He's on a urology rotation, and there he was, right alongside Martin's Dr. Starker. I would never have expected him to come back to Ohio once he left for college."

"It's just as I said on Sunday. People are full of surprises."

"I guess they are. Who would have imagined he'd become a doctor? Just like *your* long-lost old boyfriend."

"Tomas. Yes." Jill considered this: was now the time? She did not want to rush through it.

But the opportunity was gone in any case. Caroline wasn't through with Clifford Delgrange yet. "It was kind of great to see him. I mean, it was weird, but also, oh, so lovely. You know how, when you're that close to someone and then you don't see him for years, it's as if he doesn't even exist anymore? I mean, I hadn't forgotten the *fact* of him, but if I thought about him at all it was like remembering a book I'd read a long time ago. It's not like the story keeps on going after you've finished reading it. The book might still be on the shelf where you put it away but you're done with it and it's done with you. Even if you pick it up to reread it, it's not a *new* experience. It's like stepping back in time. And that's how I felt when I saw Clifford. I wasn't only seeing *him* after so long—it was also like getting to meet my own old self, because that was who he was talking to. I even *felt* like her, for those few minutes. It was amazing. For about ten minutes today, I was in the presence of my seventeen-year-old self. Before Harry. Before Jacob. And then—whoosh—that girl was gone. Do you know what I mean? Does this sound insane?"

"I do know what you mean. It's not insane. You caught a glimpse of who you were. We don't get those very often." Jill hesitated. "And perhaps there was a glimmer of who you might be now if that story had not ended years ago?"

Caroline laughed. "Oh, that story had a built-in endpoint. There's a good chance the main attraction for me was that Mom disliked him so. That, and the fact that he was the first boy to show any interest in me."

"And he recited Emily Dickinson. And wrote you love songs."

"That too." Caroline sighed. "Come to think of it, he might have been the *perfect* first boyfriend. I was lucky, wasn't I?"

"I'm not at all sure it was luck," Jill said. Impulsively she added, "You are someone who invites love." She blushed, although there was no one to see it.

"Jill! That's an amazing thing to say. And it's so, oh, I don't know...."

"Unlike me?"

"That sounds harsh, doesn't it? Oh, dear. It's just that you usually eschew sentimentality."

"I do." Jill said this gravely. And then quickly, before she gave herself the chance to change her mind, she said, "Caroline, dear, there's something I must talk to you about. Something I would be grateful to have the chance to...to run by you."

"Sure," Caroline said. There was an expectant silence.

"Oh, no, not when you have only a few minutes—or really a few seconds by now, yes? You're busy with Harry, and your husband will be home soon from his no-doubt brilliant success in the Pacific Northwest. Could we meet at Jojo's again for coffee, do you suppose? Perhaps tomorrow morning, before my first class? Or late afternoon, when I'm finished teaching?"

"Tomorrow's hard. I'm sorry. Along with all the usual stuff, Jacob and I have our counseling appointment after Harry's nap, and Martin's going to keep him at his place—he insists he's up to it—so then we have to go back over there to pick him up, and by the time we get home, it'll be—"

"No, no, of course. I understand. Whatever's good for you. You tell me what will work. There's no rush." An untruth.

"How's Friday? Late afternoon?"

"Friday's fine."

"Around three, then, after Harry's nap?"

"Yes," Jill said.

"Jill?"

"Yes?" Was she going to ask for a precis? After she'd specifically declined to have the conversation now? *I'll say: It's complicated. I'd rather not attempt to summarize it.*

"Don't bring Harry a present. He will be delighted to see you, I guarantee it, without your giving him anything. Every time we drive past Jojo's he shouts, 'Jill!' and wants me to stop the car. Every time I take him to Rose Park he remembers all the walks we've taken there with you. He loves you, okay? He loves you for yourself."

"Okay," Jill said. But with great effort to sound nonchalant. Unmoved.

She was trembling when she hung up. Because of the kind thing (but it was more than kind—it was something more pure than *kind*, not kindness but…goodness?) that Caroline had said. And also because she had done it, she had paved the way—she could not now pretend that there was not a subject she was meeting Caroline at Jojo's to discuss. She would have to tell her, she would have to talk about it.

And it was not, after all, *advice* that she was seeking—this was clear to Jill now that she'd set a place and time to talk. What she wanted was to hear herself out. To say aloud what Tomas had proposed, to pay attention to the way she felt when she heard herself speak of it. When she heard herself speak of it to someone who was not Tomas. To find out if what she felt—if the happiness that flooded her when she was all alone with her own thoughts—was real and could be trusted.

And then she realized: she had not apologized to Caroline for what she had said on Sunday that had so upset her.

But Caroline had not seemed hurt or angry—had she?

Well, she would apologize nonetheless. On Friday, before anything else. She would apologize, and then she would tell her everything.

Tomas called that night after the children were in bed, with stories of Lucie's triumphant performance in the school orchestra—she was a tiny girl with a quarter size double bass that still appeared to be too big for her—and Katerina's home run. "I hope it's all right, calling," Tomas said. "I don't know how much breathing room is enough breathing room." She told him she didn't either and that she was glad he'd called. He asked if she was still thinking over the question he had posed last Saturday and she said yes, of course she was, that they would talk about it more over the coming weekend. "Tell me about your life," she said. "I don't want to think right now. Thinking is making me crazy."

"I don't want to make you crazy," Tomas said.

After she hung up, she climbed the stairs, her dog at her heels. It was still early but she was exhausted. Exhausted and wound-up, a bad combination. All she wanted was to sleep—*O Sleep, the certain knot of peace*—but she knew she would not be able to, not for hours. Every night she fell into bed, exhausted, and then lay awake for a long time, thinking, imagining her future.

Her future! She would not have thought there was a *future*. Only a more-of-the-same, not-bad (no: quite *good*) life. A life she liked—a life for which, at past fifty, she was grateful.

She had not been looking for another one. She had never entertained the thought that there might be another one, a completely different one.

And yet it seemed there was.

She thought about the final two tercets of Caroline Lieb's "Any Which Way." She hadn't yet marked up the drafts of the poems Caroline had left with her. She would, before Friday. But she would have to remember to tell Caroline that even before she'd taken a pen to them, these lines had impressed themselves upon her, had stayed with her for days:

> *Like a drawing of a bird, that black vee, nothing*
> *but a gesture, something*
> *like a metaphor. The details don't matter—only the non-*
>
> *sense of it, the gone, disappeared, unknown of it. The clown*
> *car packed up again. The road folded back into the deck. No*

magic words, not even patter—nothing—and it's done, it's done, it's done.

It wasn't done, she wanted to tell Caroline. It wasn't ever done.

RIGHT BEFORE YOUR VERY EYES

I was in the second grade, seven years old. My dad—for the record—was thirty-three. He wrote books, so he was always locked up in his study, his typewriter clacking. **(As J. talks, he folds a sheet of gold paper.)** *This was 1987, before typewriters became extinct.* **(Acknowledges the audience's curiosity about what he's doing; indicates partially folded origami piece.)** *Oh, this? Give me a minute. I'm just learning how to do this—it's quite an interesting art form.* **(Resumes folding.)** *Anyway, on this day—for once—we were at home alone together, and I suppose my mother must have left him in charge of me. I remember that I was in my room, playing* **(origami piece vanishes as J. says *playing* and is replaced by a small stack of 80s era baseball cards, which J. begins to flip face-out so the audience can see what they are),** *and my dad came in and started telling me a story.* **(Pause, cards in both hands.)** *I mean, I loved my baseball cards—I used to spend hours, whole afternoons, studying them, sorting and resorting them, and ranking them—but a story! I liked a story—I still do—maybe more than anything, and my father was a professional storyteller. Who hardly ever told me any stories. So I stopped what I was doing* **(cards in one hand)** *and devoted all of my attention* **(cards are replaced on *attention* by the nearly finished origami piece, which J. resumes folding)** *to my dad. Who told me the Story of the Phoenix.* **(The folded paper is revealed to be an origami bird, a golden phoenix. Music cues and J. floats the paper phoenix to the center of the stage as he tells the story in the persona of his young father, speaking to his own younger self.)**

It is said that only one phoenix existed at any given time, and lived for many years—five hundred years, a thousand years. But when its time came, the phoenix would build a pyre nest, set it on fire, and allow itself to be consumed in the flames.

(J. snaps fingers and the origami phoenix vanishes.)

She was alone in the apartment, working. Every morning was now set aside for this. With Harry in half-day day care this autumn at the Jewish Community Center, she was guaranteed four hours a day on weekdays, minus the drive there and back for drop-offs and pick-ups (and when Jacob was at home, which was more and more often now, he took care of the drop-off—and he'd get Harry up and fed and dressed too, which gave her an extra hour—but of course when Jacob was at home, he'd come back after he had taken Harry over to the JCC and sometimes he forgot that he was not supposed to talk to her when she was working, and she had to remind herself that they were both still getting used to this, and that she shouldn't snap at him when he asked, "How's it going?" or, "So, what exactly are you working on right now?" or told her about something he had seen/heard at the JCC that morning or had thought of on the drive home). On weekends when he wasn't traveling, he and Harry would go off together in the morning for a couple of hours so that she could work then too. They'd finally bought a car of their own, a ten-year-old Camry, after Martin started driving his again—they'd grown so accustomed to the use of his car while he was recuperating—and Jacob would pack Harry into it and take him "to have an adventure," which was sometimes just out to the playground and then grocery-shopping, but Harry didn't seem to mind.

Today Caroline figured she'd have a good two hours, maybe even three, of silence: Jacob planned to run several errands after he dropped Harry off. There was a new poem she'd been trying to get right for days, and she was sitting staring at the page she'd typed and printed out, a pencil in her hand, changing *swim* to *float* and back again, and *flight* to *escape*—and thinking neither one was right—and wondering what the poem would look like if she re-lineated it. She pushed the sheet of paper aside and returned to her laptop, an expensive new one Martin had bought her for her birthday "and also to celebrate Harry's first job"—which was how he referred to the JCC program (he'd ask Harry, "How was work today?" and Harry would answer soberly: "Good. Lenox and Willa played with me at the sand and water table and I got *very wet*"). The poem was still up on the laptop's screen. Caroline considered it. What would happen if it took up less room widthwise? What if she cut each line arbitrarily—or almost arbitrarily, after, say, five words? Or maybe six. But was that silly? (It was silly. Jill would say so, wouldn't she?)

There were mornings when she felt the whole undertaking was silly. She'd ask herself why she was bothering (arranging and rearranging words on a page? *Swapping* words? Staring at a single word or phrase or line until the clock ran out and it was time to go get Harry?) and then she'd ask herself if Jill Rosen ever felt this way, and finally one afternoon she asked her. "At least once a week," Jill told her, so cheerfully that Caroline could not decide if she was telling her the truth. If she was, it might mean that everyone felt this way sometimes—often?—about their own work. About whatever work they did. Maybe even people who built houses sometimes thought, *Oh, dear lord, another house. Does the world really need another house?*

Jill told her it never got any easier (Was that supposed to make her feel better?) She told her that no matter how many poems you had written, no matter how many you had *published*—no matter how recently you'd written the last one—it was never easy, starting a new poem. "New poem, new doubts." She said it gaily (but she said everything gaily these days). "New poem, new problems. New poem, new—"

"I get the picture," Caroline said.

"I never promised you a rose garden," said Jill, still maddeningly cheerful.

The truth was, even on her worst writing days, she was happier than she'd been in a long time. She didn't talk about this—couldn't talk about it, not even to Jacob. It seemed to her that *happiness* was not supposed to be the point, that one did not write poetry in order to be happy (surely J.T. Rosen didn't!). Even so—even when the work was going badly, as it was today—Caroline was so glad to be doing it she never thought of setting it aside, of giving it up once again.

She was also happier, she knew, because she had the time alone in which *to* write (the time alone in which to do anything—and if she chose to use that time for writing, the very act of *choosing* made her happy, too). She thought of Jill, who had kept writing sacrosanct, at the very center of her life. Just as her father-in-law had. Neither of them knew what it was like to try to find a place in one's life for this sort of work; neither of them had ever let anything or anybody interfere with it.

Well, that was not strictly true—not anymore. Just as *she* was at last carving out a place in her life for her work, Jill and Martin both were *un*carving the places—the well-regulated, private, quiet places—they'd made for themselves so long ago. Martin had let *her* in, hadn't he? And his grandson. And Jacob, in a way he hadn't ever been let in before. He had invited Jeanie in. And all those students who so worshipped him.

And Jill had invited Tomas. And not only Tomas: everyone and everything that Tomas brought along with him.

Months ago, Martin had told Caroline: *I used to have all my eggs in one basket. Now I have several baskets and every one of them is full of eggs.*

Maybe she was happier because writing poems—trying to write poems—had taken some of the pressure off her life with Jacob, and off being Harry's mother. That basket, those eggs.

She used to wonder if it had been Martin's writing that had kept him going after Gloria had left him, after Jacob had stopped speaking to him. But when he spoke of eggs and baskets, she realized that it wasn't until after both his wife and son were gone that he had even really noticed them. And so she was glad she'd never asked about his writing in the aftermath of those departures, glad that even after the great intimacy between them last year—after she had seen him (heard him, touched him) at his worst, at his most fragile—it had seemed to her too personal a question.

Which perhaps it was. But it was also the wrong question.

She looked again at the typed page of poetry. The poem's title was "Losing Farther," a reference to Bishop's "One Art." *Lose something every day.* She'd thought of "One Art" when she'd helped Jacob write the portion of his new show that was about the first trick he'd ever figured out—because "One Art" was the first poem she had taken apart and then put back together to see how it worked. It wasn't the first poem she'd read, and she'd read it long after she'd *written* her first poem (after she had written many poems, all dreadful). "One Art" was the straw that broke the camel's back, the poem that made her want to *be* a poet, not just fool around with poetry.

She'd told this to Jill when she was her student. Jill had scoffed. "It's a wonderful poem, certainly. But a poet isn't made by an encounter with one poem. You were already a poet or you wouldn't have thought *to* take it apart."

But wasn't that just how straws breaking camels' backs worked, too? It wasn't the last straw that did the breaking; it was the accumulated weight of all the straw before it. Still, without that final one, the one that tipped the scale, the camel would have plodded on, one step after another, carrying its burden through the desert.

None of these will bring disaster.

She was eighteen when she read the Bishop poem for the first time, thanks to Clifford Delgrange, who gave her the *Complete Poems* as a birthday present right before they broke up when he left for college in Chicago. Jacob had been only seven when his father did the phoenix trick for him. But one was who one was. It was only a matter of being shown the way. Or—to continue the metaphor of the camel—of laying that essential straw.

The flaw in this metaphor was the idea that who one truly was was a burden to be carried.

The brokenness was troubling too.

(Still, there might be a poem in it, she thought. Another poem, for another day.)

> *After three days, the phoenix would rise from the ashes, reborn.*

(J., still in the persona of his father, produces a book

of matches from his shirt pocket.) *Would you choose a phoenix, please?*

(As himself, speaking to the audience) *I was so disappointed!* **(Moves stage left—speaks as his child-self 'to' his father)** *Is this a trick, Dad?* **(To audience)** *I hated tricks. I'd been to plenty of birthday parties where there'd been 'magicians.'* **(Magic wand appears in his right hand; he waves it over his left hand and a bouquet of paper flowers appears in it. Irritated, he tosses the bouquet over his shoulder and it vanishes—and, as he continues to speak to the audience, he waves the wand and makes other objects quickly appear and then just as quickly discards them: a handkerchief, a folding hand fan, a pair of silly oversized plastic sunglasses.)** *The first time, I was excited—I thought, 'Magic! I love magic!'— but oh my God there wasn't any 'magic'! The stupid magician was just trying to play tricks on us.*

(Wand vanishes; J. moves into place again as his father, speaking to young Jacob.) *What makes you think this is a trick, son? I'm telling you a story. This is my* prop **(tapping the matchbook, which is once again in hand).** *Look at me, Jacob. Pay attention. You can get back to playing in five minutes. Come on—go ahead, choose a match, any match.*

(As present-day Jacob, addressing audience) *So I picked a match.*

It was possible that marriage counseling had cured them, though Jacob couldn't see how, not when the "homework assignments" the therapist had given them had been so asinine, and when by the end of every session they were both so angry and so hurt. In fact, while they were still seeing her, it had seemed to him that their sessions with Dr. Derring not only did not do them any good but actually did them harm. As she forced them to talk about how they felt and what they thought of each other and everything that had transpired between them since the last time she had seen them, Jacob had sometimes found himself thinking of the year of chemistry he had taken to complete his science Gen Ed, how in his weekly chem lab that whole year he'd had the feeling that at any moment what was in the beaker he was stirring might explode and blow them all to bits.

As they talked, coaxed on by Dr. Derring's questions—by her *And how did you* feel *when he said that?* and *When you asked her to marry you, what were you* imagining *your future would be like?*—he felt as if he could *see* electrons being set free, kicked out of their orbits: all these invisible particles of their marriage, all these particles of *themselves*, that were not supposed to be visible, suddenly forced out into the atmosphere between them, which instantly became charged and dangerous. And then for hours, even days, after a session, there would be a swarm of subatomic particles furiously buzzing in the air around them.

Which was why, by late spring, they'd stopped going. Although Caroline had not put it that way. For her it wasn't a cloud of charged particles; it was a "manmade mountain" between them, one they were making with the marriage counselor's help—"just shoveling more and more dirt onto it." She sat beside him on the couch one night, hours after their last session, once they'd gotten Harry down, and told him that it had begun to seem to her that if they kept unloading every grievance and going back over "every inch of how we got here and what made us who and what we are, just digging and digging until we've dug up everything and then dumped it all out between us, we won't even be able to *see* each other across this colossal, ugly mound of dirt anymore. And we won't be able to move it out of the way either because it's a *mountain*. So by definition it'll be unmovable. I think we should cut our losses and quit marriage counseling while we're still ahead."

They were *ahead*? Ahead of what? he wondered. But he didn't say it. He said, "That seems like it might be a good idea." He said it carefully— neither eagerly nor reluctantly, but not noncommittally either. He sounded serious. He said it like he meant exactly what he said. He did mean what he said.

And so they had quit marriage counseling even though they hadn't stuck with it for very long—not even six months, less than half as long as Caroline had sworn they would. And somehow, on their own again, they seemed to be all right.

Was this because they'd had just enough counseling to help things get better, but not enough to do them harm? Or was it more like the way, if you stopped pounding your head against the wall, the absence of the pounding felt so good you just forgot that you'd felt bad before you'd started?

His mother-in-law had predicted that going to counseling would be the death of their marriage. She thought they'd gotten out "just in time," which infuriated Caroline (and Jacob knew he shouldn't—so he didn't—point out that this wasn't really any different from what she had said herself). Jeanie also thought that "sending Martin home" (Caroline corrected her: "We didn't *send* him anywhere—he *went* home") had done their marriage much more good than Dr. Derring had. For all Jacob knew, Jeanie was right.

But for all he knew, too, it was his own slowly improving relationship with his father that had turned things around, because this mattered more to Caroline than he supposed he'd ever understand. Or maybe things were better simply because Harry was a little older and required less of her—or because he'd started day care and she'd found that she was able to endure the separation from him. She could see for herself how happy he was to go to "school" each day and play with other kids instead of with his mother or with him or one of his grandparents, and she had discovered that she could be glad about this and not hurt or sad—or anxious or resentful—as she had confessed, one day in counseling, she had feared.

Maybe talking about everything they'd talked about in counseling (maybe *even* airing all their gripes about each other, talking about how angry and sad and frustrated they were, *talking* about what they were afraid of—casting all of those charged particles into the air around them—or, as Caroline said, building that damned mountain) had been useful after all. Even if it hadn't ever felt that way while they were doing it.

Or maybe, left to their own devices, they would just have *gotten* better. The way a cold got better, whether you did anything about it or you didn't.

My relationship with my father was complicated. I mean, my father was complicated, but the way I felt about him was, too. I wanted to be around him, I was interested in him—at that age, I'd go so far as to say 'fascinated'—but I'd already learned that any interaction between us had to be on his terms. So even though I wasn't interested at all in what by now I was sure would just be a stupid trick, like the ones the 'magicians' at Ryan Showalter's and David Pearl's et cetera birthday parties had performed (**top hat appears in left hand, wand reappears in right**), *the only thing to do was to humor him. He'd lose interest in playing tricks on me soon enough, anyway, and go back to his room, back to work on* (**both hat & wand vanish**) *The Book.* (**Pause; visibly thinking.**) *But you know what? It'll be much easier for me to take you back in time with me to that snowy day in 1987 when I was at home alone*

with my dad if one of you would come up here and 'be' me.
(**J. selects a young, male member of the audience.**)

(**Continues, with spectator in position as young Jacob**) *Go ahead* (**'becomes' his father, matchbook in hand again, extended to spectactor**)—*pick a phoenix.* (**Tears out the match the spectactor/young Jacob has pointed out and hands it to him, then closes the matchbook.**)

So, the phoenix reaches the end of its life cycle and builds a nest. (**Gestures for spectator to return the match to him. Spotlight is tight around both.**) *All of a sudden, the nest and the bird both ignite* (**as J. lights the match and hands the spectator the closed matchbook**). *The phoenix burns* (**shaking out the lit match**) *until it is no more.*

(**Opens his hand—the match is gone.**)

But now the bird is reborn in the Arizona city that proudly bears its name....

Wait! That's not how it goes. No—the bird is reborn where it originated. Open your matchbook. You've had it in your hand the whole time, right? I think you'll find the bird reborn—still covered in ash.

(**J. allows spectator to react to the burned match, still in the booklet. Then takes the matchbook and, as present-day Jacob, speaks to audience.**)

I touched it—very hesitantly. It had just been lit, so

it would be hot, I thought—but it wasn't hot anymore, and also...it was firmly attached to the matchbook—it wouldn't come out. Somehow it had reattached itself! But he had pulled it out, hadn't he? I looked up at my father, who said **(in father's voice now)**, *And that is the story of the phoenix, rising again.*

His management team was skeptical about booking the show, which Caroline had titled for him *Closer Up With Jacob Lieb.* They weren't downright opposed to the show, or at least none of them would come out and say that, but Josie, who had been his manager for years, said no, they could *not* "just book it," as he'd asked her to. Not in place of his usual act. He argued with her, reminded her that he'd been threading bits and pieces of the new show into his act for a long time now, promised her that nobody was going to feel cheated.

But she wouldn't budge. Nor would the others, when he tried to talk to them about it. They'd closed ranks. And Caroline, when he complained to her, surprised him: she said they were right, that no matter how much of the new show he had tried out on his audiences, as a whole the show was something different altogether now. Before, he had been sneaking bits of monologue around his tricks. Now the tricks (as showy as some of the new ones he'd devised were—*and*, she said, it was as if, because they *weren't* the main thing, he had felt free to come up with some more sensational, elaborate ones, and some that were expressly comical) were a part of something bigger. For that matter, all the subtle, sly ones that had been his stock-in-trade for years were now also a part of something bigger. "If it's not going to be *trick trick trick and let me tell you something cool about this next illusion* and then *trick trick trick* and *I'm going to share a secret with you, my friends. The best moment as a magician, the moment that gets you hooked on magic, is when you say* is that your card? *and they say* yes" —by now Jacob was laughing in spite of himself (she sounded just like him)—"then we need to be clear about it, we need to *call* it a one-man show and not a magic act and you can't have your team book it the way they always book you."

It was her idea that they produce the show themselves and do a trial run—a six-show run, to be precise, in January—and to book it here in town. The theater she picked out was a beautiful old one, the smallest of the three in downtown Kokosing and the only one—not just in the city but for many miles around—that had been designed for live performances and not for movies. The theater wasn't in the greatest shape—it was dusty, and when the lights were up in the house you could see that the carpets were worn thin, almost bare in spots, and the upholstery was faded; the gold molding was chipped and the paint was peeling—but Caroline had done due diligence: a month before *Closer Up* would open, a well-known opera singer on a solo tour in the Midwest and South would be in the theater for two nights, singing jazz standards with only a piano and a standup bass (an experiment for her that was a much bigger risk than the one he was taking, and which Caroline called a good omen) and *she* had made arrangements for a cleanup in advance of her show in the theater. It was a lucky break (and maybe even a good omen). And the little theater had plenty of history—if not *gravitas*, Caroline said, then "at least really good performance vibes." Anna Pavlova and Isadora Duncan had once danced on its stage; the Barrymores and Sarah Bernhardt and Mae West had acted on it.

Caroline took it upon herself to talk to Josie as well as both of his booking agents, getting them all to agree that if the run here was successful they'd move forward—not immediately to New York or LA, but to Philadelphia, Boston, Chicago, Houston (Caroline had a made a list, he realized, surprised, as he stood nearby, listening; he was even more surprised when Mack, one of his agents, evidently countered with some smaller cities and he heard his wife say, "Pittsburgh? Omaha? You've got to be kidding me—you're thinking way too small"). He wondered if she had prepared for these calls by talking to Martin or Claire Alter, or to both of them. He'd asked her not to talk to Martin, but only about the content and form of the show—not about this part, about business (he hadn't even thought of that). She had wanted him to "bounce" some of his ideas "off" his father; Jacob had had to tell her that there was no *bouncing* with his father, that he'd catch what you threw at him and then put it in his pocket if he liked it—or else let it fall and roll away if he did not…or else he would catch it, sneer at it, and wind up for a pitch and then *throw* it away. Caroline had said, "Oh, please," but even so she had agreed not to let Martin know what the show was about.

When she hung up after the call with Mack, she looked so triumphant, so ebullient, he just couldn't ask her what had gotten into her. What if she *had* asked for Claire's advice, or even his father's? Why shouldn't she ask? She had helped him write it—it was her show too now.

Ticket prices were high, but they were promoting it, in part, as the hometown debut of a show that would eventually be seen "coast to coast"—a *see-it-now-while-it's-within-your-reach* event. And it was working. With the show still more than a month away, four of the six nights had sold out and the other two were more than half sold. They'd limited the house to seventy-five per night—which was still probably twenty more than was ideal, Jacob worried, because so much of the magic was still close-up magic—his specialty. But they couldn't afford to make the audience any smaller, not given the cost of producing the show. And Caroline had persuaded him to set aside an extra ten seats as cheap rush tickets for high school or college students that would be distributed by lottery each night.

It was impossible not to be anxious, and Caroline kept saying that he shouldn't even try—"A little anxiety never hurt anyone," she said, so jauntily and confidently blasé that he was taken aback. This didn't even sound like her. It might have been (more?) advice from Claire, whom it *did* sound like. And could this possibly be true—that anxiety never hurt anyone? (It did not sound true.)

Still, as he chopped vegetables for a salad while Caroline basted the chicken he had put into the oven an hour before, Harry beside him standing on a chair tearing strips of lettuce, Jacob felt the balance shift, felt himself tilt toward Caroline's confidence, her optimism. The show was done—written, rehearsed, booked, promoted. He had practiced every trick until he could do it in his sleep (he did sometimes do tricks in his sleep and woke up with a start) and they'd made sure the tricks were so embedded in the show there'd never be a moment when the audience would think *here comes another trick.* The tricks were surprising; they were *good*. Interesting, smart, fresh, strange. Some of them were beautiful. Some of them were funny. The show was *done*—it was ready. And the press release they'd worked so hard on had already led to two national stories and four more calls for interviews the week before the opening. There'd be people coming from newspapers on both coasts and from a weekly magazine. And the first and last nights would be videotaped, so there'd be clips for the promotional video that would be made when he moved on to national bookings. He'd sat for several interviews with local TV news and talk shows—there'd be clips of those too for the promo reel—and the *Herald-Tidings-Messenger*, the local paper, had interviewed him and was going to run a big story the Sunday before the opening. He was scheduled to be on the local PBS affiliate station the *day* before the opening.

Everything was good; everything was ready.

Caroline was humming as she closed the oven door—finally relaxed, he thought, about the dinner party she had fretted over for the last two weeks.

"What's left to do?" she asked.

From her perch by the window, Delirious trilled out what sounded like an answer to the question, and Jacob said, "That's right, Leery—we're all set." He leaned over and kissed the top of his wife's head. "I think we're good in here. I'll dress the salad right before I put it out, and I'll keep an eye on the chicken. The bread's already on the table, on a cutting board. I put the bread knife out too. And filled the water pitcher. So there's just the table."

"All right then. I'll go set the table." Caroline beckoned to the bird. "Come on, sweetiepie, come over here"—she tapped her shoulder—"and keep me company."

Obediently, the bird took off from her perch and flew to Caroline's shoulder.

"You should take *that* show on the road," Jacob told her. "Harry, kiddo, you want to help Mama and Leery set the table or you want to keep on helping me with the salad?" But Harry was already clambering down from the chair.

"Mama and Leery."

"I'm going to put Leery in her cage in a few minutes," Caroline whispered to Jacob as she moved past him.

"Good thinking," he whispered back. As if the bird could understand them even if she heard them.

Harry had no such qualms. He'd heard his mother, and as they left the room he said, loudly, "Good idea. Leery has bad manners."

Ah. Quoting his grandmother. At Thanksgiving, Delirious had serenely perched on Caroline's shoulder for almost the whole meal, then suddenly hopped off and skittered across the table to Martin's plate, gracefully sidestepping salt and pepper shakers, bowls of cranberries and mashed potatoes and both Martin's wine glass and his water glass, and stepped up onto the lip of Martin's plate, where she began nibbling at his turkey. Martin yanked his plate away and said—no, shouted—"What the hell?" and Caroline said, "Martin! Stop—you'll frighten her!" and Jeanie said, "Don't yell at your father-in-law. What do you expect if you let that bird walk around on the dinner table eating out of your plates? It's disgusting," and Caroline said, "Mom, you're just making things worse." By then Delirious had taken off and was flying in panicky circles around the room. Jacob's father said, "My God, what's wrong with her?" and Caroline told him to hush, she would take care of the bird. She stood up to try to coax her down, onto her outstretched finger, and Natalie said, "You really let her eat off your plates?" and Jacob's friend Ben, the juggler, said, "Man, is that true? Every night, or only sometimes?" and his new girlfriend, Amy, said, "Just dinner? Or three meals a day?" and Jeanie said, "If you're going to let the bird sit at the table, you should at least teach it some manners, don't you think?" but neither Caroline nor Jacob answered any of them. Harry stood up on his chair and cried, "Don't hurt Leery, Mama," and Caroline said of course she wouldn't hurt her—"I'm just going to put her in her cage and let her rest there while we finish dinner"—but it took a good fifteen minutes before she could make that happen.

They'd had everyone over at Thanksgiving except Jill, who'd been in Iowa with Tomas and his family. The episode with Delirious wasn't the only rough spot. Although Caroline liked Ben's new girlfriend, Amy, a lot better than she'd liked the last two, Anya and Danielle ("at least this one smiles"), Amy had said several things that Jacob could see irked her—Amy was a dancer and a yoga teacher, confident that she knew more than any of the rest of them about "health and well-being," offering her expert opinions over dinner—and Natalie responded to each one of her pronouncements with sarcasm ("Oh, I too believe that good posture is the foundation of a good life. What a coincidence!").

Natalie had been invited to bring her new boyfriend to Thanksgiving dinner—he was a psychotherapist she'd met the first week in her external clinical placement—but she had declined. She didn't want to "jinx it," she told Caroline. She said she'd bring him to Jacob's opening "if we're still together by then." Caroline told Jacob that it must be serious if Nat was worried about jinxing it and if she was even thinking that they might still be dating seven weeks out—"not to mention that she actually used the word *together*." Jacob didn't say a word because he knew there was nothing he could say that wouldn't get him in some kind of trouble. He'd gotten into trouble at Thanksgiving when Natalie, in response to Jeanie's question about what an "external placement" was, said it meant that she had her own patients now, and Jacob didn't stop to think before he spoke—he said, "You've got to be kidding me"—and Caroline said, "*Jacob.*" Natalie said, "No, it's okay. I get it. It's a lot to wrap your mind around, right? If it makes you feel any better, Jacob, I do have extensive supervision," and while he was able to keep himself from saying, "Yes, it does," or, "Thank God for that," when Natalie added, "But you should know too that I'm told I'm actually a *fantastic* therapist," both he and Jeanie burst out laughing. Then Caroline was mad at both of them.

Thanksgiving was the first time they had ever entertained more than two guests at once, and so for them to throw another dinner party two weeks later seemed improbable—but here they were again, without Natalie and Ben and Amy this time, but with the addition of Jill and her fiancé. The party was in her honor: she was leaving town in January, having worked out a deal for an early retirement. His father had told him she was taking a financial hit. "Not that it matters, I suppose, since she's marrying a doctor." Jacob said, "A *country* doctor, Dad." His father said, "All I can say is, she must really want out."

Or she just wants in to something else, Jacob thought but didn't say.

Once more they'd set up the two folding tables, pushed together in the living room and covered by a heavy linen tablecloth that created the illusion of a proper table. Caroline had filled a ceramic jug with flowers she'd rushed out to buy this afternoon, and everybody's dishes except Harry's matched (thanks to a gift of six expensive place settings from Martin, one of numerous household gifts he had insisted on bestowing upon them after his post-hospital stay; they had two sets of six wine glasses now too, one set for red and one for white). Caroline, who had been surprisingly relaxed about Thanksgiving—it had been her own idea to move the celebration from her mother's place to theirs, and to include their friends along with both their parents—had been a nervous wreck about tonight. Suddenly she was glad to have the fancy plates and glasses. She wanted Jill to be impressed (well, that was Jacob's word for it; Caroline's was *happy*).

She had worried about every aspect of this party since the minute she'd announced that she wanted to host it. She'd worried about the menu, the seating arrangements, the cheap folding tables. She'd worried about whether Harry should be put to bed beforehand or forced to rest during the day and then kept up for dinner (as if Harry could be forced to nap!—or *would* go to sleep if his Pop Pop and Gammaw, not to mention his pal Jill, were coming over). In the end Jacob had persuaded her to let it go, to let Harry stay up all day *and* for dinner and let the chips fall where they might.

And so far, so good, he thought as he looked around the table. Delirious had been safely secured, the roast chicken was delicious, and everyone was talking at the same time, all the conversation seemingly convivial. He had opened the third bottle of white Burgundy his father had brought. Caroline had fretted too over the last few days about whether it had been a mistake to have invited Martin, who was acerbic about Tomas (he unfailingly referred to him, Caroline reported, as Jill's "childhood sweetheart")—but how could she have left him out? She asked Jacob this as if he were the one who had suggested it, when he had stayed resolutely quiet. If she'd left Martin out, she would have had to leave Jeanie out too, wouldn't she? she said. It wasn't fair to include one parent and not the other, was it? She *wanted* both of them there: she wanted this to be a family occasion, wanted her whole family to send Jill and Tomas off, with love and good wishes. Jacob stayed silent while she worked it all out in her mind. Out loud.

Aside from Martin's declaration, "Ah, at last! The childhood sweetheart!" when he was introduced to Tomas (who had only laughed and reached out to shake his hand—and Jill, following his lead, did not rise to Martin's bait) and what he'd said when Caroline asked that they all raise a glass to Jill ("Hear, hear," he said, "but I must register my disgruntlement over this retirement. You're far too young! I wish you'd change your mind"), he'd been on his best behavior. And when he "registered his disgruntlement," Jacob noted the sharp warning look that Caroline flashed at him, and noted too his father's mute apology to her—a shrug, both eyebrows up, an almost imperceptible shake of his head—and marveled as he always did over both the wordless communication between them and Caroline's ability to scold his father, wordlessly or not, without angering him. If his mother had mastered this technique years ago—if it had even occurred to her try—how differently things might have gone.

But his mother was not Caroline.

"And when do you pack up and leave?" Martin asked Jill now.

Caroline answered for her. "Right after Jacob's show, which Jill says she wouldn't miss for anything in the world."

"I would like very much to be able to see it myself," Tomas told Jacob. "I have not given up hope that I may find someone trustworthy to stay with the children so that I can. My son Adam will be back at college from his winter break by then—but honestly, even when I leave *him* in charge, I worry." He took his fiancé's hand and smiled warmly at her. "You would think, would you not, that Jill would tell me I am worrying over nothing, but in actuality she is more of a worrier than I."

"I'm not a *worrier*," Jill said. "I'm just wise to the babysitter, whom I know entirely too well. He's likely to have them all organizing protests for higher allowances, later bedtimes, and better desserts by the time their father has returned."

"You see?" Tomas asked them. "Who would have guessed she would take to this so quickly?"

Caroline was the only one of them who'd met Tomas before tonight, on his one previous visit. It was impossible for him to get away, so it was Jill who did the traveling. For this visit, his eldest child had generously surrendered part of his own break, which started earlier than Kokosing State's, to watch over the younger ones, Tomas explained, while their father paid a visit to their soon-to-be stepmother, who was still grading final portfolios. Her last set of final portfolios.

Caroline had pronounced him "unexpectedly charming" when she'd come home after meeting him last summer. That had made Jacob laugh. "Unexpected because the Great Poet isn't?" But Caroline had swatted him. "Unexpected because he's from Iowa and has all these kids and lives on a farm. I was expecting hale and hearty and, I don't know, plainspoken."

Well, he wasn't "plainspoken," except maybe compared to Martin (there was no need for him to pause and define any of the words he used or offer a footnote that elaborated on a passing thought). And now that he had met him, Jacob saw what Caroline had meant. Tomas *was* charming. His charm was of a different type than Martin's (or what he had been assured—by Claire, by Caroline, by Jeanie—was Martin's). Jacob would have said of himself that he was immune to charm (certainly he was immune to what he'd been told was his father's) but the way Tomas had met his eyes and clasped both of his hands and smiled at him with such warmth when he'd opened the door tonight had surprised him—charmed him, he guessed.

And he watched Tomas now as he managed to charm Jeanie, which wasn't easy when Martin was around. She was laughing and—could it be?—blushing, too, as Tomas told her how impressed he was that she had raised Caroline all by herself and had done "such a splendid job of it." How proud she must be! he said, and Jacob listened closely as Jeanie responded, telling stories about Caroline's childhood and youth that Jacob knew by heart. Of course, they were brand-new to Tomas. But even so, the way he listened—as if these were the most interesting stories anyone had ever told him—was remarkable.

It was the quality of his attention, Jacob thought. He'd never seen anything like it. *I'm all ears,* Tomas seemed to say as he leaned forward to the person he was talking to. *And what I am about to say to you is for your ears alone—there is no one else, in this room or beyond it, whom I'd rather talk to.*

"Caroline is an extraordinary young woman," he was telling Jeanie now.

"I know," Jeanie said. "You're absolutely right. But thank you."

Jacob glanced at Caroline, who was smiling as widely as her mother was. Jacob was shocked. No impatience, no embarrassment? Not even disapproval of her mother's *thank you*?

"Jill has spoken of her so often! And, I must tell you, using the kind of superlatives my exacting fiancé never employs. It is clear that Caroline is exceptional. But along with the quality of her mind and of her writing, I can also see for myself—and I have heard from Jill, too—that she is among the most devoted and attentive of mothers. And the credit for this must go to you." He turned now to Caroline. "You would not be who you are without your mother. You know this, yes?"

And to Jacob's amazement, his wife said yes, she knew. And the look that passed then between her and her mother was one Jacob had never seen the two of them exchange. Was it possible that Tomas's kindness and good nature were infectious? That his warmth might spread throughout their living room?

Harry too was affected, and he was an even tougher room to work than his grandmother was. In the presence of both Jeanie and Martin, he could be counted on to have eyes for no one else—but he seemed to be mesmerized by Tomas, who listened to him as closely as he had to Jeanie. He laughed at his jokes, too—the one about what cows did on Saturday nights and the one about where generals kept their armies ("in their sleevies!")—and he told Harry one: "A duck walks into a coffee shop and orders a piece of cherry pie and a cup of cocoa, and the waitress says, 'I'm sorry, sir, but how are you going to pay for that?' And what do you think the duck says?"

Harry was rapt. "What does the duck say?"

"Why, he says, 'Just put it on my bill.'"

It took his son a minute—Jacob could see him turning it around in his mind, frowning, making a quiet noise that came from the back of his throat, the sound of a machine humming, as he concentrated—and then his face transformed and he threw back his head and laughed. "Put it on my bill!" he cried. "Mama! Do you get it? Put it on my *bill!*"

While the adults had coffee and slices of lemon cake that Jacob had made with his son's help this morning, Harry kept climbing down from his chair and running to get one thing or another to show Tomas, who exclaimed over each item—a Playmobil magician and his cape and wand, a picture book about llamas, a tiny hard plastic Superman—as if it were a marvel.

"Harry, you may show Tomas one more thing," Caroline said, "and you must choose carefully because it really will be the last thing. After that, your father is going to get you ready for bed."

Jacob braced himself for the inevitable wail of protest—but Harry was so thoroughly under his new friend's spell that he said, sweetly, "Yes, Mama" and raced off to his room to make his final choice. "That's incredible," Jacob said. But no one was listening. Martin and Jeanie were bantering, also sweetly, and Tomas had turned the light of his attention toward the two of them together. Caroline had inclined her head toward Jill's and the two of them were nodding, smiling, talking in near-whispers. Jacob stood to clear the table. He heard Jeanie say, "You never did" to Martin—Jacob had missed what it was his father hadn't done.

"I did, I did, as God is my witness, my dear Jeanie," Martin said, his hand over his heart.

"Since when is God your witness?" Jeanie said, so affectionately Jacob paused to study both of them.

"A figure of speech," his father said. He laughed. Tomas laughed too.

Jacob reached for Jill's plate, and as she glanced at him—just for a second, as he took the plate, they held each other's gaze—the displeasure he saw there (it might have been distaste or irritation, even anger—he didn't know her well enough to know for sure) unnerved him. Wasn't she pleased that her fiancé was making such a good impression on them all? But then he saw her glance flicker toward Martin—toward Martin, then toward Jeanie, and then back. *She's jealous*, he thought.

He carried a stack of cake plates, the top one criss-crossed with everyone's forks, into the kitchen, wondering what Caroline would make of it. If she would make anything of it—if she would trust that what he'd tell her he had seen was what was really there.

And then he shrugged—*leave it alone; don't say a word*—and went back for the mugs. Harry had returned to the living room with a geode Martin had given him, and while Tomas made appreciative noises concerning its beauty and the cleverness of Harry to know not only the word *geode* but also *crystals* and *quartz*—though Harry said *kisstells* and *courts*—"Those are hard words to say, hard words to remember" (which inspired Harry to reach further into his well of vocabulary knowledge and produce an approximation of the word *sedimentary*—and Tomas laughed, "Oh, I see. You were holding back on me"), Martin was firing up a disquisition on the differences between geodes, nodules, concretions, and vugs.

"Don't show off, Martin," Jeanie said.

"Why not?" Martin said. And then: "I'm not."

"You are, a little," Caroline said, at the same time that Jeanie said, "What are you, three years old?"

Caroline dropped her voice to speak to her mother but Jacob heard her: "Still, you could get off his back."

The spell had passed. They were all becoming themselves again.

"It's time to say goodnight," Jacob told his son. "But you know what? You'll see your new friend Tomas again soon, because next month we're going to take a trip to Iowa, where he lives. You and me and Mama. We're going to go to a wedding, because Tomas and Jill are going to be married."

Tomas opened his arms and Harry stepped into them. "Sweet boy," said Tomas. He planted a kiss on Harry's head. "Yes, you will come to the wedding, which will be on the farm where I live with my children, where your mama's friend Jill is going to live." Harry looked over at Jill. He looked doubtful.

"It's true, Harry," Jill said. "I'm going to live out in the country. Isn't that funny? I think it's funny."

"We all think it's funny," Martin said.

But Harry's eyes were on Tomas again. Tomas said, "I'm hoping your family will come to visit us there often. This would make Jill very happy. It will make *me* happy."

"Every day?" Harry asked.

"Well, maybe not every day," Caroline said. "We have to take a plane there, and it takes a pretty long time and plane trips for three people are expensive. But we're going to go there in the middle of January—that's not very far away from now."

Jacob bent to Harry and said, softly, "Time for bed now, kiddo." He took his hand. "Say 'goodnight, everybody.'"

"I want to go to the farm," Harry said.

Tomas said, "You will. In not too many weeks. I think you're going to like it, too. You can think about this as you go to sleep tonight. Think about the animals we have there. We have llamas and goats and horses. And dogs—we have many dogs. Every one of my children has a dog of his or her own. Oh, and we also have chickens. And ducks. We have a pond, and the ducks like the pond very much."

Harry cocked his head. He looked thoughtful and somber. Then a sly look came over his face. He opened his mouth and a little laugh escaped before he said what he'd thought up.

"Plane trips are expensive," Harry said. "But that's okay. You know why, Tomas?"

"Tell me."

"Because you can *put it on their bills*."

And then, triumphant, Harry allowed himself to be led away.

That was the start of my career. Because after my dad went back into his study—'I'll take those matches, son. You shouldn't play with matches'—I couldn't get back to my baseball cards **(produces them again, in place of matchbook).** *It had been a trick, sure, I could tell, but it had been a good trick, unlike the ones I'd seen before. I couldn't concentrate on anything until I figured out how my father had done it. I got hold of a book of matches* **(cards are replaced by matchbook)** *and I worked on it. I went through I don't know how many books of matches* **(multiple books of matches appear on** *many,* **and J. begins lighting matches, allows them to flame briefly before they disappear, one after another)**—*we had a whole drawer full of them, I discovered when I went looking.* **(Gestures to spectator to reveal contents of his pockets, and when spectator checks his own pockets, he produces many matchbooks, as well as various other small items—batteries and assorted screws and nuts and bolts and nails and rubber bands—and as J. indicates where they can be put down, he also keeps lighting matches.)** *My mother was furious when she realized that I'd been spending time alone in my room lighting matches, but she couldn't stay mad because she was so impressed. She said she'd never seen anything like it.*

(Quickly runs through phoenix trick again, wordlessly, with spectator in young Jacob's role.)

And, you know, it wasn't the illusion itself that was so interesting to me. It was the process of figuring out how it worked—and the fact that I could figure it out all by myself. And after, I started to learn the basic moves of magic **(demonstrates each very rapidly)**—*palming a coin, false transfer, tear and restore. Soon I was getting one* *of my parents to take me to midtown, to the great magic shops there. More often my mother, who was easier to convince and more available—my dad, as I've said, was almost always in his study working except when he felt like coming out, and that didn't necessarily coincide with when I needed him.*

By the time I was old enough to persuade them to let me get around the city by myself, I was a regular. (**J. begins to fold another piece of paper—a white piece this time.**) *By the time I was thirteen I was taking the subway down to Flosso-Hornmann, the oldest magic store in the world—its roots went back to the 1860s in Germany. It's gone now, but it was the greatest place on earth, I thought. Jack Flosso would demonstrate any trick I was interested in. There was another magic store, too—Tannen's, which is still around— and I used to go there too. I spent all my bar mitzvah money at those two stores. By then I was performing in public—by then, I was a professional magician.*

(**J. reveals that he has made an origami dove. Music cues again and again he floats the paper bird to the center of the stage. Wordlessly he demonstrates to the spectator that he should snap his fingers, and when the boy does, the origami dove vanishes.**)

When he and Caroline were first dating, she had read to him from Jill Rosen's books, wanting him to love the poems as much as she did— which of course was impossible. Nobody would ever love those poems as much as Caroline did, Jacob had thought then. And now? He still thought so. (Until Tomas had come along, he had thought no one would ever love the *poet* as much as she did.)

Caroline was asleep beside him, hours after everyone had left, after their successful dinner party, and he'd been thinking of his show— but somehow a few lines of one of Jill Rosen's poems had wedged themselves into his mind. He hadn't even known that he remembered them:

> *What is not foretold is ever after told, the same old*
> *Same old story, the inevitable chicken crossing*
> *Road after inevitable road—so black, so white, so read*
> *All over, over and over again—and wanting to see time*
> *Fly. There it goes, a clock with wings, pitched right*
> *Out the window. Nobody makes choices anymore.*

It was almost certainly from his wife's favorite of Jill's books, *In the There-and-Now*—her second book, published long before she had become Caroline's teacher. He supposed he was thinking of it now because of something Caroline had said as she fell asleep. "How else could it have gone?" she'd murmured. She was already half asleep. "Once Tomas found her, what else could have happened?" But there were plenty of other things that could have happened. Jill and Tomas might have talked once and been done with it. They could have become friends, happy to have reconnected but not upending anybody's life. But Caroline was asleep before he could say any of this, and perhaps it was just as well—perhaps it made her feel better about Jill's leaving, which she dreaded, to think that it was inevitable.

Nobody makes choices anymore.

It was funny how just because the line was from a poem it sounded true. He was tempted to get out of bed, to look for the poem—he could picture exactly where Jill's books were in the bookcase; Caroline had put them right beside his father's—to check it against his memory and to read the rest of it. To see if it was more than what it seemed, a string of the sort of jokes his son and Jill's fiancé had told each other gleefully at dinner. Perhaps that was why it had come back to him tonight. Wasn't there a joke Harry liked about a boy tossing a clock out the window?

He wanted to see if time flies.

And what about their own lives, then? What if he and Caroline had never met? What if he had picked a college somewhere else, gone five hundred miles in some other direction? Would he have met someone (like her? unlike her?) in North Carolina or in Maine? Would he have married *her*, had a different child? Not had a child?

Or had it been inevitable that he and Caroline would meet, fall for each other, marry, have a child? Have *this* child?

Everything seemed inevitable after the fact, didn't it?

But then nothing *was* inevitable until after the fact.

Caroline slept. In the next room, their son slept too. Jacob lay awake. He thought now of the moment he had first known that he loved her. Not the story he told himself—the story he and Caroline both told, the story they had long ago agreed upon. That was the story of the night they'd sat together in his kitchen studying art history and he had told her who he was—whose son he was. That was the story of the night he understood he could not get along without her—the night he had "caught up" to her. She had already loved him; she had already told him that she loved him.

"I'm always just a little bit of ahead of you," she'd say.

The same old/same old story.

But Jacob, lying in the dark, knew this was not the truth. He knew that he had loved her before this. He had loved her before she had loved him—before she had known she loved him, or before she had told him (for all he knew, there was a truer story for her, too).

His true story took place weeks before that night. It took place on the night she had first seen him perform—his last performance, as it happened, in Kokosing. His last one until next month, when his new show opened here. That show had also been downtown, in a restaurant and jazz club closed to the public for a private party, a political fundraiser.

It wasn't long after they'd met. They hadn't been to bed yet—they hadn't even kissed. She had not yet read Jill's poems to him. Or her own poems, for that matter. They'd had coffee a few times, one meal out, a few uncommonly long telephone conversations. They'd held hands, spontaneously, as they left the restaurant on their one real date, and it was the day after that that he had called and asked her—he remembered feeling shy about it, and that this had surprised him—if she wanted to see his act. He hardly ever had a booking locally, he told her, so this was the rare chance to see him in action. He remembered that those were the words he used—"in action"—and that she had said, "Of *course* I want to go."

And he remembered the event, a black-tie party. Rare for Kokosing, but it was an election year. It was mostly table magic he did for this sort of booking: table magic and a lot of patter about the magic—working his way around the room from one rich guy in a tux to another, chatting with them, teasing and flattering them, sitting down beside one tight-faced rich guy's wife in a two-thousand-dollar black dress and urging her to go through the deck one card at a time. Moving on to the next rich guy's wife, her hair pulled back so hard her eyes narrowed and slanted—making jokes, handing her the cards. "This next trick? *You're* going to do it. I can tell just by looking at you that you have the makings of a magician." And to the husband at her side, his hand around a thick glass: "Watch her, sir. This could change your life." He looked good in his own tux, he knew that. And he was good at what he did—of course he knew that too.

But Caroline didn't know, not until that night. She was excited, he could see. He glanced at her as often as he could during the show and he could see it then. He could see it still when he found her afterwards. But girls—women—always enjoyed seeing him perform. They were always impressed; they always looked at him as if *he* were magic. So it was not because of that that he began to love her. It was after they had left the party, when they were sitting in a coffee shop downtown, not far from where the show had been. Not a coffee *house* and not a hip bar or a nice restaurant with candles and a wine list—though no one would have carded them that night, looking the way they did, he in his tuxedo and Caroline in a short, tight black dress she had borrowed (from Natalie, but he hadn't known that then). No—he saw this only now, as he lay awake thinking of that night—he'd intentionally picked someplace where the luster would fall away fast, where they sat under fluorescent light and the table was greasy and the coffee was both weak and bitter, the pie chemical-flavored. She sat across from him in the booth with its sticky vinyl seats and she kept looking at him the same way she'd looked at him during the show and right after it when he had come to find her at the table in the corner where he'd left her.

He had been testing her. He'd needed to see what would happen and he'd needed to know then and there, before they got any closer. Because although every girl he'd known since sophomore year of high school liked him when he was onstage, he could always see them downshifting when he was through performing—shifting, one gear at a time, until they were barely managing to be polite. Fifteen minutes, tops, after his show was done they would be bored with the real-life version of him.

Was it because he was boring? He didn't think he was boring. He told funny stories and he was careful not to be long-winded (careful not to be his father). He knew he wasn't stupid, and he wasn't humorless. He wasn't homely. He might not be the tallest or best looking guy around, but all his life until he had left home people had told him he looked like his mother, and while he could not see the resemblance no matter how hard he looked for it (she was tiny, blond; he had his father's build, his father's coloring—he was built like a wrestler, compact and strong-looking, and he had his father's olive skin, black hair, dark eyes), he knew his mother had been—maybe she still was—beautiful. If he had, as they said, "all her features," how bad looking could he be? No, the problem was that real-life Jacob Lieb was a big letdown after they had seen the other one, the one he was in performance. That one was so much bigger (*You looked taller—it's weird, I thought you were taller*), so much better, so much *cooler*, so much more exciting, charming, elegant, poised—so much funnier, and somehow even handsomer, than his ordinary self. He disappointed them. He couldn't help it. It was—he almost smiled to think of it—inevitable.

Except it wasn't.

With Caroline, that night, as they sat talking in that crappy diner, he understood something he never had before: that there weren't two versions of him. He understood this only because she did. Because of the way she looked at him, the way she talked to him, the way she listened to him, the way she asked him a million questions that made him want to ask her a million questions. She had seen two sides and not two versions of him, she seemed to be telling him, and both sides were interesting to her. Each one complicated the other in ways she was curious about, excited about. *And what else?* she seemed to be asking him. *There's more, isn't there?*

He turned toward her in the dark. He could just make out the outline of her face, the shape of her hair, her shoulder. Did she know then, too? That soon?

The question he'd wanted to ask everyone who'd ever been disappointed by him, who'd ever been disappointed *in* him—*What is it you want from me?*—but which he'd never asked (because he thought they wouldn't know? or because he didn't want to know?), he didn't have to ask her. Not that night, not ever. He knew what she wanted. She wanted *him*, whoever and whatever he might turn out to be.

I was sixteen when I decided I wanted to try using a bird in my act. (**Spotlight tightens around J. as he speaks.**) *But instead of getting a dove* (**holds out his hand—the origami dove reappears**), *the way I should* *have* (closes his hand around the origami dove), *I brought home a cockatiel* (opens hand to reveal an origami cockatiel with a high, tall crest). *And instead of having a bird for my act, I ended up with a pet.* (Music cues and he floats the origami cockatiel just in front of him.) *A cockatiel is useless for magic but makes a very good pet.* (Removes a lighter from his pocket.) *This is more efficient than a match.*

(He ignites the paper bird in midair)

If I'd wanted a bird for magic, I should have gotten a dove. Which I did just recently—at long last.

(...and in place of the flaming paper bird, a live dove appears. He places the dove on the spectator's shoulder, allows time for reaction. Stage goes dark briefly before the show resumes.)

AFTER THE FACT

Never sing that sad old chorus
Never play those twelve-bar blues
Never tell me that what you do
You do for us
And don't say goodbye
Like it's the news

—Jay "Goody" Goodman, "Never Say"

Caroline was at the kitchen table making lists—lists of presents still to be shopped for, decorations to be hung, cookies to be baked for Harry's daycare party, groceries to buy for cookie-making (which she and Harry were going to tackle on their own—a first) and for dinner on Christmas Eve with her mother and Martin, and also brunch on Christmas Day, when Natalie would join them too (with her new boyfriend, the therapist, before bringing him to Christmas dinner with her family—another first). Jacob's dog-eared, marked-up cookbooks were spread out around her—they had planned the menus for both Christmas meals last night and she was copying all the ingredients he'd need onto her master shopping list—and so were all her lists, on five by seven index cards, and a box of colored markers.

She finished the grocery list, but the lists of gifts were more unwieldy. Jacob had told her that he'd had friends when he was growing up whose parents had given them a little something each of the eight nights of Hanukkah and she was determined to do that for Harry, so she had a list in blue of small toys (action figures, model cars, add-ons for his wooden train set) and another list, in red, of ideas for his Christmas presents. And she still hadn't settled on the right gifts for her mother or for Natalie, so each of their names was followed by a list of possibilities. Jacob's list, in orange, was full of question marks and cross-outs, and it kept getting longer. She'd already bought a gift for Jill—a hardcover copy of Naomi Shihab Nye's *Words Under the Words* she'd found in the best secondhand bookstore in town, and she had put a leather bookmark stamped with Jill's initials in it, on the page with the poem "So Much Happiness." (In her inscription she had written the first line of that poem—*It is difficult to know what to do with so much happiness*—and, under that, *Love to you from your devoted student and friend Caroline*, and the date.) Jill was flying to Iowa to be with Tomas and his children for Christmas, but she'd be back to finish packing and for the closing on her house—which she had sold to a newly tenured professor of linguistics, a single woman, just as she'd hoped—and they planned to have dinner then. It would be Caroline's last chance to see her before the wedding.

Jacob was amused by her efforts to teach Harry—and all the children he came in contact with—about the Jewish part of his ancestry when she'd had to teach herself virtually everything about it (he couldn't be much help; his parents had been bagels-and-lox Jews, never celebrating or observing anything). She'd bought Harry two picture books about Hanukkah and she'd been reading them to him at bedtime every night in the run-up to the holiday. This was the first year he was really old enough to understand, so she was giving it her all.

It was a year of many firsts, she thought as she added *some small gift for N's boyfriend so he doesn't feel left out?* to the to-do list, then copied it to the gifts-still-to-be-bought list.

She was glad for Nat—glad, and truly surprised. The new boyfriend, Stan, seemed like a good guy. He was smart, too. He was completely different from anyone Natalie had ever dated. (Jacob said it was a good thing he was a psychotherapist—that if Nat ever had kids, an in-home shrink would be helpful. And Caroline had to remind him that Natalie was also going to be one.)

Jacob watched her work from the doorway to the kitchen. Delirious was up on her perch in front of the kitchen window, grinding her beak in her sleep; the new bird, the pale gray ringnecked dove they hadn't named yet and who looked like a distant relative of Delirious's ("Delirious's slow, much bigger, dull third cousin once-removed," his father said, while the rest of them referred to the new bird for now as Jacob's "assistant"), was pacing the floor of its large cage, still acclimating to a new life and a new line of work.

On the kitchen floor, under the table by his mother's feet, Harry was playing with dinosaurs. A memory came to Jacob of sitting on the floor playing while his mother sat making *her* lists. She was a great list-maker too. Had her lists been color-coded? Had she concentrated so hard on them? Caroline found her list-making soothing. Had this been true of his mother? He might ask his father.

Could he ask his father? They never talked about his mother. They talked about Harry and Jeanie; they talked about the city that was so improbably now home to both of them. They talked about restaurants, they talked about baseball, they talked about the progress of his father's book. His father had stopped asking him about the show after Jacob had responded a great many times, without losing his cool, that he wanted him to be surprised, and by silent mutual agreement they did not speak of Caroline after an incident in which his father implied he knew her better than her husband did and Jacob lost his temper. Otherwise, there were only a few subjects they avoided. They never talked about Jacob's decision to leave New York at eighteen, or about the period, before Caroline intervened, when they hadn't spoken.

And then there were the subjects Jacob *wanted* to avoid but that his father insisted on bringing up. His incontinence, for example—which he spoke of ruefully now, and yet without shame. "Well," he said first thing one morning when Jacob met him for breakfast, "it looks like I may have to sleep in a diaper for the rest of my life"—and Jacob could not think of anything to say except, "I'm sorry," and, "I'm going to order an omelet—how about you?" His father had also wondered out loud one night when they'd met for a drink whether it would be possible for him to get a hard on now—and Jacob had said, "Really, Dad? Must we?"— and then announced, a week later, at breakfast, that it wasn't. "At least not on my own," he told Jacob, "and so far I haven't had the opportunity to try otherwise. Not that I'm so sure I want to." This time Jacob was sure "I'm sorry" wouldn't be sufficient, so he said nothing at all.

It was Caroline's opinion that his father had changed drastically since his diagnosis, and that Jacob had changed, too, as a result of what his father had been through. It was Jacob's opinion that his father had changed *some*, and that he had not changed not at all. It was true that it had been briefly frightening, and there was a minute there when he had contemplated, for the first time, the possibility of the old man's death—and yes, sure, it had shaken him. But in retrospect the time between the diagnosis and his father's being cancer-free seemed to have been about an hour. And while the recovery from his surgery seemed to have taken forever (and didn't in fact seem to be *over*, either—not if his father couldn't get it up and was still peeing in his sleep), and having his father living with them had been brutal, he could see no way that it had changed *him*.

Caroline didn't give him enough credit for deciding to meet his father halfway. More than halfway. But Jacob didn't say this—he had made the decision never to argue with her again about anything having to do with his father. This was something for which he could give their marriage counselor credit: she had taught him that there were things it was better not to say and not to hear (although he was sure that hadn't been the lesson Dr. Derring had intended).

And so they had reached a truce about his father.

Just as he and Martin had reached their own truce. They got together regularly now, just the two of them, and Martin was included in every family gathering, just as Jeanie was. "Who needs more than one parent?" Natalie had remarked at Thanksgiving. "With one of each, you've got it covered. It's so terrific how much you guys all *like* each other, too." Martin had beamed at her. He'd pronounced her "perfectly delightful." He actually told her to feel free to bring her patients around. "We'd be happy to serve as a good example for family happiness. Wouldn't we, Jake?"

And Jacob had thought, as he often thought lately, *Is he for real?* But everybody laughed, so he laughed too.

Wondering how seriously to take his father was new. In the past, there had been little question of how he should be *taken*—the default, with Martin, was sarcasm, jokes with a sharp edge, purposeful outrageousness—but it seemed to Jacob now that he had understood nothing of his father *except* that he should not assume that he meant what he said. But was he now to believe that he meant everything he said?

This hardly seemed possible. Even Caroline, he was sure, would not claim his father as a paragon of sincerity. No—that was Tomas Vítámvás's role in their extended family, Jacob thought. He must have chuckled to himself because Caroline looked up from her lists and said, "What?"

"Nothing," he said.

"You laughed. Are you making fun of me and my lists?"

"Absolutely not. I love you and your lists. I was just thinking about Jill's fiancé."

"And that's funny?"

"How different he is from my dad."

"Martin doesn't like him."

"He's only met him once."

"Still." She started to say something else and then she didn't.

"You remember that I'm meeting him for dinner tonight, right?"

"Of course. My mom's coming over here and bringing pizza or something. We'll be fine. You go have fun with Martin."

"Fun," Jacob said.

"I'm having fun," Harry called from under the table.

"Go. Go get dressed."

Reluctantly, he pushed off from the doorway. Seeing his father was fine—but it was never fun. And something nagged at him, the whole time they were together. Something in their conversation, in the way his father talked to him or looked at him, would leave him wondering, each time he left him, what it was his father wanted from him. He was already giving him so much, he wanted to tell him. His time, his willingness to listen even when he'd rather not. His sharing Harry with him. Sharing Caroline. Jeanie.

His whole life, he thought as he changed from sweats into good jeans and a sweater, he'd had the sense that his father wanted more from him than he wanted to give him—than he knew *how* to give him. Even when the answer to the question *What does he want from me?* seemed obvious—*he wants my company* (when what *he* wanted, at age four, was to continue building the block tower he was working on, or to go down to the third floor of their apartment building to see if Roberto was at home) or *he wants my attention* (when, at nine, he had other things on his mind: his baseball dice game, say, when he was about to roll out the seventh inning of a playoff, or a re-ranking of his baseball cards—or the chapter of *The Time Garden* that he'd just started reading, or a new trick he was trying to master—or even just homework he needed to do) or *he wants everything between us to be all right again* (as if, in his youth, Jacob could remember a time when everything had ever really been all right)—there was always more to it than that. There was always something else he wanted beneath the surface layer of wanting. The result of this unease was that while he might leave his toys or reluctantly abandon the notion of playing with Roberto, and go out for a walk on Riverside Drive, if his father was in a "quiet walk" mood, or on Broadway, if his mood required an "*interesting* walk," or to the Museum of Natural History or the

Central Park Zoo or whatever else his father had decided on ("Just the two of us, Jakey, how'd you like that?"—a rhetorical question, even four-year-old Jake knew), even at the age of four Jacob *kept himself apart*. He didn't really keep his father company. He was with him and he was not with him.

Just as he would not fully pay attention when his father stood in front of him until he set down whatever he was doing and listened, watched—*Look at me, Jake, I'm talking to you*—even when he did look, even after he had learned to act as if his father had his full attention.

And here he was, a grown man, putting on his socks and boots, going out to dinner with his father, willing himself to *be* with him, to be fully present, when he was with him. To listen whether he wanted to or not. To try not to disappoint him. To try not to be disappointed *by* him.

Did that mean he'd changed? And what about his father?

When he arrived at the restaurant, his father was already there. He used to like to keep people waiting. He was drinking a glass of red wine—he'd given up Scotch since his ordeal and was toying with the notion, he'd told Jacob, of giving up drinking altogether. Jacob said, "Hi, Dad—you're looking well" as he sat down across from him. Martin said, "Jake"—just his name, but with real pleasure, as if there were no one in the world he could ever be happier to see—and Jacob thought for the first time in his life: *Maybe what he wants is just to be happy*.

Maybe what his father wanted from him now was his permission to *be* happy.

And maybe he deserved to be. Like anyone.

Jacob was out late. Much later than Caroline had thought he would be, much later than usual. Her mother was long gone—she'd stayed just till Harry went to bed—and Harry had been asleep for hours now, long enough for her to have a watched an entire movie (it was the kind of stupid romantic comedy she liked—Hugh Grant doing his impersonation of an inept suitor—and Jacob couldn't stand). Finally she'd put Delirious in her cage and covered it, then covered the dove's cage, and headed for bed herself. She had just closed her book and turned out her reading light when she heard Jacob come in.

"Still awake?" he whispered from the doorway.

She sat up and turned the lamp back on. "Everything okay? It's so late."

"Yeah. It was weird. We had a good time."

She patted the bed. "Tell me."

"There's nothing to tell." He did not move toward her. "It was just—it was just good."

"But weird?"

"*Therefore* weird. Don't worry about it. I'm going to get ready for bed. You can go back to sleep."

When he returned, stripped down to his underwear and smelling of toothpaste, she said, "I'm not *worried* about it. I just want to know why it was good."

"It was just a conversation," Jacob said. "Who knows why it was better than it usually is." He got into bed and tapped her knee. "I'm beat. You going to lie down and turn off that light?"

She did. She turned sideways, toward him. His back was to her and she put her arms around him. In the dark, she said, "I watched a romantic comedy."

"With your mother? That must have been fun."

"No. She left. She only wanted to see Harry. She was going to meet some friends from work for drinks, I think."

"I'm sorry you had to watch a romantic movie alone."

She kissed his neck. "Ha. Better than watching it with you."

He was silent for long enough so that she thought he was asleep, but then he said, "Did you know that Houdini was so devoted to his mother, he never recovered from her death? His friendship with Arthur Conan Doyle—the guy who wrote the Sherlock Holmes books—

ended because of it, because Doyle's wife claimed that she could bring Houdini's mother back with a séance. And he went for it, but then she 'brought her back' and described her as wearing a big cross, which was a pretty seriously stupid move, given that Cecilia, like Houdini, was Jewish. Also, the day of the séance happened to be Cecilia's birthday, but the ghost apparently didn't mention it."

"Did your father tell you this tonight?"

"Actually, I told him." He slipped free of her arms and turned so that he was facing her. Except they couldn't see each other in the dark. "He was talking about his mother—my grandmother. And about my Aunt Anna, who he's been talking to a lot lately, he says. She might even visit. He wants us all to get to know her, he says. She has daughters I've never met—my cousins. He said, 'You should know your grandmother's other grandchildren.'"

"What did he say about her—your grandmother?"

"That he still misses her. That he still thinks about her all the time. So I told him about Cecilia, and about the Doyles. And you know what he said?"

"How could I know?"

"He said, 'That's too bad. I bet Houdini could've used a friend.' That's weird, right?"

"Why is that weird?"

"Oh, come on. You know that it's not like him. You know what he would have said before."

"No. What?"

Jacob laughed softly. She could feel his breath on her face when he laughed. "He would have asked if I happened to know that Arthur Conan Doyle was a doctor and that he'd based the character of Sherlock Holmes on one of his old teachers. He would have told me that the teacher had the ability to diagnose a patient just by looking at him."

"Are you making this up?"

"No. It's true. But he didn't tell me."

"But why would he have to tell you if you already know?"

"When has that ever stopped him before? The point is, he didn't say that. He said 'Houdini could have used a friend, I bet.' And he said, 'No one ever gets over the loss of his mother. No matter how he loses her, or why.'"

"He was talking about you?"

"I think so. Yeah. For the first time."

Caroline reached up to touch his face in the dark. "The first time since when, Jake?"

"A long time. Years. The last time might've been when you made me call him, after all that time we hadn't talked."

"All that time *you* hadn't talked to him."

"Fine. Right. But since then, neither of us has talked about her. It's like we've been pretending she never existed. But tonight we talked about her for a long time. And *that* was weird because I'd been thinking I was going to bring her up tonight. And then I didn't have to, because he did. So I asked him what I'd wanted to ask."

"About why she left?"

He was silent.

"Jake?"

"Not that. About the way she used to make lists."

"What are you talking about? What lists?"

"All kinds of lists. Just like you do."

She put her hand on his shoulder. "Jake. Sweetheart. What does that have to do with anything?"

"It doesn't. I don't know. I was just thinking about it."

"You've never mentioned it before."

"I never thought of it before. I hadn't remembered it, until today."

"What else did you talk about?"

"I don't know. A lot of stuff. But it was like all of a sudden we both wanted to talk about her. About things we remember, but also finally to say out loud, to each other, that she isn't ever coming back. That she's just *gone*. We'll never see her again. She's done with us."

She brought her face even closer to his, so that their noses were touching in the dark, and whispered, "Jake. I want to tell you something."

And she told him, finally, about writing to his mother after Harry was born. About how she'd waited and waited for her to respond and how—of course—she hadn't. He didn't interrupt her and he didn't move away, and when she was done talking and he still didn't say anything, she whispered, "Are you mad? I've been so afraid that you'd be mad."

"Mad? I'm not mad. How could I be mad? I'm just—I'm just sad that you thought she would answer, that you waited for her to. I could have told you that she wouldn't."

"How could you have told me that? You didn't know. You still don't know. You and Martin think you're sure, I get it, but—"

"Caroline. She left as soon as she could tell herself that I didn't need her to stay."

"But you did need her to stay."

"I said as soon as she could *tell* herself that. I don't know what I needed. I don't know if I needed anything by then. All I know is that she must have felt like there was just no reason to stay anymore."

"You don't know that for sure."

"I don't know anything for *sure*. I'll never know. I'm only guessing."

"I was so sad," Caroline told him. "Sad for you and sad for Harry. And for Martin. I don't know why I thought I could fix it—why *I* could make her care."

"I don't think it's that she doesn't care. Dad thinks she doesn't, but that's not the way I see it."

"It isn't?"

"No. I see it as impossible to know. We're fooling ourselves if we try to explain it, if we try to make it simpler than it is *or* more complicated than it is. Even my stupid guess about the timing of her leaving. We just don't know. We can't know."

Caroline began to cry. She didn't know if she was crying because she'd thought they *would* know someday, if she had believed until now that there would come a time when Jacob's mother's disappearance would make sense—when the idea of anybody disappearing would make sense. Or maybe it was that she hadn't understood until now that she hadn't given up, that she was still waiting, hoping for an answer to her letter. That Jacob's mother, Martin's wife—Harry's other grandmother—might come back. A little bit back. She might want to hear about her grandson. She might want to know her son's wife.

She could not imagine how Gloria had been able to walk away from her whole life and begin again. Would she have said—if she had been willing to say anything at all—that she had *had* to do it to save herself? Was her unhappiness that vast? Was her unwillingness to explain why she'd left a product of her selfishness? Or did she feel that if she let even a tiny corner up from where she'd battened down the hatches, she would be endangered, she would be snatched back up into what she'd left behind?

"It's like she looked around and saw that nobody was watching. Like she saw her chance to slip away and she just took it."

Jacob stroked her hair. "Like an escape from prison?" he said.

"More like magic. Not a magic *trick*—not an illusion. Like actual magic. She just…disappeared."

"That's the word my dad used, too." He was still stroking her hair. "He said, 'I don't want you to ever think that because you've had one parent disappear, you're in any danger of the other doing so.' He put his hand to his chest like he was pledging allegiance and made a promise to me that *he'd* never disappear. 'You can't get rid of *me*,' he said."

"Like you ever thought you could."

"Are you laughing now or crying?"

"Both, I guess." She rubbed her cheek against his so they both had her tears on their faces. "I promise I won't either," she said.

"You won't disappear?"

"You can't get rid of me," she said.

"Nor you, me," Jacob told her.

"Promise," she said.

"I promise I won't disappear," he said.

"So this is it, then. This is all of us—our family. No Gloria."

"Yeah," Jacob said. "It's just you and me and Harry. And Martin. And your mother."

"And maybe your Aunt Anna."

"And my cousins I've never met."

"And Delirious—don't forget about her."

"How could I? And Delirious. And my new assistant."

"That's right. Soon enough she'll be a real part of the family too. I guess she'll need a name then. Oh, and don't forget about Natalie. Natalie and Stan."

"I'll think about that," Jacob said.

"And Jill and Tomas? And all those kids?"

"Maybe. We'll see."

"And that's plenty, isn't it?"

"That's plenty, yes," he said. "It's enough."

"Because it has to be."

"Yes. But also because it is."

It was ridiculously hot in the apartment when Caroline returned from her afternoon of shopping. She set down her bags and yanked off her scarf and hat and shrugged out of her coat, saying out loud, "Why is it so hot in here?" even though she knew no one was home. She'd asked Jacob to take Harry out until dinnertime so that when she got home she could hide presents without having to rush.

Jacob always said the apartment was like a New York City apartment, that *they* were always overheated in the winter. But she hated doing what he told her everybody in New York did, what his own family had done when he was growing up, which was to throw open a window or two. It was so wasteful, so unreasonable. But the heat could not be turned down. The only remedy was to bring the cold in.

She glanced at the clock in the kitchen—it was not even five; she still had an hour, plenty of time—as she headed to the window there. It had been a beautiful day, sunny and cold, the kind of day she loved best. She hoped Jacob had bundled Harry up and taken him to the park instead of the science museum as he'd planned. Who knew when there'd be another day like this?

She'd gone to the mall that was an imitation town, where one strolled outdoors from store to store, and although she usually hated shopping, the day had been so lovely it was almost fun. She'd exited the Lego store into sunlight so fierce she was momentarily blinded— she had actually ducked into a store that sold nothing but inexpensive accessories (where she was dazzled—dizzied—by the racks of sparkly, glittery earrings and barrettes and purses) to buy a pair of cheap sunglasses, the plainest ones they had. Even so, there was a sprinkling of colored gems along the temples.

The sun was going down now, the sky turning blue-black. She reached over the sink to open the window but it went up only a couple of inches before it stuck. She had to pound it with the heels of both hands. When it gave, she yanked it all the way open, but as she did, the screen dislodged itself and fell. She watched in dismay as it tumbled down into the courtyard, right into the bushes there. She'd have to go downstairs and get it—but right now she had to get those presents hidden.

The blast of cold air into the hot apartment was wonderful. She stood breathing it in for a minute before turning away from the window, promising herself that she'd go get the screen as soon as she put everything away.

And then she would get dinner started. Jacob was cooking, as usual, but she could wash and pare vegetables, she could put up a pot of water for pasta and take out the roasting pan, the big saucepan, the olive oil, the can of tomatoes, the garlic. That way, as soon as the boys got home,

Jacob could take over in the kitchen and she could tend to Harry. Her mother and Martin were due at six thirty—they were fitting in an extra celebration before the holidays, this one for her mother, who had just gotten a promotion. Caroline had bought a bottle of Champagne (well, sparkling wine—Martin had taught her to buy Cava or Prosecco) while she was at the mall, and now she went to get it and put it in the refrigerator. She took four champagne flutes out of the cabinet. It would make her mother very happy to be toasted.

Though Jeanie was *already* happy—it was remarkable, really, how happy she was lately. She was thrilled about her promotion—she had a new title, too—and the raise that came with it. And last week Martin had shown her a draft of the novel "about her," and she was very pleased—she was *proud* (you'd think she'd written it herself). She kept talking about how he'd made her "a star," and Martin didn't seem to mind it—he seemed amused and touched by it—and wondering out loud who would play "her" in the movie version.

"You've sold it to the movies already?" Caroline had asked Martin the first time her mother said this. "I thought it was a first draft."

"I've sold nothing to anyone," Martin said. "I haven't even shown the manuscript to my agent yet."

"I'm thinking positive. I'm thinking big." Jeanie was grinning. Martin was grinning too.

Everyone was thinking big. Everyone was in a good mood. Martin had been positively buoyant when he announced that he'd finished his first complete "showable" draft of the book. And Jacob, who was already jumping out of his skin about his show, had gotten a call two days ago that had excited him so much he'd grabbed her and danced her around the family room after he hung up the phone, and Harry had shouted, "Dancing party!" and jumped up from playing on the floor to dance with them. The call was from Josie, his manager, about a TV producer who was "displaying some interest" in him. "What kind of interest?" Caroline asked as he spun her around. "Displaying how?"

"I don't know. He's talking to my team—that's all she said. They're 'in conversation.' But if something comes of it, our lives could change."

"Change how? What exactly might come of it?"

Jacob pulled her toward him, kissed the top of her head, then dipped her. "Who knows?" he said. "A sitcom. A variety show. I have no idea. But I'd definitely be able to stop traveling." Wasn't that what she wanted? he asked her. They were still dancing. Harry was jumping up and down, shaking his hips. "We might have to move, too," Jacob said.

"*Move?*"

He spun her. "Haven't you always wanted to get out of here? Aren't you the one who says, 'Why can't we live in New York?'"

"I said that years ago. When we were there for the first time."

"You say it every winter. You say it every time I tell you that gray winters aren't normal. That a New York City winter's chock full of freezing cold and sunny days."

"I'm *joking* when I say that. And you always look so mournful when I do that I tell myself, every year, I won't say it again."

"And yet you do. And I don't feel mournful anymore." He pulled her close again. "Though it might not be New York. It might be LA. Where it's *really* sunny. But never cold."

"*Jacob*," she said. "I'm serious. Would we really move if you got a TV show?"

"Anything can happen." He released her and bent to Harry. "You want some spinning too?"

"What about Martin? He moved here for *us*."

"If we go? If we go, he can come too." Jacob spun Harry, who cackled. And what about her mother? Caroline asked him. "Her too. Everyone can come. We'll buy a great big house and we'll all live in it together."

"Oh," she said. "You're joking."

"Who knows?" He stopped spinning Harry and brought him close to his chest, then flipped him sideways to cradle him the way they used to when he was a baby. Harry screamed with laughter as Jacob rocked him.

"Look, Mama, look! I'm a baby."

"Jake. Is this really going to happen?"

He stopped rocking Harry. "I'm going to put you down, buddy. You're too heavy to rock like a baby."

"I'm not a baby," Harry said. "Mama. Are you listening? I am not a baby."

"I know that, sweetie," she said. "Jake?"

"No, probably not. But you never know."

You never know. Two days had passed since then and she hadn't mentioned anything about this conversation to her mother or to Martin. She had done a pretty good job not thinking about it herself. If he'd heard anything more, he would have told her. There was no point thinking about it until then.

She was stashing Harry's presents—Legos, more dinosaurs (including a four-foot tall T Rex that came with a remote control, for Christmas), a Playmobil stone age set, small Superman and Batman figures, Matchbox cars, a battery-powered wooden engine for his Brio trains, and way too many books and puzzles—deep in the back of her bedroom closet when she heard Delirious calling to her. *Damn it*, she thought—she'd been so busy she had forgotten about her. She'd been making little whistling sounds since the instant Caroline had put her key into the lock, but what with hiding the presents and thinking about dinner and worrying about Josie's news, she had tuned her out, preoccupied. Now Delirious was shrieking. "I'm sorry, I'm sorry," she called to her from the bedroom. "In a minute, I promise." She put one of Jacob's presents—the poet Donald Hall's book about the baseball player Dock Ellis, which Jill had told her about—in her underwear drawer and heaped her most uncomfortable bras over it. The rest of his presents (another baseball book—a novel by Robert Coover—and a cookbook and a set of knives he had been wanting, and a sweater so soft she thought he might not complain, for once, about getting clothes for Christmas) she stuffed inside a trash bag and buried in the hamper in the bathroom.

"First things first, right?" she told the bird as she opened the cage. Delirious chirped—she never stayed angry long—and jumped onto her shoulder. "There you go. No harm done. Want to help me start dinner?"

In the kitchen, Caroline turned on the radio. The dove—they had decided they would call her Faith—was asleep in her own cage, in the kitchen's sunniest corner. Practicing with Jacob every day exhausted her.

Caroline sang along with the radio as she chopped the ends off Brussels sprouts and asparagus spears, snapped the tips off green beans, split a head of cauliflower into chunks. *No one else, no one else, can speak the words on your lips....*

She filled the pasta pot and set it on the stove, fetched the roasting pan for the vegetables and the pan for the sauce. As she bent and straightened, crossed and recrossed the kitchen, Delirious warbled and whistled in her ear, holding on tight. Caroline opened a can of tomatoes, and just as she was tossing the lid into the recycling bin, she heard the boys come in. Caroline called, "In the kitchen!" and she heard their voices, but the music was too loud for her to hear what they were saying. Then there was a crash—Harry must have been moving too fast and bumped into something—and a shout from Jacob, over the music, saying, "He's fine, he's fine!" before she even had a chance to be alarmed, and then before she could form the thought, *But something broke—what?*—Delirious, startled by the crash, flew off her shoulder, straight up, and then she was heading for the window, still open, still unscreened—Caroline had forgotten all about it, *how could she have forgotten about it?* She screamed. Jacob and Harry both came running.

But the bird did not fly out the window. She dropped suddenly, onto the perch they'd hung across it. She teetered there, her wings trembling—and then she was aloft again, but only a few inches off the perch, flapping her wings, staring out the open window.

Then she let herself back down onto the perch again, and turned her head to look at Caroline, who said, "Come here." Until she spoke, she hadn't known that she was crying.

"Go slow," Jacob whispered.

"Delirious. Sweetheart." Caroline extended her hand slowly, straightening her index finger toward the bird. Her hand was shaking. "Come here. Come on over here to me."

The bird hesitated. She looked out—oh, it was so cold out there! The wind ruffled her feathers. She stared out into the darkness, out into the great world beyond. Her crest was standing straight up. She turned to Caroline and then back to the great world. And then she lifted off her perch—lifted herself high and made a graceful turn and flew directly to Caroline, landing on her shoulder.

Jacob crossed the room in a few long strides. He closed the window. And, absurdly, locked it.

Caroline was still crying. Now Harry began to cry, too.

"Mama's okay," Jacob told him. "Mama's fine."

From within her cage, Faith made a sound they hadn't heard her make before. It sound like laughter. *Heh heh heh heh heh heh heh.*

"It's not funny," Harry shouted at the dove.

Caroline, still trembling, spoke to Harry. "It's all right, baby." She bent toward him, Delirious digging in hard to stay with her as she did. She kissed the top of her son's head and looked up at Jacob. She mouthed the words, "My God. It could have been—"

"I know," he said. "I know." He wasn't even whispering. "It wasn't, though."

"I am not a baby," Harry said.

"I know you're not." Caroline straightened up. On her shoulder, Delirious pecked at her ear, then chirped once, loudly, into it.

Caroline looked at Jacob. "It was close, though, wasn't it?" she said.

"It was, yes," Jacob said. "It was very close."

Acknowledgments

I am indebted to The Ohio State University for many things (principally, of course, for what I think of as the still remarkable fact that for over three decades I haven't had to worry—as before then I had worried constantly—about how to keep body and soul together). I'm grateful to have had the chance to be a part of building and maintaining the uniquely supportive creative writing program there, and to devise and run an interdisciplinary program that has given me the opportunity to work closely with artists from all corners of our sprawling campus. But what has most delighted and amazed me is having been able to meet, teach, advise, and mentor so many interesting young writers, some of whom would later become my dear friends. This has been one of the great sustaining joys of my life.

Close-Up began—in my mind, if not yet on the page—when a then twenty-year-old undergraduate English major spoke eloquently in class one afternoon about the practice of magic as an art form (and then performed an elegant, confounding trick for us). That was a long time ago, and in the years since, the magician-writer Joshua Jay has continued to astonish me and to make me proud. And I am thankful to him for his cheerful and exhaustive responses, often from farflung places, any time I had a question about magic or magicians in the course of working on this novel.

I am grateful, too, to the Corporation of Yaddo, which provided a home away from home at a crucial time for me. And to Glen Holland, Grace Herman-Holland, Scott Herman, and Sheila Herman—my bedrock. To Scott Raab, who might as well be part of the Herman family. To Tammy Carl, Eva Tibor, Rita Bourland, Brock Kingsley, Nick White, Memory Blake Risinger, Jim Phelan, Shari Goldhagen, and—as always—M.V. Clayton. To the wise and generous Kate Nitze. To my literary soulmate, Mike Kardos. To the indomitable Marian B.S.

Young. To Allen Gee, Rosellen Brown, and Donald Jordan (a book could not have a better trio of godparents). To Filippo and Russell Lepley-Pelacchi, who have made my life sweeter, more joyful, and more beautiful. And, in memory, to Cody and Molly and Ella Lucia— beloved, one-of-a-kind companions.

About the Author

Michelle Herman is the author of the novels *Missing*, *Dog*, and *Devotion*, and the collection of novellas *A New and Glorious Life*. She is also the author of three essay collections: *The Middle of Everything*, *Stories We Tell Ourselves*, and *Like A Song*. Herman has been awarded an NEA Individual Artist's Fellowship, multiple Ohio Arts Council Individual Artist's Fellowships, the Greater Columbus Arts Council Grant in Fiction, and the *Hadasash*/Harold U. Ribalow Award for Best Jewish Book of the year, among many other honors. She writes a popular parenting column for Slate and teaches at Ohio State University in the MFA program she co-founded, and where she also founded and directs an interdisciplinary program in the arts. Find her at www.michelleherman.com

CSU Press was officially formed by Columbus State University in 2021. The Donald L. Jordan endowment was established, in part, to aid in the development and creation of the press. We are extremely grateful to Mr. Jordan for creatively conceiving how CSU Press could be a viable publishing venue for the Donald L. Jordan Prize for Literary Excellence. DLJ Books is the first imprint of CSU Press and will always retain this designation. Mr. Jordan is a prominent Columbus businessman, and he is also the author of the novels *Negative Space* and *Fearfully and Wonderfully Made*.